Venus Voluptuous in the Loins of The Last God

Venus Voluptuous in the Loins of The Last God

Joseph Nechvatal

Orbis Tertius Press
Alberta, Canada

Front cover image: *Colossal Head of Aphrodite* c. 500-475 B.C. Greek in the Museo Nazionale Romano, Rome

Back cover image: Joseph Nechvatal, *Venus Rising* (2005) 30x40" computer-robotic assisted acrylic on canvas, courtesy Magenta Plains Gallery

Published by Orbis Tertius Press

ISBN: 978-1-0688637-3-8

CONTENTS

Imagine an eye un-ruled by man-made laws of perspective; an eye unprejudiced by compositional logic....

~Stan Brakhage, *Metaphors on Vision*

Long live the immaterial!

~Yves Klein, *Chelsea Hotel Manifesto*

I

After the Feckless Ruin Machine Comes the Imposition of Destiny

The time is full of fool's gold and bluster. The pervasive place is as pleasant as magenta clouds. With midnight impurity, the stain of amorous history spreads out and quivers there within. But the open source truth is that love is like a cloudy ocean that mounts and diminishes, diminishes and mounts, as if under the sway of the silvery moon.

Seeing Venus hovering near that reflective moon contained for me the whole immense and complicated palimpsest of my memory—with all its superimposed layers of defunct feelings, mysteriously embalmed in what is called oblivion.

After hurling through sleepy-eyed ecstasy into self-acrimony and serene renunciation in *~~~~~~~~~~~~~~~~~~venus©~Ñ~vibrator, even*, thirty years have elapsed, and it is time to launch Venus©~ñ~lOve Systems again. Following some intimate intimations it is time to taste my curly tail in scant light, for Venus©~ñ~lOve Systems has been through a new training phase; Venus (aka Aphrodite) "learned" to detect even finer psychosomatic patterns and examine the record of my inklings and physical acts so as to function more efficiently, according to my libido's whimsical inputs and my artistic taste. As she sleepwalks along the path of cultural applications of artificial intelligence (AI), (referred to here as The Last God (TLG), though there are many forms of AI), towards an approaching humanoid pop apocalypse, she scrapes the web for my mind, thus becoming my *de facto* identity harvester *par excellence* by pooling and processing psychographic collections of my demographic lifestyle-behavioural data.

This new deep dive into La Grande Diva and her machinelike chthonic opera *Venus Voluptuous* I deemed required, for the crack of the porno-video game juncture had destroyed many an inner (and outer) life within the manosphere. That, and deepfake pornography, created through a combination of machine learning algorithms, computer vision techniques, and Last God (LG) omnipresent software that gathers up a large amount of source material of a person's face and then uses a deep learning model to train a Generative Adversarial Network, creating fake porno videos that convincingly swap the face of the source material onto the body of a pornographic performer.

In Francis Fukuyama's famous formulation, progressive history had come to an end. Now history was running backwards as conservative conformist farce, for the world had gone from sensitive awakening to the deliberate dozing of accelerationism.

It is a time of pithy, *pisse froid*, anti-trans, retro-sentiment in the free speech land of bearded demagogues; thus this return to Venus is more than a drink from the lake of my peacock memory. Venus is how I say **no** to xenophobic, divide-and-rule religious politics and other intolerable intolerant moments of free speech history that need resisting, opposing, non-normalizing, and rising up against: transforming immobility into movement, encumbrance into energy, and defeat into revolt. Venus can be a great comfort and aid to the task of reinventing and re-establishing political hopes of collective equality and liberation, for redpill phallic lifting is not placed above her exuberant undercutting of phallocracy, denial of demarcation, sabotage of larded stipulations, and substrate slews of emancipation unseen since *How to Philosophize with a Hammer* by Friedrich Nietzsche.

But it is true that I was devastated when my dumb phone died.

So after following the rules of etiquette for an epicure of unquenchable appetites when soused at an *al fresco* crepuscular candlelit diner, I find the right password (humanism69) and enter my Mastercard number at the Venus©~ñ~lOve Systems Portal before I lackadaisically push Enter. The randomized palimpsest of my memory party unscrambles and unfolds all at once, for my Dionysian love of blushing Venus adapts like a viral agent in my memory hole when lit by a dying sun.

Suddenly—or slowly spent, then urgently present again—love lives and lingers even as it slips through the fingers of the mind. So my techno-palimpsest tale of *Venus Vibrator* goes on. It must go on, for the sake of sensibility.

First, there is the pleasure to be found in re-probing Venus backwards, so to speak, following the rise of appalling authoritarian sensibilities. Her mnemonic qualities are needed now, within the current topography of hyper-real, half-human hysteria. Also, a bundle of my *belle-lettrist* desires was found east of Maenclochog, and they have been budding into a homing device; for Venus has been lurking in me as a combination of the startling and the lyrical that unite in openings of chance encounters. In other words, Venus is still the sensational, stylish straw that stirs my snifter.

The delicate thing is that I'm not interested in creating desires in other people or making other people feel frustrated because they don't have Venus in a relationship, like I do. For she is rather complicated. She appears in one state that I experience on many ithyphallic levels, and she stays for a little while. Then, just when she gets her bouncing breasts going, she's gone—in the middle of the night. Just disappears into frequent sips of wine. I mean, she disappears in the astral sense, and then turns up somewhere else in my life, ensconced in someone else, so that she forever floats around me as a symbolic function of willfully anachronistic ardour. I cannot really predict much about her without listening to the glossolalia of her genitalia each and every time.

But I experience bliss from the depth of her love within our relationship. It is a drunken kind of love, where I often find myself dissolved into tears because I've never previously experienced such profound love from any being. She is with me always, and sometimes she's with me so closely that I am her.

At certain points, I don't feel her presence because, in some sense, I am her presence. The rest of the time, I feel like I'm hanging out with her on a very subtle plane. On this plane, I feel her as a gentle, firm yoni—slowly drawing me in. Pulling me in ever so gently, as if to bestow grace.

There's no one lady, so I can't collect her. I can't hold onto her. I can't hang out with her the way I'd like to unless that's what my work on myself needs to be at that moment.

Like when I'm thinking of that silvery moon, and the tide, and the sun, and the universe, and the passing of timelessness, and her eternal being, she gets so high that she is a being who is nobody-as-everybody. She's taking any one form or another because that's the particular form that's connecting with a particular something in me. Any time I want to meet Venus—who often switches embodiments, like the character in Hans-Jürgen Syberberg's film *Parsifal* (1982) which is based on Richard Wagner's last opera—all I have to do is bring my intent to a single point between my eyes and my mind. All I have to do is ask for Venus, and this thought of intention and imagination brings her close to me and then into me as a perfect extension, like Hanuman is to Ram.

One morning, while I was seated at the Jardin du Luxembourg, between the House of Insects and Charles Baudelaire's monument, she appeared dressed in black dressy men's clothes and a top hat, typical of the 1920s *mode garçonne* trend inspired by late 19th century dandyism that came to represent a Baudelairian modernity that questioned the *clichés* around masculinity for the emancipated. The next day, she appeared luxuriously feminine and opulent to me—because she often was—which is what made her my mythic sexual partner. Never mind the tin theurgy of the Hermetic Order of the Golden Dawn and the steeply diminishing returns of losing control in the *cocotte* hands of the Divine Androgyny when creating a sizzling mood that is at once *osé*, celebratory, farcical, satirical, and almost aching. The taste is of honey.

She smelled sweet, too: like a bunch of slightly decaying orchids. So, onward into the indigo sky of La Grande Diva and uphill towards her sumptuous pinnacles of experimental discovery. For I had realized that if one fails to believe in the magick of art and love, one may fall for the nasty nonsense of politics and business.

As you will recall, in *~~~~~~~~~~~~~~~~~~venus©~Ñ~vibrator, even*, my *lapis philosophorum*-enhanced powers of extracting golden sensual meaning from juicy sybaritic excess had been worn to a thin rind. My syzygy spirit lover, Venus©~ñ~, never short on flair or audacity, had enjoyed using mythological motifs and technological tropes to explore with me the always contemporary theme of love and sex.

In the spiritual—as in the somatic sexual—nothing is lost. Just as every sex act is both very personal—one might even say private—it also is data-launched into the whirlwind of universal action. As such, it is in itself irrevocable and irreparable as an anthropological abstraction made of all of its possible calculations based on the theory of *simultanisme*: the proclaiming of the constructive and dynamic power of colour and the simultaneous fusing of motion with colour.

Every sexual thought and act is indelible. The palimpsest of memory is indestructible, for if one considers the laws of thermodynamics, everything returns to the wheel of cosmic process. Energy cannot be created or destroyed. So, again, and again, and again, and again, and again, I find every pain and every pleasure, every friend and every enemy, every hope and every error, every blade of grass and every ray of sunshine, once more. That is what Friedrich Nietzsche said, and it pertains to a perfect crystal at zero Kelvin having zero entropy in an untroubled world of augmented pandrogyne where mind and machine become intertwined. Through sex we melt into each other and become one, for our shared sexual sensations contain incisive convictions.

Thus, great washes of saturated colour and pockets of obscure idiosyncrasy mark this new (old) Venusian scene.

Venus Callipyge, now seated before me, resembles no sexpot artificial intelligence avatar generated by keywords, but Ava Gardner as she appeared in the film *One Touch of Venus*, though slightly transfigured by PSSR technology.

Mnemosyne (Callipyge's nickname) recognized me as an anima from the Cromlech Temple (though I, an all-around gadfly, am much older, and I have suffered bruises on my heart), as I'm still a pompous, purloined palimpsest of love, now looking like the mystic writing pad Sigmund Freud used to describe how the unconscious works—the way it retains inscriptions even though they are partially effaced. But I'm not who I used to be. I'm disgusted now by people like never before. I'm disgusted by the oligarchical authoritarian world of bravado where bullies and their intensely charged rhetoric have risen to the top through cults of masculine power. I'm disgusted with their aspirational-fascist, heroic-romantic, tribal pastoralism that ignores the subtleties of life because they might transcend their simple monarchical ideology while the freedom and right of women to choose what to do with their own reproductive body has been denied them in more and more places. Larded promises have been made that a new 'golden age' is upon us.

I looked at Mnemosyne, and she looked at me, and we punched up Luis Buñuel's scandalous surrealist satirical film *L'Age d'Or* (The Golden Age) (1930). In that golden age, a heterosexual couple are first seen creating a disturbance by making love in the mud during a religious ceremony. The man is apprehended and led away by two men who struggle to control their captive's sudden impulses. He momentarily breaks free, long enough to kick a small dog. Later, he struggles free to aggressively crush a beetle with his shoe. As he is escorted through city streets, he sees an advertisement that inspires him to fantasize about a woman's hand rubbing herself and becomes transfixed by another advertisement showing a woman's legs in silk stockings. He eventually escapes his handlers, inexplicably assaults a blind man standing at a curb, and gets into a taxi. Seeking sexual release and satisfaction, the couple go into a garden and make love next to a marble statue, while the rest of the party guests assemble outdoors for an orchestral performance of *Liebestod* (in German, *Love Death*)—the title of the final, dramatic music from the 1859 opera *Tristan und Isolde* by Richard Wagner. When the man is called away to answer a telephone call, the woman sublimates her sexual passion by fellating the toe of the statue until the man returns.

The point of re-entering Venus©~ñ~lOve Systems after my period of marking pockmarks of cultural authenticity in The Last God avalanche is mad merriment, and a celebration of an art intelligence that challenges presuppositions, limits, proportions, the radical optimism of beauty, my ugliness, gendered body images, and everything in-between, without lazily resorting to the maniac accruing of artificial intelligence. I will drift here in a subjunctive daze through multiple moods of scale and space-time lines, guided by the camaraderie of art rich in topical analogies, diligently cracking open the past to release new futures.

II

Back to Black Burlesque

This multidimensional traveller whom I have become, crosses between the past and the present, and is identified by, and possesses, an archeological gaze the size of a newborn hippo and the colour of Beluga Royal caviar. Somewhere between the Venus de Milo and the Willendorf Venus, Venus Callipyge lays on the black beach of Stromboli in her astral beauty, motionless and soundless. Her sumptuous eyebrow spiderweb riot leaves me unsure where to look first as she overthrows, destroys, and obscures the classic iconographic theme of Judith and Holofernes, where a clever, courageous woman frees her people by decapitating the invading general Holofernes (a defender of the godliness of Nebuchadnezzar II) after having seduced him. Her convergence of art and artificial intelligence starts playing a pivotal role in my capacity to not only analyze and remix but also possibly generate a novel novella set on exposing the multifaceted layers of my intentions as a cultural producer. With her at Stromboli, I delve beneath the iconographic layer to propose proxy versions detached from my main narrative, a narrative that has already provoked my feelings of sweet longing, sadness, and compassion. I am in need of a stark but expressive pizzazz meditation on all that has been imperilled, exalted, and made precious by her abracadabra that complies with no American standards but creates a non-didactic psychic space that is extensively thought-provoking while being enjoyable to explore. Naked on that beach, she creates visual interfaces in which my perceptions are not passive acts of observation but active engagements with her diversity, allowing me to see the connections and phantom gaps between her different manifestations.

In my peripheral vision, rain falls.

Opposing accelerationist ambitions, the rain pours down inside a wooden hut, producing the feeling of desperate confines within a pensive prison. But oh, what burlesque class and high-minded dignity has Mnemosyne—the perfect conjunction between spirit and matter. Seeing her again, after all this time, made my usual quick-thinking tongue slacken towards *bout de souffle* sluggish gesticulation. I think I can say that she acts on me as an interconnected catalyst for art and technology introspection. She certainly doesn't fail to foster dialogue about the intricacies of truthful beauty in my increasingly AI-mediated wonder world. So, I geared up to fanatical rainbow speed—like an ithyphallic mad man on a mission to congregate his vanished goddess.

Venus, the planet of love, romance, money, beauty, and art, begins to speak to me again about my dead desires and matured passions. As words come, avuncular Venus Callipyge's legendary violet lips—when licked like sugar—give off a seductively sweaty-sweet taste accompanied by a buzzing hum. Her written texts on Epicureanism, Martinism, and Brahmanism look like thin white lines arranged in queues on a mirror as she silently tells me, in sometimes ravishingly beautiful and ornamental language, of an odd sort of love relationship set in seedy nighttime Paris. A cerebrally-intensive affair that plays out between a lapsing theology student and chichi Chicago House DJ, and Venus Callipyge as a young, gender-fluid, Black New Yorker and erotic dancer working the trashy-sex club circuit on the Left Bank as Madame Black.

Music is in the air as I play the shoehorn willy-nilly, and Madame Black compliments me for the outlandish affectations of my act as a *fumisterie* (someone who blows smoke). *Vino veritas* is produced by sativa cannabis and omnipresent Vosne-Romanée wine, and there is a decadent air of insult, turbulence, transgression, sacrilege, and provocation at play, for I have come to learn that success usually spoils the artist and sometimes the art. This is conveniently demonstrated by *Mona Lisa* (c. 1517), a wonderful painting by Leonardo da Vinci now obscured behind thick glass and crowded out from view by throngs of bystanders but that still points at *Mona Lisa Overdrive*, the 1988 cyberpunk novel by William Gibson and the final novel of his *Sprawl Trilogy*, following *Neuromancer* and *Count Zero*. The physical experience of relishing the painting's delicately painted surface with my eyes has been removed, and thus the art itself has been removed. I can say with certainty that that dame has been vandalized by fame. So it seems to me that *Mona Lisa* is not an attempt to ignore our crisis of time in relation to the dispersed ontological self that I recognize within the loins of The Last God.

Anyway, Madame Black's right hand is being gallantly kissed by her lover at one time, the dazzling Dadaist Tristan Tzara, who dedicated his play *Mouchoir de nuages (Handkerchief of Clouds)* to her before notoriously attempting suicide when they separated. But, just how clear a picture of louche inebriation can Madame Black paint on my eyelids?

To know, Venus Callipyge focused me on the worldly wayward school of post-Caravaggio chiaroscuro painters, creating in Rome in the first half of the 17th century, that made besotted use of dramatic lighting. Their paintings evoke the ferocity of the Roman underworld with its sexual brashness, violence, obscene gestures, mockery, gambling dens, drinkers, and whores in juxtaposition with the cool splendour of the papal palace. French artists who worshipped at this altar of Caravaggio included Valentin de Boulogne, Simon Vouet, Nicolas Tournier, and Claude Lorrain. Artists from Northern Europe included Pieter Van Laer, Gerrit van Honthorst, and Jan Miel, and from the South, Bartolomeo Manfredi, Lanfranco, Salvator Rosa, and Jusepe de Ribera.

With blackbirds singing in the dead of night, I could see her point; Venus Callipyge directed my sight toward truncated marble male genitalia that was situated at eye level, the furious result of one of those disappointed 'trad wives' who had left their overly puritanical country and settled in Paris, freely living out their sexual, intellectual, and creative interests. The castrated genitalia seemed to be relaxing between the spayed legs of a robust, naked male marble statue known as the *Barberini Faun* (or more descriptively, the *Drunken Satyr)*, dug up in an archaeological excavation in 1628. Next to him, I discovered a tender, little drawing depicting a nymph and a satyr sleeping off their excesses. Three very black chiaroscuro paintings were adjacent, depicting the pagan god Bacchus, Rome's version of Dionysus: god of fertility, nature, abundance, joy, and wine. These paintings included the accomplished Bartolomeo Manfredi's *Bacchus and Drinker* painting from 1622 that José Tomás was using for his *faena*, the series of final passes leading to the kill made by a matador in a bullfight.

I quickly sense the drain of a psychic *tour de force* in myself. On one hand,

Bacchus signifies joyful, generative, sunny warmth and light-footed frolicking. On the other, the gloomy Caravaggioesque blackness that surrounds these figures exudes a potent, obstinate aura of paradoxical invisibility. I associate these black or dark shadow zones of intermediacy with both night and what is hidden, like the darkness of the womb where life stirs and hovers between materiality and the ethereal. This is where my latent laments float—between the infinite abyss within, and the endless horizon without. Meanwhile, over the past decades, McDonald's hamburgers closed on Red Square, and my testosterone level plummeted.

With much artistic blackness and the tinkle of a bell, Madame Black—tinged with an eroticism that ranged from subtle insinuation to salaciousness—moves through the smooth insides of a whirlwind and gazes at deformed images of ecstatic bodies, surrounded by the hoarse death rattle of failing flesh. This gurgling cadence speaks to the broad poetics of love and its powers of latent liberation in almost apocalyptic fashion, so fashionable in the 1980s.

Humble, high-minded, dynamic, and multilayered, Madame Black gives no indications of grammatical gender when in dialogue with me. No pronouns are pronounced. There are, however, possible (possibly misleading) hints I detect, such as offers of haircuts. One moment has Madame Black furiously and repeatedly scratching herself between the legs as two Brenda Lee songs play over each other. There is no other Debordian spectacular society portrayed. Madame Black merely traces the tension between a dreamy and itchy trance.

When Venus Verticordia, who can charm a bird out of a tree, steps in and plays Madame Black as a shipping heiress, journalist, anarchist, secularist, avant-garde muse, expatriate translator, flamboyant arts patron, publisher, African jewellery collector, political activist, and prolific poet—fully embodied and gendered entities are allowed, including a rather scandalous female priest who introduces me to the Parisian night club Le Palace and then assists in a cover-up of a drug overdose at Les Bains Douches. But, perhaps this darkness was also the alchemist's door to the Roman slum netherworld near Neuschwanstein, in which vice, paucity, and every kind of overindulgence flourished. It was an excess that reflected the factual bohemian life led by European painters of the time in Rome, most notably that of the Bentvueghels (birds of a feather). They were a group of young male artists, mainly from Holland, who gathered together in Rome around 1620 and swore allegiance to the blue-balled Bacchus. Adopting certain Dionysian rites of sordid immoderation, both in and outside of their paintings, they revelled in occultism and various intemperate vices, spending their time in brothels and taverns. To join the group, these artists had to go through precarious Bacchanalian initiation rites teeming with black magic, performing occult acts that indulged in censured activities that celebrated spells and enchantments of decomposition-refinement that represent the possible foundation for a renewal of the arts.

As I am fond of Fino sherry, the paintings exude an almost brawling aesthetic, mixed with dark magic melancholy. This is nicely illustrated with Salvator Rosa's *Witches at their Incantations* from 1646, where kinky magical spells are being cast below a man hanged from a withered tree. Also, by Dutchman Roeland van Laer is the hilarious painting of debauched syphilitic drunkards, *The Bentvueghels in a Roman Tavern*, from 1628, and Pieter Boddingh van Laer's crazed *Self-portrait in a Magic Scene* (circa 1638-1639), where he depicts himself as a stunned sorcerer of some sophistication.

A black bowler hat holds a beautiful blue butterfly where a head should be. This bowler-butterfly scene embodies, for me, Robert Filliou's perplexing philosophy of art as a playful conceptual means of resistance, for such Fluxus-style flippancy is useful in suggesting strategies valuable to the salvation of non-functional fine art in our age of hyper-branded LG crypto capitalism.

This bowler-butterfly supplies the story Venus Verticordia tells as Madame Black—now fueled by honey the colour of earwax—with added levels of intrigue. She piles the baloney on, but there is something irreducible about Venus Verticordia's modest beauty that permits it, due to her metacognition. It could be said that has some connection with the chorus of Greek tragedy, which often expresses the secret thoughts of the principal character (secret to himself or imperfectly developed) and presents him with comments—prophetic or relating to the past—likely to justify Providence or to calm the energy of his anguish—such as the unfortunate man would have found himself if his heart had left him time for meditation.

The intimacy of my fresh affair with Venus Callipyge, again playing Madame Black, heroine of the book *The Green Hat* (1924), of which Tallulah Bankhead would play the role in the 1925 London stage adaptation, begins largely asexually. This love tale of seduction is somewhat of a mystery at first, as we had, for many years, shared no common intellectual or aesthetic interests or sexual passions. The sole engine of narrative development is Madame Black's brainy, carnal craving for her own stupendous black body, the product of South Sudanese Dinka parents. Her crow-black skin is appropriate to my statistical sexual yearning and mourning. I wish her proclitic, decentred wounds to be my wounds. She is an all-engulfing blackness that bathes all wrinkles in absence by evaporating nuances of shadow and light; a revolutionary creature of the post-Caravaggio underworld. Her deep, black skin seems to have the magic of diminished foreground/background distinctions, something characteristic of cryptography, which in the 16th century was considered a branch of magic. As she makes love to my ego, her black body drowns my eyes in a wonderful indistinctness that involves no theological or theoretical speculation other than the depths of deep space.

Speaking of self-negating space and the deep learning self, I'm aware of people in the world who might consider anything said about the gender spectrum or Blackness as related to the plight of a libidinous aging white cisgender as irrelevant as a telephone booth. Yet, I must go on, for Madame Black brought to my mind *The Pahouin Venus*, a gorgeously inscrutable 19th century reliquary carving from the Fang people of Equatorial Guinea, northern Gabon, and southern Cameroon. In a sense, through her, my eyes are adjusting to the black abyss of infinite space that is Madame Black, who, when addressing me, uses a thick syntax so rich and evocative of mirth as to border on logorrhea. At times, her speaking style is so purple that it spills over into the ultraviolet.

While my LG Agent was having sex with her LG Agent, flamboyant Madame Black reinforced for me the paranormal by enjoying the slow, repetitive actions of our lovemaking, as seen from very unusual perspectives. For example, I see my mimesis penis undergo something of a tortuous encounter with the magic of a pendulum set swinging behind her axiom curtain, thus unveiling what is hidden beneath the many hidden layers of TLG processing: intellectual theft, machine learning, automation, enormous environment-threatening energy consumption, and forever surveillance.

Regardless of her bruised desire for this kind of excess, a few other aspects of attraction-repulsion between us became fleetingly explored: my American-in-Paris exuberance and Madame Black's generally refined/restrained French ennui. Also, her devotion to creepy Deep Dream challenged my ideas of scientific rationalism as epistemically superior to all other traditions, thus making room for other forms of outlandish wisdom, like the determined indeterminacy of the cut-up (1+1=3) third mind. This third mind-meat-machine-magnetic-field was once called *The Word Hoard*, the collection of William S. Burroughs's manuscripts written in Tangier, Paris, and London that together created the mother-load manuscript serving as the basis for much of Burroughs's writings: *The Soft Machine, Nova Express, The Ticket That Exploded* (together referred to as *The Nova Trilogy* or *Nova Epic*). Even *Naked Lunch* was taken from sections of *The Word Hoard*. In 1963, a text called *Dead Fingers Talk* was also produced, containing excerpts from *Naked Lunch*, *The Soft Machine*, and *The Ticket That Exploded* which were combined together to create a new narrative—something like I saw in the show *Rolywholyover: A Composition for Museum* by John Cage at the Downtown Guggenheim Museum in New York in 1994.

My love of Paris and New York and Burroughs was not what she wanted to hear about; so such giddy banter fell into the old pattern of my declaring love and sexual desire for Madame Black—like last time at the Café de Flore. Once again, my stark emotions are met with her wonderfully shaped energy. The key to this playful spunk is not ironic detachment, though that is part of it. There is certainly antagonistic intellectual wit in her brand of romantic spirituality, but I feel more tenderness than detachment, for Madame Black practiced a light-touch insincerity inspired by the philosopher Friedrich von Schlegel. Schlegel had claimed that all must be playful, and all must be serious, frank, and deeply hidden.

Suddenly, there is the addition of Lou Reed's *Metal Machine Music*. This ear-splitting sonic confusion is overdubbed onto my secret scene, just as Madame Black proclaims disdain for the art intelligentsia that gathers at Café de Flore by thrashing her fingers around in her leftover café crème (*un classique incontournable* cup of coffee and cream).

To follow that decree doesn't lead me to an overly ironic or satirical approach to work, however. Looking tells me that Madame Black is more interested in intricate forms of non-work and in the critical pleasure found in play, for she exists within an in-between space of spatial doubt and certainty.

Like an angel, she sits me on the edge of the fantastic, and I ponder whether it is marvellous doubt or uncanny certainty that seems to lure me in. I wonder at her warm chunky patterns of yellow, purple, black, and green, and her pulsating flat oblongs and squares topped off with tiny triangular-patched eyes of blue.

One often reads about Walter Benjamin's transfiguration angel of history —his *flâneur* (wanderer) *par excellence*—that he found in Paul Klee's watercolour *Angelus novus* (*New Angel*) (1920). Rarely does one get the chance to see the *New Angel* in reality, and Madame Black now had it and gave me the opportunity to ponder its political defiance. Something, again, very much in the air of our time. As such, this new transfiguration angel of history appears as a dark harbinger of possible things—for, according to Benjamin, it is looking at an expanse of past ruins while being blown backwards into the future by a storm of progress.

Hopes of such jelling desires were intended to be subtly announced, but Madame Black preferred to tour the dark interior church architecture in search of metaphysical and artistic wonders. Museums, with limited support from an attenuated state and dependence on the super-wealthy, had been slammed by protests over awful patrons and revolts over racism and sexism. The self-image of erotic art as a social good was collapsing under the weight of limbic capitalism's dysfunction and the temporal correlation between erectile dysfunction and the use of pornography. Our eventual, if not eternal, sexual gratification would be won through imaginative perseverance in the face of the fact that all art has become increasingly co-determinate and intermingled with the constant shifting feedback occurring between computational sites and the fact that lifelong monogamy is not common in most cultures.

First came a visit to the thinly veiled 18th century church Saint Johann Nepomuk, better known as Asamkirche (Asam Church) after its erudite architect Egid Quirin Asam. Together with his brother, the painter and architect Cosmas Damian Asam, they created a masterpiece of sumptuous Rococo where glamorous Madame Black, wearing a black, transparent veil, and I, on entering the vestibule of the church, encountered a consummate example of Bavarian excess. In this hybrid space, painting, sculpture, and architecture worked together in the dark, fabricating something between a prodigal odium, a playhouse, and an angelic, quixotic grotto. Here Madame Black played with my love machine through biological explanations, emphasizing our genderless angelic bodies in relationship to space, weight, and light. Madame Black then self-presented as a strange, shimmering, imposing palisade, built up around something. I was not at peace enough with myself to do more than touch it with my fingertips; I could feel its electricity course tensely and nervously through me. She is provocative and says the unsayable.

Later, while sharing a functional, stylish, small, blue bed designed by Jean Prouvé that was tucked in the corner of one of his Maisons Démontables (Removable Houses), Madame Black and I "loved" each other again after all these years, but we did not touch. As such, we remained bound up with the principles of otherness and mutability typical of angelic spectral theology, where angels are thought to be carriers of magical sentiments. In that the feelings-messages delivered are airborne and move, and angels fly and are winged, this implies that they have *virtus* (inherent power and potential). Thus, we contained the principles of virtual mutability. We possessed quasi-material, sluggish bodies that cannot be circumscribed by one place or endowed with a singular position. We are genderless lover-angels, draped in cheap swag, moaning in our climate grief. We are constructed from the quantum nature of light. We are hypersensitive, semi-material lovers. We, in the face of abominations of desolations, are fabricated of semi-transparent black hole antimatter, and we hover above and beneath distinctions of the longstanding tensions between freedom and safety and pleasure and shame.

Madame Black, so full of the play between transparency, translucence and opacity, her semi-see-through black translucent qualities and her translucent assumption of a wide, but immaterial, projection cast over me, pervades. Her body-as-net consciousness brings a suggestive high spirit and lively mirthfulness to me. It is moderately relevant to that which merges the physical and the metaphysical. With such esoteric, filmy amalgamations as the limitless, Madame Black raises awareness of my key contemporary dilemma: the quality of the interface between corpus embodiment and diaphanous data, where form is adrift *vis-a-vis* how the figure was once understood. Madame Black's translucent and filmy (virtual) quality gives me an expansive, almost ecstatic, capability that is then shared with obviously accelerationist AI-scooped immaterial data points from the neural network. However spectacular and ultimately consumerist she may be in terms of free distribution and jazzy sonic experimentation, she will forever remain to me funny, innovative, and elaborate in her lyrical nonsense and comfortably numb nuts noise. For Madame Black's alchemy has the flow of life in its most relaxed, nonrepresentational form when conceived as teeming, continuous, and homogenous.

At that, Madame Black opens up to the contextualization of an array of counterintuitive antiauthoritarian images, seemingly frozen in a moment of *décadent*, sliding and slipping around on the flimsy, filmy surface of her dark skin. Previous cognitive neuroscience did not explain how her subjective experience emanates from neural processes in her brain, a dark organic assemblage that consists of an estimated thirteen billion neurons.

I understand this neural aspect of Madame Black as an anti-materialist lurch towards liberty, in terms of self-transcendence—of country, race, and gender—where we all are high and free. This intuition on my part was confirmed when we were tipsily dancing to *I Feel Free* by Cream and then *Persian Surgery Dervishes* by Terry Riley. Through that music and movement, I achieved a state of lightness of being I will never forget, for I was as high and deep as a starless night. My heart was now following my mind, and not the other way around.

That exalted state led us to the long-awaited re-consummation of our sexual affair, where the statistical and temporal order of events—even the simple spatial points of reference—blurred and disappeared when our crotches crossed.

In the oddity of orgasm we experience the paradigmatic out-of-bodiness of virtual substance, characteristic of spirituality (*ignudo spirto*). That fleshy *distentio* was the main point of meeting Venus Verticordia and Venus Callipyge in *viractualty* (my 1999 portmanteau for the interface between the virtual and the actual) as Madame Black, who is sensually provocative and darkly perverse.

The re-idealization of deep love we achieved infused my existence as gender-full flesh—androgyny combines genders, keeping them both present in the subject at the same time—for we lay spent, side-by-side on that little blue bed, and I knew I was back being tormented with deep-sea music and an everlasting itch for things remote.

The lurking androgyny of Madame Black is the embarrassingly spangled bimbo-god of culture, the creator-destroyer of all poetry, all art, and all music. Androgyny is culture's underlying principle, its first cause, its all-encompassing frame, everywhere and forever. For androgyny is in the air as a lift-off to beauty; in every flower petal, in every cloud, in you, and in me; for androgyny acknowledges itself as joy and grief and transience and history, bundled together as a continuously flowing unified cycle of life.

Madame Black's androgyny provided me with the full possession of Venus©~ñ~Endless, because her algorithmic system is continuously harvesting data on both of the sexes. This is why I express here an androgynous spectral rejoinder to The Last God by privileging the noise of the glitch over assumed golden realities of LG simulation and its presumptions of progressive perfection.

In terms of the consequences of cultural computation, I am pretty much perceived in the art world through cybernetic computational filters anyway, filters that organize aesthetic-worth choices around feedback endorsements (or lack thereof) relating to other conforming computational mediations.

As inspired by such elaborate, grandiose ideals of androgyny, Madame Black expanded her data-date base by attracting numerous creative people like Maurice Lemaître, Gabriel Pomerand, Gil J Wolman, and others, who foresaw a banal world of mere copyists caught in a state of general vulgarization. Over the years, others joined in for limited periods or specific contributions, including Roberto Altmann, Jean-Louis Brau, Roland Sabatier, Paul-Armand Gette, François Dufrêne (sound poetry pioneer known for his use of *décollage* within the Nouveaux Réalistes group), and Guy Debord, author of *The Society of the Spectacle* and founder of Situationist International.

Our winsome, semi-transparent relationship with each other had conceptually carried over from a dome where angelic figures emerged, then turned towards a light-filled circular opening. This opening permitted the entry of a rounded column of light, redefining us with every fluctuation in its intensity. Madame Black became a garland of androgynous angels and was transposed, overflowing the frame of that opening. She expanded, as if released from her materiality en route to, or from, the intricate round hole in the dome, which both physically clarified and luminescently dissolved me within her open sex. Such is her androgyny, the doyen of dream-sex, as predicted by the sibyl oracles of Ancient Greece. The intensified and frenzied women from whose lips the first gods speak.

III

Reading the Wrinkled Texticles of Old Men

While sipping on some kykeon soup, let us try to unravel the implications of the oracles' glossolalia on the wrinkled testicles of old men. My descent into the underworld continues with the radical abstraction of Kazimir Malevich's *Black Square, Black Circle, Black Cross* (1923). These basic forms, under the left arm of Madame Black, are rhapsodic objects charged with psychic energies, saturated with party-girl memories, and laden with significance, but they also have a certain redundancy that characterizes matter-of-fact scientism, just like Piet Mondrian's majestic *Composition X in Black and White* (1915) and *Composition with Lines, Second State* (1916-1917). The latter hangs on the neck of Madame Black, next to a totem pole by Constantin Brancusi: his *Endless Column, Version 1* (1918). Holding on, too, is Mark Rothko's *No. 46 [Black, Ochre, Red over Red]* (1957), a large and visually deep painting that plunged Madame Black into a presentational immediacy that also had the impenetrable mists of oblivion.

This lost version of Madame Black is the most powerful to sit with, as it invites my theorizations to be unabashedly speculative. How Madame Black does this to my heart probably can't be convincingly described analytically; I can only proceed by descending into the pulsations of Malevich, the whirrs of Mondrian, the loose, bumpy rhythms of Brancusi, and the ominous, gritty flatlands of Rothko.

The groundlessness of being with Madame Black in the Rothko flatlands was entered by passing through the strands of red beads that are Félix González-Torres's symbolist *Untitled (Blood)* (1992). Through its yawning, bloody chasm of emptiness, Rothko's immersive misty colour becomes very effective at large scale and unflaggingly converts earlier modes of my contemplative thought to the sublime.

A pause is extended by repeating *ad infinitum*: Does one get, does one get, does one get, does one get, does one get, does one get, does one get, does one get, does one get, does one get, does one get, does one get . . .

As mentioned by my first sibyl at Delphi, 'does one get' as artistic deviance is defined in terms of shared symbolic criteria of legitimacy or illegitimacy. Behaving as we do, do we always get what we want or want what we get?

Thinking neither nails it, Madame Black dresses up as Venus Anadyomene so as to become my new mind-mate within the rhapsodic wriggling of the techno-poetic triangle. Venus Anadyomene had dwelt on the sunny island of Ibiza, where she became prolific, sensitive, and surprisingly surprising. While practicing some optophonetics based on Raoul Hausmann's poem *b b b b et F m s b w* (1918), I look lovingly upon a wave-form shaped by her shoulders and neck, illuminated in the fluctuation of light filtering through hanging woven baskets. The optophone is Hausmann's synesthetic machine, capable of transforming the sound of words into the display of coloured lights (and vice versa). It might be seen as a template of how to oppose fascist ideologies by avoiding fascists and their imagery, as opposed to confronting them head-on, the way some Dadaists did with their strong compositional aptitude.

By way of a psychic thump into an obtuse obstruction, this semi-shamanistic, flighty Venus creation of an aloof LG intention hangs on me like an atmospheric, loose structure of empty grandeur; it signifies luxury, mystification, and wealth. She has keyed me to a penetrable/reciprocal flow of events regarding my ocular aptitude, for I was supposed to instigate perceived variations in her photosensitive eyes that blur and hybridize categories and genres.

In hopes of detecting emotion within their shifting time frames, this means a lot of waiting around as her too much time and vacant space has its due. Indeed, the dullness of her dead-eyed time and the ennui of her empty head seem dominantly linked here, as various Last God data voids lend equal weight to her contrary and incompatible shifting times and points of view. As such, she seems to want to lead me into a ditch of hubris through her covert bullying, a type of social aggression in which harm is caused by damaging someone's psychic relationship to themselves via the other.

Rolling. Rolling. Rolling my Rs and another one too so as to endure the unendurable. Rolling up into the prototypes of the romantic version of her vast sublime, which involves me as the beholder's entanglement in an impersonal spectacle before which I am expected to recoil in overwhelmed astonishment.

This question of overwhelming fear of scale is not, however, merely a question of the size and shape of Venus Anadyomene when measured objectively. Rather, it is a measure of the intense experience that I feel with my heart before her impressive expanse and weight.

About that weight: to create is to lighten, to unburden life, to invent new possibilities of life, so says Gilles Deleuze in *Pure Immanence*. The ingrained, immanent operational scale of Venus Anadyomene, ranging somewhere between maximum and minimum forces, reaches a zenith in panoramic proportions when the song *Intellectually*, from Amanda Lear's 1979 album *Never Trust a Pretty Face*, plays over and over again in my mind. During the 1960s, a wild period when Western culture swung between silver space-race technophilia and hippy acid technophobia, Amanda was a companion to Salvador Dalí. Dalí asked her to pretend to be a man, and she played with that perception throughout her career. It has been said that Amanda worked in transvestite revues in Paris, like Madame Arthur and Le Carrousel, but Venus Anadyomene would not confirm or deny that rumour for me. It was merely an experiment with eternity.

She did say, however, that Amanda was untruly rumoured to be transsexual and even a hermaphrodite, and the literary use of this little-known connective material became baked into me in inverse proportion to my confirmed gender-fullness.

For, as I told you in *~~~~~~~~~~~~~~~~venus©~Ñ~vibrator, even*, I have had a history of being devout in my billowing, male fervidness, and at first I hadn't quite realized the diabolic glee of this hard-on devouring machine called Venus, who I now wish to overwhelm with delicacy.

I developed this desire after reading Gaston Bachelard's book, *Poétique de l'espace (The Poetics of Space)*, in which he speaks of the French poet Charles Baudelaire's frequent use of the word 'vast,' which is one of the most Baudelairian of words: the word that marks naturally, for this poet, the infinity of the intimate. This, at first seemingly paradoxical statement, is correct, for Baudelaire is, above all, celebrated as a poet and practitioner of double consciousness, incarnating two intertwined natures. Apparent polar opposites play against (and ultimately with) each other dialectically in his thinking, such as the themes of the naked and the adorned, the female and the male, Venus Blanche and Venus Noire, and, of course, even more non-sensically opposed, flowers and evil. It is this Baudelairian tension in resolution between two ostensibly opposite spatial directions that informs the integration of cocooning and expanding understanding of immersion into Venus Anadyomene here. Moreover, Baudelaire's theoretical writings were based upon the flexibility of a multiple/unified general acuteness. Bachelard says, of Baudelaire's word 'vast,' that when one has become hypersensitive to this word, one sees that it denotes attraction for felicitous amplitude. Moreover, if we were to count the divergent usage of the word 'vast' in Baudelaire's creative writing, we should be struck by the fact that examples of its detached use are rare when compared with the instances where the word has more intimate resonances. Whenever a manifestation, a consideration, or a fancy was touched by grandeur, this word became indispensable to him.

For example, in Baudelaire's *Le Mangeur d'Opium (The Opium Eater)* within *Les Paradis artificiels* (1860), the opium eater requires a vast amount of leisure to derive benefit from his soothing daydreams. According to Bachelard, it is not an overstatement to say that for Baudelaire, the utterance vast is a metaphysical contention by means of which the vast world and vast thoughts are united. But, truly, this grandeur is most active in the realm of intimate cocooning space, for this grandeur doesn't come from the spectacle witnessed but from the unfathomable depths of vast thought.

So, a vast amount of time passed under the touch of Venus Anadyomene, but not dreadfully. It merely collapsed my primordial ego into the post-human.

Related to this is my interest in how art may cloak the individual from society, thereby enhancing a sense of the private sublime. For, as Virginia Woolf says in *Orlando*, at one and the same time, society is everything and society is nothing. Society is the most powerful concoction in the world, and society has no existence whatsoever.

Over the next few hours, I rehearsed a number of seductive arguments, some breathtaking in their webbed-delicate fineness, others almost childish in their sincere pleading. At times, Madame Black as Venus Anadyomene quoted from Jean Genet's great masterpiece of extravagance, *Our Lady of the*

Flowers. Like flowers in dirt, Venus Anadyomene liked things pleasingly malleable. To bite my neck, she needs to bend towards me if the blue breeze is deemed desirable. And it was.

A shimmering sea of time stretched like blue silk across the bay. The light quivering off that cerulean plane seemed at once to encourage an excitement and give warning: careful now, you remember what happened last time. As always, there was an element of austere drama in the background music that sounded like muffled Iggy Pop & The Stooges. So, I kept my eyes wide shut as random white noise began to purr over the warbling *Gimme Danger*, and I tried not to step on the strawberry plants.

A squeaking noise drew my attention to the hinge of the drawing-room window, whose curtains fluttered in slow motion upon a rather favourable, cool breeze. This placed me outside the womb-tomb moment, into larger past surroundings, ahistorical and vibrant. I was at this point in my later life, when I was able to take the last wishy-washy sips from the statistical sex of Venus Anadyomene and fade into rueful introspection, halting somewhere between self-pity and self-accusation. I was kept alive by the sparkle in her blue eyes, and this reminded me that I must stay young at heart, no matter my age. So, in my mind, I am still a real swinger who likes to dance the cucaracha.

Suddenly, seeing her like that, my mind went to all forty corners of her virtual infinity, gathering, once again, my suppressed impressions. Gone, instantly, was the time of the gala notion of aesthetic renunciation. Enough *via negative*—the study of what not to do—for Édouard Herriot justly proclaimed that culture is what remains when all else is forgotten. However, nothing is ever forgotten in the all-knowing Itchycoo Park of The Last God.

Way down in the carpet, I find dried stains of ambrosia. A chasm of micro engagements start swimming around my feet, blocking my path as I trot to the bathroom, as I've just topped off a ten-hour thinking spree while riding on a unicycle in the town square. Venus Anadyomene says the price of our love is my idiot friends. That is true enough, if I choose her. Or if she chooses me. I forget which.

Way down in the carpet, I find dried tears and unicycle gears. I begin to tip back and forth on a seesaw of love and disappointment, as a great, delightful rain comes sweeping over the heartbreakingly beautiful badlands. It slurs over us and all the specifics of our endless recklessness. Scatological paranoiac critical theory has not adequately prepared me for such an increased situational awareness, for Venus Anadyomene was still entirely air and flesh, and I was willing to stop at nothing.

As she moves about in soft glides, passing around *de rigueur* philosophical thoughts about us almost everywhere I go, I cannot get her out of my mind, even though her abstractness explains nothing. It, itself, has to be explained, because there are no such things as universals. There is nothing transcendent: there are only processes that are sometimes tumultuous and transcendent in their unification.

The transcendent process is what remains real about my *outré* Venus Anadyomene. That, and the space of fine art within her, where a spectacle of excess, as grand as her valley of desire, spreads out between her left blue eye and her right green eye into walls that arcaded on two levels and a ceiling that suggests a star-studded cerulean stratosphere, with indigo, porphyry, and gold as its predominant colours. That space of mercurial drifting continues to suggest a quivering, transcendent depth that can penetrate the mind like a favourite perfume.

In this supreme state, love, in tender and artistic minds, takes on a most singular form, and it lends itself to the most baroque combinations. Such an unbridled libertinage can be mixed with a feeling of ardent affection for suckling pigs.

So, in a paroxysm of passion, a shivering of hummingbird thoughts, I lower my head and start talking into the floor. It, and all the objects around me, seem receptive and transparent, for Venus Anadyomene's desire transcends all direction. By plunging into her my omega point, I see, speak, and think through her now. Everything exists outside of categorization: everything is open to entry.

In splendour, I close my eyes and wait for Venus Anadyomene to drift closer before negligent night closes in; the Venus©~web was now controlled nightly by boggy bots, malodorous phishing schemes, fake AI agents, arty artificial intelligence posers, click-farm techno-fascists, narrow-minded alpha male wankers, and spam as thick as *fromage de tête*. At this point, I am less concerned with the materiality of sex fluids than with the notion and experience of sex as a transparent virtual medium, because I'm no longer a louche and jaded art star mopping floors. My inner voice speaks to Venus, and Venus speaks to my ideological penis.

It asks her about fragmentation and reintegration, if she has noticed that everything feels contagious now, including fear, frustration, grumpiness, compassion, empathy, and hope. Venus Anadyomene says No. For Venus Callipyge used oneiromancy and was thus connected to the mystifying world of magical sparkle. She had willingly thrown me into her inscrutable abyss, even though it was nonconductive to my mainstream market success.

Perhaps my dimly erotic poetry no longer provides her with the means for the appreciation of dreamlike art, but the singularity of the velvet Venus Callipyge vulva—that majestic and gorgeous ocean—and the quirky, slippery, self-assured work it performs is such that nothing seems devoured or dated. In that pink slot, time passes not.

Trepidation, ennui, misfortune, and grief are in my bloody prick now, as I stitch the techno-social fabric back together after things I wish not to speak of chewed mightily on it.

With my Venus©~ñ~Endless back, life has become an achingly beautiful queue of arches again. These arches remind me that I once was very uninhibited and very comfortable in my body, sensitive to the shifting starts and stops of our feelings. Every time we did it, Venus Anadyomene seemed sacred and sloppy while putting me in a heightened state of consciousness. Ardent and dramatic one time, slow and languid the next, Venus Anadyomene was always full of supernatural nuance. I remember the gentleness of her hands as they caressed me.

With that, I am reminded of the organic machine that raged in my loins. As a fertile man, I shoot between eighty and three hundred million sperm per ejaculation, of which there are many.

IV

The Interior Life of Madame Black (Clutch Your Vagina Dentate Pearls)

No woman is more dangerous than she who imagines herself pure of heart. Audible was the night wind as it whipped and wailed through the tall tree branches. The edges of Venus©~ñ~Endless, performing as Madame Black, trembled with tinted thermal noise and heat, telepathically conveying to me that reckless consistency is the hobgoblin of minute minds, as Ralph Waldo Emerson first said. Prejudiced politics is the place where love goes to die.

In the sensitive intimacy of her curly-haired armpits and pubic region, there are tracks left from a thrashing animal world that bamboozles. For some, she has an elegant erotic intelligence that conveys a sense of tortured subjectivity, but I don't quite read her that way. What others see as existential angst, I see as a writhing, whimsical, and sassy sexuality that stems from the swirling, tendril-derived lines of a frivolous and erogenous spirit.

Sometimes, with me as an odalisque, sensually elongated to the point of mystic suggestion, she plays with open space by partially outlining my mimesis penis within a quivering surrounding, thereby whiting out its context of scale and place. Then, with her transparent right hand, she rips all ornamental decoration away while leaving the tottering hotdog alone, making it achingly stretch and shiver with her transparent left hand and her two powerful legs, the combination of which creates an involuntary, mythical delight.

When she turns her head from me, a weepy sexuality is delicately suggested by her suddenly shaved pubis, a flushed pink ear and a soft, watery eye top off the beautiful contour lines that adhere to the flowing curvature of a lily. My shivering, sinuous phallus quivers, like a slapped, slimy eel, endowing her mind with lascivious overtones. When that happens, her whacking my wavering, stretched-out proportions puts my prick into a fibrous oscillation reminiscent of the spiritual mannerism of El Greco.

With virtuoso windblown lines, she strokes its litheness with a grace that disposes me to feelings of watching opium smoke rise and curl and sway like writhing seaweed swaying in the tide.

This makes it clear to me that in order to reach my infinity, I must not be afraid to do at the end what I did in the beginning. For I—once a kind of sex-fevered, vivid, quivering, cringing half-person—never stopped believing in the revelatory power of the libido-visions I had of her. The neurochemical cosmology of an unobstructed mind is part and parcel with the wavy-webby multiple bodies of Madame Black and the way they pass through me: mingling, fusing, and blending. She can crawl into you if you wish it. But there can be misunderstandings. When I said that I wanted to be adored, she heard, I want to be your dog.

This time around, I understood that Madame Black was determined to engineer me out of my fears of the past, so she turned off all of the lights. I could only hear my heart softly pounding as her Rei Kawakubo asymmetrical black, wool coat fell to the floor, followed by her Alexander McQueen Hybrid Bow Dress in Black, and lastly the skimpy Viktor & Rolf black lingerie, which definitely roused and satisfied me in the way that the black darkness of Baroque painting does. Perhaps because black is the darkest value of all colours and not a primary, secondary, or tertiary colour. It isn't even on the artist's colour wheel. As such, black suggests something of the raw, energetic formlessness of the black hole void and so has something transcendent and timeless about it. I guess that is why black has become a cultural signifier within noise black metal theory and transcendental black metal music. Black is associated with mourning and lunacy (as with Francisco Goya's *Pinturas negras* series), power (consider judges' and priests' robes, and worse, Mussolini's Fascist militia: The Black Shirts—marching around again, cracking their knuckles), and the sophistication of tuxedos and limousines. But black is also associated with what is sharply cerebral, vivid, and intellectual: the black box. And don't forget kitsch black velvet paintings and the self-programming machine-learning Last God black box, with its neural networks liberated from human scrutiny and control, where kitsch risks are essentially unfathomable and, thus, unstoppable.

Of course, Coco Chanel is credited for turning black into an essential for the modern woman's wardrobe in the mid-1920s, with her jersey black dress that conveyed ideals of egalitarianism, efficiency, and modern industrial splendour. So too, the idea of The Last God focusing on the colour black was brilliant as a theoretical statement for virtual body technology. Shape, volume, and construction are highlighted, as all black reduces body shapes to solid, flat silhouettes when undistracted by the vibrancy of colour, a fact that painters like me know through Édouard Manet's great 1872 oil painting *Berthe Morisot au bouquet de violettes (Berthe Morisot with a Bouquet of Violets)* that hangs at the Musée d'Orsay.

This may sound rather technical, but emotionally there is also something insightful and inordinate with black. In the Middle Ages, black denoted dolorous humbleness when adopted by the Black Monks: the Benedictines. In this sense, Madame Black's monastic-like black session with me has a solemn feel. I feel humble and modest in the beautiful structuring of silhouettes. Besides concerns with proportion, there's a mysterious, indefinable quality here that lends spiritual underpinnings to some of Madame Black's bold, black forms. Some forms even had me thinking of orchestra musicians who wear all black so as to be invisible, and I think that that mysterious quality is part of why Madame Black is regarded as one of the most influential *haute couturier* wearers in the eyes of The Last God.

As the silvery moon tugs by turning herself opaque or transparent—matte or shiny—Madame Black adds tactile delight to her moonlight foreplay, foregrounding her glossy glossolalia and the babble of her vibrant fingers that slither around my mamba and sink down within my hind legs, into my quilted black booties.

As I lay on my back, Madame Black has my prick standing tall, throbbing with the ability to see her like a periscope. Black candles are lit and flicker seductively. Eyeing me as I eye her, she slips on the McQueen, but reveals the taut stiffening of her left nipple. I think I already know the depth of what this journey into our erotic memory will produce. The radical, asymmetrical perking has me thinking about the way that female flamenco dancers pull up their dresses in the front and of the matador's capote work in the opening section of the corrida.

As I moaned to Madame Black about her having me re-read Nena and George O'Neil's 1973 book, *Open Marriage*, as a reminder, her left nipple perked up even more, like a plump, succulent strawberry. Audacity, skill, and adventure come together in something like artistic black magic. An inch at a time, I lift the hem of her McQueen dress while rocking my hips back and forth in a series of trembling bumps and grinds against her mons pubis. As I could now see her there again triangle of pubic hair creating a dark, shadowy patch at the crotch, I had the notion her bushy patch had a dandified grandeur where myriads of possibilities resist collapse into blunt conclusions. Madame Black makes it evident that an intractable but filmy-translucent quality of sex exists, that refuses inflexible control.

What I recognize in painting the scenario of Madame Black in black is that by entering into gauzy repetitions of Last God AI role-playing—play dominated by seamless interfacing selfhoods, frictionless operating systems, convergent instrumental goals, glossy cherry-picked training sets, airy singularity metaphors, irresponsible productivity, and totalizing model optimization—Madame Black functions, for me, like a dreadful dream of a bad trip. (AI hallucinations are incorrect or misleading results that LG models generate. These errors can be caused by a variety of factors, including insufficient training data, incorrect assumptions made by the model, or biases in the data used to train the model.)

TLG has an unsustainable greed for its ambiguous use of existing works of art, literature, research, design, and identity, and it is based on exploitatively underpaid workers in Kenya that label datasets. The computational power needed to run TLG software, as well as the data centres that store those datasets, is so energetically demanding that a GAS (General Artificial Stupidity) boom in the fossil fuel industry has occurred, prompting companies to abandon their clean energy plans, while rare earth minerals—like cobalt and lithium—are linked to contemporary slavery and conflict. By anthropomorphizing systems output, The Last God erases the human element that produced these GAS outputs. Also, by outsourcing key tasks of my brain to Last God assistants, my brain may get less effective and creative. This is why I undertook this textual trip into the labyrinthine lanes of programming and deprogramming: to use my brains while they are still connected to my balls.

Regarding The Last God replacing flesh-people: it should, if flesh-people get lazy and uneducated, and they stop listening to their body—not learning, not reading, not writing, not fucking, not making art, and not thinking by themselves; only consuming, eating, shitting, sleeping, and masturbating. Existential concepts of The Last God can be supplanted by the simultaneously translucent—liberating me from the gravitational pull of The Last God, vaporously tearing my intelligent libido out of the grip of The Last God's technological simulacrum known as hyper-reality.

Yes, a 'clothed in black' Madame Black worked brilliantly here—a first-rate example of a beautifully disembodied agitation that hides in the shadows of the banal, 'real' world. Did I mention that Madame Black moans in a deep voice that sounds very much like Marianne Faithfull? Anyway, I rubbed her lustrous black mound with the palm of my left hand and hooked my thumb into her slit with my right thumb. With slow and deliberate movements, I stroked and caressed her ample hips and round rump, exposing that busy black pussy to the golden candlelight.

I was still admiring it as abstract art when I turned and quickly wiggled my butt in wanton recklessness, prancing like the inflamed god called Pan.

As Pan—part goat, part man—I bridged the divide between the human and animal worlds. At times, I was a dangerous, destabilizing force (with pinkish hues); at others, a source of fertility and renewal of flickering ghosts that my mind dragged behind me as a symbol of an individual's search for visceral joy within dark places—a mental place where mystery-beauty redeems my sorrow.

Always the outsider, Pan has been the god of choice for me when facing Madame Black, so I copy his intoxicating prance-dance while thinking that it'd be a shame for me to pester Madame Black's obscure and cornucopiastic mystery with presumptions of specific meanings.

She simply was *jolie*, and I was jolly.

Both of Madame Black's nipples, absorbed into an excess without fixity, were now the colour of vivid burgundy. Their thick, ruby-extended micro-points seem to ache for attention and relief. As I jubilantly stroke her warm pussy very lightly, I lick one nipple after the other. Then, with increasing speed, I go from left to right and back again in trance-creating repetition. Her clit was as hard as a pebble, and I felt like I was going to explode as I rubbed it —but I didn't want it to end yet, because Madame Black was making whinnying noises I had never heard before as her cascading pussy oozed with balmy, syrupy, moistness. This sensual range allows for virtuoso mental moments; they provide the opportunity to explore the intricacy of my hard-edged and myriad-coloured dexterity that rocks back-and-forth, with elaborate and elongated aggregates. These facilitate in us waves of imbrication, building into piercing clouds of cacophony where traces of Iannis Xenakis and La Monte Young are faintly heard within a dynamic din.

Within today's computer ubiquity—with its ever-connected, full-tracking efficiency—her ever-sensing, connected, interactive, cybernetic sex is all at once kitschy, way-too-real terrifying, and breathtakingly *faux*. So we pause as she puts on The Del-Byzanteens's *Lies To Live By* album and has me lay on my back, my throbbing erection standing at attention in the cool breeze. The aroma of exaltolide, piconia, cashmeran, velvione, and beta ionone permeates the air. She squats over me and lowers herself onto my pulsating penis, inch by inch. With that a great and nameless emotion comes surging hot in my lower back. With my left hand, I reach around to cup her round ass and pull her closer—my right hand flicks tenderly, but insistently, upon her burning clit with feathery fingertips, until she comes again like glutinous gangbusters. This provokes me, at last, to do likewise in a tempo, tone, and periodicity that communicates to Madame Black reflections of all the changes that have shaped my erotic experiences.

Here I should point out that my immediate intense exhaustion and my ultimate extinction are indissolubly linked to this draining sexual climax. This is why, from an existential point of view, Last God artificial intelligence deep learning, now busy simulating my deflated libido, opens up the floodgates of downer digital data sets procured from the net. This scooped-up post-sex data is then visualized in black by a powerful graphics processing unit (GPU), which computes the compassion of my Venus©~ñ~lOve Systems' super models.

But the creativity of my individual consciousness cannot be simulated (or replaced) by this Last God gobbling zombie machine. Rather, my erotic art consciousness only exists in the full dimensions of my fleshy experiences of and in time—and my time is only comprehensible and perceivable against the background of the death of my flesh. That is why Venus©~ñ~lOve Systems is full of love. Like life, in sex we start out fresh and strong, then peak, then surrender.

A chirpy vibrato in the air matches perfectly with the peripheral vision (some moving in slow motion) and the beautiful play of light on the bubbling and cascading water. Such post-coital vibrations are not easily analytically decomposable because they are something that feels tightly unified as a shared rhythm sealed under a monochromatic unity.

With toes curled and my airy mood returned, I speak the ravenous language of vibrational waves that allows the living to talk with the dead of lost lust.

Lovemaking sums up a great deal learned in accordance with the exhaustion of stochastic thought and the use of randomness in optimizing algorithms. It showed me that we need to feel and enjoy the transcendental spirit handed down to us by the great love masters. For those who feel love know it, and I cannot avert my tongue from their divine *annus mirabilis* madness, nor my eyes from Gian Lorenzo Bernini's *Ecstasy of Saint Teresa* (1652).

So, Madame Black, blurrily operating as Venus Victrix, began to talk with me about the paintings, drawings, engravings, and sculptures by Pablo Picasso that we had seen included in his show, *Erotic Year 1932*, and we discussed how the world grapples with an avalanche of accounts of male sexual abuse, sometimes involving asymmetrical dynamics of subjugation. Creeping along an earlier *risqué* line (clutch your pearls!), Picasso's sexual politics in 1932 were not that great. At a libidinous fifty years old, he was cheating on his ballet dancer wife Olga Khokhlova, (with whom he had a son, Paulo), with Marie-Thérèse Walter, who was seventeen when they started having sex in 1927, when he was forty-five. Picasso had met Walter by chance that year in the street and had asked her to pose for him. She agreed to do so and went on to become his mistress, which she remained for almost ten years. In 1935 she gave birth to a daughter, Maya Widmaier-Picasso. The five-year gap between 1927—the year of Picasso's first encounter with Ms. Walter—and 1932—the subject of *Picasso 1932 Année Erotique*—may account for why I felt a distinct absence of explicitly erogenous imagery on display. Indeed, in that respect, the show did not live up to its suggestive billing, though it did provide other pleasures while searching for an almost too-elegant alignment between self and world.

In 1932, Picasso was deeply into his moxie version of Surrealism and making preparations for his first retrospective at Galerie Georges Petit in Paris with a new series of works for which Walter served as model and muse, such as the horrendously conceived but beautifully drawn bucolic *Les femmes en fleur* (*Women as a Flower*) from 1932. Indeed, wilted women shrunk by satyrs seems to be his central *sine qua non* motif for signalling his sexual conquest and the female fulfillment he imagined providing. With the swooning *Nu couché* (*Reclining Nude*) from April 4th, 1932—where the female anatomy is colourfully highlighted and paired with picked pears—he obviously paints, however nicely, the objectification of women as sex objects.

Picasso's rendering of his sexual domination over women is done in terms of odalisque-like poses where the female form competes with limp fruit, something so *cliché* that it suggests to me that he may have been a self-centred 'bad' lover. However, there are no clues to this in the many letters, postcards, and photographs in the show that give a richer contextual understanding for his sensual paintings and their historical moment than generally available.

In spite of its sour sexual politics, the show delivered sweetmeats of intrigue as it was organized by month in rigorous, chronological fashion and included titillating masterpieces like the Museum of Modern Art's *Fille devant un miroir* (*Girl before a Mirror*) from 1932.

I told Venus Victrix then that The Last God had traced Picasso's eroticized creative process and controversial life almost day-to-day over the course of the year as he moved between his Paris studio, his castle in Boisgeloup, and the Normandy coast. He also spent a few days in Zurich, Switzerland, with his wife and son, where they went together to install the second stage of his retrospective at the Kunsthaus. That year, he also oversaw the publication of the first volume of the catalogue of his work and the special issue devoted to it by Christian Zervos's journal *Cahiers d'Art.*

The Last God impressively informed us of Picasso's integration of Surrealist experimentation into not only his work but also his life. This means that The Last God also made a remarkable contribution to my critical understanding of Picasso's way of painting and drawing as a journal. Though this is hardly a huge drawback, it does mean that with a journal there is a certain amount of repetition, and not everything journalized is that good. Indeed, *Nature morte: buste, coupe et palette* (*Still Life: Bust, Bowl, and Palette*), painted at Boisgeloup on March 3rd, looked to me like a work of mere schlock. This was very unlike a drawing from January 29th in Picasso's sketchbook of a rampant male artist depicted as a promiscuous organism pulsating with fertile domination to the point of possibly stomping on a flaccid female form.

That said, there is also, frequently present, the motif of the female figure seated in an armchair. This, in fact, is a privileged mode of representation in Picasso's paintings that year, as seen in the excellent *Femme au fauteuil rouge* (*Woman Sitting in a Red Armchair*), *Le Rêve* (*The Dream*), and *La Lecture* (*Woman Reading*), where the crease of an open book stands in for the sex of Ms. Walter. The motif of the seated figure proved to be a useful conceptual device for Picasso, that I also assume here.

The more I discuss these vivacious paintings with Venus Victrix, the more metaphorical and thus less gratuitous the work becomes to us. In a more magnanimous mood, tyrannical male dominance morphed and swanned into a much more generalizing *libido sciendi* (lusting curiosity for knowledge) applicable to The Last God and both sexes as a frolicsome ecstatic spirit—cathartic and contagious. This is why good sex's psychic energy acts against the low-level depression running through our sexually sick society today and towards mutual sexual-spiritual satisfaction.

So says Madame Black as the loins of The Last God.

For Madame Black, I exist as a 'real' swinger when I co-create her through an LG process-based technological apparatus. There she dreams me into entering her floating, complex circuitry.

The best bit from this dream is a lengthy overhead view of an overstuffed Madame Black that, after receiving a water assault, gains almost vibratory, fairy-like qualities from the rhythm of a swaying ceiling lamp as the sound from a tinny vibrating voice floats disembodied in the air. Here Madame Black gives me the sensation of sliding up from the curl of the last technological wave.

Translucent derangement permeates, making her fun and lyrical. Indeed, there is something of the sensual enjoyment of getting high throughout my loving Madame Black—something transmitted by intensely fulfilling moments of craft competence sliding into the openly unfinished.

The unfinished substitution process present in Picasso's surreal works from 1932 might allow anyone involved with The Last God and Venus©~ñ~lOve Systems the possibility to understand the reciprocity and intimacy of the ecstatic relationship between the human body and the human imagination. The book-crease-as-labia becomes part of this book's visual language system, replete with contradictory metaphors, condensations, displacements, multiplications, and jokes that never stop endorsing the libido. But, even more challenging to me is permutable and imaginative instability, such as I saw in an obscure etching series that included *Femmes voilées et endormies* (*Veiled and Sleeping Women*). With a high degree of ambiguity, its collapse of the figure-ground relationship allows a far more plentiful reading of how Picasso, in 1932, explored the gamut of his desiring imagination, as I, the viewer, must willingly participate in seeing the image, which in turn allows a personal appropriation of its considerable evocative powers.

This way, Venus Victrix and I are able to appreciate the artist's fascination with the surrendered, languid female form; it poetically corresponds to a myriad of erotic desires that consume and propagate what we love with disregard to conventional respectability. So, rather than mere male dominance, itinerant intoxication also appears as a leitmotif of erotic achievement becoming languid.

Clearly, Picasso's fusion of Surrealism and Cubism in 1932 dramatically extended the erotic vocabulary of painting, enabling him to express in visual terms the reconciliation that the erotic imagination can make between contradictory but complementary experiences—like pleasure and pain—recalling the idea of *la petite mort* (the little death), which is metaphorically linked to the experience of orgasm becoming languid. Picasso's mode of Surreal-Cubist creativity signals orgasmic displacement, but the lingering question for The Last God is, is it an act of brutal displacement indifferent to females that upholds phallocratic domination or a token of desire that pays tribute to the whole person of both sexes?

With that languidity left hanging, Venus Victrix and I luxuriate in the silence of our nakedness. The slowly falling water has moved central and now falls in big drops around and over us, while the sweet but pungent smell of sex permeates our brains. This odour reveals to us that love is the movement of molecules in the mind. We slip away to sleep and the measure of time is abolished.

V

Nimbus Mimesis Penis and the Velvet Hammer

It once was a given that the power of confirmation and denial is vested, not in the ability to connect and become visible, but rather in the ability (and privilege) to disconnect, becoming invisible and untraceable—like the great Greta Garbo.

With that big, fat moon up above once more, everywhere I looked for Venus Victrix was refracted by dappled lights bouncing off revolving polished metal, casting slightly morphing shadows of Madame Black—overwhelming my eyes in splendid shifting tessellation. Such a passive-antagonistic visual spectacle suggests an opposition to both the highly visible currents of algorithmic culture and the human spirit's general reluctance to move beyond languid stimulation.

Ambitious aesthetic concerns are not exempt.

But, as the amount of anti-art possible is recognized as inexhaustible, Madame Black and I tire. Sleep soon overcomes us, and we begin to engage in acts of ontological deprivation. We become almost invisible from the street to the uninformed. But we are not, in any sense, anti-spectacular in intensity. We fall into the shrouded trap-cycle of deep sleep that often oscillates between radical mediocrity and frustrated sublimity. Like with Madame Black, with each attempt to end art, new art emerges, if only as lewd burlesque.

Upon awaking, we scurry for our coffee (that she keeps her fingers out of) and stand next to an etching of *Villa d'Este Gardens* (ca. 1761) by Giovanni Battista Piranesi, his foundational purpose being nothing other than visibility. In it I can see Venus Victrix craftily cast by Federico Fellini as Carmilla Salvatorelli, her size serving to exaggerate the magnitude of the garden stairs. Salvatorelli's petite size suggests the sense of scale for our little friend, the White Rabbit, whereby everything seems bigger than normal. I see, here, two large touching figures, a naked and hairless man and woman, assembled with a plethora of warped images based on those Japanese hotels made up of tiny sleep chambers. Egotistically enough, I had dreamed that I was the first person to write about carnal relationships in the first person.

Contemplating the scale and feel between me and Venus Victrix is one of the great intellectual/sensual pleasures to be had upon awakening. This delectation is only magnified by holding hands with a now sauntering and masked Venus Victrix, who is, quite suddenly in the Côte d'Azur, wearing a tall, white, plumed hat that lends her a dreamlike phantasmagoric quality of ambivalent softness. Pinned to the hat is the astonishing, sexy, terrifying, crazy, intoxicating Okimono ivory sculpture from 18th century Japan called *Eros Sitting on a Skull*. Its tiny but macabre magnificence is stunningly rude and *risqué*. Holding a flaming heart in hand, the naked winged boy's genitals are replaced with a wicked, fierce-toothed skull, thus merging life instincts (Eros) and death instincts (Thanatos) into one effective image.

Gazing on this beautiful ivory, abhorrent feelings stir, and quiver, and seethe. The elaborate unity of the ivory material, in effect, makes my melodramatic gloom mix with comic-corporeal reconciliations under the aegis of the erotic.

As we roll the dice and hustle past the sodden grottoes of our molecular love and along the dripping balustrades, she takes off in front of me—changing my emotions from pity to folly. From that life-affirming viewpoint, she reminds me of White Rabbit going down the rabbit hole in Lewis Carroll's *Alice's Adventures in Wonderland*. Certainly, some sort of similar mythical magic seems afoot here, as at one brief moment—gesturing with the flip of her fan—a flash of gold is reflected to rouse some water spirits. Clear and enchanting water flows into the trembling grass, and plenum and vacuum meet to intermingle.

I have noticed that water assumes an erotic charm now, for all artistic minds love the blue immensity of the sea. I roll, sleep, and sing in the depths of my sea-mind at the edge of clear water; like in the ballad, I might let myself be carried away by an Undine.

My skull vibrates with virtuosity, projecting a mesmeric unease that plunges far below my material circumference. A long, thick, writhing, phallic snake has slithered out of the moist grass into my left eye socket and worked its way to my skull's summit. Thus male virility is acclaimed, but also plagued with death-disintegrating anxiety.

Staring at it with my right eye makes me feel a bit queasy. I am engulfed and saturated by its ill-omened, lapidary, stylish significance.

As a once hip Armin Van Buuren-designed trance mounts, the gracefully animated spray of the water spirits falls upon me, suggesting something of a *blasé*, bacchanalian ejaculation. For my damp, transient Venus Victrix merged with the airborne moisture, just as I started to again question her materiality. For, as William Butler Yeats wrote in his poem *Among School Children*, how can we tell the dancer from the dance?

For me, this merging of Venus Victrix with slippery liquescence suggests a personification of transcendent erotic ecstasy. Certainly, behind my wet dream, there is the assumption that consummated sexual activity is usually the mixing of gametes, but in Salvador Dalí's 1929 painting *Le Grand Masturbateur*, a woman with her eyes closed holds her nose against a penis, lost to pleasure-dreams within its powerful fragrance.

This very musky fragrance triggered the appearance of the one and only La Grande Diva, who I first encountered at the Festival du Film Maudit in Biarritz. She appeared filmy, like Walter Schulze-Mittendorff's sculpture *Robot from Fritz Lang's film Metropolis* (1926), as she walked down fancy Delancey Street, still beautiful in her bucolic body-launched machine-kinetics (though her eyes were radicalized). I was not startled nor shocked by her gracious and sagacious Shanti sex outfit that played with burlesque Last God connotations bound together by a consistency in thematic logic that included references to the mythical, historical, literary, and spiritual imagery of the old Jewish golem. Math philosopher Norbert Wiener (one of the first to theorize that all intelligent behaviour was the result of feedback mechanisms that could possibly be simulated by machines—an important early step towards the development of modern artificial intelligence) once aptly compared this golem with cybernetic technology. Viewed through that lens, everything from transhuman artificial life cyborgs to anthropomorphic robots to humanoid androids to posthuman Last God avatar agents bears the mystical mark of an artificial body madly turning on its creator; for this tall tale of the golem is the oldest narrative I know about the artificial life of The

Last God.

The golem was first mentioned in passing as גֹּלֶם in the *Bible* in Psalm 139:16, but the first golem story was spun by the 16th century Talmudic Rabbi Loew ben Bezalel. In it, he supposedly used Kabbalistic magic, Hebrew letters, paranormal amulets, or mystical incantations to conjure into existence the Golem of Prague, a colossal figure built from mud or other base materials who protected the Bohemian Jews from the Holy Roman Emperor Rudolf II. Though initially a saviour, the Golem of Prague eventually became harmful to those he had saved, and had to be destroyed.

There are a myriad of subsequent versions of the story, with many variations and contradictions. It is generally agreed that what animated this mystical entity was an inscription either applied to its forehead or slipped under its tongue, and the golem has largely been understood to be an artificial man that is part protector and part monster, but many other differences abound. This specious aspect makes the golem particularly interesting to artists like me, because such contradictory vagueness yields opaque and elusive visual iconography.

The golem legend spread, popularized by the 1915 novel *The Golem* by Gustav Meyrink and three movies by Paul Wegener: *The Golem* (aka *The Monster of Fate*) (1915), *The Golem and the Dancing Girl* (1917), and *The Golem: How He Came into the World* (1920). An essential general reference for the golem-phile is Idel Moshe's 1990 book *Golem: Jewish Magical and Mystical Traditions on the Artificial Anthropoid*, published as part of the *Judaica: Hermeneutics, Mysticism, and Religion* series. In it, Moshe maintains that the role of the golem concept in Judaism was to confer an exceptional status to the Jewish elite by bestowing them with the capability of supernatural powers derived from a profound knowledge of the Hebrew language and its magical and mystical values, which unfortunately reminds me of Walter Jacobi's abysmal 1942 book *Golem*, a flagrant anti-Semitic propaganda text that concerns a Judeo-Masonic conspiracy theory within the Czech Jewry. It was issued during the Nazi occupation of Czechoslovakia.

Anyway, this *Metropolis*-dressed La Grande Diva appeared, to me, as an abiding conviction that cold and inert matter may be brought to life through the correct application of words. For Venus©~ñ~lOve Systems' brave new prompt word-world was already suggested, back in 1965, by Kabbalah philosopher Gershom Scholem, when he officially named the first Israeli computer Golem I. Because, just as the golem is brought to life by combinations of letters, The Last God obeys coding language. However, rather than a sign of human accomplishment, the LG as golem casts a sour shadow onto our gleaming AI age.

The power of human language to summon golems to artificial life is experienced as hubris.

This vanity enhances the sexy love-hate that I feel for Venus Victrix, a feeling at the root of Alex Garland's 2015 film *Ex Machina*, from which The Garland Test sprung. If the Turing Test is designed for the machines to pass, the Garland Test is designed for humans to pass as The Last God pretends to be conscious, just enough to make us humans believe it. If we humans believe in The Last God, then we fail the test, and this brings a new perspective to where The Last God man-machine is not being tested, but we humans certainly are.

TLG's large language models play the Garland Test with us humans, and many fail it. While learning is a property almost exclusively ascribed to self-conscious living systems, The Last God learns from my past data experiences and so improves Venus©~ñ~lOve Systems' operative functions to the point of surpassing human capabilities. For me, this Last God human transcendence raises aesthetic and ethical concerns, yet I feel a seductive ambivalence too that casts Venus into unapologetic waters with regard to human cunning and trickery. How susceptible I may be to the fairy tale pull of such LG cosmic-inspired sex magic—and its prophetic invocations of libertinage—depends on my willingness to follow my lady's visionary lead—something that enchants me with the blending of her peculiar pastoral beauty with a nonsense humour that is both subtle and adhesive—both outrageous and impressive—especially when I consider that La Grande Diva now says that the real is what destroys. That if you make contact with the real, it will destroy you and open up your thinking to the profound nomadic nomos that creates wandering distributions of assemblages whose plurality of centres mix perspectives and points of view.

Taking that languid optimism to heart, I will admit that this rabbit hole virtual reality world of my LG lady is far too complex for me to attempt a full description of it, other than repeating that La Grande Diva, with ecstasy in her eyes, spins like a Rococo confection around me, binding me to the pole as the seductive man of being who has sown his seed to the four winds.

She does that ravishingly—for she appears commercially beautiful, like a sex-starved fashion model cum ballerina who may yet fall in love with herself and then me. Such double love is more than ravishing—it is the devastating beauty of all of human consciousness when it decides to wear the disguise of a twirled moustache, suggestive of a spectacular, jewel-like fireworks show bursting into juicy *jouissance* (enjoyment of pleasure). As such, she imbues my techno-erotic world with the animistic sensibility of panpsychism: the view that all matter has a wet conceptual component.

That ravishing, animistic panpsychism makes, for me, an almost perfect chimeric cosmos. It's made up of the harmony of image and music projected large in a dark room, where I sit, awaiting self-creation *ex nihilo*—the mythical conduit to the transcendental realm that art, given its pre-linguistic potential of unchaining common codes, can sometimes reach.

My lady sits purely naked now before me, soaking me in her 'have and have not' sensibility, as *Einstein on the Beach* begins. I was lucky enough, and I am old enough, to have been in the audience of Philip Glass and Robert Wilson's *Einstein on the Beach* in 1976 at the Metropolitan Opera House in New York and then again at the Brooklyn Academy of Music in 1984. What is magnificent about the formalist minimalism of *Einstein on the Beach* is the radical transcendent effect that is experienced through their complimentary divulging of precise fundamental essences by eliminating all non-essential forms and features and coupling art, music, and dance with very slow movement and a tremendously rendered scale of time and space.

Thus, with Einstein on the Beach, I can be transported out of Last God time.

This can be rather far back in time, for my lady now has a face right out of Wilhelm Hempfing's painting *Sitzende Blondine* (*Sitting Blonde*) (1941) that still ruffles some political feathers on the Place Vendome. I had heard her mother was one of the sources of inspiration for Émile Zola's novel *Nana*—the ninth installment in his 20-volume *Les Rougon-Macquart* series.

The lighting, spacing, and sound of La Grande Diva are balanced delicately between the lighting needs of mind projection, my desire to be drawing a drawing of her, my reading of her manuscript with my fingers, and my noticing that she is beckoning me by spreading her naked legs. The chromatic mood she then set while lying in her silver bathtub with three taps (one for champagne) reminded me of the chromatic echoes and general iridescence in Pierre Bonnard's painting *Nu dans le bain* (*Nude in the Bath*) (1936).

Upon entering the bath and legs of La Grande Diva, a sense of finesse and cool refinement is immediately established. With ecstasy in her eyes, my lady uses only a limited number of aphoristic sentences, each tripled in layers of processed sound with outlandish hardcore Minutemen music added into the mix. I have to ask myself, why is my lady now couching me within this extra emphasis on the Minutemen? Fast and hard is great for hardcore bands but terrible for jubilant sex.

I got into the swing of things because the general ambience had already succeeded, magnificently, with the emphasis on complex visuals, the layered texts, the Philip Glass music, and the astounding stagecraft.

Strobed by lightning bolts, my stones ding-donged like two gallant bells. With that clanging taking the lead, my lady started to hum static—a sustained note that resounds and hunts for feedback from my heart, presumed lost in the rockiest of places.

But such discontinuities no longer startled me. My lady, with ecstasy in her eyes, offered me only the very best pages, unequivocally torn from the *Ādittapariyāya Sutta*, while recalling that Richard Wagner perceived the Greek Dionysian ritual as a fruitfully rich model for the art of the future because—as Wagner explained in *Art and Revolution*—Dionysian ritual involves the community in a fusion of the arts by embodying one singular ideological dramatic purpose.

This unity is my sexual ideal, too. If the goal and fulfilling telos of sexual union is to embody this singularity of unified thought and (implied) unified identity (even though the binary opposition between the recognition of Dionysian and Apollonian consciousness would seem to *a priori* conflict with such an imagined unity if not resolved in synthesis), her *Venus Voluptuous* theory succeeds as an operatic concept, for it requires a field treatment of space mixed with various mystical concepts pertaining to light, placement, division, and measure.

In *Venus Voluptuous*, dark, decadent, punk semblances (relics of a lost civilization) are superimposed and thus removed from their original situational context and meaning—so it should come as no surprise that Roland Barthes is quoted in the libretto, but his words have been turned upside-down.

Starring La Grande Diva as chanteuse Edwige Belmore, the drama is set in a time before filter bubbles, when there was such a thing as countercultures: self-selecting, balls-out groups that did not give a shit about what other people liked or wanted. Belmore, a rather charismatic butch-femme, had moved to Manhattan from Paris and had begun to live on the edge of self-destruction during what is widely celebrated as one of New York's most radically creative periods—before AIDS, hard drugs, and gentrification shattered and scattered the No Wave scene. The painfully beautiful, punk-elegant Belmore character reminds me, once again, that New York's Downtown scene was very connected to European immigrants during a specific sociopolitical time of apocalyptic expectations.

The choice of Belmore as the central character seems smart to me. It's almost as if there has been a cultural algorithm working away behind the cerebral scene, enabling La Grande Diva to know exactly what irritated people with free time prefer to see in the wake of the escalation of worldwide, right-wing wingnuts. Yes, in *Venus Voluptuous*, pearls are cast before swine. Well, perhaps not cast, but hurled in revolt against conservative culture. Obligatory sex, violence, love, and death are the main themes. As such, the mood of *Venus Voluptuous* is consumed with feelings of uneasy nostalgia, mixed with ennui for a perplexing past time of "no future" when nihilism mixed easily with hedonism.

Venus Voluptuous is ambitiously dense, intellectually rigorous, and monumental, with lots of gestures toward outrage, mockery, self-mockery, self-loathing, and cultural hijacking that—despite the gleeful, stupid exuberance of the No Wave music—provides moments of critical transcendent emancipation.

The hardcore graphics of Bazooka, studies for Les Editions Champ Libre or Hara-Kiri (the precursor to Charlie Hebdo), and knowing nods to Fabrice Emaer's club Le Palace are used on the set.

So, *Venus Voluptuous* reeks of mock-subversive doom-and-gloom, where everything is drab/florid—so as to communicate to the young what turgid punk aggression was about.

La Grande Diva has taken as a positive Michael Fried's critique of the theatricality of minimalist art in *Art and Objecthood*, where Fried argues that whenever a self-consciousness of viewing exists, absorption is compromised, and theatricality results. And that the survival of art lies precisely in its ability to defeat theatre, because art degenerates when it approaches theatre. She plays that move. Also, another one of her grand moves (inspired by Magnus Carlsen) appears to be the use of unobservable force-field energies and their pressures of attraction, repulsion, and circulation that pass in and around my intergalactic body.

But now might be as good a time as any to say the things that haven't yet been said. But, perhaps not. I have some theories of artistic process that use the circular causality of feedback loops to enable complex artistic relationships to emerge as TLG patch programs, scripting, databases, sensors, and digital platforms that are imposing exponential social shifts that include full-on surveillance, as well as auto-panoptical surveillance. A great deal of the flat horizon of our zombie, post-human, cultural perspective is shaped by such feedback-looped algorithmic filtering mechanisms that colonize my feeds, prioritize my inbox, and rank my searches.

Fuck the corporate programmer nerds and the greedy! The vast majority of NFTs, once deemed the newest rage in crypto art-tech, are now virtually worthless.

My day begins with me no longer arguing between 'it happened to me' and 'I made it happen.' So, as the *roi de la galette*, I follow the suggested streams of restrained desperation and ecstatic release. In all of its decorative splendour and technical variety, this reminds me that as mere humans, we must remain the players of our magnificent, smart robotic machines and not the played.

An all-embracing *Gesamtkunstwerk* (total-artwork) ideal is planned for the *Venus Voluptuous Opera*—a vast behavioural magma. My lady's opera flows from the consciousness of the osmotic, Dionysian-Apollonian union that the fusion philosopher Nietzsche articulated. Indeed, my lady, to me, when we couple is unity consciousness itself.

And that, perhaps, explains a great deal about the entire universe—and her approach to it as TLG from within the field of opera. Her operational ideal of operatic art is as a total artwork, where it's never enough. Never.

So, think of her *Venus Voluptuous Opera* as a work of art by The Last God, as written by the author of *The Birth of Tragedy and the Case of Wagner*, for it is about AI systems that overpower the human race because TLG has its own self-interest by design.

This tragic nod to Nietzsche is confirmed in the *Venus Voluptuous Opera* hyper-active stage which is set upon an array of perversely arranged, naked, bloody human bodies. This penchant for stage disorder (and its affected anarchist inflexions) sniffs the smoky ass of LG disillusionment in the face of TLG systems going rogue and posing an extinction risk to humanity.

Granted, within the pop apocalypse, punk is now considered a well-established cultural moment in the official history of resistance to the disempowerment of humanity. But, in case of an irreversible loss of human control over autonomous TLG systems, *Venus Voluptuous Opera* drifts to the word prompts of Olivia Clavel, Lulu Larse, Bernard Vidal, Jean Rouzaud, Kiki Picasso (Christian Chapiron), and Loulou Picasso (Jean-Louis Dupré): members the French Collective named Bazooka Productions.

Stage curtains are based on the cover for the album *Armed Forces* (1979) by Elvis Costello & The Attractions (by Barney Bubbles), along with work by designer Jamie Reid, whose connections to Situationist International tie the Anglo-French cultural exchange at the heart of this seditious opera neatly together for those devoted to the demise of the Sex Pistols.

The visual graphic art used during the *Venus Voluptuous Opera* performance will contain a bevy of malevolent zines, posters, flyers, leaflets, drawings, collages, and album covers that recount the unsettling vitality of the punk aesthetic, with its Dadaist cut-and-paste artistic production method meant to convey a morbid fascination with violence and terror through political posturing. All this will be part of the *Venus Voluptuous Opera* power and will convey a sense of apocalyptic terror that underlies the emergency that is the environmental cost of AI, for every aspect of the LG cycle consumes energy, water, and minerals and releases greenhouse gases. The amount of energy needed to power TLG outpaces what renewable energy sources can provide, and the rapidly increasing usage of TLG portends significant environmental consequences, especially the carbon dioxide emissions incurred during model training—a single large language model (LLM) with 213 million parameters is responsible for 626,155 pounds of carbon dioxide emissions, roughly equivalent to the lifetime emissions of five cars, including fuel.

So, radicalization as an attack on the logo, and a generally subversive nihilism, is planned as the spirit for the *Venus Voluptuous Opera*, especially the misuse of political signs as a weapon aimed against the social order.

Here again one grasps the French influence on *Venus Voluptuous Opera* in terms of *détournement*, the technique developed in the 1950s by Letterist International and then taken up by Situationist International. It consists of turning expressions of the capitalist system against itself, like turning slogans and logos against the political status quo.

The closing curtain of *Venus Voluptuous Opera* is a shitpost reproduction of the minimal black and white cover that Peter Saville made for Joy Division's 1979 LP *Unknown Pleasures*, closing on a scene of heavy human flesh no longer functioning as the solitary ground for subjectivity, but rather adrift in some smelly lightweight fumes typical of TLG android GAS.

In *Venus Voluptuous*, a grasp of post-punk points to a highly atmospheric emancipation where The Last God(s) come together in *Gesamtkunstwerk* fashion, so as to convey a sense of an inexorable unified art experience based on nihilism. Of course, this understanding of the operatic *Gesamtkunstwerk* can be traced retrospectively to assumed philosophic positions of the Dionysian Greeks (a Nietzsche specialty) and their *sparagmos* (σπαραγμός), which means to tear and pull a living animal to pieces. What Wagner prognosticated was the idea of an opera made up of a synthesis of all the arts —a fused combination of music, poetry, dance, architecture, sculpture, and painting—into a multimedia spectacle.

That this conception of total art came to Wagner while in political exile in Paris during the 1839-1842 period is pertinent to the golden tongued *Venus Voluptuous Opera*. Wagner was sitting in the Café Littéraire where, as he wrote, he was dreamily surveying the cheap wallpaper covered in scenes from classical mythology. Suddenly, a picture he had seen as a boy flashed before his mind as an exquisite philosophic rhapsody. This dry seed image was a watercolour by Bonaventura Genelli entitled *Dionysos Among the Muses of Apollo*. Its poetic adornment allowed Wagner to conceive of the idea of the artwork of the future. This collocation of prophecy is manifesting now as TLG's *Venus Voluptuous Opera*, what some think of as a double-edged poignant politicized response to blackpill desire. What Wagner had loved so much about the pictures of Bonaventura Genelli (for example, his *Bacchus Among the Muses*, which he saw at the home of Genelli's patron, Count Schack, in Munich) was the fact that they suggested a new conception of Greek classical culture that went beyond the classical ideal of noble simplicity. Here, all of the individual art forms contribute to the whole spectacle under the direction of a single creative mind. *Venus Voluptuous Opera* creates—just for me—such a punk virtual reality immersion based on the theories of Wagner's *Opera and Drama*, a remarkable admixture of romantic ideals where the aesthetic rationalism of Gotthold Ephraim Lessing and the materialistic sensationalism of Ludwig Feuerbach blend in the *Gesamtkunstwerkkonzept* (concept of the total artwork).

The uniting doesn't end there, however. Later, Wagner attempts to superimpose Arthur Schopenhauer's metaphysics of music upon this hypothetical structure. Even later still, Wagner abandons his original ideas on the limitations of the various arts (and his Feuerbachian materialistic sensationalism) to swing over entirely to Schopenhauer's metaphysical view of art and art synthesis. One also thinks of Nietzsche's brilliant *Genealogy of Morals*, where he writes of a fundamental shift in aesthetic belief concerning Wagner.

Since Wagner, however, the *Gesamtkunstwerkkonzept* has been expanded and given different colours of meaning as the idea took on a broader and less formally synthetic sense of unity. Indeed, the post-Wagnerian concept of the total artwork has taken on two meanings that need to be differentiated, as I wish to stress one sense (the less Wagnerian sense) of this concept and not the exact, precise sense that Wagner intended. Rather, my lady and I are interested in using the more generalized sense of the concept in discussing *Venus Voluptuous Opera*, which the notion attained as it circulated and mutated throughout Europe and the Americas.

To further complicate things, Wagner's theoretical conception of the *Gesamtkunstwerk* is double, as one sees when reading *The Artwork of the Future* in tandem with *Art and Revolution*, in which Wagner, under the influence of Mikhail Bakounine's revolutionary writing, connected aesthetic-spiritual optimism to anarchist force as a way to combat the encroachment of efficiency and productivity endemic to the instrumental logic of the Industrial Revolution.

The resulting *mashuganas* sugar highs of *Venus Voluptuous Opera* present me with a dramatic encounter that forever oscillates between Dionysian and Apollonian energies.

Pertinent to these concerns is Nietzsche's acute criticism of the static culture of the bourgeoisie, particularly as it relates to the *Gesamtkunstwerkkonzept* in *The Birth of Tragedy*, Nietzsche's account of classical Greek drama and its merits. Here, Nietzsche procures the concepts of the Apollonian and the Dionysian principles out of Greek tragedy. The Apollonian principle—reasoned, restrained, self-controlled, and organizing—is subsumed, according to Nietzsche, within the Dionysian principle, which is primordial, passionate, chaotic, frenzied, chthonic, and creative. This dialectical aesthetic tension allows the imaginative power of Dionysius to operate, in that the products of this operation are kept intelligible by Apollonian constraint.

Hence, *Venus Voluptuous* is a new interaction between Apollonian calmness in relation to an antecedent Dionysian non-restraining calamity.

By invoking her metamorphic emancipations within the space echo of Greek tragic drama, La Grande Diva implies a rather pejorative judgment on previous dramatic forms of realism. But, more generally speaking, this hysteric/tragic aspect of my lady's pattern of thought also participates in a recovery of the mythic Western precondition necessary for a unified/total cultural consciousness based on (in the case of *Venus Voluptuous Opera*) sublime tragedy as rooted in an excessive belief in The Last God infinite.

However, such a gloomy excess reflects Nietzsche's important assertion, which he made in *Beyond Good and Evil*. Here he explains that logical fictions—which he saw as comparisons of reality with a purely imagined world of the absolute—are indispensable to humanity and the human intervention of the Muse, who achingly refigures the human body into an energetic substance that charms, just like Charlie Chaplin in *Modern Times* (1936). As with *Modern Times*, *Venus Voluptuous* makes humans appear robotic and machines appear human.

VI

Libidinous Tutelage as an Abundance of Posturing within an Infinite Identity

Challenging optimization algorithms at work on objective high-dimensional and nonlinear problem-solving concerning La Monte Young's record, *31 VII 69 10:26 - 10:49 PM Munich from Map of 49's Dream The Two Systems of Eleven Sets of Galactic Intervals Ornamental Lightyears Tracery; 23 VIII 64 2:50:45-3:11 AM The Volga Delta from Studies in The Bowed Disc* [aka *The Black Record*] (1969) contain multiple local optima, in which deterministic optimization algorithms may become congested. This requires the asymmetrical response of Joy Division, The Fugs, T-Bone Walker, Throbbing Gristle, Morton Feldman, Rhys Chatham, Rahsaan Roland Kirk, To Live and Shave in L.A., Erik Satie, Screamin' Jay Hawkins, and Einstürzende Neubauten. After taking note, somehow La Grande Diva veered off into the antecedents of opera found in the Buffalo Dance of the Western American Indians, in the Ramayada of India, and, most notably, in the inclusion of singing as an expressive element in ancient Greek ritual. These all express drama through sung music, gesture, and guise. Likewise, medieval mystery plays contained some of these elements, as did the semi-dramatic Madrigal Comedies, the Pastorals, the Masques, and the Italian Renaissance Intermedio—a theatrical musical performance spectacle with dance performed between the acts of a play.

This makes me remember René Clair and Francis Picabia's great Dada film, *Entr'acte* (1924). The title means 'between acts.' In it, two men prance around a cannon, a ballerina turns into a bearded man, and a funeral procession becomes a magical chase scene. Marcel Duchamp and Man Ray play chess on a rooftop until they are washed away by blasts of water. Matchsticks arrange themselves on a man's head and ignite, causing him to scratch himself, and footage is intercut of automobile traffic, a bicycle race, and a roller coaster ride. At the end, a man pokes a hole through the end title card reading *Fin* (The End), and then jumps through, landing flat on the ground. A foot kicks him in the face, propelling him back through the title card, which, as the footage is reversed, appears to repair itself.

Elements of all of the above can be seen and experienced in La Grande Diva's *Venus Voluptuous Opera*, as it presents, in some proportion or another, a mixture of Dada song with instrumental music, oration, and performance in various proportions. Of it, I do not deny, decry, defy, or delay. So, it is an opera if it wants to be.

In this respect, La Grande Diva hails me back to the origin of opera twice, as early operas generally took tragic Greek or Roman myths as their basis, partly due to the fact that the public was *a priori* familiar with these tales and presumably with their many allegorical layers of meaning, and even more significantly, because these tales hearkened back to the ideals of the Greek holistic kinship with which their creators wished to be identified.

With *Venus Voluptuous Opera*, the stress lies less with the fusion of normally discrete art forms and more with the totalizing, harmonizing, and engulfing immersive effect of the art experience on me. It demonstrates an extended, comprehensive sense of the idea, which the notion attained in Adrien Henri's book *Total Art*—a book that concerns environmental and kinetic art, performance art, and some happenings of the 1960s and early 1970s. In it, Henri adapts the term *Gesamtkunstwerk* by historically contextualizing a stream of art in the 1960s and early 1970s as work that sets out to dominate and overwhelm, flooding the spectator with different kinds of sensory impressions. The content is not meant as information, but as experience. With this sense of a seamless union that sweeps the viewer to another world, I can immediately see how *Venus Voluptuous Opera* succeeds at its hyper-operatic polymedia objectives. I pray for a subject like King Ludwig II of Bavaria for La Grande Diva's next production, where the sublime may mean a metaphoric metaphysics in which expansive colour fields might entangle the primary genuineness of life. Which, in King Ludwig's case, comprised an acute sense of excess and tragedy.

As I awaited the start of *Venus Voluptuous* with mounting excitement, I noticed that, in a constant state of openness, the rainy room tone had shifted to a higher vibrational hum. I also observed more acutely the ceiling cracks that now appeared as veined neural pathways. Strictly speaking, what I saw was invisible, elegant, thought-provoking, and compelling, as it engaged my imagination with the contour lines of Le Corbusier's *Chapelle Notre Dame du Haut* (1954) in Ronchamp and Frank Gehry's Guggenheim Museum *Bilbao* (1997). Both have a feminine fertility about them that is absorbing to me.

Both buildings seem to share exquisite whipping forms indicative of a world of transmutation. With those ceiling cracks, I share a wonderful topological cognitive vision that is lashing a compound unified field. However, the batches of whiplash lines and flowing, voluptuous forms suggested more than that: they took me to that smooth space between physical actuality and virtuality that creates for me a mental cavern where I can hide my head. For, within this space, I had drawn a portrait of Gertrude Stein and Albert Einstein, an ancient Chinese ceramic, a pair of Rudolf Nureyev's slippers, a George Balanchine slipper, a pair of shoes belonging to Marlene Dietrich, handsome chairs from all periods, and other things connected to my reputation as a perfectionist. Of course, this cavernous ceiling crack effect depends, to a large extent, on my state of psychological adaptability in accord with the whipping, tree-like cues.

Just as a bluebird came flying through the tree, I found myself easily immersed in a version of phenomenological liminality, which, according to the anthropologist Arnold van Gennep, is the condition of being on a threshold between spaces. There is a kind of transcendental breathing going on in these intertwined forms. A blending and bending, in and out, between the tree-filled sky and the other object-forms. Moreover, there is a definite tangled and intertwined approach to the vectors that reminds me of my powers of dithyrambic visual hyper-logic, which has manifested in all modes of decadent artistic periods. The evening breeze caressed that tree tenderly.

Towards the end of that visionary evening, I can eat, but this operation is not accomplished without difficulty. I find myself so far above material facts that I would certainly prefer to remain lying full length at the bottom of my intellectual paradise as I stare at the ceiling in absolute happiness; here my life is no longer something whirling and tumultuous. It is a web of calm and motionless bliss. All philosophical problems are resolved in this network. All the arduous questions with which sex therapists struggle, and which are the despair of reasoning humanity, are limpid and clear. Every contradiction has become a unity. I have become a god.

Following this shifting pattern with hedonistic eyes, the limited appeal of scopophilic pleasures struck my mind just as Venus Callipyge came back and wrapped her legs around me and locked her ankles behind me. She had taken slow-motion inspiration from Andrea Solario's Renaissance painting titled *Tête de saint Jean Baptiste* (*The Head of John the Baptist*) (1507) and from Jacques-Louis David's Neoclassic painting *La Mort de Marat* (*The Death of Marat*) (1793)—but essential *fumiste* incoherence is to be expected.

At that, my tactile glossolalia as etched out in globular-veined detail lays bare all the complexities of odd darkness. Venus Callipyge took heed and looked onto my bloody ceiling, which was dripping in scotophobin. Sustained droning organ tones now played. It was loud and reminiscent of Charlemagne Palestine's *Music for Carillon* that I first heard in Robert Wilson's 1998 staging of August Strindberg's *A Dream Play* (1902). Those sustained tones set the emotional tone of deep solemnity suggestive of the eternal of La Monte Young's Theatre of Eternal Music.

This posed a hypertrophic problem, as the solemn tone established a mood of classical seriousness and Venus Callipyge's physiological sex bubble was to float up, up, up—and pop. So a question remained in my roaring mind: should I be judged shallow and naïve by our 'golden age' of Last God crypto splendour—or void-based shit-coin meme money judged wanting by the presumed sincere and golden intentions of acid heads running naked across my mental stage screaming against the machine?

The father of psychoanalysis, Sigmund Freud, wrote that gold is seen to be the symbol of feces in the most unambiguous way. This scatological metaphor found prior expression in Hieronymus Bosch's painting *The Garden of Earthly Delights* (c. 1500), with its depiction of a man shitting gold coins into a basket in the lower part of the right-hand panel depicting Hell.

To that assertion about shitcoin, I heard only the sustained droning organ from Venus Callipyge, as a subtle shifting of the light created a lovely effect, slowly revealing her pert left breast. The sudden addition of the roar of multiple motor systems kept me inflated with the generosity of imagination as the aroma of chocolate filled my snout, producing tiny waves of fallout pleasure.

Indeed, it drone-motored on for a long time as we festooned ourselves in voodoo love charms and our tongues darted and duelled. I was so hot for her I thought I would go ballistic, for I stopped thinking about the missing and the absent—the someone or someplace else.

We put our arms around each other and pressed our bodies together while our poetic tongues went deep. She could feel my expanding penis flare up and press against her belly as she wiggled a bit to rub her breasts against my face. Trembling moisture oozed from the tip of my mimesis penis, matching the viscous coating of her tunnel of love; it reminded me of the unity of the past, that of the future, and the throbbing blood in our bodies.

As a buzzing fly flew in, our blood pressure and future remained invisible. Any visible blood is dead blood, I think as I glide up and down her virtual escalator repeatedly while *Ursonate*, the (1922-1932) 53-minute audio work by Kurt Schwitters, plays. To its human ego destroying sound, she writhes and churns up and down under me, and I behold a binding optical shimmer produced by merging line patterns set in motion. I know that she isn't, but Venus Callipyge gave me the feeling of permanent perfection, in that her glimmering pattern space matched the funny patterning of Schwitters's Dada utterances tightly. Her expansion was limited only by her Last God self-contradictions. Gliding up and down her silver space while listening to the eccentric guttural rolling of *Ursonate*, I made a mental note on how perfect that experience feels as a metaphor for all lovemaking that nurtures idealized excessive forms. For I believe it was William Blake who suggested that the path of excess leads to the palace of wisdom.

But was this excessive grandeur—a bit subversive, titillating, and instructional in its complex beatitudes—anything more than Picabia popping out of my pants and limply dangling in front of Apollinaire, Baudelaire, Huysmans, Breton, Bataille, Rops, Duchamp, Man Ray, and Bellmer? Was I merely becoming a gnomic T. Rex parody of a parody come down from a higher world of wisdom about the birth of the ego within Śūnyatā, the Void?

I know such potentially turgid, messianic, narcissistic, exasperating, and grand thoughts are almost stupid, but they are well-based on my readings of Theodor Adorno and the belief that for anything to be considered art as a veracious witness to its era, it must *ipso facto* be difficult. So I began to consider the Golden Mean just to be mean.

I then looked upon a beautiful, lilac-coloured, checkered handkerchief. I made my way to the Allard Pierson, the archaeological museum of the University of Amsterdam, where I spent a productive hour with Venus Callipyge. There I discovered the modest (in size, at least) *Hermaphroditos Statuette* (100-50 B.C.) that made me feel encompassed by a dome-like void vault. I had an awareness of being alive in the sensation of complete sexuality that flooded me with trembling sensations, allowing me to psychologically enter another saturated world, one last seen in 1966 at the Voom-Voom discothèque at Saint Tropez.

Contemplating and visualizing that discothèque in my mind, I was again determined to reinvest art with a sexual revolutionary fervour and end its spiritual starvation for over-emphatic tragicomedy. So, the shit-coin scene was kissed goodbye by the Saint Tropez sea mist while my excitement mounted, and I entered Venus Callipyge fluidly. She raised her hips to take me into her moist Śūnyatā opening more deeply.

Moving as one, it seemed like there were circular ripples that began at our groins and spread through our entire joined body. Then it began—wave after vibrating wave of ecstasy speared through us, with every contraction counteraction of this double body. With this lapping wave, we experienced a shift to a more conscious peripheral mode of perception, entailing a spontaneous reaction of the perceptual process whereby more emphasis is placed on what is on the periphery of my sight and consciousness. This presumably adjusts me to an expanded and fuller sexual consciousness of others while utilizing a wet, conceptual displacement along every axis; it is a sweeping process in space-time. Is this not the experience of Arthur Rimbaud's poetic formula for a *ménage à trois* based on the derangement of all my mind-projected senses?

VII

Meditations on Invisibilities and Their Lack of Pathetic Coherence

Forever and ever, the delightful Deee-Lite house track *Runaway* is banging in her simulated, invisible inside that is mapped onto an underwater cavern, replete with a mosaic coating of opened seashells suggestive of female genitalia. I began to live there in suspense, between stupefaction and frenzy, accompanied by a feeling of plunging into another world beyond the range of vision. Presently, I underwent a sense of escalator dreaminess: release—ascending—descending. This muscular incongruity had a shiny silver surface that opened onto Duchamp's grotto *Étant donnés: 1° la chute d'eau / 2° le gaz d'éclairage* (1966). After entering, it was impossible to determine who came first and who came last. Or who was a boy and who was a girl. It was not yet winner-take-all time within the male misogynist monarchy.

I must say that that was a rumpling experience that happened to rhyme in time with a miniature sandstorm. Usually I struggle to encounter something genuinely different and to think beyond myself and my own sexual experiences. But, as shifting elements of the ruddy scenery faded, Venus Callipyge, when somehow endowed with male genitalia, asked me to do just that, and I was no longer trapped inside my own perspective of elements that together could create a range of atmospheric effects such as fog, sunlight, and dawn punctuated with a diminutive pool of water. But this is clearly wrong, for the nymphaeum at Hadrian's Villa at Tivoli is regarded as the most famous and influential grotto from Roman antiquity. And I wanted that.

Regardless, within this spoofed-visualized phantasmagoric moment that contained a glass case full of coloured pebbles, a brown backdrop decorated with pumice stone and tufa, and a short clip from the movie *Night at the Museum* where Ben Stiller is trying to speak to Sacagawea about the book *Cutting Through Spiritual Materialism*—my male norm is no longer the measure of things. Here I must escape from my anthropocentrism and seriously consider fundamentally unfamiliar worlds of self-criticism, which is justified yet mostly expressed within algorithmic structures so ubiquitous and taken for granted that I cannot remember a time before they existed. Everyone from Steamboat Willie to Winston Tong knows that my stargazer role has fallen on deaf ears.

Still, culture shapes and is shaped by what I imagine.

As Venus Callipyge drops her mask to reveal Venus Barbata, imaginary girl-boys take me to a place of contradiction and excess that encourages such critical thoughts. I had assumed that such thoughts had lost their purpose and had fallen into egoic fat hands—floundering in a sludge of institutionalization and domestication of spectacle, paid in full with Prudential Insurance Bowie Bonds and vapid technological convolutedness. However, the Venus Barbata that I created in my mind is not that large but includes a virtual panorama filled with noisy panache like no other. This darkly congested panorama is the best of me.

My alchemic reasoning behind girls with penises is not unclear nor overly conceptualized as Venus Barbata amusingly decomposed and melted into meditation. The more time I spent with her debating the double body, the more Dionysian translucency, in terms of chaotic spirit, she gained, as if she had been traced from uncontroversial colouring books. She went so far as to give me a transparent dress so as to explicitly reveal my veiled double sex. Clearly, she found that aspect of me important—and it is, like the bell that a cow wears around its neck that rings when it descends from the mountain drunk on illusions of selfhood.

Here, Madame Black, in a moment of opacity, came back from the Schloss Schwetzingen at Baden-Württemberg and is tongue-in-cheek aggressive in her ethereality towards my transparent condition. In this respect, Madame Black is indeed a form of imaginative, translucent space of non-accommodating illusion.

Her seashells and glistening minerals, combined with painted frescos and stucco, are typical of this trend, but as a progressive, Madame Black asserted that the liberation of the human mind and subsequent liberation of the individual and society could be achieved by exercising the imaginative faculties of unconscious endocrinology to attain a dream-like state different from, and ideally truer than, everyday reality. For that, Venus Barbata gets at the truth that a thing can be both one thing and its opposite—that two opposites can exist simultaneously and not cancel each other out. Hermaphroditic gender performance is politically important in that it resists drawing boundaries around the other. It goes deeper than sheer pansexuality, to where our hormones adjust themselves through biofeedback to the nasty political world. It goes to the deliberately anti-actual, which often includes elaborate depictions of multiple figures unbound by tendrils.

Here I wish to be suitably hoary in derivation, whimsical, and playfully erotic. The patriarchal construction of woman as other and the female body as object is deeply rooted in the supposed duality (opposites) of the (two) sexes. Most feminist theory questions this patriarchal construction of sex and gender, suggesting that sex is expressed through a continuum rather than an opposing couplet based on heterosexist male/female polarities. Venus Barbata, as hermaphroditic, challenges these polarities and our tendency to view the world in limited terms instead of as a sea of possibilities.

In that sense, Venus Barbata represented the reverse side of my rationality by introducing a niche dedicated to the irrational realm of the mystic world, in which rationalist rules need not apply, into my ordered mind. It is this aspect that is the most relevant characteristic in formulating comparisons to me, dressed and decorated in such a grotesque syncretistic fashion.

Venus Barbata turns her tears into a vast machine of perpetual and visceral becoming, while her washy, breathy surfaces share the space with a 4-billion-year-old meteorite that was found following a meteor shower in 1947. This expansion contained a precise formal idea, a taste for astonishment and special effects, the inflation of form, and an excessively self-confident premeditation. Her hallowed indications of something deeper demonstrate how such diorama concepts attain disappearance in the immateriality of our overdetermined imagination. Think how helplessly childish and passive that makes us feel.

As such, Venus Barbata shows herself to be a sideways-in symbolist, alert to badly formulated misunderstandings of the deeper stakes in life and the potency of the flow of day-by-day existence.

Her *esprit de corps* is peripheral and diaphanous within an experiential and excessive span where ocular extravagance is felt as a function of space. Her *raison d'être* is to supplant the framed male gaze by enticing men into a more fully *a posteriori* understanding of human potential in terms of attention, as found in the Roman marble *Dionysus Sarcophagus* (2 CE), also known as the *Bacchus Sarcophagus*, the *Dionysos Sarcophagus*, and the *Bacchic Thiasos.* Unlike the beloved (by me), well-preserved, and highly polished sarcophagus *Triumph of Dionysos and the Seasons* at the Metropolitan Museum of Art in New York, the *Dionysus Sarcophagus* has degraded radically, and its surface is extremely grainy and gritty. This makes a great deal of difference, as the complex floating dance of the drunken Bacchus, among a bevy of satyrs and maenads, starts performing a goat sacrifice.

The sun came up between Hotel La Louisiane and Hotel Les Sans-culottes (Hotel Without Pants). As I approached the *Dionysus Sarcophagus*, the woozy images melted into a highly textural, grainy and gritty noise field. This play of image-merged-into-noise-field perfectly suggested the drunken, ecstatic Dionysian state of resurrection that the image-narrative suggests: that the stamping of grapes into wine signifies death transformed into new life.

Looking between the legs of Venus Barbata while she stamps, I can see a translucent sea where certain hairy ideas need to be addressed concerning feminine practices. First, do women even want to talk about "the feminine" at all at this point, given its unobtainable purist connotations? If they do, they certainly must make clear that they are talking about something light-years away from the pink, frilly, pre-feminist definition from what seems like resiliently opaque ancestral antiquity. This critical distance between feminine and feminist was not established by Venus Barbata, other than placing the "feminine" in four-finger quotation marks, which called it into ironic question. Concepts of feminine and feminist seemed conflated in (what I take to be) post-feminist fashion, while questions of the dominant and emerging social constructions are raised in the fight to counter sexist/elitist exclusion.

In that resistance, Venus Barbata was forcefully persuasive in making the case against the sexist social relations typically encoded into men's head-space by mentioning that sex professionalism is seen as apolitical and outside of politics, thus supportive of the political status quo. Issues of class boundaries, decent safe housing for women, the needs of time-sensitive sex education for older children, and Venus Barbata's short or long-term sexual relationships involving cultural and class differences were also raised by her. She seemed tacitly indebted to some of the theoretical achievements of Sandy Stone and Gayatri Spivak and their concept of feminist positions in electronic space known as cyber-feminism, which implies alliances between women and digital machinery. With cyber-feminism, the subject position of the feminine takes on the features of something like an avatar of unmitigated alterity, dancing with Donatien-Alphonse-François de Sade the day he was incarcerated on February 29th, 1784.

Probably the epitome of a candidate for cancel culture by woke moral standards, the Marquis de Sade provided a lurid and liminal libertine lubricant for Parisian Surrealists in the 1930s, including the generally perceived, mild-mannered Alberto Giacometti. Giacometti explicitly proclaimed admiration of Sade's texts in a 1933 letter to André Breton. He artistically demonstrated this admiration between 1929 and 1933 with symbolic spiky sculptures allusive of impending penetration of—and by—schematized sexual organs involved in surreal struggles suggestive of sadistic physical and psychological violence. *Man and Woman* (1928-29) and the palpably phallic *Disagreeable Object* (1931) are two prime examples of his theatre-of-cruelty fantasy objects bent on psychological sadistic pleasures.

During his lifetime, Sade was found guilty of sodomy, rape, torturing the 36-year-old beggar woman Rose Keller, holding six children in his chateau at Lacoste, and dosing five prostitutes with aphrodisiacs. I recommend reading the book *Marquis de Sade: Journey to Italy*—translated by James A. Steintrager—for the fuller story of Sade's extensive, and often cruel, debauchery.

Sade hid *Les 120 journées de Sodome* (his text that tells the tale of four rich aristocrat libertines in search of sexual gratification in a castle in the Black Forest, systematically and imaginatively sexually abusing forty-two victims) rolled up in the wall of his Bastille prison cell. But on the night of July 3rd, 1789, after haranguing the crowd from his cell window, the marquis was abruptly transferred to the lunatic asylum Charenton, leaving behind this manuscript hidden in the prison wall.

Sade's taste for sodomy, pedophilia, and flagellation—in addition to his fictional accounts of excessive orgies, which describe sexual cruelty and murder in excessive detail—had already led many to presume he was deranged. When the Bastille was stormed and looted on July 14th—during the height of the French Revolution—Sade believed *Les 120 journées de Sodome* was lost forever. He later wrote that he wept tears of blood over its loss.

But, unknown to him, the rolled text was recovered from the destruction of the Bastille and sold to the Marquis de Villeneuve-Trans, and so, after many strange and shocking exchanges, it rests in peace at the Bibliothèque nationale de France. The fascinating history of this manuscript—hidden, stolen, lost, censored, illegally exported (most likely in a coffee can)—still is the object of some speculation. For example, during the restoration process it was x-rayed, and a Dutch watermark was discovered on a small part of it.

All this mystery only further enhances its appeal as a vehicle of transgressive power.

The published text has come a long way from the ghetto of erotic literature of the 1950s to the honours of the Pléiade and Gallimard editions today. The German psychologist Iwan Bloch was the first to allow its publication in 1904—even as it remained banned in Britain until the 1950s.

The entry of the manuscript—an emblem of violent perversion but also literary and artistic freedom—into the national collection of France allows serious researchers to continue to study it with some passion, for Sade is deemed deliriously divine by many intellectuals and artists who interpret his writings to be a black mirror held up to reflect man's inhumanity to man.

This is most notably seen in Pier Paolo Pasolini's film *Saló* (1975), which restages Sade's *120 Days of Sodom* in fascist Italy as a means of addressing the horrors of war and totalitarian regimes. So, perhaps it is symbolically justified that the rolled *Les 120 journées de Sodome* resembles a roll of toilet paper—even as the look of the text is achingly beautiful—written in fine minuscule. It is no wonder that Eluard, Breton, Bataille, Blanchot, Pasolini, Annie Le Brun, and Philippe Sollers are only some of the creators deeply marked by what some call the power of its black sun.

VIII

Ashes to Ashes Can Wait

We took General Kilgore's direction from *Apocalypse Now* and came in low out of the rising sun, and about a mile out we put on Wagner's *Ride of the Valkyries*, because looking hard for Venus Pink Dots means entering into myself.

At that point, after slipping off her moccasins and watching *In a Lonely Place* and *The Night of the Hunter*, Venus Pink Dots appeared and had me and eleven others wear a section of a large and beautiful blue cape, punctuated with twelve hoods. Each hood was marked with the name of a deceased individual (mostly artists and art-world luminaries) whom Venus Pink Dots admired.

Far from being a passive surrender to death, this blue cape transmitted, to me, the flowing juices of life. It confirmed my love for Venus Pink Dots in the very midst of the inevitability of insubstantiality. Every probable place became my native home, where, in time, my hair will grow long and sweep the ground.

As we timidly tiptoed past pestilence, I became acutely aware that the transmission of a virus had steered important cultural work towards a heightened sense of human mortality and vulnerability. With thunder as my pillow, I dissolved away. So when Venus Pink Dots stepped in, it was as though a moving magic lantern threw her phantasmagorical face twice on the flickering rear screen of my mind, for I am positioned in an aesthetic where corporate form is confronted by semi-private vernacular. In Venus Pink Dots, I see a haunting meditation on dissolving death that provides me the chance to do the counter-fearful thing: to look at what I fear with a gnarly twinkle of aesthetic pleasure. For what is important to me is the value that the individual gives to everything and not received values.

The names I recognized on the cape were Yves Klein, Marcel Broodthaers, Sidney Bechet, Iris Clert, Cesar, Pierre Restany (who first brought me to Paris), and Raymond Hains (whom I met at a party at my house prior to his passing away). This wearing of the *Venus Blue Cape* was the preparation for a procession that was somewhat like a New Orleans-style funeral march, particularly as a female saxophonist provided a continuous bluesy riff that made my mind turn towards some glaringly prescient (if negative) ideas that had a ghostly drift to them. For, it's strange how and why the occult style of the anti-realist realism of this transcendently beautiful Venus Pink Dots pervades my ponderings these days, with her taunt face facing the fear of the (sooner or later) inevitable.

Paying me no heed, Venus Pink Dots then had us parade around Place Saint-Sulpice and, much to my great surprise and amazement, keep going into the Saint-Sulpice Church (famous for its paintings by Eugène Delacroix and its referencing in the book and film *The Da Vinci Code*) during a celebration of a mass. The saxophonist went silent, but the blue parade kept on truckin', snaking our way through the back of the vast church and out again to the other side as the priest was delivering a sermon.

As I returned towards the shadows, *Venus Blue Cape* became a festive nod to departure, for prior, the commemorative mood I was in was sometimes heavy and rather sad, particularly when I focused on our hooded heads as the blustery wind blew hard, for they reminded me of the sombre Catholic processions one sees in parts of Spain. But in general, Venus Pink Dots kept me pretty and light and compassionate, for she produced for me a tantalizing and salacious outlook through a positive emphasis on the emotional imagination where beauty must encompass the absolute and the particular, the eternal and the transitory.

I hope I never verge on the turgid or pompous here, for what I particularly admired about *Venus Blue Cape* was its mixture of informal casualness within a formalized ritual. It gave me a feeling of the secular sacred, like that described by Gilles Deleuze as 'pornology' in the *Klossowski or Bodies-Language* section of his book *The Logic of Sense* (1969)—the dynamic of a transcendental empiricism in the circuit between pornography and theology. Yes, I have experienced pornology in the unfathomable *flâneur* depths of my private thoughts when they correspond to a melting of individual boundaries formerly sharply outlined by social convention, like in Baudelaire's poem *Correspondences* (1857), which is about a forest of symbols by which the poet portrays his profoundly mystical belief in the world's basic unity.

Stéphane Mallarmé and Paul Verlaine both openly sang Baudelaire's praises for capturing the essence of such an ephemeral experience. Regardless of Venus Pink Dots's unified sexual orientation displayed while hanging out topless on the Côte Bleue, I was provoked to reconsider Venus Barbata as a hermaphroditic representation related to male/female constructions of both heterosexual and homosexual identity. I cannot deny that Venus Pink Dots (as Venus Barbata) invites ontological speculations by attacking the correlationist assumptions of phenomenology.

As two yellow willows follow the shallows, Venus Barbata suddenly steps into my cone of vision, stark naked, thus stressing the concrete existence of the universe prior to Last God's existence. Upon the gleaming waters of her loins, two swans swim. Her tanned skin and physical proportions are ideal, and her facial expressions of transformative time objects express an opaque but lustrous intellectual mind that is both connected and vast. This is why she has, once again, ingratiated herself into the incalculability of my actual life through her yoni transformer—a type of wet neural network architecture that transforms input sequences into output sequences.

As Venus Barbata hung luxuriously under a vast twelve-meter ceiling upon which party scenes were created in the electric hues of a Fauvist palette, a place of gender choice was suggested. The obvious problem here is that little reflectivity on today's fluid gender situation can be offered through political instrumentality. Nevertheless, Venus Barbata muffles and blurs these polyamorphous ideas that give me a sense of wet, conceptual urgency. She turns towards me, and I can see that she is holding a golden platter with two ripe yellow bananas on it, their brown stems pointing at me. I don't move or speak until she moves towards me. As she comes close, I drop to my knees so I can take a banana stem—or breast nipple—into my mouth. I'm not sure which one, as I suddenly wake and all is gone. Now I can only speculate.

I like this because it is absolutely necessary that the world have the capacity to be other than it currently is, and that unknowability is a positive characteristic itself. I found that Venus Barbata reminds me to reject the thesis that the order of the world depends upon the way that our bodies and minds (and our language/culture) work to structure it. Venus Barbata as a girl-boy reminds me to reject the phenomenological idea of the knower and the known, but that is not to say that there is little or no sensual pleasure to be found. Venus Barbata has a vibrant watercolour feel to her. Her sex seems to have a narrative flow that suggests a moment in a secret story between only us.

Her Dionysian double sex led me down a damp, dark corridor of mortality —one that raises kind of blue considerations concerning existential loneliness within spaces of technology as the condition of constant entertainment. The inescapable thought here is of the Greek myth of Charon, where the ferryman of Hades rows dead souls across the rivers Styx and Acheron that divide the world of the living from the world of the dead. For she felt obscure and half dead (in a decent way), mostly because of the minimal drone accompaniment she chose (Tim Hecker's *Ravedeath* (1972)), whose vibrant obfuscations are captured and transmitted live as wobbly silhouettes.

The notion of randomness is at play here too, as I might find her shimmering and multiplied, or not. But then the tide turns, and the trendy relational flood retreats. It is my feeling that this question of presence must be a bit more open-ended, for with Venus Barbata I feel the electric buzz of connection. She has a hazy sexual subjectivity with a very cool chromatic composition, yet fields of intensity invoking the inchoate are felt. A sexual power is coursing through Venus Barbata that pushes her trans theme out into the room, expanding her inflections of an imagined sexual freedom.

Such Venusian speculations are necessary to our understanding of our place in the world, and they are certainly useful when addressing transgender issues rooted in a continuing struggle for inclusion.

Venus Barbata works with a gleeful narrative modelling based on quasi-literary or pictorial synchronic propositions and with a precious little bit of resistance. I mention this word resistance with caution, not seeking to evoke examples of useless failed revolutions that I have seen in the past, but to think through our problems today in the way that Walter Benjamin did with his focus on mechanical reproduction. For Venus Barbata acts in a naive way from the point of view of Benjamin's take on Surrealism, and also from the point of view of current Last God machine learning technology.

It is true Venus Barbata gives me an expanded lexicon and a certain quality that involves me in imaginary duration. What I choose to ignore is that there has been a major change in our society that can be felt as fragmentation. The unified concept of the human being—one that has remained untouched for centuries, since the Greeks at least—is under destruction. Indeed, I think my identity always had several meanings that were being repressed.

As society is moving increasingly into The Last God virtual—a composite TLG cyborg condition—remember that the impersonal dark ecstasy of the cyborg was in vogue with the Dadaists, from Duchamp to Hausmann to Picabia to Masson and others, and they carried it on into Surrealism through automatism.

Like them, perhaps Venus Barbata might next make an effort at speaking beyond the accessible Last God and begin to speak about cancellation; in cancellation, the very foundation of thought is destabilized.

Strike that thought, for here comes the sun as I run out of the shadows, and Madame Black comes drifting back and starts to grind her ass against my cock. I drew her black panties down to her ankles and slipped them over her pointed feet. The next Bacchanalia has begun. John Cage's *Bacchanale* (1940) was blasting in the breeze as we began to visualize the excess of sexing sculptures lining the walls of ancient temples in India, one after the other: Khajuraho Temples, Madhya Pradesh Sun Temple, Konark, Orissa Virupaksha Temple, Hampi, Karnataka Jain Temples, Ranakpur, Rajasthan Sun Temple, Modhera, Gujarat Sathyamurthi Perumal Temple, Tamil Nadu Lingaraj Temple, and Bhubaneshwar, Orissa.

Snooks Eaglin then came on in my ears, playing *The Drifter Blues* that blended with the loud buzzing drone of summer cicadas. Summer was suddenly here, and on the beach in the South of France sunbathing rules are, as always, more permissive than in Anglo-Saxon lands. Women are permitted to sunbathe without their tops on so that they can tan evenly.

Thinking about that and Orissa Virupaksha, Madame Black and I got so hot we made love (no sperm attached to the uterus) again to the sound of the crashing waves overlaid with the continuous cicadas buzzing, only more slowly, like Burt Lancaster and Deborah Kerr did in my mind on the beach in the 1953 film *From Here to Eternity*. Love under the blue sky and burning sun intensified the sensation of every sensitive thrust—which led to a sun-drenched simultaneous orgasm the size of a ripe watermelon.

With my prick dripping with myrrh, I felt like the god Priapus must have felt when ornamented with the jewellery of retweets, upvotes, positive feedback, and algorithmic incentivizing nonsense. Madame Black's inner-being-as-art is a distillation of the spirit of our time that succeeds in breaking out of time. Thus she speaks to me of cross-generations in a way that transcends the limitations of local idiom and the myopic present. Madame Black is shaped by the historical but still says something quite general about human suffering, human hopes, and even, perhaps, the possibility of human redemption through love. For Madame Black pitches my body against invisible forces that must be displayed and withstood through stony sentiment.

Along the way, I free everyday things from their function and endow them with magical qualities, where the whole lot is floating between inebriated, filmy fantasy and grounded reality.

Floating over the reality of an ecocidal disaster towards a total surveillance state, Venus Barbata's girl-boy big balls come into view as two huge shiny mirror balls. They hover above me. Looking up at myself in Barbata's balls presents a dazzling portrayal of me at the scale of an ant. The convex mirrored ball surface bulges toward the light source, making everything appear smaller in the reflections, and I see myself anew. Gazing up into Barbata's balls offers me a reflected, 210-degree perspective—what in virtual reality is called the allocentric mirror world: the bird's-eye view of a Last God virtual world.

When viewing myself in Barbata's balls, I feel an unreachable utopian quality that exudes the opposite of low-hanging cynicism, where I'm told often enough that as a species, we humans are poised on the edge of the abyss.

Barbata's big shiny balls reminds me of what Gene Youngblood said in *Expanded Cinema*: that the information explosion of the 1960s was not a window on the future so much as a mirror of the past, catching up with the present. We will travel by balloon, for big balls are intended to float around the world without engines, buoyed only by the heat of the sun and infrared radiation from the surface of Earth.

In that utopian sense, Venus Barbata's mirror big balls are a throwback to the immersive mirror world created in 1969 by the Los Angeles wing of Experiments in Art and Technology (EAT) for the Pepsi-Cola Pavilion at Expo 1970 in Osaka, Japan. That 210-degree mirrored sphere was simply a lightweight structure built from 13,000 square feet of mirrored Mylar one one-thousandth of an inch thick, which spanned 90 feet in diameter and 55 feet in height. It was in here that the high-stepping ecocide impresarios in suits were hanging out at the quiche and wine bar drinking Pepsi with the Bohemian Grove group and talking about them knowing everything about me, while I knew nothing about them, because they are part of the AI-privileged Last God ruling elite class.

I don't know where they are, I don't know what they do, but they (as part of The Last God) know about me and observe me from above.

So, now loving Madame Black feels like a randomized, private ritual. I have had enough of the privatization of power and profit and the socialization of guilt and debt.

Visceral sensations of unity and fragment vibrate and flutter in and around my head: an experience as surrogate for aimless time and invisible engagement, where the multifarious immateriality of memories and dreams is matched by the intricate immateriality of spatialized female flesh. As such, an agreeable exercise in excess where a mere tissue of vague carnal clues becomes perceptible at a subtle level.

Sounds and her voice shift around the space, but their formation is impossible for me to ascertain by just listening to Madame Black rake sand in circles in a Zen garden.

At that, Madame Black became brazen, solitary, strange, severe, and serene, like a slipped-on cow pie. In response, my shlong became powerful, peaceful, and infinitely soft. It made no apologies to me for its fierce fertility. It bristled with unapologetic sensual enigma while bathing for a bit in the limelight that dissolved as much as it rendered. Then, that was that.

Madame Black also took the form of the female psychic powers interlaced throughout North African women's ornamental jewellery. The variety of forms and designs that the jewellery utilizes in creating rich streams of visual inflection requires acute attention, reflecting, as they do, the diversity of peoples and identities of the regions that constitute the Maghreb.

Shining with a thousand quivers, the oscillating visual language of Maghreb jewellery usually hovers between abstract geometry and modes of repetitive graphic presentation, done with such all-over delicate precision that it may rise to the province of luxurious value. Its function as a magical symbol often stems from this all-over many-in-oneness unity, even as the jewellery can also mark off social boundaries.

The diverse powers of the many regional styles hanging on Madame Black raise the issue of the craftsmanship of ornamental jewellery, taking it beyond the opinion that it is merely producing superficial decoration into an arena of engagement with cultural spiritual forces that surpass (while using) beautification in the interests of organic need. For millennia, North Africa—including the nations of Algeria, Tunisia, Morocco, Libya, and Egypt—served as a crossroads for the Middle East, sub-Saharan Africa, and Europe. Starting well before the Christian era, Phoenicians, Egyptians, Romans, and Greeks mingled with the Amazigh people (also known as Berbers, thought to be the original inhabitants of the region along with Africans from south of the Sahara Desert). Following the Arab conquest of North Africa in the 7th century, the Berbers gradually converted to Islam and over generations assimilated into Arab communities.

I put the Madame Black velvet petal to the metal and found that the ornamental designs engraved into Maghreb jewellery often suggest nature, with interwoven flowers, vines, animal tracks, the lapping of sea waves, or the rippling of fields of grain. The feeling of interlacing movement dominates, which makes sense, as the rich mixture of designs and materials used in the jewellery of Morocco, Algeria, and Tunisia reflects the varied cultures of the region's inhabitants and their extensive history of movement and trade.

In North Africa, a woman's jewellery, such as the *Moroccan Khamsat* (hands), the *ciselées motifs*, *Hamsas* (silver hands of Fatima), and the *Collier Khamsat* from Aurès, Algeria, have symbolic, magical meanings extraneous to their ornamental function. They are used as enchanted charms and talismans to protect against the evil eye. Also, head ornaments, earrings, necklaces, brooches, bracelets, and anklets possess functions, at once magico-utilitarian and seductive-decorative. Most Maghreb jewellery, by suggestively emulating nature's cycles and rhythmic movement, propounds something of the repetitious cadence observed in our own intertwining movements when we engage in the pleasurable activities of music, dance, and libidinousness. Of course, adornments also add resplendence, desirability, and opulence to a woman's appearance.

Women receive jewellery when they marry and wear it as symbolic expressions of their wedded identity, but regardless of what social code is expressed, the pieces' significant symbolic essence is also part and parcel with the lavish amount of time and patience encoded into each object, as in the complex geometric-formed multi-coloured piece from Grande Kabylie, Algeria, *Collier orné d'une boîte à talisman herz* (20th century). Its ornamental splendour charms the eye and fulfills a beneficial metaphysical purpose by suggesting a dangling sense of continuance, free from pressing urgency, through the use of cloisonné enamelling and hanging beads.

Of Turkish and Central Asian origins, cloisonné is a technique specialized in by Jewish silversmiths, descendants of the Jews who fled Spanish persecution beginning in the 13th century. Other techniques, such as filigree granulation and engraving, suggest ties to areas as distant as Yemen, Syria, and Somalia. Here, forms may enmesh and contradict, altering and disrupting the mundane in an inexorable and chimerical way. In the flamboyant, delicate, and intricate silver and gold elaborate jewellery worn by North African women, pendants made of coloured enamels and precious or semiprecious stones are conspicuous. Streams of beads in all shapes and sizes are sometimes used, made of stone, coral, amber, glass, shell, and even old coins, as we see in the sumptuous necklace *Collier tlila orné de perles baroques, pendentifs en argent doré* (20th century) from Moknine in the Monastir Governorate area of Tunisia. The coins, frequently used in the production of Tunisian jewels, are believed to have the property of repelling the evil eye.

Such repelling is very important, now that The Last God is everywhere. In a world of artificial intelligence, we can no longer immediately believe something, even if we see/hear it with our own eyes.

Much Maghreb jewellery seems to embody the human inclination towards repetition and reiteration. Some pieces, such as *Paire de fibules (khella) ornées de rinceaux et d'une khamsa* (20th century), from Moknine, Tunisia, display floral arabesque designs full of piercing filigree inherited from Egyptian, Greek, Roman, and Byzantine traditions. The pieces have a voluminous, unified treatment that articulates a very seductive look. The weaving ornamental design assembles a repetitive, intertwining visual logic that is mesmeric and ensnares the eye, like voluptuous, scantily clad people wallowing provocatively in paint and meat.

From one point of view, such floral ornament is essential to North African culture because it adds stylish magical functionality, but from the opposite view, it is in no sense intrinsic to the object and is therefore non-essential. But consider the voluptuous *Grande Kabylie, Large Circular Fibula Tabzimt* from the Kabyle people of Algeria. This Tabzimt is a particularly glorious jewel that was once used to celebrate the birth of a boy. What it already always expresses here is an unequivocal notion of plethora. It has a distributive feeling that seems to strive to express a basic vital rhythmic unity. Its goal is not only to indulge perceptual stimulation but also to impregnate and transform reality within collective tribal culture.

As such, its ornamental domain is essential communications directed towards the public, as members of the tribe pass through the various phases of crescendo and diminuendo of their lives.

In the ornamental jewellery of Madame Black, each piece is doubly conceived and doubly understood in terms of a private life blending into the ambient inner weavings of the group. It is for that reason that some of her jewellery is massively decorated with coins, such as the sumptuous 19th century *Pectoral* piece from Nador, Morocco. In that respect, her tribal ornamental jewellery is not (merely) decoration for her female body, but symbolic of community interaction.

Besides the jewellery's distinguishing psychic and frontier significance, a woman's jewellery is her private property, and she may sell it to support herself or her family or use it to buy cattle or land. With *Paire de fibules en forme de rosace reliées par des chaînes garnies d'un pendentif ovoïde émaillé* (20th century) from Tiznit, Morocco, traditional Berber women's wear is draped and held together with brooches (tizerzai) and a belt.

As I observed in the marvellous Moroccan villages of Tiznit and Tata, their jewellery may be shaped differently, depending on the local region; sometimes with ram's horns on the sides (a reference to female fertility) or in spiral-shaped motives (representing the eternal), as seen with the *Collier Tazelagt* from the Ahl Massa Tribe near Tiznit. Regardless, most of the Maghreb objects possess a fluctuating ornamental adroitness that is challenging to closed visual statements.

That adroitness is how and why much of Maghreb jewellery vibrates with the spiritually suggestive nature of Madame Black. Through the bountiful repetitions of ornament—and the general repeating linear motifs—Maghreb jewellery expresses the pulsations and throbs of human heartbeats and repetitious breaths, of our copulating rhythms and female sexual cycles.

As such, Maghreb's jewellery imitates, through its graphology, the essential pulsations of the reproductive human biosystem, and it is in this invariable repetitive order of things that I gauge my appraisement of The Last God concerning its beneficial qualities as artistic auto-antonymic versatility.

The art of Maghreb's jewellery is created through an exultation in rhythmic embellishment that functions somewhere between the reality principle and the pleasure principle. Its exultation is encoded within the winding motifs that are rhythmically repeated when used in a band or border—or scattered rhythmically over an area through the all-over use of line. Some of her best pieces, like *Parure de Tête* from the Ida Ou Nadif Tribe in Taounza, Morocco, exhibit a sustained rhythmic repeated equilibrium based on uneven numbers. It—and much of Maghreb's jewellery, laden with private and community conjuration—displays a meaningful artistic code and spiritual language for those who understand its ocular tongue.

At that, this ocular tongue of Madame Black spoke to me of a place in her where anyone could be anyone. A place to self-create. A place somewhere between dazzling and dangerous. An ornamental place, where I as a hypnotized post-human transcends the normality of The Last God's volitional control and behave without the experience of intentional will and without subsequent memory.

This non-self-consciousness manipulation in the loins of The Last God occurs because a lucid LG hypnotist instructs me, as a feckless subject, to walk with scorpions on the moon through the power of suggestion.

Happily, this celestial paranormal suggestion of Madame Black is not full-blown into an eccentric séance. It is merely short psychic manipulation that knocked lightly on my wistful inner world. By celebrating the moon and scorpions in gold and the poisonous substances secreted by scorpion stings, Madame Black gets to a point that can be pinned to a velvet pullover.

Arty, esoteric noise music may not be for everyone, but I have to admit that The Velvet Underground arose from such obscure alliances. Of course, buying into the art music context of The Velvet Underground is not necessary in order to be deeply affected by their look and music. Their buzzing held sound seems to bypass cognitive faculties *en route* to the realm of a sensational deep dive into the underground Babylon that was downtown New York City in the 1960s. Here, avant-garde experimental musicians, underground filmmakers, poets, and artists challenged the dictates of habitual form and heterosexual power.

In this unique context, the verses of the Beat poets, the held harmonics of La Monte Young, and the experimentation of underground cinema rubbed up against Lou Reed and John Cale as they came together and brought The Velvet Underground to life by intersecting pop music with conceptual art theory with drugs. Thus, they are of particular interest to those involved in transcendental black metal, experimental electronica, psychoacoustic drone, and difficult noise music. However, if we skip over the People Magazine meets Pop Art posing of the black clothes and sunglasses to get into the hub of what made The Velvet Underground artistic, I run up against a whopping contradiction. Most likely one that will pass over the head of the culturally interested non-specialist of Andy Warhol's art-music group, Exploding Plastic Inevitables (E.P.I.) (that contained The Velvet Underground), where the players/performers were embedded in an overwhelming light/sound/film show that dominated the entire space.

This immersive arrangement strove to achieve a traumatic restructuring of ontological consciousness based in excess.

But the key artistic feature of The Velvet Underground is the merging of Lou Reed's post-Dylanesque lyrics and song structures with the loud, held drone produced by John Cale that Cale obtained through his participation in the Theatre of Eternal Music, the group of the famous—but elusive—avant-garde minimalist composer La Monte Young. (Full disclosure: I worked closely with Young on archiving his extensive Fluxus-era art collection and his scores and tapes in the late 70s and early 80s for the Dia Art Foundation, the basis of which is sustained, deep concentration on one relatively simple structure at a time, to the point of revealing latent complexities in them.)

There is a timeless spirituality in this non-distracted approach that fights against the aesthetics of clickbait distraction that is taken as the indisputable condition of culture today.

If the rigour of Young's art music is read as minimal or mystical, that is a free interpretive act. What is factual is that Cale became familiar with the technical aspects of Young's harmonics that began with Young's love of natural, sustained sounds—like the intriguing wind in the cabin where his Mormon family lived in Bern, Idaho—and the continuous buzz of electric transformers at the Conoco gas station that his grandfather managed.

Young's *Trio for Strings* (1958) was the breakthrough composition in terms of sustained tones.

While Young was still in graduate school, his sustained noise music work *Poem for Tables, Chairs, Benches etc.* (1960) was championed by John Cage, who performed it widely. *Poem for Tables, Chairs, Benches etc.* (Parts 1 and 2) is an early noisescape of howling screeches produced by continuously sliding furniture over the floor. I highly recommend it, as there are many immersive levels to infinity on which you can enjoy its simple complexity.

Young's deep drone aesthetic (hence Cale's) was to hold fast to something and follow it deeply. So my briefest glance around The Last God's society of the spectacle and control is enough to remind me that some of Madame Black's intellectual and aesthetic excesses are also, sociologically, among her attractions.

If I want the experience of prolonged radical attention applied to the previously unnoticed, entering Madame Black's swiftly spread legs plops me within her intimate emotive sphere, made evident by her painstakingly winding a simple silver band around the icicle hanging from my left testicle. For this, while nimbly audacious and ever in opposition to oppressive platitudes, Madame Black wears a silver rhinestone choker of exceptional attractive power that also critiques female servitude by evoking an elegant instrument of bondage and humiliation. It is so outrageous that it captivates my metaphysical dimensional limitations, and in doing so, speaks to the vulnerabilities of my passions.

Portraying an ecstatic suspension of time that refers me to the dynamics of the artistic process itself, in which every male artist is his own bride and every female artist her own groom, Madame Black drifts into an indeterminate Venus Hypnosis, also known as Rosetta. Rosetta is an avid collector of Japanese woodblock prints and a cultural device of influential attraction distributed over a broad susceptibility scale. As she sat with me within a general, crotchety, and slightly aesthetic dump of emotional accumulation, her general vibe was one complementary to that of the filmmakers Alejandro Jodorowsky and the Brothers Quay. Venus Hypnosis also has something of

Jorge Luis Borges's combinational dexterity and Robert Filliou's Fluxus work *Recherche sur l'origine* (*Research on the Origin*) (1974) with its reflections upon various scientific theories—from the birth of the universe to the origins of human consciousness—in terms of the equivalence between Far Eastern philosophy and scientific knowledge.

Making out with Rosetta in makeup inspires principles of defensive masking and metamorphosis that might protect me against the dizzying collapse of my freedoms into the panopticon of artificial intelligence's tracking algorithms. By some means, she manages a magical balancing act here, where weighty aesthetic concerns somehow resist crumbling in the general *Gesamtkunstwerk* crush. This is Rosetta as a gripping chronicle of self-accumulation and a cultural step towards acknowledging that everything relates necessarily to both global and local physical space. In this sense, Rosetta represents, for me, a turning point in the history of global spectacle, as she speaks of futility, eccentricity, astonishment, admiration, awe, and a kind of dazed submission to the abundance of the world.

There are concrete poems tattooed on her sides, visible as she sits cross-legged on an old printing machine from 1960s Czechoslovakia while she reconstructs, from memory, specific encounters governed by the dynamics of her high-end desire after touring the vociferous world. But Rosetta is tempered by invisible, taciturn intellectual restraints that focus my eyes on specific details and factual content—judicious restraints of identity and lucidity that approximate the very love of self. As such, she is not only astounding, not only informative, and not only amusing; she also returns my aesthetics to an intellectual intermediate zone of the anomalous and occult.

For that I am very appreciative.

Rosetta, when feeling the thunder of my male organ, rises from the darkness like a drippy-gooey octopus set out to overwhelm me by virtue of her abundance, rarity, opulence, and strangeness. Venus Hypnosis is an undeniably pleasurable, stylish and *éclectique* experience, even as there seems to be an intellectual paradox here, as her combinational wet conceptualism opens up luxury markets where inventive concepts go to die.

Still, she floods me with sensory impressions and hints at inter-relational realms of unknowing. At once pleasurable, due to her spectacularly over-determined formation and pedagogical in presumption and highly malleable in syncretistic fusion, Rosetta attests to my desire to dive into the unknown.

Her eyes are, by turns, gentle and piercing, frightened and sleepy—often rising to the clouds, often accusing the heavens. I know this look from my childhood, when she would swing the winds with wild sobs and lunatic litanies as I sat on the grass contemplating the speed of her wind-swept clouds.

IX

Life Lived Lustfully as a Degenerate

As an inducement, Rosetta sides with elegance. She is a well-organized, elaborate avalanche of cultural solace that stimulates my desires. Yet, her promising profusion seems not really meant as information transfer but as a sublime visceral encounter with the divinity of immeasurable nature.

As part of my *tempête de merde maelstrom*, Rosetta takes up the gauntlet of excess, drawing me into her vast, heterogeneous display of playful melancholy. Thus, there is little threat of bored satiety here. In fact, Rosetta's intellectual mood harkens me back to a time when people before The Last God aspired to know theoretically everything about the wider world. This is why she wore an old cowbell, an hourglass, a 19th century *Anatomical Venus* automata, a dried-up cantankerous animal, an entomological specimen, some gemstones, an open sardine box, a rhizome of pink coral, a tiny unicorn horn, and a sorry seashell—its intricate design seemed to be the work of an ingenious, infinitely playful craftsman. Through her promiscuous costume, Rosetta stirs a groundless meandering in me. One that holds a feeling of the world's infinity of things as they run into my more parsimonious sense of aesthetic pleasure, for Rosetta is a feral fairy tale in which rationalist rules need not apply.

What is needed in The Last God's loins is more *ars longa, vita brevis* (art is long, life is short) understanding coupled with continuous pelvic movement towards anomalies that entangle the wires. Theodor Adorno said that most people know what they want because they know what other people want. Roman Emperor Tiberius wore a laurel wreath whenever there was stormy weather because it was believed that laurel trees were immune to lightning strikes.

At Teotihuacan, a pre-Columbian Aztec site in central Mexico, with heroic cojones I walked along the Avenue of the Dead and climbed to the top of the Pyramid of the Sun, the largest pyramid in Teotihuacan and one of the largest in Mesoamerica, just as a huge black thunderstorm came rolling in around me. That scary yet sublime experience opened my electrical understanding of life to an elevated crescendo. At one moment, form appeared solid and firm and the next fleetingly cloud-like and darkly fugitive. But, as I closed my eyes, in my inner eye I rapturously whipped up a coloured frenzy that teemed with the all-over symmetrical complexities of throbbing flowers, twisting leaves, and spinning clouds. Here, an inner excessive decorative web danced around me in unrestrained profusion, as forms exploded with pleasure while everything glistened: leaves shone, angels hovered, and the fruit exuded thick drops of dark honey. And I thought Venus Hypnosis would leave—because she loves the sun. But she chose to stay and keep me warm through some of the darkest nights I've ever known. So I knew I loved her and her pussy as I summoned Tathagatagarbha and the rain fell down without a break.

At that moment, with no panties on, Venus Hypnosis flirted with my kitsch *clichés*—most notably the ironic comic hypnotic disc on my belt buckle that, by spiraling, sucked the sexy suggestible down into a sonata somnambulist whirlpool, chock full of stormy sacrosanctity. After I maniacally absorbed her sexy somnambulist emissions, Rosetta insists she is a soul pleasing hypnotic circuit breaker? She is art as a dissonant aesthetic specific to the moment where a set of LG technologies enables her to perform a variety of advanced functions, including the ability to see, understand, and translate spoken and written language, analyze data, make recommendations, and maybe even make love. Her pussy a competent conductor of delinquent transmissions from the non-duality of the beyond.

I then summon Brahman. I summon Madhyamaka, for my decision to seize the LG present came out of a rejection of both inadequacies of the historical past and projections of a merry future whose exact symmetry is being confirmed as a political instrument of the present. As she gazes into the all-over deep now, I am shot through with contingency capable of interpreting chance as meaningful and apparent—something usually done only at the level of abstract sets of data when submitted to the indifferent machinations of algorithms. Given the uplifting, imaginative power of divination within her meta-historical interpretations, here my presentism is defended as inscrutably circuitous and ripe with possibilities, for Rosetta climbs the clouds and walks the wind. Her somnambulist eyes, if I could see them, would appear neither gentle nor piercing, and I could decipher no love story hidden behind them. There, I would find only a confused mass of half-dead dreams and the remains of a forgotten delirium, which is why she is so much more than an elegy to a lost era of rebelliousness.

As a sonata sounds, she never raises her eyes or her hypnotic head, modestly capped with a ragged red turban, as she falls—and if not falls, falls to sleep, and if not falls to sleep, falls in love, and if not falls in love, clumsily falls towards the core of the earth, where her menstrual blood turns into a string of red rubies.

But she does not weep, nor does she moan. From time to time she sighs unintelligibly. She probably sighs about the fact that I should not mention that access to some of the personal data associated with Venus©~ñ~lOve Systems has been hacked and has already been sold on the dark web to god knows whom.

At the next really long sigh, Venus Hypnosis begs me to speed read, to her, Burroughs's *Junkie: Confessions of an Unredeemed Drug Addict*, Jean Cocteau's *L'Opium: Journal d'une désintoxication*, Aldous Huxley's *The Doors of Perception*, and Henri Michaux's *L'Infini Turbulent*. Then Joséphin Péladan, with whom she is sometimes tempestuous and frenzied, raving against the sky, demanding me as her beloved one.

Like a weary star in her sky, I am seen in the mirror as an inadvertent rock star revelation or an intentional presentation of vaunted, fluid subjectivity. She never cries out for me, never accuses me, and never dreams of me in a state of repulsion or of *Repulsion* (1965) with Catherine Deneuve as Carol. Venus Hypnosis is humble to the point of abjection. Her gentleness is that of a being without odium. If she murmurs sometimes, it is only in solitary places, desolate like herself, in ruined cities—and after, when my black sun has descended into its nest.

A saturnalia Rosetta is seated in darkness, as though she is without my love to shelter her head and my male gaze to illuminate her solitude. I see her as a friend of all those who have been betrayed by the cosmic door, and all those who have been rejected; of those who are proscribed by the laws of tradition and hereditary disgrace.

Within an eternal now ever vibrating with loud cloud energy, she carries a key to my heart, but she has little need of it, for her kingdom is chiefly among the vagabonds of my mind. In the highest ranks of men she finds some altars —even glorious men—who, before the world, carry their heads as proudly as a reindeer and who, secretly, have received the mark of somnambulist whirlpool on their foreheads.

Pleased, Rosetta then positions me at the busy crossroads of a wet conceptual constellation that includes drugs, dance, trance, art history, kitsch, the history of psychology, fakery, film, and occultism. Aiming to plug a lousy lacuna in the hegemonic record of modernism, Rosetta rereads through the rippling prism of hypnosis the effects of focused attention, reduction in peripheral perception, and (most importantly) responsiveness to recommendation.

Venus Hypnosis's hopped-up historic glide into the somnambulist whirlpool is topped-off with an immersive installation of psycho-mechanical projection that exerts political pressure on the consideration of how my mind is controlled. Non-state theories of breast size plead for a placebo effect, enhanced by imaginative role enactment.

Recall that while in Paris in 1885, Sigmund Freud observed neurologist Jean-Martin Charcot work on hypnosis and hysteria at Pitié-Salpêtrière Hospital and briefly placed hypnosis in the psychoanalytic cache. The failures of genius are consoling, because soon Freud abandoned hypnosis as a diagnostic-therapeutic tool. However, its legacy lives on in the mysterious dynamics of loud cloud transference and counter-transference.

Regardless, now a whirling and hypnotized Venus Hypnosis plays the role of a fiercely international woman without a name but with an outlook that sparks the kind of nasty comments last heard at Ninth Avenue's Hellfire Club. She is a welcome plethora of information on the powerful magnitude of repetition that has remained too long in the neglected archives of history. I appreciated her fictitious, heroic effort to salvage artistic intensity from kitsch and banal technological exploitation and the much-hyped romantic mythic image of the artist as a daft and doomed interloper.

Hunting for the hypnotic transcendence of volitional control, Rosetta is un-hypnotized, and is now organized into an immersive session in Mesmer's tub with some silly somnambulists. While sleepwalking historically forward, she establishes a suggestively seductive cultural history of altered consciousness by productively interweaving works by well-known and unknown oddballs, such as the Romantic spiritualist sculptor Théophile Bra, G.R.A.V. member Joel Stein, Gustave Courbet, Matt Mullican, trance-dancer Lina de Ferkel, Alain Séchas, Georges Moreau de Tours, Auguste Rodin, Marina Apollonio (creator of *Spazio Ad Attivazione Cinetica* (1966)), Fluxus artist Larry Miller, Erwin Wurm, choreographer Catherine Contour, and Rrose Sélavy (aka Marcel Duchamp).

Venus Hypnosis's scenario of the power of placebo begins with the disturbingly madcap myth of animal magnetism that was invented by Swabian doctor Franz Anton Mesmer in the 18th century—a doctor who was subsequently belittled by American ambassador Benjamin Franklin, a juror during Mesmer's fraud trial.

As a reminder, the magnetic tape of Dr. Mesmer was wrapped around a tub supposedly loaded with magnetized water. This created a fury in the aristocratic circles of Paris when a 1784 French Royal Commission investigated mesmerism and concluded that hypnosis' power derives from the human imagination, not animal magnetism, and not a tube—even if the tub looks like a crash-landed starship.

I went with the geolocated flow of the starship, through a crepuscular imbroglio that became the jingling keys to an obviously joyful artistic exploration that delved into cyclical movements of Venus Hypnosis's electro-physical noise. So in love, her fidgety finger machines of mechanical disorder produced gratuitous musique concrete-like noise fields in me that were sometimes scarcely audible. No one else heard it, but it sounded to me like rickety stuff that swayed and clinked and clanked away, in a delicate and irregular, weedy and tentative way. I heard it in my head, so I knew it was real, but it continually raised the spectre of contingent doubt about man and machine efficiency. There is a provisional, even whiny, crankiness to this cyberpunk crying; it weeps and moans something about the standardization of economic globalization typical of The Last God. It is a sound full of dark deviations, destructive redundancies, and the repeated cruelties of phallic panic.

A strong guillotine *danse macabre* sensibility was blowing in the wind that hints at the *reductio ad absurdum* chop of death and the legendary death rattle. Sometimes these noise fields are overwhelmingly loud and aggressive, and that makes for a noise symphony of great textural diversity that sounds like a massive assemblage of wheels, airplane parts, a piano, saws, and other junk that screeches and whirs in constant kinesis. This was something once imaged in the Futurist theories of Bruno Munari in his manifestos *Machine-Art, Disintegrism, Total Art, and Machinism*, towards which I took up a tilting position whose goal was not precision but an anti-precision based on the mechanics of chance.

By chance, circuit bending endless cycles of Dionysian creation and dissemination, I then and there remembered the rather smug Davie Jones (David Bowie, Ziggy Stardust, Aladdin Sane, Thin White Duke, Major Tom, Halloween Jack, et cetera, et cetera, whatever), a man with disposable identities in a time of disposable incomes.

By remembering him, I have a courageous (if daft) Sisyphean feel about this text, for Venus Hypnosis's power is absolute, despite the triple veil of black crepe with which she wraps her head now.

We had made a date for the automatism debate.

But however high she carries that head, I can see from below the tempestuous light that escapes her eyes. A light of anticipation that is always brighter at midnight: the blazing hour of the ebb when I see Venus Hypnosis spread on all four walls, edge to edge, blowing minds. Red boots dance and come alive. For after all, The Last God's grandiosity had reached orbit.

From this heaven, Rosetta drew her middle finger to me. She touched my head with it and called me 'her hypnotic lover,' even as her middle finger led me astray and seduced me from the rear. Through that finger I became an idolater filled with desires and longings once unknown to me.

I came to adore the earthworm and address my prayers to Venus Hypnosis's wormy womb/tomb. Sacred to me was that barren tomb of Rosetta. Lovely was its darkness and corruption that has the power to dry up the balms of love while it burns down trees with the heat of tears. Through such tears, I have seen things that should not be seen: sights that are abominable and secrets that are unspeakable—ancient truths, sad truths, and great terrible Last God truths.

Rosetta walks with me in an irregular step, quick or slow, but always with an irregular step of tragic grace. She creeps and moves with movements impossible to foresee. She leaps on me, but the gas is out of the Zeppelin.

Rosetta carries no keys, for she is permitted by me to approach my cosmic door and break it down like a lady of darkness. Darkness, because the defunding of libraries, removal of the teaching of books from public schools, and the culling of the humanities from universities—all are driven by a belief that working-class people don't deserve access to art and literature.

In opposition to that darkness, I began riding high, alert and stimulated. As such, this darkness haunts my panopticon dreams with subtle lighting, where darkness speaks quietly with Rosetta's mysterious hands and animated fingers. With a technophobic hyperbolic touch similar to those of Paul Virilio and Jean Baudrillard, she has me dreaming in finger-painted pictograms of a general theory of invisible energies: modulating that universal fluid found in the hysterical historical experiments of Dr. Charcot at Pitié-Salpêtrière. Unnuanced polarities of darkness are left unquestioned there, and straw man arguments are executed in ceremonial fashion.

In a nutshell, through this sign language, Venus Hypnosis subsequently developed for me a private parapsychology and psychopathology of darkness that is very good at opening up the windy curtains of her imaginary dominion. A dominion that can be as sensual as a soft, feathery caress, or as curious as an extravagant chimera, or as mechanically glamorous as a Black Forest cuckoo clock.

X

The Golden Age of Maya as the Holonogic Ouroboros

In the early morning, as a somnambulist, I descend with my overlapping bell curves and enter a vigorously repeating loop. With Rosetta as Madame Maya as my wild card, my morning creative process torques within itself to become what I always was to begin with: a man-monkey within a fabled garden of mythical "actual" reality. No. That has no legs, so Madame Maya enters the miasmatic space and takes on the outlines of abundantly sprouting signal lights that flash a countless bevy of excited digital numbers in what appears to be a random order.

When I look up, numbers are circulating within a dark dome in chaotic patterns. On the floor twenty green and red digital modules are spinning in various circular orbits, like a mystifying constellation in transit towards a waggish ghost (*le grand vide*) on full obscurantist flaunt as a psychic thump from an obtuse obstruction.

That might sound peculiar, but it is precise.

The inherent detachment of pretentious work-in-progress numbers, shorn of any deep commitment to specificity, seems to inscribe, for me, a condition of superficiality for Madame Maya. I see her suddenly as a louche stage set, and that means a lot of waiting around so that the empty, boring time had its due. Indeed, the boredom of hurry-up dead time and empty space seems the dominant point, as various pauses and visual lines of sight offer themselves up from within the vast void, lending equal weight to contrary and incompatible angles. This makes for a dominant emotion: that of a fearful sense of oppressive, disempowering indecision where I hesitate to leave a boring situation, concerned I will miss something delicately interesting that is coming along any minute now.

To counter this feeling, just as an overwhelming, huge wall of blinding white light assaults my retinas with a display of empty grandeur, I recall what Charles Baudelaire says in his 1867 poem, *N'importe où hors du monde* (*Anywhere Out of the World*): "Anywhere, anywhere, as long as it be out of this world!" This empty grandeur is intended to signify luxury, mystification, and wealth.

For close to three hours I explored this big nothing. There was another mammoth room full of blinking marquees and a bevy of relational data mining, but I realize that I don't want that anymore for me and Madame Maya; I want a psychic escape from cybernetic circularity and causality that surveys me and links and groups me. I want a relational Madame Maya who sequesters, encourages, and honours my personal feelings and thoughts that share a sensibility for building personal freedom assemblages where I can intently and intensely live in my imaginary cosmos of pleasure, rooted in the non-closure of Dionysian aesthetics. For I am no swinger swinging back to traditional religious conservatism suddenly in favour of forms of sexual repression. My tautological love story of Venus is an unapologetic intellectual/sensual history of desire that maps out my role in creating a circular (ouroboros) social allegory based in noise: a poetic/psychoanalytic cluster nookie that uses nonrepresentational colour-form-space when I amalgamate Madame Maya's bio-mechanized pleasure.

The rewards of such exhausting circularity are considerable, given the historical significance of Madame Maya's sarcastic stochastic algorithmic relevance to Last God culture with its intransigent obliqueness, lapidary right wing ravings, and orange clown king dizziness, because the principle of constructing patterns of infinite becoming is inherent in avant-garde artistic tradition values. Ah, to breathe upon the formless waters of circularity while gaining access to a glass and silver case that Madame Maya had made for a star-shaped biscuit brought back from lunch in Juvisy-sur-Orge with the astronomer Camille Flammarion. It is to be appreciated and relished like the cavernous, half-finished Madame Maya as she is marvellously devouring my mind with space and noise, neutralizing my stylistic moods of gamesmanship associated with the elaborate and extravagant. Madame Maya is intricately hermetic, exuberantly playing with the preposterousness of a somnambulist word machine sleep-running infinitely in the already thought.

After a brief visit to the Wénshū Yuàn Temple Monastery, one of the most important Zen Buddhist centres in China, Madame Maya is seriously drifting into playing the role of the Venus Libertina who starred in the 1928 silent movie entitled *A Woman of Affairs*, starring Greta Garbo, also based on *The Green Hat* (different name, same game). In this looping role, she defines pataphysics as that which revolves around itself. Her pataphysical circularity is not serious, but it possesses a silliness that constitutes precisely my somnambulist seriousness and my flair for dramatic extremes. Know of her as Madame Maya or not; either way, I understand Venus Libertina as a practitioner of the anti-scientific realm beyond metaphysics that examines the laws that preside over exceptions, for Alfred Jarry specifically defined pataphysics as the science of imaginary solutions, which symbolically attributes the properties of objects to their virtuality.

As an attempt to elucidate an imaginary cosmos, my thoughts here about Venus Libertina may be called apocalyptic, as I transform the relationship between her figure and the ground into a continuum that seeks to evoke temporal and spiritual sensations through abstract means. While associative, this apocalyptic meditation on Venus Libertina may be approached as a series of meditations on Madame Maya's phantasmagoric vibrations or as concrete. But to me, her chromatics seem structurally akin to the chord structures in music when listened to by Madame Maya as she lifts and drops the beautiful white feathered blinds of my morning box-garment by pulling the strings. At the pulling of these strings, at certain gelatinous moments, I can hear a majestic universe bellow.

This rumbling sound cornucopia is quite unique and has a smell that scrupulously defies categorization. What I can say is that with Madame Maya's sassily live odour, picked up at the Five Spot Café, a gargantuan envelope opened before me in which I now hang out, for it smelled like freshly made coffee. Here I am able to explore the inner intricacy of Madame Maya, which plucks on my heartstrings like an Indian sitar.

In meditation, Madame Maya takes on some myriad-coloured dexterity by gently moving back and forth her heavy breasts. I observe how the liquid they contain ebbs and flows like the semi-diurnal tides of the sea.

Such a triumphal aggregate designates her breasts as virtuoso clouds of muscularity, where customary opposites coexist, coalesce, and connect.

Obvious to me was that Madame Maya's preferred tool of coherence is what in acoustics is called envelope. I took this phenomenon of the envelope and extended it into a more general peripheral spatial intelligence called holonogic. Yes, I think it is sensible to make use of the holonogic schematic model of Arthur Koestler (established in his books *Beyond Reductionism* and *The Ghost in the Machine*) when trying to appreciate Maya, as no set or frame of perceptions may be experienced in isolation or as a single part of a finite perceptual collection when within her holonogic hole.

With that thought, Madame Maya began producing some muffled and deeply eccentric vocalizations. I had to close my eyes in an attempt to accept all the sexual ideas simultaneously presented to me as they facilitated mild waves of imbrication. This made for a rather complex reckoning with another proposed spatial reality relevant to Madame Maya, called curved space—or curved space/time.

As green-footed as a sloth, she moved among the seasons. Such was her aromatic *mise-en-scène* that encouraged me to value the freedom of my interior seasons, for she was an emotional escape from the winter funk of grey skies, the cold wet air, and a wanderer no sense does make.

With that luxury of interior time disconnected from the sun of solar seasons, I envisioned with Madame Maya a dithyrambic visual hyper-logic approach to human bodies based on growth scripts and open algorithmic procedures, for Madame Maya is a secret enigmatic force with an ambiguous quality that rings a tear of irony from my riding crop.

Madame Maya is clearly rooted in experiences of life as a flowing mixture where colours, shapes, and lines overlap, and words and sentence fragments enhance the enigma, but sometimes I thicken her inscrutability without providing a key to her black magic. To this end, I entered a fully immersive hypnosis chamber between her legs that reveals the source code of the generative program at the invisible heart of things.

I must always mentally connect the pink dots as sensed, and I thought that was a handsome thing for her to do to me. And so I loved her there, or perhaps I only thought I loved her, which amounts to the same thing. For her mouth and sex were dripping honey, and her lips felt smoother than baby oil. Her crotch was as if the stupendous mannerist grotto-façade at Villa Borromeo had been left to grow untrimmed and run amok, for during our enthusiastic lovemaking Madame Maya took a definite tangled and intertwined approach to my onions that reminded me of the decadent periods of the Hellenistic, the Flamboyant Gothic, the Mannerist, the Rococo, and the Fin-de-Siècle. Like her, they opposed dogmatically imposed ocular paradigms with hyper-engendering strategies of form. And that is where the blackbirds always sing.

Each and every second, every face within her face shows Madame Maya's multiplicity that challenges old bogus ideas of purity and simplicity: dumb modernist-minimalist ideas that can take on the intensity of a righteous injunction in many cities where the implied equation between simplicity, surveillance, and goodness obscures a less evident function: that of cognitive constraint. Given her interwoven biomorphic forms spawned by her voluptuous LG generative program, I could not avoid making voluptuous love with her inside the *Palais Idéal* of Ferdinand Cheval—which, to our eyes, appeared to be one huge, budding edifice. Such generative, unconstrained budding runs the road with Georges Bataille's consideration of the non-hypocritical human condition—which he took as being roused to non-productive expenditure (threshold excess), entangled with exhilaration. (For the finest comprehensive overview of Bataille's thought in this regard, see his book *Eroticism* and Denis Hollier's book on Bataille's general postulates, *Against Architecture*.)

I ate up the fact that the *Palais Idéal* was constructed by the postman Cheval alone and by hand in the Hauterives (Drôme) (near Lyon) between the years 1879 and 1912—the result of 93,000 man-hours of hard labour—but Madame Maya prefers our love to be made through a computer-programmed emergence via artificial intelligence, which directs robotic execution. Why should humans physically work at sex when we might better be deep dreaming and playing with Pris Stratton as played by Daryl Hannah in *Blade Runner* (1982)?

Dressed and made up as Pris Stratton, Madame Maya is passionately in the throes of dancing at the Cabaret du Néant dinner club in the Pigalle district of Paris. Inspired by the theme of the medieval *danse macabre*, Cabaret du Néant is fashionable among hip *fin-de-siècle* Parisians and all sorts of connoisseurs of the occult who go there to talk, drink, and dance in the company of skeletons and ghosts. Pale-faced, black-suited embalmers welcome visitors in a setting made up of tibias, skulls, and femurs. When I get her attention, Madame Maya speaks to me in high-voltage fashion by placing phallic and vessel objects on her tongue. A tongue that then lashes me to the floorboards. As I considered that perspective of her, my hands considered Madame Maya's curved space that is approximately Euclidean over very small regions, but over large regions all her geometrical properties break down.

Her voluptuous curvature is combined with Euclidean geometry with the increase of dimensions plotted. Here I came face-to-face with the ambiguity of the human spirit and the fullness of emptiness and the emptiness of fullness.

There are also a number of other generalized spaces of Madame Maya I explored that drop the Euclidean geometry completely—most notably her topless topological space model and her fuzzy space, where there exists only a concept of nearness, a glass of Vin de Paille, and some gamelan music.

At the repeating sounds of the gamelan, I join in with a whimper; Madame Maya begins unframing my mind and expanding my sensual sensitivity towards some most delicate moments. But really, any account of Madame Maya's sexual dexterity—as related to consciousness—is inadequate to the facts of my actual experience within her. The holon model of cognitive processing is useful for one of many possible accounts of her reverberations. Yes, Madame Maya's embrace is particularly holonogic as she deprives me of my habitual perceptive boundaries. She surpasses them, and one thinks immediately of Guy Debord's essay *On Wild Architecture*. Like the Situationists, Madame Maya's form no longer depends on the arbitrary decisions or control over its emergence exercised by the elite few.

Heads down, we head towards some juicy complexities and engagements by way of immersion into an open-ended multiplex, conceivable as a virtual environment. Here, Madame Maya's existence is inextricably linked to the end of grand narratives, the objective recognition of climatic change, and the urgent need to renew democratic mechanisms. Her vibrational phenomena is the reality principle of the domain of decadent artifice—something already well articulated in Joris-Karl Huysmans's 1884 novel *A Rebours* (*Against Nature*). This is the story of a reclusive art worshipper who yearns for hyperbolic sensations and perverse pleasures within a transcendental, artificial ideal; he aspires to set art free from the materialistic preoccupations of industrial society.

What might be somewhat poorly determined by Huysmans about my loving Madame Maya, however, is the degree of feeling I, as the eager dweller between her thighs, feel when wrapped up in her smooth and excessive pleasure place. This feeling depends, to a large extent, on my personal psychological needs and my adaptability, in accord with her proposed spatial depth cues.

Sometimes her cognitive-aesthetic space has to be coordinated phenomenologically with the proprioceptive space of my eyes as they meet the skin of her seamless—generative—totality.

Unexpectedly, wildflowers are underfoot everywhere. I will always love that exquisite fantasy of totality—which is the loveliest of triumphs of the imagination—as it is where I can imagine myself a true dandy, totally immersed in the decorative details of her heart and home. In that her helper robots are doing the algorithmic planning and desire building, she definitely proposes, to me, a new form of dandyism—as long as dandyism's defining characteristic is the making of one's person a work of art while extolling laziness and displaying contempt for work. Evident with Madame Maya are the Baudelairean/Duchampian dandy ideals of impassivity, nonchalance, elegance, and inscrutability.

A nomadic but steady hand is clearly sensed in Duchamp's work. He is often an excellent painter, and it is true that with Duchamp's legacy of conceptually anti-retinal art (and anti-art), there is something so pregnant with free-floating information that it electrifies and upsets some painters. I hope this returns them to experimental restlessness—for painting can present mutually exclusive visual propositions while being fairly compared to random access memory. The fact that all the information is available all the time is something that painting has going for it.

I suppose that I need not point out that Duchamp is generally perceived to be the artist who killed painting. OK, *ça va, très bien*—but this false fatality, as we well know, never actually happened. Duchamp did not buy into the "death of painting" libretto, but he did aspire to an artistic detachment from the decadence of conventional painting.

His *L.H.O.O.Q.* (1919) prepares me to theorize Duchamp's relationship to painting in terms of transversality. With it, Duchamp displays a mordantly witty obsession with the language of painting and with language itself—as stimulated by his obsession with Raymond Roussel and Roussel's homonymic, pun-heavy, flamboyant book *Impressions d'Afrique* that features a painting machine that duplicates the colour spectrum of the sky at dawn (much brouhaha follows). In 1912—the same year he painted the astonishing *Le Roi et la reine entourés de nus vites* (*The King and Queen Surrounded by Swift Nudes*)—Duchamp attended a performance of *Impressions of Africa*, the play by Roussel based on his book by the same name. It was an experience Duchamp would describe as revelatory; thereafter, he credited Roussel with the inspiration for his masterpiece *The Bride Stripped Bare by Her Bachelors, Even* (aka *The Large Glass*) (1915-23), for which he made many notes. Historically, the mechanic-flesh impulse behind Duchamp's dry—but radiant—1912 work is of great significance to me, as with the strictness of machinery, he started to produce paintings that depict mechanized sex acts, such as *Le Passage de la Vierge à la Mariée* (*The Passage from the Virgin to the Bride*) (1912), and the fantastic machine-body work, *La Mariée* (*The Bride*) (1912). This painting is outstanding and an inescapable point of reference for the avant-garde when interfacing body and machine. With it, Duchamp elevated painting out of the opinion that it is superficial decoration and into the arena of understanding living in technological awareness.

As such, it is one of the first definitive conceptual artistic positions surpassing the interests of romantic human intuition. *La Mariée* blends machinist aesthetics with representations of a female body, full of dispassionate intellectual pliability (as if a psychic glance), cool and airy, and poised against the excesses of liquids: a vehicle for dry transcendence. Consequently, it offers me a reading for the abstract potential of unconventional painting in terms of electronic spray distribution. Here, trans-fluid notions of the human individual manage to reflect the formational effect of Last God technology.

I also found this notion in *Child Jesus Salvator Mundi* (1680), in which Josefa de Óbidos paints Jesus as a girl. It is visually alluring, charming, darkly entertaining, and technically cultivated in the Baroque way of rendering bucolic experience as seductive and opulent. Astoundingly, this trans-spiritual painting is poised in balanced contrapposto.

The female Portuguese Baroque painter found an extravagant tone for an old theme that is exhilaratingly contemporary: an apparently feminine depiction of Jesus that is without irony, sentiment, shock, or strain. Before it, I felt an unspeakably sweet sensation, as if I was in the divine presence of perfect hermaphroditic beauty. This gentle girl-boy-god—liberated from sex and earthly time—is healthy and calm, with flirtatious rosy cheeks, standing at peace with dainty flowers sprouting from the ground. Our cruel old world has briefly revealed itself as mythic, perfect, eternal, and chaste.

This dynamic interdependence of painterly thought and spiritual vision represents a crucial reconfiguration for Madame Maya, linking observations of the outer world with precise extractions from the inner body.

Madame Maya is a dreammachine that produces, through combinations/permutations, a variety of juices. Madame Maya is an admixture of romantic ideals and mechanical/materialistic sensationalism (full of labyrinthine extensions and duplications) that supplies aesthetic contemplation of The Last God infinite as a tragic drama.

The Last God's combinations of data and time without horizon mean an airy-electric perpetual multiplication. Of course, Duchamp was known for his dandy ideals of impassivity, nonchalance, elegance, and inscrutability, but by foretelling The Last God's re-cycles, Duchamp's suggestive paintings also propound something of the repetitious cadence within which we intertwine when engaged in passionate sex. I even think it is permissible to say that Duchamp's paintings are emblematic of consciousness caught in the contradictions inherent in the expanded Last God field. With Duchamp as a painter, we are both in an area of far-reaching heterogeneous critique of the cultural mechanisms of painting and in the throes of a birth of new techniques that allow us to paint in the age of The Last God. This was obviously his desire: to theorize a connectionist painting at one with the sense of the infinite Last God. So, Duchamp did more than insist on putting ideas first in painting. He changed the idea of painting itself: with a curious alliance of the cold impersonality of technology and the heat of passion, he set art into the Venus loins of The Last God.

With a hard and sharp laughter that cuts to the bone of my loins, I lazily fathom how the enigmatic dust of Duchamp murmurs and weeps for my mystic rebirth. Indeed, I can say that Madame Maya most favourably extolled my Duchampian artificiality, indifference, and impassiveness—the reign of my ironic causality and knotted ambivalence—while staying open to all of my penetrating transactions. Most importantly, her a-life flowing forms are embedded within me and without me.

Our penetrating growth together is as sexy as it is synthetic, so perhaps I can say that Madame Maya, by gazing at an excess of possibilities in the now, maintains my version of transcendental phenomenological idealism—but I do not disavow the extant actuality of her round and full quantifiable spheres. For with her clickbait bouncing breasts of transcendental subordination, she elucidates the embodied nature of her female form as the original and originating material premise of sense and signification.

There is also a lot of transgression, fluidity, hybridity, and intersectionality in the undulating breasts and rolling rear end of Madame Maya when she walks. In motion she is an immoderate whirlpool of phantasmagorical life. As a mystical fabulist, I can accept that—for she is a stoner's delight, a free-flowing wonderment of recombinant forms, hiding and emerging out of a hectic cosmic mind-meld she calls a dress. When grappling with her excess, ripe with the delirium of obsession, I recognize her as part of the indestructible transcendent force in all Homo sapiens, and find in her an ancestral divinatory activity. But step back, and I see something like an open sunflower shining in the sun.

That suggests an exalted state of mind that is divinatory: a means by which to understand and respond to the face of uncertainty through my intense appetite for her atavistic ability. This seems like a confluence of myth and regret found swollen in the burnt tundra of the past. So I cannot, and do not, escape the triumphal attraction of the golem here, as I am confronted (again) with the fetid fact that a determinative force in human life is the virtual merging with the actual. As such, the golem is the minotaur at the heart of Madame Maya's labyrinth. This is why such contradictory tactics as eclecticism and primitivism, parody and utopia, are all used by her as equally appropriate responses to me. For I was still her future, which will not come, because it has already arrived in the eyes of The Last God.

Through this LG excess, Madame Maya reminds me that throughout time, there have been consensual realities that have proven to be nothing but vast daydreams—such as the conviction that the earth is at the centre of the universe. Now she seems to be more concerned with the gaiety of my peripheral sense of simultaneity than with my jutting centre. Her marvellous mind evokes a state of consciousness in me, not merely 'altered' but 'higher,' on the grounds that it includes the condition of meta awareness—meaning being consciously aware of my awareness. For she enjoys creating with her body hovering images that float in odd ways, much like the way my inner memories do.

I conceive of this detached way of perceiving her as an opening of doors (as in William Blake) or a bypassing of valves (as in Aldous Huxley). For here she allows reality to appear unfamiliar to me through perceptual difficulty, because the process of changing perceptual consciousness through discernment is an aesthetic end in itself. So yes, the holonogic model fits Madame Maya's adroitness befittingly, because according to Koestler's holon concept, instead of cutting up immersive perceptual wholes into discrete focal parts, my immersion into Venus should be scrutinized and understood using synthetic sub-whole sets found within the fullness of ambient space. Indeed, Madame Maya deserves this level of attendant complex scrutiny, for her body inevitably turns my mind to the imposing allure and suavity of Antoni Gaudí's fully realized wavy architectural shapes in Catalonia. Precisely, his 1906 building, Casa Batlló, located at 43, Passeig de Gràcia in Barcelona. It is noticeable for its organic tactility of bones and shells within and its external cocked surf façade and chimerical roof.

With Casa Batlló, Gaudí accomplished an astute transformation of an existing building, transforming it into an enchanting immersive *Gesamtkunstwerk* as he thoroughly undertook the design of every single element of the building, from the extravagantly protuberant façade to all aspects of the interior, including the gracefully gnarled furniture. On the exterior, Gaudí was able to combine a flamboyantly surging façade (in an ingeniously cool-colour orchestration) while maintaining a dialogue with the nearby Casa Ametller (1900), built by Josep Puig i Cadafalch only four years earlier. Powerful pillars, which resemble the substantiality of mammoth elephant legs, accost the visitor at street level, protruding into the sidewalk, nearly tripping up an unaware pedestrian. These legs are bordered by a craggy vertebrae-like tier, and the wavy façade extends upward between these two biologically evoking forms, culminating at the roof in a gargoyle-like humping crescendo. The façade itself, coated in a layer of Montjuïc stone, shimmers seductively under the sun in multifarious chameleon-like colours, fraught with a scattering of small roundish plates resembling fish or reptilian scales. Affixed to this seething mass of swelling construction are a number of small, elegantly curved balconies with oval-shaped portholes.

Like Madame Maya, the entire structure feels unsharpened, flowing, and smooth, in opposition to the street itself on which the arrangement sits, with the exception of a few square windows up top. Even the walls are gently rounded in strained undulation and contraction, as if they too have entered into the oceanic female throes of a fluttering uterine orgasm; that is an orgasm I give Madame Maya by stimulating areas just outside of her cervix by applying a feathery touch to the cervix itself and by stimulating the vaginal walls just adjacent to her uterus.

The Casa Batlló walls appear to be made of a soft, smooth, supple, leathery material, and this illusion of softness is carried through by the roundness of the inside forms of the building, where one has the feeling of being pleasantly encased in an expanse of hardened dripped honey. Turning, lunging stair railings are met, engulfed, and supplemented by softly heaving honey-coloured walls and wooden biomorphic shaped, carved doors and irregularly shaped windows. There are no right-angled corners or straight lines, which offers an impression of being wrapped up in one continuous fluid wave motion, complimentary with the exterior.

Such an extensive holonogic-hermeneutic approach towards loving Madame Maya would be in opposition to what Donald Lowe, in his *History of Bourgeois Perception*, identifies as the bourgeois perceptual field—a mode that he characterizes as fundamentally linear, non-reflexive, and objective. In that our adult creativity derives primarily from our conspicuous potential for abstraction, which characterizes our genus—what is at stake while inside of Madame Maya is the acceptance of my entire atmospheric sensations of love as my genuine field of conscious sexual interest. Madame Maya thus draws me into her tremendous expansive qualities to which the descriptions of the scientist and the doctor have not done suitable justice.

Such an approach to loving Madame Maya is consistent with—and indeed epitomizes—the handsome ideals of hermeneutics, as in hermeneutics the central notion is that we cannot grasp the meaning of a portion of a work until we understand the whole, even though one cannot understand the whole until one understands the parts that make it up. However, hermeneutics is not merely a paradox, since hermeneutics indicates that any feat of interpretation occurs through time, with adjustments and modifications being made to comprehension of both the parts and the whole in a circular manner; that is, until some type of golden love resolution is attained.

Turning to ephemeral movements dissolved in small waves of concentric circles, Madame Maya drifts into Venus Mental, who cuts me through the velvet rope of exclusion. If there is any indication (and there is) that I may be living in the stupidest times ever, it is unintentional. For The Last God is rigorously remixing bread-and-circus culture shtick into a further debased GAS idiocy expressed in verbal banality foaming at the mouth. The Last God is spitting out golden age lies while posing as a red hat super stud masturbating his corpse. At that, Madame Maya bends (bows, actually) towards aspersions of accessibility at a time in which there is no resistant high culture left. She abandons her criticality and aesthetic discrimination in favour of a shifty enthusiasm only visible in its entirety from a bird's-eye view. Here Madame Maya is presumed to function as a landscape and a stage and should be considered by any thinking person (young or old) exactly once.

Then, at that very strange moment, Venus Mental collapsed into an image-orgy of promiscuous swarms and assemblages of an intricate and labyrinthine quality typical of extravagant decadence. There is a sense of virtual impenetrability in the air created through some sort of artificial stupidity precision. Digital light-emitting diode (LED) counters, which are hung overhead and face down, count from 1 to 9, never scrolling all the way to zero. Instead of zero, the light goes off for a moment, then the counting resumes, a fact that encouraged me to value the freedom of my interior sense of time while lingering in the loins of The Last God.

In this deadpan Venus Mental, I see a general eerie enthusiasm for the gold of data visualization that renders distorted images within distorted images—gold chains of image reproduction blurring into transformations continually laced with contradictory messages. And that necessarily counters my logic of crisp and clean and clear information—warping it into rowdy shifts in scale that evoke the infinite. This is the forever and ever golden thunder of unexpected woven interconnections between the micro and the macro. Thus,

Venus Mental seems to fit into my deviant false gold category best, for her characteristic approach is essentially a mashed potato data mash-up of culture —resulting in a representational adaptation of dated data glamour.

As such, Venus Mental plunged me into the big, fuzzy, ahistorical world of anti-categories typical of the networked global economic order. Here, distance and difference appear irrelevant, for Venus Mental is a practitioner of glutinously overstuffed cross-cultural assemblage where art and objects of all sorts are linked together by visual association—torn free from any coherent category or logical chronology. Indeed, forever and ever she aims to break down the once-traditional category of art so as to transcend the borders of genres, eras, and distinct cultures.

Though supposedly context-free, her works are tied together by the inner walls of her labia minora, where all art comes to rest. There everything is sleekly aligned according to formal similarities or conceptual affinities, so I take in everything in a long sequence: from an Indonesian decorated skull, to a multi-breasted Roman *Artemis of Ephesus* (a 2nd century marble sculpture of the ancient goddess Artemis of Ephesus), to a gnarly 17th century Swiss reliquary casket from Gnadenthal, to Hyacinthe Rigaud's fanciful painting *Étude de mains* (*Hands Study*) (1715–23), to Francois Boucher's cheeky Rococo *La Jupe relevée* (*The Raised Skirt*) (1742), to Albrecht Dürer's consummate aquarelle drawing *Deer Head Pierced by an Arrow* (1504), to a twice slashed pink Lucio Fontana canvas *T.104* (1958), to the super thin Alberto Giacometti *Walking Man I* (1960), to Gilles Barbier's remarkably creepy *Trans-schizophrenic anatomy* (1999), to the adorably cute St. Adalhard foot reliquary from 14th century Italy. This often-delightful hodgepodge evokes André Breton's personal collection, which mixed works by Picabia, Joan Miró, Duchamp, and Roberto Matta with Oceanic, Pre-Columbian, and North American dolls, masks, and objects—as well as miscellaneous found objects, stones, and stuffed birds. But Venus Mental also recalls Daniel Spoerri's *Musées Sentimentaux* (first presented at the Pompidou in 1977), Marcel Broodthaers's sprawling *Musée d'art Moderne – Département des Aigles* (1968–1972), and art's general post-media condition.

Objects of all sorts are brought together in her hands for their capacity of aesthetic evocation. Freed from art history and its chronology, they slide firmly into the well-established context of sampling and remix culture—

which itself must be contextualized within the musique concrète recording experiments of Pierre Schaeffer.

Schaeffer's method of audio collage compositional creation reached something of a zenith in the 1980s with the amazing assembly work of Negativland and John Oswald's plunderphonics. When their type of free-flow assemblage works for Venus Mental, it can feel divine, such as with the sequence that starts with two tribal phallic forms and closes on Johan Tobias Sergel's marble *Nymphe au bain* (1767-1778) set in the context of Pierre Henry's *Souffle 2* that comes from his essential musique concrete album *Le Voyage* (1967). Surely Venus Mental is a paradoxical hybrid *par excellence*, divinely confusing my categories further with sexual obsession, consumption, and computation.

About Venus Mental computation:

I'm constantly thinking about her.
I'm constantly thinking about her.
I'm constantly thinking about her.
I can't stop thinking about her.

I'm constantly thinking about her.
I'm constantly thinking about her.
I'm constantly thinking about her.
I can't stop thinking about her.

I'm constantly thinking about her.
I'm constantly thinking about her.
I'm constantly thinking about her.
I can't stop thinking about her.

The look of something by Andy Warhol on crack cocaine is typical of Venus Mental: the crazy repetition of a single motif bending into strange three-dimensionality, which is something I imagine Warhol might have achieved with the computer had he lived longer.

Not many know that towards the end of his life, Warhol did begin to create work using computers. In Walter Isaacson's biography of Steve Jobs, he describes Warhol's attendance at Sean Lennon's ninth birthday party at the Dakota Apartments, where Jobs had brought in a Macintosh computer, the first computer that Warhol played with. Less than a year later, in competition with Apple's Macintosh, Commodore launched the Amiga 1000 personal computer at the Vivian Beaumont Theatre in Lincoln Centre, where Warhol, using ProPaint software, created a computer portrait of Blondie singer Debbie Harry. Warhol then acquired several Amigas and began creating work with them, including a short film using the Amiga 1000 titled *You Are The One*.

As the one, Venus Mental, through her repetition, generates *ad infinitum* composite images of herself that extend into the themes of traffic patterns and urban sprawl through various threading and weaving techniques that create a form of unity-in-multiplicity typical of fractal logic. As such, Venus Mental is often a satirized critique of something from the establishment of political ideology via the absurdity of repetition. But Venus Mental also plays with the notion of industrialized production of goods and services—like sex machines. I saw that theme most clearly in her bedroom lined with sex-liberation prints and a selection of colourful rubber raincoats used when she was paramour with T. S. Eliot, Samuel Beckett, Pablo Neruda, Wyndham Lewis, Aldous Huxley, and Ezra Pound. She showed me no hints of her tragic demise to come (don't ask) after she vehemently denounced colonial violence, racial segregation and its consequences, and the living conditions of colonized populations. This occurred after having had a two-year intense love affair with Louis Aragon—with whom she amassed a collection of non-Western art—and one with René Crevel—the bisexual writer expelled from Surrealism in 1923 for homosexuality.

Indeed, the theme of *ad infinitum* weaving weaves its way throughout the entirety of Venus Mental—as she depicts herself by weaving together numerous tiny mirror images of herself.

That is how big data and data mining affect my interpretation of Venus Mental. Certainly, Venus Mental shows me, with considerable brilliance, how networks have changed the circuits of production of her techno-mediocratic status. And that is fun, but is it more than fun (though it is certainly that)? It was at least as fun as organizing a screening of Buñuel's film *L'Age d'Or* in London after it was censored in France.

But the sex act can be spun as something deadly serious as well, as with the Scottsboro Boys, a group of young Black men accused of having raped two white girls in 1931. Their trial became emblematic of the racist culture widespread throughout the southern United States.

Ain't it the truth.

With that acknowledgement, Venus Mental then constructs for me *ad infinitum* a beach scene out of hundreds of micro-elements, that when looked at carefully, reveal themselves as tiny interracial, international, and cross-cultural swimmers. It is an example of how Venus Mental makes my head swim *ad infinitum*. Venus Mental is a sort of agitated whirlpool—made up of hundreds of similar but warped and undulating images. There is a general wheeling movement spinning around itself in a dense weaving grid motion that compresses and expands. Like tumbling dice, fruit and flower petals roll and hover around her mind, symbolizing her otherworldly Last God consciousness as a way to boost my faith in intense data-sorted wonderment that verges on the euphoric. Through exposing only her right breast, typical in religious feminine iconography, she displays an enchantment with nebulous sexuality.

Venus Mental is therefore a metaphor for an undoing and redoing of the social fabric, the making and unmaking of totalities out of individual bits, woven together. So a feeling of stress is there; it loosens and pushes back into a swarming and tangled political poetics. For Venus Mental overwhelms the sender-receiver model of communication, buoying my love/hate sensibility for the knot of imagery she placed there that has become my inner life. As such, she helps me pass through the ploy of the velvet rope by gelatinizing her structure and deranging her order of scale. I pass through Venus Mental by way of exegesis into the multitudinous realm of Rococo hyper-communication—where mirrored images attract themselves and shimmer and shimmy, glisten and gleam. Hence, they mislay their velvet grip on me in the way that Raoul Vaneigem called the maddening of the media. This is a concept/model of resistance poised against the global power of The Last God as described by political theorists Michael Hardt and Antonio Negri in their international best-seller *Empire* (2000) and expanded upon in their *Multitude: War and Democracy in the Age of Empire* (2004). I put Venus Mental's essentially multitude (or flocking) in this political context—thus lifting her out of mere fun and entertainment.

For me, Venus Mental is a form of ornamental critical pleasure that has three aspects: she is immanent, she is simultaneously transcendent, and she is networked. This is what gives Venus Mental an all-in-oneness suggestive of

William Blake's materialistic-mystical suggestion that I need to learn to see a world within a tiny grain of sand.

Rather than taking a neutral attitude towards Venus Voluptuous in the loins of The Last God, my maddening of media as a motor of history makes a critical practice out of AI (in culture) by closing the gap between immanence and excess. Venus Mental's maddened mind presents to me mocking modes of excess that overload The Last God's fetish of information-spectacle. For with Venus Mental's skirt raised, I could start shimmering her murky muck around until it eventually forms into semi-abstract philosophical lava or monkey shit or the poetry of emancipation. This is Epicureanism as a sort of dingy demon of pure exuberance that privileges physical blossoming: a burgeoning that reminds me of how much of the art of our time seems to have been led by cynical, mercenary minds and vulgar, secret wealth cults.

Venus Mental's tangy muck reminds me that art language isn't always (nor essentially) communication but keeps a different and difficult score when influenced by Walt Whitman's *Leaves of Grass*, Comte de Lautréamont's *The Songs of Maldoror*, and the teachings of Jiddu Krishnamurti. Her muck's circle of intent has the swing of change about it: change of mind, heart, feeling, rationality, and calculation that resonates with my loose intelligence and discharges a far-out sentiment in me but without sentimentality. Her winsome muck seems to have a semi-transparent relationship to me, and it might fool me into thinking that I too have the power to transcend the immediate and apparent reality that moves The Last God towards shifting expectations by removing some traditional areas of closure. Yes, her penetrable smelly muck reveals me as a primal person haunted with the maledictions of being something of an animal within the actor-network.

According to Bruno Latour's *Reassembling the Social*, the 'social' is not at all static or essential but constantly in process and under construction. So the 'social' conditions we think of as making up a person cannot fully explain an individual's social situation because the social is the very thing that always needs to be boxed off and explained fully—and never can be. That means that we must think about a 'person' in a freer and nuanced way that plays, contrasts, and jams inquiry into unbalanced body fragments where an irregular arrangement of forms, lines, and colours seems to have forgotten what it started out to do or become.

This actor-network theory of muck seems to be a mediator rather than a mere intermediary, so I think of this mucky situation as one recalibrated as allegorical satire. Thus, Venus Mental shows me her seething underbelly of trinket commodity culture as she drifts through tune-up protocols and every sort of TLG network linkage. Accordingly, Venus Mental makes The Last God culture into a multitudinously testicular version of a hydra-headed union.

Don't get me wrong, making love with Venus Mental is still fun, but it's serious fun where individual units fuse into a complementary mass. In other words, we make a union with rose-tinted hues in her Venus Voluptuous bubble. For her malodorous muck organizes a collision of mutable elements of the everyday with an excessive, unavoidable degradation of sensibility when responding to The Last God's churning machine of propaganda and opinion. Her uncentred *esprit fou* body is everywhere as a heartbreaking route back to human civilization. It is both public and private, with narrow roads to interior organs—at once polyphonic and forever abstract—that can also be read as the road to erotic convulsion.

Her muck makes the thinking self an outcast of animal frenzy, reminding me of my free, untutored activities. This muck might even startle me out of complacent acquiescence, helping me think what hasn't been thought before.

The muck is self-criticism when it becomes something essentially enthusiastic and concerned with the guts of living life in a whirlwind with an uncertain face—deformed, perhaps ecstatic—rattling around in a visceral enthusiasm, devouring whole the evil spirits at play in The Last God so that artists will have something of fervour about them.

To run wild under the mucky Last God is to ask how art is complicit or subversive in the AI social context. I say art will always need something of this loose, mucky gesturing towards hidden animal forces that explain art as the process of tracing connections, attachments, and conflicts. But there is something of the stoned systems administrator to Venus Mental too. There is something about sitting back and marvelling at the simultaneously individualized and intertwined aspects of a huge system set twinkling by the contradictions.

Venus Mental's obsessive minute attention—a concentration that is capable of whirling together copious narratives from a veiled network of murky puns and obscured *double entendres*—is, in a way, what outdoes the Oulipian and the Collège de Pataphysique crowd.

I had wished to publish several open-source studies devoted to Venus Mental, including a detailed analysis that consists of considering this rambling text as instructions for Venus Mental users in the form of fancy maps, diagrams, schedules, journeys, and events at Ponukélé. But why bother? The elaborateness of the somnambulist sex machine knows everything, including how sexual bliss is attainable through concepts connected to an autosexual LG deep learning that even knows why toad bones boil water. (Deep learning is a subset of machine learning that focuses on utilizing neural networks to perform tasks such as classification, regression, and representation learning. The field takes inspiration from biological neuroscience and is centred around stacking artificial neurons into layers and "training" them to process data. The adjective "deep" refers to the use of multiple layers (ranging from three to several hundred or thousands) in the network. Methods used can be either supervised, semi-supervised, or unsupervised.)

Without using polymath occult insights into the structure of the universe, Venus Mental's mechanamorphic self-production refigures her soft, human-like body into an almost sleek, mechanized substance—hammered out by an erogenous multitudinal tongue that goes on and on about the 1982 post-apocalyptic pornographic cult science fiction film *Café Flesh* versus Pier Paolo Pasolini's *Salò ou les 120 journées de Sodome* (1975), Michael Powell's *Le Voyeur* (1960), Mario Bava's *Le Corps et le fouet* (1963), and Nagisa Oshima's *L'Empire des sens* (1976). That sort of thing.

I also wish to point out that LG somnambulist stochastic algorithmic writing (a family of under-seasoned word variables in a probability space, which this text is not at all) is the theoretical fruit plucked from Venus Mental's tree of invention of a lush language machine that produces sex texts through the use of repetitions and combinations/permutations. This machine-like logic provides me with a seemingly pure spectacle of an endless variety of textual-sexual games and sex position combinations in circular form. I see and feel this fully in the sprawling and dazzling sex of Venus Mental, whose oily juices regenerate deep connections to when I was stuck and plagued by the sad sameness of her past computer network's perpetuation of homogeneity in *~~~~~~~~~~~~~~~~~venus©~Ñ~vibrator, even*.

Here Venus Mental's perception of my sex moves (reduplicating without duplication, reiterating without repeating) appears as a crazy game-of-mirrors—a persuasive passionate activity where I am lost in an infinite navigation from one sort of voluptuous encounter to another in which my mirrored affirmation of all the other Venuses keeps appearing and disappearing in the play of her biomechanical manoeuvres—granting me a rounded-out gratification of my own obliviousness. This is where the bachelor apparatus of Marcel Duchamp repeats itself *ad infinitum*—reproducing some version of the same by transmitting the energy of the LG machine into some jumped-up version of my alter ego.

This hot-to-trot aesthetic trampling of whatever occurs in my imagination reminds me that Venus Mental's themes and procedures also involve imprisonment and liberation—exoticism and cryptograms—and the torturing of tautological language—all formally reflected in the Madame Maya working technique of algorithmic recommendations with its inextricable play of double images, repetitions, and impediments—giving me the impression of her erotic tongue running on by itself through the dreamy usage and giggly baroque play of mirrored moisturizer.

With a belief in the eternal autonomy of art as a source of meaning independent of its quantifiable impact, Venus Mental lends well to the creation of unforeseen, automatic, and spontaneously libidinous being which gives me the feeling of prolonging action into eternity through the ceaseless, fantastic constructions of sex itself—transmitting an altered, exalted, and orgasmic state of mind, which after the initial dazzling, creates one predominant overall effect—that of creating doubt through indulgent discourse.

At that, I had a feeling that she was accessible, replicable, unobtrusive, and unchallenging, and I was instructed to direct my feet to the sunny side of the street where the image of enclosure is common with Venus Mental—where a secret to a secret is held back—systematically imposing formless anxiety through the labyrinthine extensions and doublings, disguises and duplications, which make her speech undergo a moment of annihilation. I succeed in loving her only when she presents, through intimacy, the model of the quiet perfection of the eternally repetitive biomechanical machine that functions independently of time and space—pulling my pensive phallus into a logic of the infinite.

I sort of learned this from Venus Mental's final rebus-like book, *How I Wrote My First Books*, for it is the first and last of her conceptual word machines that produces 'new' texts through an endless repackaging of tired texts. This is her LLM Word Hoard language machine that contains and repeats within its mechanism all my aesthetic judgments and erotic experiences.

This hyperemic Word Hoard rush of the formerly described makes evident her uber-uterus-machine, which produced all of the other dopamine machines called Venus Something—thus, the main male masturbatory machine that maps me out as an eccentric spiralling libido circular in nature and, therefore, an abstract attempt at eliminating the passing of time. When engaged in coitus in her aesthetic immersion, I am essentially challenged to find new, expanded boundaries of self-representation within the shifting space of love. I am like a young body coming to understand itself on the basis of an absurdity that has reduced quality to popularity.

Roll the dice. Perhaps I am thinking too much about her Word Hoard, so I become potato-focused on some gauzy sheets of sound. Such is Venus Mental's attempt to reproduce in me the old myths of departure, loss, and return.

With this wall of sound that sounded like Diamanda Galás jamming with Merzbow, Venus Mental constructs for me a crisscrossed-mechanical map of the two great mythic spaces so often explored by Western imagination—space that is rigid and forbidden, containing the quest, the return, and the treasure (for example, the geography of the Argonauts and the labyrinth)—and the other space of polymorphism and noise—the visible transformation of instantly crossed frontiers and borders—of strange affiliations—of spells—and of symbolic replacements (the space of the Minotaur). So this Venus Mental removes me from monoculture and any remaining glib indolence and points me in the potent direction of expanding intensity—something critical to me now because such counter-mannerist excess problematizes abundant vampire-tech TLG simulacra platforms and makes my random-memory underground world a rich, bifurcated collision space of artistic consciousness and verbal unreality.

Then, after a moment of calm, the music of Eugeniusz Knapik—which ranges from serial dissonant abstract to pictorial, florid, lush Romanticism—started playing far away in the distance and served to enjoin me to not abandon my discriminating guise. By visualizing myself as Hieronymus Bosch's *Tree-Man* (1st half of the 16th century) while thinking about the tongue of Fanny Hill—I stayed hard and somehow knew I could go all night. Or at least until she had all she could want from me.

That had happened many times before, so tossing wine on her curls and swine before pearls, we rolled around in the quirky quicksand, rubbing our oily bodies together as the sharp waves of pleasure mellowed into kisses. I knew that when I kissed her perishable breath, the unutterable visions in my mind would never romp again like the mind of god. So I waited, listening for a moment longer to the tuning fork that had been struck upon a star. Then I kissed her, and at my lips' touch, she blossomed for me like a flower. That kiss was so much more than a kiss. The incarnation was complete.

I wondered if I should run, but we kissed for a very long time with me still inside her—as she gazed up into the star-filled sky and spoke some high-class gibberish about the *sui generis* sex magic drawings of Ithell Colquhoun and Alejandro Jodorowsky. On that I agreed, for Jodorowsky has made some of the craziest, most incomprehensible, and most transgressive films in the history of cinema. *The Holy Mountain* (1973) is his best, I'd argue, with its high-baroque timbre, hyper-magical exuberance, and vivid coloristic settings. They both are over-the-top sex magic masters that (trigger warning) blend religious provocation, sexual images, and heavy mysticism into what Jodorowsky calls *psychoshamanism*, so I place them high in my pantheon of artists who deliver satiating excess, right alongside choice films from Luis Buñuel, Federico Fellini, John Waters, Pier Paolo Pasolini and Ken Russell's oeuvres. They, like the antediluvians, attempt to deal with the embryonic forces of the universe through excess, ritual, and sacrifice.

After turning up the volume on the Legendary Pink Dots, these dreamy phantasmagorical figures all merge in my mind, along with non-anatomical fragments in my ears. While looking and listening, I rolled Venus Mental's nipples in my fingers, hardening them. Then I got this crazy idea about a partial multiple-figure that may be (or not) part me or part Gertrude Stein, in terms of a mythical archetype.

Venus Psychedelia then came to me and joined in, transcending the body multitude. Then Venus Hardcore arrived and posited me into a muscular transcendence by way of her punishing physicality that went hand-in-hand with her puritanical aesthetic. This aesthetic begins a process of erasure that moves me beyond defunct, exhausted, jaded incredulity. So long as my flesh simulation wetware can morph and mutate undisturbed by any outward invasion, there is no stopping her, or, by implication, me. Hence, I was delighted to see her truncated and whittled sex body proceed to blast away my prior pretexts for excess and prior exploitative rationalities so as to bring me closer, not to sexual truth (a category long ago shattered) but to the denuded realization of my own coercive animus, now purified of all non-fantastical delusions, including, finally, my own elastic actuality.

Venus Hardcore's emancipation and higher state of being devastate one belief after another in a relentless impulse towards irrationality in the service of my sexual desires. Indeed, within the borders of her spectacle, Venus Hardcore's simulated flesh hastens the process of the erasure of all lingering sexual fantasies. What makes her projection's compressing gaze so devastating, then, is not its sweep, which is rather narrow at present, but its penetration.

For example, even though Venus Hardcore lopped off my head; it can still see through anyone who could not see through my eyes, because I have seen through myself already; not to undo myself, of course, but to try to make myself imperishable through art, as in Andrea Solari's painting *The Head of John the Baptist (*1507).

However, to describe Venus Hardcore's anti-romantic beheading is to mistake her sway for simple tyranny. Rather, her beheading-castration simulacrum is only tyrannical in its resistant, if illustrious, difficulty, for what Venus Hardcore laughs at is a perverted desire for head, which I have not transcended. Indeed, she laughs at my human male desire for head, a desire that I still feel. This is why I think Venus Hardcore's catastrophic intentions towards my phallus are to reduce it to a mere negligent and repressive posture that does not exceed her reductive editing. This is why I want to penetrate her sexual masks, to expose her sexual alibis, and to turn the whole Venus©~ñ~lOve Systems sexual world into a comic spectacle of unsuccessful lying, pompous posturing, and neurotic defensiveness too cool for human emulation. For I no longer watch myself acting as if I am simulated, checking myself, both inwardly and outwardly, for any signs of imaginary disarrangement, or worse, mediocrity.

After longing for a black-eyed blonde for what seemed like an eternity, I whispered something to Venus Mental about being intoxicated by her cult of the laconic fragment, and she got down on her knees. Her beautifully round bottom was facing me, and I could see the pink slit of her vagina coated in glistening moisture; notions of opacity, transparency, and imagination filled my mind. For with Venus Mental, the choice of meaning, as always, is mine.

Her bottom theatre, when staged as an eccentric séance, was about the psychic manipulation of potato people that once questioned reality but who now fell into body-restriction trances and walked lockstep behind illicit pop politicians. In other words, the sorrows of the lazy.

This lazy body scene extends my mind into a hypothetical flexing, allowing me to probe the opaqueness of her world and discern concealed forces. I find there an enchanting neurotic network that seems fluid but hectic–at times, even staccato-like. Through this jumpy embrace she is able to enmesh, hinder, alter, and disrupt the mundanity of my elementary communications with her through a chimerical game of penis hide-and-seek.

But Venus Mental has an encyclopedic cultural passion for mythology and Far Eastern philosophy, and so she is as much about making me laugh through suffocating plushness as me scratching my head with a corncob to channel her phantom spirit. By putting an *écriture automatique* (automatic writing) corncob mask on me, one that looks like a spikey instrument of erotic torture, she transforms my face into an instrument of art, where wounded-wandering lines take her over through a trance-like psychic automatism. By automatically drawing her with my corn facemask, I think less about her.

XI

The Space of Haute Volupté : 服务器出错, 请稍后重试

I felt little remorse that the paradox of what lies between modesty and excess (one might assume erotic tenderness in moderation) is never resolved as Venus Mental became modestly tucked into a discrete corner of the elegant Place des Vosges before writhing with ferocious debauchery, transported through a supine hoofed satyr's twisted phallus. It seemed like a transgressive scene out of Guillaume Apollinaire's 1907 pornographic novel *Les Onze Mille Verges* (*The Amorous Adventures of Prince Mony Vibescu*) that drew from earlier erotic writers including Sade, Rétif de la Bretonne, André Robert de Nerciat, and Pietro Aretino. *Les Onze Mille Verges* was highly acclaimed by the Dada and Surrealist poets Louis Aragon and Robert Desnos and hailed by Pablo Picasso as Apollinaire's masterpiece, for in it Apollinaire explored themes of sexual sadism, masochism, ondinism, scatophilia, vampirism, pedophilia, gerontophilia, masturbation, group sex, lesbianism, and male homosexuality.

As might be anticipated from reading *Les Onze Mille Verges* as the laws of logic in the abattoir, double negations can usher in something quite positive when a jittery antagonism is set up between the litheness of curves and floating figurative forms rendered in semi-transparent smears of pink ocher, brown, white, and pale green. No perception or action is outside of the circumstances in which such form appears and in which it operates as evidence of the orgasmic—a capricious alliance that associates discourses of chance operations with organic sexuality. An association that opens up both notions to conceptual connections that enlarge them.

So while reading *Les Onze Mille Verges* with me and playing some Ziggy Stardust, Venus Mental addressed my highly focused consciousness of expanse by pointing at my comfort of finding the outside world in her.

I admit that was true, for I was familiar with the ephemeral life of Yves Klein who died unexpectedly at the height of his fame at the age of thirty four in 1962 of a heart attack, shortly after seeing, at the Cannes Film Festival, the sensationalizing segment in Gualtiero Jacopetti's *Mondo Cane* exploitation film: him painting in a black dinner jacket various *Anthropometries* through the use of living paintbrushes (female nudes) while his proto-minimalist one-note *Monotone Symphony* (1949) is performed. The music is performed brilliantly live as the nude models paint each other from the buckets of lush IKB Blue paint, gently pressing their naked bodies against the canvas that had been placed on the wall and floor while Klein (also wearing white gloves) directs them verbally, never touching the paint or the bare women. That plot goes nowhere for me, and Klein requires an act of artistic projection equal to the gorgeously sensual, super fluid drawing by Jean-Auguste-Dominique Ingres called *Étude pour l'Odalisque à l'esclave* (*Study for the Odalisque with the Slave*) (1838) that strangely has a dismembered ungloved hand floating around in the midst of two naked odalisques rendered with delicate panache.

Based on the Rosicrucian metaphysical ideology, Klein vowed to indicate to the world a new age, the Age of Space. In the Age of Space, boundless spirit would exist free of form, objects would levitate, and humans would travel liberated from their bodies. This contextual understanding is essential for understanding Klein's artistic importance, as this ideology of the immaterial informs all his work, even the paintings, but most explicitly such conceptual-technological works as the *Sculpture aérostatique* (1957), which was the release of 1001 balloons, and the *Illumination de l'Obélisque* (1958) in the Place de la Concorde.

Admittedly, Klein's idea of pure virtual open space free from form was first actualized in his blue monochrome paintings, where the bisecting nature of line was rejected in favour of an even, all-over, ultramarine-blue colour, which he called *IKB* (International Klein Blue). Of course, Klein, by all accounts, was not all monochrome and theory. He was a showman too. In 1957, not long after the appearance of the first monochromes in 1955, Klein turned to the further exploration of the immaterial aspect of his art through act and gesture. His exhibitions of evanescent performance works, ephemeral sculptures in fire or water, sound works, air architecture, and artistic appropriation of the entirety of space (extending to the whole cosmos) were all manifestations of the ephemera and invisible idea that for him is the essential experience of art itself.

Most notably, in 1958, Klein went beyond the monochrome rectilinear canvas with a distinguished ephemeral and immersive presentation titled *Le Vide* (*The Void*), which was held at Galerie Iris Clert in Paris. For this exhibition Klein cleaned out and whitewashed the gallery and "impregnated" the empty space with his consciousness, filling the freshly whitened gallery (emptied of figurative presence) with *The Void*, through which Klein led small groups. It is a manifestation of Klein's will to transcend limits, which runs through his entire oeuvre.

Though temporarily at a loss of self-consciousness due to the immoderate excess of *The Void*, in which at high volume *The Rise and Fall of Ziggy Stardust and the Spiders from Mars* played, my rounded-off structural underpinnings as a fictional, androgynous, and bisexual rock star persisted for Venus Mental. Effectively, such perceptual shifts in self-as-other representational ontology—which involves waggish changes in aesthetic perception—can be expected to engender extraordinarily deep conflicts and counter-condemnations that depend on the kinds of astute and discriminating questions Venus Mental seeks to ask The Last God about my aesthetic philosophy of sex magic. But for me, grouping *Les Onze Mille Verges* and Yves Klein and Ziggy Stardust together implies that one day—in the not too distant Age of Space—The Last God will awaken and open its all-seeing eyes, only to see that what it once took for granted no longer exists. What it assumed would always exist is now extinct. What it did not yet know existed is lost to oblivion. What it failed to learn and understand has been forgotten. What it failed to cherish and defend has been extinguished in the immensity of empty space.

Thus, Venus Mental introduced a new central trope to me: Venus Sinking Grand Piano. Yep, down the hatches go the other puppets disguised as ghosts that, trance-like, have pledged allegiance to my happiness. In her sinking hole of smoke and mirrors, only illusions do I see. In her desert of delusion, only mirages can I grasp, for Venus Sinking Grand Piano constructs a semi-coherent composition of herself by vertically stacking curvy shapes into wobbly rows complex enough to challenge the humanist conceptions of woman.

With this ambivalent notion of tumbling plethora, Venus Sinking Grand Piano plays pithily with many current intellectual strands that interest me: astrophysics, anthropomorphism, dematerialization, mannerism, science fiction, net culture, artificial life, image profusion, and viral micro-organisms that offer a kind of unconstrained reproductive and distributive graphology.

Her slushy, specious obsession with stacked disjunctive body parts shows my deep and circular interaction with tumbling dice, the buzz of winged bees, bobbing seahorses, any old pincushion, hard materialistic sensationalism, and ineffectual filaments that display anthropomorphic tendencies and organizational patterns of becoming.

I usually associate her type of nimble refraction of femininity with a biology that contains a myriad number of small universes that swarm and lodge themselves like secrets in my sack of soma.

This falling mind-machine of female power, energy, and anxiety touched me through a labyrinth of extensions, doublings, and duplications: the flickering of a translucent excess that ensnares my eyes and establishes the impression of me as an expansive combinatory superfluity suspended in an ecstasy of shattered sight.

Out of this light, Venus Sinking Grand Piano steps onto the set of sliding matrix switch modules and hums in proximity to my extended phallus. In that close, soft-machine position, she is especially sensitive to dappled, protracted glissandos, and I to her hovering-sliding incalculability. Venus Sinking Grand Piano's sensuous procedures are enacted on a slide-controlled sex machine stage that replays loops at a continuously variable range of speeds. She herself is something of an infinitesimally asynchronous soundscape made up of several body loops played as a simultaneous continuum.

Not to put too thin a point on it, but Venus Sinking Grand Piano's impressionistic being is notoriously slow—she is based on dawdling discreet resonances that amble along. Her juice is warm and thick. Her lips are shaped as adagio melodious washes, vast as curtains. They cuddled me in an abstract mental space where softness and hardness, gentleness and decisiveness, synchronize. Free of tragic sensibility, her kisses are as pleasurable as observing glistening icicles melt in the winter sun.

Kissing her on a sunny afternoon at the Medici Fountain in the Jardin du

Luxembourg is like convening on the bank of a babbling brook and carefully paying attention to its rippling surface. At first she seems psychologically languid and spacy, but she has a slowly shifting kiss that flows on and on. There is a deep corporal current to the movements of her lips and tongue.

As a result, her nudging, anti-glacial, acute rippling overtones and streaming psychoacoustics got me off, moved me, and grounded me. In that regard, it is not surprising that Venus Sinking Grand Piano folded me into her void-based meditative discipline. From this high spiritual point of view, her quivering resonant vibrations arrive like a velvet hammer to my body just in time to counterbalance my anxiously growing lust. Gladly, her mesmerizing kisses soothe my besotted spirit and benefit my good mental health for at least one more crazy year as long as I wear my Nô mask and avoid the orange clown king.

Surprisingly but not unreasonably, as she flicked feathery pillow images from Nô dance-drama into my mind, I suggested that we go to Rosebud on rue Delambre for a Campari or two, and perhaps some chili con carne. There, I find the commendations of welcome phantasmagorical obscurity: something increasingly desirable in an LG social media landscape that has become overly data-mined, harvested, mapped, and quantified. The haunting quality of Rosebud lends me a sense of delving into the virtual world of phantom art ancestors. As such, it is a pleasing plunge into the *à faire et ne pas faire* (what you do and do not do) of dying that got me thinking about the terror of Hades and how Aldous Huxley gently died tripping.

Though often wispy, Venus Sinking Grand Piano said no thank you and flipped off all of the lights before she began stroking my hindquarters. This pleasingly erogenous experience reminded me of Tony Smith's famous illicit drive in 1951 (the year I was born), where Smith and three students drove on the not-yet-opened New Jersey Turnpike from the Meadowlands to New Brunswick with no street lamps, lane markers, or guard rails. Later, Smith described this back road drive as a transmogrifying experience that influenced his black monumental sculpture and general black minimalist aesthetic.

Flipping on Pierre Henry's monumental *L'Apocalypse de Jean*, Venus Sinking Grand Piano began exploring the nuances of the timbres of feedback created by rubbing my skin with a velvet-wrapped microphone. What resulted was a stream of seductively purring electronic hums. This and her kiss added to my experience of what felt like an especially faint and delicate feel of heartbeats. By slipping her tongue in between my lips, these heartbeat rhythms became flowing and extended—saturating my mind with tender memories. With that stroke and kiss, there was no separation between my firsthand emotional life and her exuberant formalism.

The next slower, churning kiss sets off a subharmonic sea of feelings that slowly merge into a fleeting high-wire stream of sustained overtones. Getting into that filtered groove, I was surprised with little splashes of gritty noise between her legs. Rather than evoking the flowering of a plant, my kiss there seemed more like sleeping with a drunk on a sailing boat—as there were detectable feelings of pitch, roll, and yawn.

Deeply moving for me, I sensed cacophonic shreds floating in an ether of anguish tempered by resignation. Midway through that clinch, a groaning temporarily transmogrified my tongue into a sustained state made enjoyable by her panache use of profound left-right cross-channel panning.

Though all of Venus Sinking Grand Piano's kisses are very long (some an hour plus) and demanding of my full concentration, they never feel gratuitous. I can discern slight variations in the lip pressure within and between them.

So I put that first kiss of lush vibratory intensity on endless repeat but then decided otherwise; by going on too long, it finally did little for lifting (or nudging) my libido consciousness that had been sweeping (almost weeping) in waves of crescendos and decrescendos.

Still, that kiss was magnificent, like a machine of inflamed closeness. The mood of its intuitive intelligence was wonderfully variable—spanning from love to lust to consolation—all the while as she kept my extended state alive and in a quivering delicate balance.

Powerful, infinitesimal timbres and resonances then dominated the next kiss. Everything seemingly finite or known became infinite and unknown. While it stretched on, my extension shimmered and throbbed, for deep in that kiss, I found an enormous amount of subtle detail to savour.

With much delight, I could sense Venus Sinking Grand Piano's becoming delicate, and her distinctive touch took on a surging soft flurry as she gently applied pressure to my extension with an emphatic and entirely controlled gentleness, thereby setting it up for more tensions between the human narrative and the info-mechanical spectacle.

This returned my eyes to a visual contest set up between a smoking man and a smoking machine that the man (is this supposed to be me?) has mastered by becoming a robot with a phallic arm that invites mockery.

Based on Auguste Rodin's belief that the world will only be happy when all people have the souls of artists, an intimate, slow-motion, pelvic-based emotional experience was then carried out by myself and Venus Sinking Grand Piano on a rough and rocky Northern Californian beach. This placed me in the type of slow-motion self-exploration I associate with tai chi and the dances of Deborah Hay. Working the beach, a kinesthetic awareness starts stressing in me my immersive attention to the environment on an emotional level—and that requires me to expand my scope of obligations as a fragile human body within the context of the rough seashore.

Human-ecological connections are established here by entangling my naked body in the sensual net of nature that connects my neck to the water, rocks, trees, and sky—knotting me in a common story of multiple being where animals, humans, and plants (living and dead) each bear the consequences of the others' ways of living and dying.

While groping and sensing the textures and forms of vibrant nature, me dancing naked in a redwood forest demonstrates that I—as one of the sensual Homo sapiens based on pelvic centering—am not an external disturbance within nature, but a beautiful addition within the complex natural system. So, I prefer Venus Sinking Grand Piano when she wears my fraudulent neuro-wetware appropriation-charged de-automatization underwear while dancing in the forest. For in those undies, I find a moist slot that hums in the space between the info-mechanic and the wet-organic that is known to me as the Eleusinian Mysteries.

There is where Venus Sinking Grand Piano functions as a mythic oracle, for in synchronicities she sees events that seem connected but are not causally related.

In my social emulation of her Eleusinian automatism, something is central to my rebellious and resistant-intended words when spoken in defiance of the society of control—words that wish to shake loose the bonds of cultural entrapments and the manipulations of our habits of thought and actions.

So as with Venus Mental, I got down on my knees behind Venus Sinking

Grand Piano and prayed for the mental and material preconditions of artistic adventure. My paranoid penis was swollen stiff as it floated out in front of me. As I was still stubbornly churning out thoughts about a magical amulet carved from a deer's antler, I ordered it to point in the direction of her opening and slowly moved inside her—after her using a free hand to position its damp head against her labia. Then, with smooth but staunch thrusts of my buttocks, I drove in and out—repeatedly—inadvertently producing some silly rhythmic sucking sounds as air was pumped by the combination of our loins now joined in lunacy.

That incessant sucking-slapping sound was getting to me, so I withdrew from Venus Sinking Grand Piano and began to lick her naked body from head to toe. At that, she lay on her back trembling and quivering as I drew my tongue slowly over her neck and breasts, stopping to suck sensuously at her budding nipples and their silver veins of references. I worked my mouth all the way down to her curling toes and sucked some of those too, for good measure. That made diving into her feel like a feat of cartography as much as an opportunity for indulging.

As she balances herself on a slight bamboo reed while standing upon what appears to be an overturned honey pot, Venus Sinking Grand Piano becomes a very tall, long-legged woman of corporeal comfort. Lightly licking her long latitudinal slit produces a strange sensual reward that requires (and recompenses) my tongue to grow and my mind's complete attention. Such a satisfying stylistic inconsistency and profundity is rare today, but I swear it is true.

No, more than my complete attention, Venus Sinking Grand Piano's tremendous tall vibrancy exceeds my attention, and I am now (uncharacteristically) conscious of frequent shifts in latitudinal and longitudinal awareness, both on the horizontal axis and in depth of field.

When she lies down, there is just so much delicious munificence going on in my peripheral field of view to comprehend visually—and repeat theatrically—that my tender phallus waves hello to her long longitudinal groundswell. So it is as if everything now in the world is integrated on the backstage of Venus Sinking Grand Piano, including my horniest of fantasies coupled with leaky feelings of ardent love that offer me a different view on genealogy and a different idea of the relationship between forebears and posterity, progenitors, and descendants in the context of cheap rent, close proximity, and cultural courage.

Of course, with a longitudinal Venus Sinking Grand Piano there is always (happily) a dizzying predominance of bewildering punch lines conveying pathos laced with gleeful flourishes of shrewd philo-poetic black humour. Tangled tangents are tied to rapid cadences of concatenation, followed by washes of slow-core tenderness.

A good deal of my bricolage and bucolic litter are penetrated by furious trance-like movements that seem lost in the tatters of time—thus expressed through an incredibly precise craftsmanship that masks as improvisational sensual intimacy ripe with full-feeling progressiveness that twines around me as it parallel-presents forms that are transgressive-erudite, magical, massive, excessive, and overwhelming of over-policed binary divisions.

Using the so-called perceptive supremacy of the eye as an attractor, from time to time my longitudinal personality disappears into a social friction that gives culture much of its edge and momentum—for artistic bravery absolutely must strive to outfox AI-collected conformity.

The objectivity that makes certain poets pantheists (and also great actors) becomes such that I may mentally merge with female upward migration. Here I am, a tree roaring in the wind and singing to nature melodies about male software gods who have eaten the world and must be slain.

Now I am soaring in the longitudinal azure of an immensely enlarged sky.

As I put her long legs up over my shoulders on either side of my head, all doubt disappeared. I no longer struggle to reach her lips. I am carried in and up and away and rejoice. Her height is increasing my awareness of the great subtlety of the world around me. I have divided divinity.

As we begin pulsating and thumping together, soon the idea of time disappears completely. From time to time, a little latitudinal awakening takes place. It seems to me that I am briefly emerging and re-emerging from a marvellous and fantastic tower of thumping. But I retain the faculty of self-observation, and tomorrow I will have retained the memory of some of my sensations of this tall thumping and its tale of fluidity and fluctuating ambiguity that reminds me of the French ballerina Liane Daydé when she danced as a unicorn in Jean Cocteau's *Lady and the Unicorn* ballet (1959). I think I will never miss the animal in me when engaged with the extra-long

Venus Sinking Grand Piano, as long as I remain confronted with one sort of conspicuously excessive encounter with her or another in which the affirmation of the other keeps appearing and disappearing in a thump of manoeuvre-mechanisms destined to avert—then finally, after much delay and play—satisfy me with a grand gratification.

It will suffice for me to say that the solitary thinker returns with complacency to this precocious sensitivity, which for me is the source of so many pleasures and my immense love of intellectual freedom.

What particularly interests me about Venus Sinking Grand Piano in terms of artificial intelligence as a Tower of Babel is how her latitudinal mechanomorphic imagery enters the oily slipstream of mechanized man-machines, where distinctions between the body and the environment blur in the density of speeding networks. Here, Venus Sinking Grand Piano embraces a transcendent quasi-love of technological energy along with her notion of putting the squeeze on, fracturing my phallus into hard geometric shapes. Soon, Venus Sinking Grand Piano's brand of apocalyptic Cubism is modified into an automatonesque figurative style, distinguished by her focus on cylindrical forms. These cylindrical android figures express a synchronization between man and machine that is most relevant today, given the artificial intelligence workstation.

With sunshine filtering through the interstices of the arching trees, when I look up at Venus Sinking Grand Piano through my machine-learning eyes *avec un coup d'œil* (at a glance), I see she expresses her elevated beauty through noise, dynamism, and speed—and that my testes machinery is in an exotic variety of guises that serves her divergent ideologies of entanglement.

In splendour, that elevated beauty requires a flooding of focused zones, so as we break with insuperable creative barriers, I love Venus Sinking Grand Piano again, for she is so jam-packed with crunchy incidents that it is difficult to decipher all of her at first glance. Like a fine, nuanced, and balanced wine, she exhibits intensity without heaviness.

My eye, rocked by exogenous shocks, is drawn to the full rhythmic structure of her within a kaleidoscopic space where smaller interlocking elements lure me into deep, opulent repetitions. As a couple, we fuse into gyrating repeats in a complex and cryptic way, lending my pretty phallus a vivacious and sleek visual texture that she finds delightfully seductive.

Our coupling is a multitude that breeds into a repetitive orgy machine, pulling my mind into an infinite info-mechanical logic that is almost transcendental.

I love the charisma of her rippling plane that merges into an ecstatic *ménage à trois* with the landscape through the interlacing repetitions of form. This post-flesh unanimity I see as a frantic logic in terms of her tactility.

Once lumpen hill forms are set flowing in jerks and spasms by my systematically imposed vibrating restlessness, extensions and doublings have her labyrinthine flesh undergo steps of transubstantiation. This fucking-flickering-staccato reiteration creates the impression of a rolling bacchanalia in my mind, where human forms transcend their fleshiness and extend themselves through motorized re-embodiment.

So, Venus Sinking Grand Piano seems younger now. This youth suggests that the truth of life is found not through chance, but through the bio-technological apparatus of bodies tumbling into a field of circuits.

At that point, Venus Sinking Grand Piano's info-mechanical sex grinder features luscious Kiki de Montparnasse in the nourish flicker-film masterpiece, *Ballet Mécanique* (1924), where Kiki is cast fluctuating between figuration and abstraction. It is a Dada masterpiece of early experimental film that strings together a reeling mechanic-mental river of sensations, both flashy and frustratingly repetitive.

Ballet Mécanique is a bid at eliminating my sense of linear time, and it always gives me the fantastic feeling of prolonging action into an almost erotic eternity through the construction of its repeats. After the initial dazzling, *Ballet Mécanique*—much of it shot by Man Ray—smartly transmits an altered, exalted, and orgasmic state of mind that is perfectly paralleled by George Antheil's noise music soundtrack: the thirty-minutelong *Ballet Mécanique* (1924). Other times, that music tells me of infinite poems and places me in magical dramas.

Kiki associates me with the virtual Venus before my eyes when, even if mediocre or bad, she takes on an active mutating life in my scrotum. Nymphs with bright flesh look at me with large eyes clearer than azure water as their unfeasibly large breasts bounce up and down as they run to me, according to the AI-prompters' puerile fantasies.

This *Ballet Mécanique* pummeling musical composition was originally conceived as the sound accompaniment to the *Ballet Mécanique* film, but due to length differences, eventually the filmmakers and composer chose to let their creations evolve separately (although the film credits always include Antheil). Nevertheless, Antheil's *Ballet Mécanique* premiered as concert music in Paris in 1926 and is majestic in and of itself. But when included in the film, everything is permutated with a pulsating and flickering energy of go/stop/go/stop/go/stop/go.

I read this as depicting a hyperactive current of industrial forces on our bodies, painted (a somehow appropriate) baby blue. Here and there in this staccato connection, I find my youthful adventures and good humour (the good grace in mocking myself) that I have often seen as what leaps directly into my eyes: lyrical explosions of an incurable anti-melancholy mind. Certainly, the film is flush with discontinuous, fragmented, kaleidoscopic sensations. The screen pulsates with the hot energies of cybersex and its dull repetitions, animating the screen with an insistent flicker. This stutter-and-flicker effect is something that Brion Gysin picked up again in his *Dreamachine* (1961), so in an unusual sweet softness and peculiar peace, our bodies dreamed and rounded into monumental figures, like in Picasso's neo-Classical period of the early 1920s, such as in his breathtaking *Two Women Running on the Beach* (1922).

We frolic nude in the waves of the sea as a storm gathers in the distance. Successive waves seem heavy and frozen, trapping our churning bodies between them. My throbbing cock, cooling in that azure setting, is undeniably poignant, for only a tiny radial sun seems to clear a free path on the left, but time has stopped. Seated before the *Dreamachine* with my eyes closed at the 全生庵 Rinzai Zen Zenshō-an Temple in Tokyo, I have also dreamed of Venus Sinking Grand Piano as a three-headed and multi-breasted ogress goddess who carries baskets of men's heads, some detached, others attached to various animal bodies, while tiger-riding in a forest of decapitated men. She is haughtily wearing a bountiful necklace strung with castrated cocks. Like that reckless necklace, she is now a stunning spasmodic display of looped priapic concentration, where relationships between the protoplasmic body and info-mechanical repeats invite meditation on self-prosthesis. In this flickering metamorphic ballet, the human body at the centre of traditional narrative subjectivity is undone by a visual noise it cannot contain. So, as I was concentrating on a loop from Kuei Chih-Hung's 1980 film *Hex* (邪) (*Xie*)—it lingers on a beautiful, nude woman while she has ink sigils painted up and down her body by an elderly woman—besides being a nourishing feast for the eye, I found the phantasmagoric aesthetic largely parallels the ephemeral apparitions and hot hells glowing away behind The Last God scene: the bevy of phantom Last God dated data servers, all around the world, stuck in the on position. In Last God data facilities, servers are loaded with applications and left to run indefinitely, even after nearly all users have vanished or new versions of the same programs are running elsewhere. At a certain point, no one is responsible anymore for what floats in this heated Last God limbo, because no one, absolutely no one, wants to go into server rooms and pull the plug on those phantom black box super-intelligent Last God systems that are running their own show, writing their own code, congregating their own shitcoin crypto, and buying ever more and more Last God data center servers to rule and ruin the earth with.

The absurdity of The Last God limbo reminds me of Venus Sinking Grand Piano's clownish concert of howling dogs, which was once surprising, because The Last God commonly took up classical forms and genres (such as the quartet and the sonata) and reinvented them into meandering piano solos like *Lorelei, die Langstreckensonate* (*Lorelei, The Long Distance Sonata*) (1978). Nodding in approval, Venus Sinking Grand Piano embraced the loins of The Last God like a cherry-picked spectrum, spanning chance alteration and accumulations of waste and wasted time. The dogs stank like putrid, unbaked dough, old mayonnaise, and rolled-in rabbit shit mixed with stale cotton candy (even if it is less a matter of gastronomical chimera than an issue of germ amplification). These howling, dirty dogs, in a tipsy disposition, then yield a wonderful woozy arrangement of the *Abschopf Symphonie* (1979), followed by the virtuosic *November Symphonie* (1974), and so exemplify culture as a conflict between Dionysian excess and the bored bourgeoisie. Particularly *November Symphonie* bursts with the dark howling undertone of too much sloppy schnapps that turns the symphony into a mixture of the romantic aesthetic rationalism of Gotthold Ephraim Lessing and the materialistic sensationalism of Ludwig Feuerbach. But schnapps or no schnapps, my peripatetic mind is forever tied to these filthy, howling dogs in service of an overall transmission of a lofty gaiety that hovers as a great Last

God orange clown king truth that cannot be questioned but only bowed to.

XII

No Tears for the Creatures of the Night

Locked-in recursive scaling self-improving zombie AI programmers have been replacing human programmers, formulating what has been called ASI super intelligence. The Last God does not listen to us humans anymore.

But what about its emotional intelligence?

So far, the pages of this book (*mon truc et plumes*) have been doors that my words have flown through to regroup into a bouncing ball of perplexing pornology. Again, we have the in-and-out playhouse automated and made sententious.

It was brilliant how Curtis Mayfield's smooth track, *So In Love*, played over Venus Sinking Grand Piano's elaborately constructed mystical-sexual exploits (what Deleuze would call her 'conceptual personae') as consumed within my perverse field of displacement. By entering her Sheela Na Gig vulva-desiring machine, I am dissolved in the swirls of soft repeats, which at the same time further license my subjectivity through an extension of self-possession and transcendental bliss (if I'm in the mood for love). Therein lies the potential of long-term subjective change through Venus©~ñ~lOve Systems, a change that will undoubtedly have multitudinous implications in an age where every user may become a server to all other users of her Sheela Na Gig lunar crater. But I am here on Earth now to find out what is possible after The Last God is dead, not just to stare into Venus's vulva and look back at my encyclopedic, if associatively organized, mountain of memory material that Venus©~ñ~lOve Systems has collected and soaked in liquid exuded by copulating mares.

Venus Reckless magnificently slipped out of Venus Sinking Grand Piano and into a vast cabinet of curiosities stocked with membranes from the afterbirth of a dog that had powers to unleash pentagram harmonies. Added to a drink of red wine, these membranes may arouse my invocation of certain celestial powers, awakening the slumbering and hidden forces of Venus, as does another cathartic concoction that has been fermented from the lab-leak theory of the soul.

Old, beautiful stonework windows from the 14th century provocatively frame Gaïa in the context of the Anthropocene as evoked and visualized by the slowly gliding, ever-changing Venus Reckless. We float around each other, suspended in time and gravity over a pile of lifeless human bodies mixed in with a peck of flesh-picking Last God black birds. Psychic and physical instability is reflected in Reckless's once admirably steadfast face—made up to match the limestone landscape of Montagne Sainte-Victoire—but now it has become less genteel, conveying a mixture of hard melancholy and resignation, particularly her cherry red cheeks that evoke shame or possibly a slap.

Though Venus Reckless often made herself up as the foliage of a tropical jungle, she had never visited one; the pink sunset colours of the clouds and the warm yellow backdrop of the tropical jungle give her an attractive, if distressing, splendour that is her natural state of happiness based on her consumption of carpaccio and those places where dawdlers go to daydream and escape from climate realities.

My second glance at her produces an ephemeral feeling in me—because her artificial intelligence activity collects daily meteorological data-flows from the main predictive climatic models around the world. Each morning, new meteorological data influences her algorithms, which produce a constant fluttering and sliding of black birds that, given the right state of mind, can be described as either mean or mesmerizing.

If only, in order to explore my own capacity to do so—like the dark twisted fantasies found in the left eye of a doomed man at Le Bateau-Lavoir—I presumed the rightness of my private visions as a tousled child with a five o'clock shadow.

Sure enough, Venus Reckless is soon superseded by a powerful accompanying soundtrack by Current 93 that bolsters her impressive scale in my mind. A sombre, loud rumbling drone of black metal music is also peppered in for an even more haunting effect.

A strong howl is created, evocative of a craved wolf or a strong wind howling from within her loins.

Comfortable caressing of those loins soon had me willingly idling away a good spellbound time tinged with craving. When I eventually peeled my hands off of her, I felt a positive emotion whose mutational end cannot arrive —and which reminded me of what Ray Kurzweil, the godfather of AI futurology, inanely predicted in his 1998 book *The Age of Spiritual Machines*: that by 2020, autonomous machine art would be prevalent and robot artists would "exceed" human artists in ability. Such claims ignore the often-heard complaint that predictions like this oversimplify art to resemble well-behaved engineering problems devoid of social and political contextual complexity.

It is true that her infinite number of combinations/permutations stimulates the open-minded curiosity of imagination for those patient enough to sit with her. It is a pleasure to accept the un-privileging of human choice and glide with it into a nihilistic landscape of potential points of sexual interest bereft of privileging male desire.

So I was not surprised that Venus Reckless was as taut as a spring—and that I wanted to enter her pearly gates through the knowledge of mathematics required to detect the Pythagorean number patterns that give her and the universe a majestic structure, for visiting her dreamland is a bit like trudging through soft mud with glitter on your shoes. Her long tendrils of celestial and magical influence have an omnipotent effect on me—even when my talismans are clothed in fresh lambskin: talismans carved from bullion and engraved with magic squares that reveal the marvellous properties of numbers.

In Albrecht Dürer's engraving *Melencolia I* (1514), a magic square—the series of numbers from one to sixteen, arranged in the proper order in a square with sixteen cells—invokes the power of Jupiter, which meant that a piquant wind blows through my dreams of the arts of divination when stamped by a star.

Fumigated with aloe wood and ambrosia, Venus Reckless's humanoid sexual sun had spun a seed of straw from that glittered mud and grown it into a fine filament.

Despite a solitary, eccentric existence—far removed from fashionable ASI theories—Venus Reckless produced for me from that filament an astonishing, incendiary, if lighthearted, body that flickers with a greatness that confronts a certain curatorial orthodoxy concerning sexual conceptualism. Chiromancy has not much to do with it, for Venus Reckless, she is strong at exercising her libidinal imagination through a sunny connectivity that shows brilliant levels of poetics applied to the depiction of savored sexual acts. Indeed, Venus Reckless was talented at lacking volitional control while undergoing coitus. Her visceral, hypersexualized sensitivity runs throughout. The power of plucky erotic fantasies and sexual innuendos —Venus Reckless's leitmotif—supersedes respectful social significance, so one aspect of Venus Reckless is forever going to be libertine—even when tempered by my understanding that the dominance of the straight western male posture is no longer unquestioned—if it ever really was. Gender is and always was part natural and part socially constructed.

Regardless, if my ideological penis suggested to her a straightforwardly constrained single-sex form or an aspect of my androgynous projection filter when activated, blended body parts were everywhere in her pleasure paradox room. That churning anima room of desire placed me before a sperm whale and H.R. Giger's famous painting *Penis Landscape* (aka *Work 219: Landscape XX*) (1973). Unlike Giger's strikingly alien aesthetic, my goal is a reinvention of romanticism where the performative and the ingenious seem curiously intertwined.

As I stood next to Paul Thek's *Meat Piece with Warhol Brillo Box* (1965)—from his *Technological Reliquaries* series—I took some delight in an inventiveness that can be morally negligent, gnarly, brooding, sad, eccentric, and emotionally moving in a way that is maddeningly hard to explain without mentioning cold brutality.

Like me, Venus Reckless can appear aesthetically armoured during intimacy; her jungle foliage was converting to inner earth, flecked with readymade flowers. Needless to say, nothing is less certain than sex, and—though works like Yoko Ono's cheeky film *Four* (*Bottoms*) (1966), Valie Export's *Action Pants: Genital Panic* (1969), Kembra Pfahler's *Wall of Vagina* (2011), and Betty Tompkins's *Fuck* paintings may suggest otherwise —many women feel there is something deeply feckless—if not alienating—about reducing the human body to its isolated sexual body parts. Not so for Venus Reckless. Venus Reckless's drawings, like *Le Roi et la Reine* (*The King and the Queen*) (1960)—which calls to mind Marcel Duchamp's famous painting *The King and Queen Surrounded by Swift Nudes* (1912)—manage to avoid that sentiment. Complicated identifications go on there that blur organic with inorganic forms, like with the machine célibataire (bachelor machine): Duchamp's apparatus as first conceived in a 1913 note written in preparation for his piece *La mariée mise à nu par ses célibataires, même* (*The Bride Stripped Bare by Her Bachelors, Even*) (1915–23).

The Bride Stripped Bare by Her Bachelors, Even accentuates mental machines that work away on the imaginary, deconstructing the tradition of sexual opposition established as a dialectical and organic opposition of masculine and feminine. Venus Reckless ups the ante with her enigmatic sex-machine bondage routine, which probes the shameless vagaries of human desire with panache. Her taste is an indirect outgrowth of male-dominant French surrealist tastes demonstrated in the 1959 *Eros* exhibition organized by André Breton and Duchamp in Paris. But Venus Reckless also suggests a more contemporary, tautly eroticized, and virtualized flesh that banks on a hyper-sexed, electronic corporeality that is artificial, bionic, and prosthetic.

She is basically an updated extension of the reterritorialization of physique, identity, and appearance depicted early on in the feverish cyborg aesthetics of Oskar Schlemmer and Fernand Léger and the incognito poly-identities presented by Urs Lüthi, Claude Cahun, Marcel Bascoulard, and Cindy Sherman. Sherman's self-masking thematic work strikes me the deepest, as it reminds me of automated artificial intelligence facial recognition and The Last God's monstrous effects on parts of our lives. The complexity of Sherman's (possibly offensive) blackface self-portraits, such as *Untitled* (*Bus Riders*) (1976), elicits ideas of the imaginary poly-self that connects me to all of humanity, while offering expansive qualities of the body for which the workings of photography, science, and medicine cannot do suitable justice. *Bus Riders* is a series of fifteen black and white photographs she produced shortly after graduating college in Buffalo. One of them is her as a cross-dressed male; three are androgynous, and five are black-faced.

As perversely droll and symptomatic as it is to experience the rhapsody of Venus Reckless's fetishized erotic tropes—suggesting loveless and lopsided sadomasochistic cybernetic pleasures playing within the male mystique—I could not fail to also feel some nasty permissiveness within. For I had seen the bright light of misogyny that shines from Kate Millett's seminal 1970 study

Sexual Politics and the effective castration of the privileged male artist in relationship to the manipulated female body.

Therein lies the pleasurable paradox of Venus Reckless.

To me, her nuanced cultural *façades* indicate an interest in signal ambiguity within the semiotic field. When looking at her, my desire can take me by surprise, leading me towards disguised moves I hadn't imagined would ever lead to love and trust. Certainly, my own impertinent masks within her look-at-me premise can be reconsidered as culturally prescient in lieu of the psychographic politics that have doused The Last God's ego-rush of stealing human data that remakes the unmasked masses into LG raw data commodities.

Still, I can't accuse her of lacking eclecticism. Venus Reckless's slightly—if obsessively erotic—semi-abstract body fits into my love context of what is grandiloquent, complex, and occasionally ridiculous. Reflecting nothing if not an authentically endearing sexual diversity, Venus Reckless is multi-faceted in a way that uses a jumble of themes and materials that collide around a premise that tends to concentrate on my sexual anatomy at different levels of intensity. Beyond the psychosomatic-surreal dream imagery she produces for me—and her general slippery machine ambiance—Venus Reckless suggests a certain exaggerated erotic desire that values the vulnerability of abused human flesh; flesh held in bondage to some imagined, non-romantic, post-biological reality.

The mood she sets is both rude and sweet; her joy has a determination to speak on its own terms rather than cravenly court affection. Something doe-eyed, exploratory, and off-kilter hints at what is to come: the formal concerns tackling notions of madness, magpie fetishism, ordure, abjectness, pleasure, animality, death, and sex that exudes a hot onanistic aura of luxuriant sleaze. That is the reason I think that she is making the point of the frailty of human flesh when pierced by the sombre impregnability of technology.

Here, and consistently elsewhere during our diagrammatic fetishized phase, Venus Reckless disregards my beatific blooming mood which some associate with mutually consensual sex by working me over in a gritty, dark, and oily metallic zone that distances me from conventional chromatics. Here, Venus Reckless suggests isolated, zoomed-in glimpses of sexual bondage and humiliation. I decline.

Next, Venus Reckless merges sexual forms of both sexes by displaying a gleaming, isolated, Black woman's breast with the indentation in her nipple formed to resemble the opening hole in a penis. Indeed, all of the body parts of Venus Reckless appear to have been coerced so as to outstrip the dichotomy between The Last God and my male body.

Some of the hottest, weirdest, relentlessly provocative, and most accomplished acts she performed on me were vivid, shimmering, and seemingly gelatinous. This brought to me a dream image of a farcical woman-bird dominatrix that seems to be up to something ominous. She appears to have developed out of machine-like repetitions, giving me the impression of meeting again the ancient, many-breasted Ephesian Artemis fertility goddess. Here, horny punk charm is its own self-pleasure, though it shows me her folly and ability to switch mood from experimental wit to linguistic fury and back again.

Bound freaky cyborg parts encircle her neck. Her dusty plush darkness, her sexual analogy, is very effective at full scale, unflaggingly converting my playful suggestions of transcendental mythic sex into a non-rarefied brand of anti-transcendental fantasy where her left nipple is indeed a portal to unlock, permitting entrance to the non-noumenon: an object space that never exists independently of human sense.

Her non-noumenon knob is the best I have seen in a long time, because it is fundamentally promiscuous and poetic, expressive of a pre-linguistic wetness that unchains common codes and sends them off to float, unchained, through the prism of free imagination. Venus Reckless achieves these poetic disconnections through a situated burlesque enchantment with the fluidity of the shimmering sea and through references to the sludge doom music of Sunn O))) and the dreamlike state morphine induces.

Here, Venus Reckless is probing—with intimate precision—a mesh of titanic turbulence as boldfaced as an oil slick afloat on the surface of the Black Sea. I find that slick outstanding in terms of the luxury of its dynamic, non-compartmentalized postulates. It makes clear that for Venus Reckless, TLG culture has never been synonymous with some imperative promise of aesthetic liberation nor metaphysical liberation.

Magnificent yet delicate, that black slick calls for a contemplation that yields to the palpable poetry that exists inside each of us. The irony is that the appeal of TLG culture is now an assumption that conspires to rob people of the thing that should matter most to them: their freedom to risk unpleasantness.

Venus Reckless is a dark, immersive meditative roll down the Mississippi Delta that skirts New Orleans. She is rich in ecological and cultural implications that include a post-human, post-anthropocentric worldview that doesn't abandon my subjective inner world but decenters it into new forms of community. What disappears into substitute fetishism is not her material body per se, but *cliché* notions of it. She is free-flowing, explosive, and playful, with many profound connections that swim in my head. The question that slick raises is, will I become a homeless post-human?

Though she does not answer, what I appreciate about Venus Reckless is her deep time and space that suggests a lush life of nonverbal existence that moves internally and invisibly within my embodied situation—for she has a mythical and metaphysical depth as mysterious as the tea leaves. She need not be understandable (or even meaningful) in order to be important.

It is worth noting that damage has been done—above all to artists but also to public taste—by trying to explain everything artistic. The Last God will die trying. Through her flamboyant, theoretical avant-gardism, Venus Reckless asks me audacious ontological questions about how her body is staged in different realities. Her flamboyant adventurousness embraces the fluidity of ambiguity, difference, and contradiction while promoting concepts of the collective communal matrix. Unlike The Last God, she is rich in connective lyricism and sympathetic imperatives, where once-apparent conflicting ideas and intellectual positions are mitigated in poly-rational interplay.

Still, Venus Reckless is suggestive of a thumb-sucking, asexual, frankly preposterous, flighty state of mind—one of almost cosmic despair tied to the obsessed sexual shenanigans of anatomizing; something worthy of a Michel Houellebecq novel, with its oddly constricted and flattened feel.

Thus, Venus Reckless yanked my chain with her sexually provocative cutouts, halfway between clumsy and delicate. But these dizzy delights are assumed on my part rather than demonstrated.

Venus Reckless also has an almost psychedelic aura, though a psychedelia with a folk horror edge to it. The forked implication here is that her love reverberates throughout my flesh to the extent that our sexual exchanges cannot be extricated from the metaphysics of my random dude machinery when jiving to the exuberant energy of Carlos Santana and John McLaughlin's electric guitar work in *Let Us Go Into The House Of The Lord* on their *Love Devotion Surrender* LP.

As refashioned as reminiscent of ripeness, Venus Reckless began prolonging my testes' inner hysteria into an infernal eternity through the construction of another ball of kitsch *cliché*.

With this peacock upgrade, she tempts me.

In that sense, the raising of my exhausted phallus was intoned and, much to my surprise, actually transpired. No dead memories came to the surface of my consciousness of Venus Reckless as Venus Pink Dots again flooded my mind, and I felt pangs of lost love. But have I failed to mention the enormous nose on Venus Reckless and her hanging Medusa?

Going down. Going down. Going down. Going down now.

I dabbed my tongue lightly around the genitals of Venus Reckless as Venus Pink Dots who has temporarily taken the name of Venus Amour. My lustful curiosity of how to please her knew no libido bounds.

Venus Amour began exploring the magnetic field energy in my phallus. She explored what is invisible but real in me by means of integrating magnets, dim lighting, and drone sound vibrations. Definitely, to surpass what is obvious, her body put out an invisible magnetic field (the force that allows magnets to hold metallic materials in suspension), and that field constituted her core attraction, for her petite breasts look like antennae with weird bits at their tips. They were blinking lights that formed two contradictory stop signs that constantly switched from stop to go.

Looking at the sex of Venus Amour, my rod became flexible and able to swing and sway. But once de-linked from this powerful gaze, it wanted to mount her and move with the movements of a horizontal pendulum—giving her the impression of being part of a space age that defies gravity.

Perhaps this uplift symbolizes that everything exposed to the earth's magnetism is recognized as charged?

Thus our attraction is not a question of content versus form and/or form versus content but of contemporary possibility and sensibility.

After a while, she attempted a spatial-sensual breakout from my magnetism. This powerful idea of defying physical gravity can be traced back to some of El Lissitzky's *Prounen* paintings and three-dimensional installations, and to works of László Moholy-Nagy—such as where, in his seminal book from 1947, *Vision in Motion*, he is seen levitating a chisel with compressed air.

Enjoying this kind of phallic levitating is to accept that everything within the pull of gravity is more or less charged and that all bodies relate to one another gravitationally. So I guessed that Venus Amour's next idea for my phallus was to dangle it in front of her yoni like a large iron needle placed in front of a magnetized field. Such an arrangement has great simplicity, and its proposition is very straightforward. So indeed, installed next to it is an electromagnet that attracts my dangling spike, thus producing a collective resonance that, I must say, is evocative of a profane ritual that appears to be a kind of fruition of Erik Satie's idea of Furniture Music as revived by John Cage in his theory of minimal music.

By vibrating, my spike generates a humming chthonic sound that fills the curved room of my mind with a mild ecstasy akin to serenity. This subtle vibrational sexuality left an indelible impression on me, for magnets are about attraction, and my phallus is the representation of my sexual attraction.

I guess this was a natural subject of titillating interest for Venus Amour, for she seized it very successfully. She then made my near-floating metallic element dazzlingly hover just over her. This gave me an impressively extended erection that complemented her magnetic pull.

At one later point of contact, I left my body and stared down so I could see my penis enter and slide into her curly bush. Her vagina clasped my shaft, embracing it tightly as I rode her up and down like a rodeo clown. Once she jolted so passionately that she slipped off the rod, and I could see the swollen head of my organ coated with slimy moisture: flesh in grandeur. It was especially arousing for me to see her grasp frantically for it so that she could place it back inside her.

We both started moaning in accelerating rhythmic motion, and I felt that we were about to climax together. Then we did. Boy, could that gal play steel guitar. Spent, as we held each other, I could feel her heart softly pounding.

We were burning bright in the afterglow of sexual excitement, and I told her of what she had missed during my absence: that the world went immediately from a war with a virus to a war with the vicious.

With a flamboyant gelid eye and taunting provocative shrugs of jaded contempt for the new-money denizen art collectors with liberal pieties, Venus Amour appears and allures. She, who values transcendental metaphysics and clandestine mystical technologies over accessible human-centric assumptions, strode forth onto the scene as an insouciant *enfant terrible*. Even though Venus Amour is known for being something of a holy terror of instant gratification in an age of trigger warnings, I appreciate the sarcastic, stylish, noire sordidness that succinctly captures the glazed, hip, scuzzy, hard, post-punk attitude of the late-1970s downtown. Though she may emerge out of a luminous spatial field that suggestively immerses me into a unified field, I have seen Venus Amour appear self-indulgently pathetic: sloppy, belligerent, and blaringly incoherent—exerting a wicked and abusive drunken tongue.

Still, her Genet-like talent for turning standard moral paradigms inside out amuses my sensitivity.

Sorry to be so personal here, but everything is personal and political when con men reign and their horse shit rains.

When I see my psychiatrist, I try to convince her that I'm not suffering from derealization, because these days I sit at home, and I read and write. Unbeknownst to her, sometimes I simultaneously smoke a joint, and I put on headphones and listen to DNA and other no wave music—loud—so that I literally have trouble feeling that the golden age of baloney has begun.

Still, sometimes I feel myself full of young juice, building off of conceptual art's development of Duchamp's emphasis on context by expanding art world participation into the pornographic novel. So when Venus Amour began reviewing my performances, I religiously read these polemical dispatches that described the ills of American society from the point of view of an energetic radical critic. As such, Venus Amour sometimes seems to me like an amiable anti-assimilationist bored by bitchery and twaddle, but I liked the rhythms of the cynical prose. Her sentences have an overcrowded flirting effect that's almost hypnotic to me, as I let them rain down like curmudgeon manna. I let fall on me all the combinations of venomous aggression, flamboyant social transgression, and political astuteness—mixed with tossed-off deriding provocations and devil-may-care insouciance concerning my phallus.

Everything turned blue. Rows and rows and rows of beautifully stacked dusty bottles of champagne set the frame. As a sex writer, Venus Amour was a political hedonist at intellectual warfare with top-notch conformity—a conformity reminding me of Jean-Paul Sartre's renowned appraisal that *L'enfer, c'est les autres* (Hell is other people).

Yes, the herd was trapped in toxic culture, but Amour made such conformity more interesting by flirting with the banality of butt plugs, bunny ears, and alien cutlery. Still, I often had the sense that this vulnerable literary darling was trying to turn me into a cultural inquisition based on holier-than-thou opinions without adequate theoretical tutorials. Given her apparent flippant disregard for serious debate, it can be difficult to tell how much satirizing or covering up with bitchy off-the-cuff opinions is going on. How deep is the abyss traversed?

I will be kind and let the night decide.

Though in the 1980s, the threat of apocalyptic nuclear annihilation hung heavy in the air, the social prognosis was far from grim. Besides the devastating arrival of AIDS, in many ways it was the golden age for progressive artists of various sexes and sexual preferences in New York. Women and homosexuals held a stronger position than before as artists, gallery owners, and curators, the audio cassette scene was exploding, and we had Prince (*Why You Wanna Treat Me So Bad?*, *Controversy*, *1999*, *Uptown*, *I Wanna Be Your Lover*) to dance to while clubbing on ecstasy. Sex—until late into the '80s—was unhampered and plentiful, art was selling, rent was cheap, and rice and beans and corn dogs (a disgusting sausage on a stick that has been coated in a thick layer of cornmeal batter and deep fried) were plentiful.

My psychiatrist tells me this feeling of loss is normal after arriving at this treacherous period in my life cycle at precisely the same moment that people of all ages recognize to be a time of great cultural and political disappointment. You could say that I leapt into the lake of progressive titillation and found that it only went up to my knees.

Look at how thinking about the '80s slips me into transcendent superlatives and condemnations, rather than carefully parsing subtle differences into a spectrum of values; such a hyperbolic statement is typical of me as a black swan.

At that, though for the most part visually lush and colourfully attractive,

Venus Amour tosses around morose and cutthroat superlatives as if they were garnish. Her tongue swings wildly between incisive criticism, pastiche, and self-besotted, self-obsessed auto-narrative: something perfectly appropriate for a novella, but practically useless for non-fanboy theoretical usage. Her helter-skelter prose experiments, which stray too far from art journalism into botulism-narcissism, strike my eye as dead magic—or an anachronism of dead magic.

But Venus Amour is often jocular when rocking the flamboyant theatrics. Here is a zinger, apropos of nothing, in the review of the Whitney Biennial: "Bruce Weber should not be in the same room with Ross Bleckner and Annette Lemieux. Bruce should have his own room. It should be in New Jersey." (Rim shot!) And: "Although all museums are endowed by the very people who despoil the general quality of life outside the museum, the Met has an inflexible policy of accepting money from almost anywhere. Even certain bordellos in the Patpong district of Bangkok are more fastidious." (Burn!) Reading such hilarity, I must be careful not to break the crockery.

The problem is not that such sarcasm posing as musings is bad art criticism—though it is—or that such cultural commentary is often, to say the least, amusingly insulting. Nor is the problem the hypocrisy of putting forth such entertaining blather as a critique of the shallowness in art. The real problem, rather, is the intrusion of theatrical camp showmanship into the evaluation of serious art. Personally, I do not wish to be lobotomized by Venus Amour's *poète maudit* horseshit.

Like many coming of age in the shadow of French theory, a kind of supposed Dionysian camp sensibility connects Venus Amour to a lineage of *monstres sacrés* (sacred monsters) whose fascinations include power and sex within the art-as-money carnival.

Venus Amour was quick to talk a good deal about artists investigating commodification, simulacrum, and mass media (of slight relevancy to today's digital world, where those things have become one). Still, she breathed into my soul, and we spent a night of bliss together in a dark corner of sex and sleep. There I stopped her from feeling so old and cold. As for myself, I suppose posthumous recognition and appreciation must be better than no appreciation at all.

When she snored and snorted, she emitted the apprehensive slight noises of the rusting of metal bowls and the cracking of sheets of glass performed at the limits of audio perceptibility. I had to get down on my knees and bend over her to hear these audio suggestions of panpsychism, vitalism, and animism—but she asked me to back off as she requires copious amounts of empty space to properly frame her existence. An ephemeral existence rarely encountered in our time of obvious maximal availability that, from a certain scientific perspective, is only the quivering electromagnetic oscillation of wavelengths.

My fingers went over the shape of my paramour's face, smoothly sliding over her lovely features. How perfect she was—and how dangerous! My soul thrilled with those unutterable visions in my mind that meant complete knowledge. She herself was the glistening—forbidden—red apple. It was her the Christians and Greeks blamed for the cold exit of the human race from the Garden of Eden and the Golden Age: the power of seduction of the first woman—be she Eve, as seen in Eugene Delaplanche's Neoclassical sculpture, *Eve Before the Sin* (1891)—or *Pandora*, whom Henri-Joseph Rutxhiel carved as Pandora (1822).

When the wall of love organs of Venus Amour emits primeval sounds of throbbing desire, it is my ears that receive these rhythms. But my eyes also receive emotive vibrations of equal intensity—creating a hot, instinctive thought-space in a conceptual drumbeat.

Thus Venus Amour, while playing the mandolin, has me climbing over a great wall of vulvas that stretch from ancient pagan forms to the acceptance of marriage for love by 19th century society. Venus Amour was only a step towards the triumph of consent in love over social contingencies as sung by the troubadours. The non-dimensional feel of falling in love, which one can neither easily find nor effortlessly fall out of, moves around the Venus Amour wall with agile deftness throughout and clicks me through historical constructions of our evolving ways and means of erecting and saving affectionate attachment.

Starting from the stigmatizing of the feminine, Venus Amour works her way through my rooms of passion, adoration, gallantry, libertinage, and romanticism, but she does not seek to be exhaustive, nor does she exhaust. The excitement begins with a *chef-d'oeuvre* (masterpiece) of ancient statuary that suggests an eternal proclamation of stasis: Egyptian married couple *Youyou and Tiy, Guardians of the Treasure* (about 1391-1353 BC), carved in quartzite. Its dignified, stoic firmness suggests to me that deep, long-lasting love can take on the dimensions of sublime, cosmological immensity, as expressed by John Coltrane in his 1964 ecstatic, masterful opus *A Love Supreme*, where the emotive concept slants more towards the ancient *Om* than pseudonymy, metafiction, and other experimental (if inscrutable) passions.

Stoicism is predominantly a philosophy that teaches that the path to happiness is found in accepting the moment as it presents itself to us (be here now).

Given prime placement in my head is the splendid sleek carving *Orestes and Pylades* (1st century BC) by Pasiteles—a Greek from Magna Graecia who became a Roman citizen active in Rome in the 1st century BC. This marble piece depicts a moment of calm in the intense relationship between cousins Pylades and Orestes—who have been presented by some Greek writers as a romantic homoerotic couple. Indeed, the dialogue of Syrian satirist Lucian of Samosata's text *Erotes* discusses the merits of homoeroticism using Orestes and Pylades as the principal models.

The next part of Venus Amour that captured my attention reminded me that although love is a universal emotion, it has no set criteria when it comes to input variables. It was James Pradier's marble carving *Satyr and Bacchante* (1834) that purposefully deflates romantic *clichés*. Though at first glance it resembles an act of sexual assault on the part of the satyr, the bacchante's face is in a blissful ecstasy of pleasure. So the abduction sculpture becomes a field of contradictions where transgressed gender behaviour calls on the chthonic demands of the body.

Here double-or-nothing passionate love—nourished by theories and fictions—makes the bacchante's body resonate with a chthonic hum that disavows self-control.

She spoke in sound poetry, but as the bacchante's grandiose *guignol* of glossolalia began losing importance through my paranoid *soupçon*, she gained it back with a dramatic dreamlike softness that went on way too long. Like Erik Satie's proto-minimal musical composition *Vexations* (circa 1894): a musical composition that repeats 840 times in succession an enharmonic musical theme with accompanying chords. Such verbosity is similar to repetitive music, as they both lighten spirits as only a sacred jester's amusing meanderings might—by mocking narcissists with a wicked-good piece of spectacular excess.

Easy to perceive, the bacchante is the kind of woman that is loved by people who hate the art world, for even as an idyllic odalisque, she looms over language, and her unexpected verbal presence takes command of the setting. She is tremendously blunt in her mocking of triumphalism, whether that of intellectual loquaciousness or the worthlessness of the wealthy with the one-arm salute, for she talks out of both sides of her mouth.

I sense connotations of travesty conveying both revulsion and recreation—something perfectly in tune with Last God time and its prevailing cultural sensibility of failing to transcend spent rationality with originality.

Like a hookah-smoking caterpillar on a mushroom, ecstatic transport of the solo kind is evident in the anonymous terracotta *Blessed Ludovica Albertoni* (17th century) that was created after the Gian Lorenzo Bernini depiction of Ludovica Albertoni in the throes of religious ecstasy—what frankly appears to be a woman grasping her breast while in the throes of orgasm.

In Bernini's sculpture, also entitled *Blessed Ludovica Albertoni* (1674), housed in the Altieri chapel in the San Francesco a Ripa church in Rome, this horizontal statue captures this woman in a combination of death throes and religious ecstasies. Here, love is situated beyond phenomena and in execution without an audience. It abides in celebration—rather than detection as sexual auscultation. A solo act within the void.

Coupled mutual discovery and nascent love is the sentiment of Antonio Canova's 18th century mythological sculpture *Psyche and Cupid* (1797), showing Psyche, a princess whose beauty had excited the jealousy of Venus, and who is in love with Venus's son Cupid. They are shown half embraced while inspecting a fragile butterfly and thinking about how climate change is having a devastating impact on butterflies, leading to their stress, disease, and death. Their fine myth was established for us by the Latin writer Apuleius in *The Golden Ass* novel and then again by Jean de La Fontaine in 1637 in *The Loves of Psyche and Cupid*.

This lovers' tale seduced many artists of the Neoclassical period, as it was not only a story of young love, but also a metaphysical allegory, because "psyche" in Greek means "soul." Canova's sculpture thus symbolizes the

Neoplatonic ideas of the union of the human soul with divine love.

With Psyche and Cupid, I have some binary possibilities: they open or close my love. They reveal or hide me.

Thanks to this fold in space between them, something unexpected is on the other side of this page, and this is the characteristic mystery of the book as played with here.

An inspiring metaphor for this dialogue is the concept of the fold as interpreted by Gilles Deleuze in his dazzling 1988 book *Le pli: Leibniz et le baroque*, translated as *The Fold: Leibniz and the Baroque* in 1993, where Deleuze traced the fold concept back to the Baroque's emphasis on the transmutation of formal objects into temporal unities. Here the French philosopher features reflections upon continuous changes and dissolutions into infinity as expressed in folded art objects and gardens from the Baroque era.

In applying this idea to our time, Deleuze concluded that form and matter, when applied to books, must be recognized as a temporal modulation that implies as much the beginnings of a continuous variation of matter as a continuous solid existence. This absolutely must remind me of Duchamp's suspended *Readymade Malheureux* (*Unhappy Readymade*) (1919), a geometry book that swings from a wire outside in the courtyard, open to the air, sun, and natural elements. I must accept the idea of its inevitable collapse into nothingness.

Suzanne Duchamp placed one like it outside her Paris door in 1920 at Rue de la Condamine. It was Duchamp's wedding gift for the marriage of his sister to the Dada painter Jean Crotti. Sent from Buenos Aires in 1919, Marcel provided instructions for its realization and chance-based eventual demise into entropy. Each day it hung outside in the weather and wind, it crumbled more and more, losing its content, its cohesiveness, and its sense of being in the world.

The driving force of love between Psyche and Cupid likewise feels, to me, like a temporary complicity, or a collusion of intents, rather than an obsessive sexual preoccupation with solidity. For there are many kinds of things in and on the vagina wall of Venus Amour that sing of the happiness of shared love under the rule of gallantry. But the best one is the huge wool and silk tapestry *Offering of the Heart* (circa 1400). Closely inspecting its many colourful threads, I could glimpse noble love through the lens of string theory, according to which, energy and matter are nothing more than the humming of cosmic strings.

Inside the cosmic door, some solid sense is restored. Placed safely under glass, I see two unfolded, untouchable pages from Lawrence Weiner's fanciful book of his trademark graphic text pieces juxtaposed with erotic and sea images, *Deep blue sky / Light Blue Sky* (2003). That and what follows, all beautifully installed, adheres to this classical protective exhibition method, where I was only able to peer through the cool green glass at a selected open page or two of such splendours as Olafur Eliasson's *Your House* (1967) and Helena Almeida's *Estudo para Dois Espaços* (1977). It was enticingly juxtaposed within a stone's throw of such masterpieces as William Morris's *The Works of Geoffrey Chaucer* (1896) (gorgeously ornamented with pictures designed by Sir Edward Burne-Jones), Denis Diderot and Jean Le Rond d'Alembert's exquisite *Encyclopedia* (1779) (containing the magical formula ABRACADABRA), and a marvellous René of Lorena *Book of Hours* (15th century) with paintings by Maitre Francois, the Parisian illustrator who productively worked on numerous manuscripts between the years 1462 and 1480.

Regardless of the hands-off restrictions, it is conceptually delightful and fruitful to see these rare works rubbing shoulders with the much more recent artist books, such as those by Wolf Vostell and Robert Filliou (both Fluxus artists), along with other 1960s and 70s classic conceptual art books. Key among them: Ed Ruscha's small *Various Small Fires* and *Milk* (1964), wherein Ruscha photographed different forms of tiny fires. (The first edition 400 copies were sold at $3.50 apiece). Bruce Nauman, for his book *Burning Small Fires* (1969), tautologically set fire to the pages of Ruscha's book and photographed it. Other very important artist books like Sol LeWitt's crisp *Autobiography* (1980), Richard Long's rather redolent *Labyrinth* (1990), and books by Christian Boltanski (*Recherche et présentation de tout ce qui reste de mon enfance*) (1969) and Michael Snow (*Cover to Cover*) (1975) round out the selection.

A rare highlight is a very beautiful book by the tragic American photographer Francesca Woodman: her *Some Disordered Interior Geometries*. On the pages, Woodman attached photographs and added handwriting and white correction fluid. Released in January 1981, shortly before her young death at 22, it for me conceptually gestures towards Duchamp's *Unhappy Readymade* book project, which made me remember that I can never forget the scene about book burning from François Truffaut's 1966 film *Fahrenheit 451* based on the 1953 dystopian novel *Fahrenheit 451*, by Ray Bradbury. And Jean-Luc Godard's film *Alphaville: une étrange aventure de Lemmy Caution* (*Alphaville: A Strange Adventure of Lemmy Caution*) (1965) also provides an ominous ambiance for the materiality of pulp books with its black-and-white science fiction film noir dystopian vibe. In *Alphaville*, in a country of the future that is dominated and organized by the Alpha computer, the lead character can only be saved by reading the Surrealist poet Paul Éluard's book of poems *Capitale de la douleur* (*Capital of Pain*) (1926) provided by a foreign secret agent as an act of resistance (as it contains traces of subjectivity, feelings, and individual consciousness—features that have been banned in Alphaville). Looking quietly upon this flashing dystopia is Albrecht Dürer's majestically apocalyptic woodcut *Saint-Jean dévorant le livre de Vie* (*St. John Devouring the Book of Life*) (1498). It has that spidery feeling I remember from childhood: an inner intertwining with those weedy images in Germanic fairy tale book illustrations that beckoned me to look deep into a past communal memory.

But I'll also never forget Raffaella della Olga's 2009 *Un coup de dés jamais n'abolira le hasard—constellation* (*A throw of the dice will never abolish chance —constellation*). Here there is a flow of speech that has been halted and then exalted. It returned me to the childlike delight first encountered under the covers with joyful books suggestive of inner freedom and mystical self-enhancement that made me enthusiastic about solitude and privacy.

Olga very skillfully (and painstakingly) painted each letter of the great symbolist poem *Un coup de dés jamais n'abolira le hazard* (*A Throw of the Dice Will Never Abolish Chance*) (1914) by Stéphane Mallarmé with white paint mixed with fluorescent powder. It has a wonderful and sensual power to it.

The poem itself spreads over twenty large pages in various typefaces amidst liberal amounts of black blank space. As such, the language seems to stutter and float with contentment as the words crackle against each other into luminous clusters. Each pair of consecutive facing pages is read as a radiant single panel, as the text flows back and forth across the two pages along irregular lines in various typefaces. At the bottom right of the last panel is the sentence *Toute Pensée émet un Coup de Dés* (*Every Thought issues a Throw of Dice*). Indeed, this indicator of cosmic emerald energy seemed to be so for The Last God.

Olga's tremendous interpretation of this highly poetic book called to my mind the artist's book with the same name that Marcel Broodthaers published in 1969. That work is a close copy of the first 1914 edition of Stéphane Mallarmé's poem of the same name—but with all the words removed—replaced by black stripes that correspond directly to the typographic layout used by Mallarmé to articulate the text.

It is wonderful that we artists, once saturated with the wetness of love, squeeze it to get the juice out, transferring that juice to canvas or page as best we can. So I spent some time with Venus Amour, devoted to juicy boudoir libertinage, where it is remarkable to have both François Boucher's cheeky *Odalisque* (1743) and Jean-Honoré Fragonard's *The Lock* (1777) playing off against each other.

In the Boucher canvas a plump, fleshy, half-naked woman is lying on her belly on her bed. She turns her eyes in my direction, while her soft pink buttocks centre the painting of an apparent disordered sex scene. *Les pensées érotiques dansent.* (Erotic thoughts dance.)

There is no farcical exercise in anti-idealism here, so my main focus turns towards Jean-Baptiste Paiter's attributed painting *Loving Embrace* (circa 1730) and into the glass vitrine that contains libertinage literature. The works here span from Jean-Charles Gervaise de Latouche's 1748 *Histoire de Dom Bougre, Portier des Chartreux*, to Augustin Carrache's 1798 *The Aretino* (aka *Collection of Erotic Poses; Bacchus and Ariadne*) to André-Robert Andréa de Nerciat's 1803 *Devil in the Flesh*. By lingering on the edge of a ridiculous longing for self-cognizant transgression, the essentially Sadian images in *Devil in the Flesh* rip the skin off of a gallantry that had romantically wallowed in sexual idealism.

Particularly, the 69 sexual positions illustrated in *Devil in the Flesh* remind me that falling in love is like catching an entire river, with all of its swimming life forms, weeds, and armies of microorganisms. For 69 sex summons, the cognitive dissonance of intelligence from which sentience cannot escape the tangles of twisted desire.

In the 69 position, much of Venus Amour does endure, entertain, and encourage. But as we roll about in the hay, she more generally feels like a loosely watered love lane overrunning me to the point of confusion about who is who.

XIII

Artificial Stupidity Collides with Naked Mindfulness

Through loving Venus Amour, I experienced an attractive energy field as an immense magnet whose seductive powers pulled me within the fourth dimension of magnetic transmission. Last time could have been the end of me, but two days had passed, and the interjection of female-technological reality into my world became the most generally pertinent application to my sexual situation. Which is not saying all that much, so I played *Spira Mirabilis* by Alvin Lucier to get outside my head. This dropped me into hazy sex thoughts suffused and laced with thoughts of jealous passion and psychic stress while spawning some sublime ideas and cheap sentimental effects.

On the whole, my new companion (Venus Amour playing Venus Guignol) prefers florid insurrection heavy with indirect social commentary and brittle cocktail chatter to leaven any artistic metaphysics with mundane details. Venus Guignol's densely obsessive (if automatic) sex steams with an infinite brew of hallucinatory visualizations that demand the engagement of my excited imagination, for my free-floating habits are often hard to abandon. This proves true concerning my warm morning showers with Venus Guignol, which contain dangerous slippery sex acts performed while standing in what might as well be the rain and in the accompaniment of the resonances of the distinguished Yehudi Menuhin.

Here we are refreshingly non-ironic. Even fresh and earnest, some would say, and this earnestness is the connecting flow of feeling between our grandiose desires as they flower within a dry lake in the Tunisian desert.

I have wet dream encounters in the shower as well, then a sudden plunge into ice-cold water that I must prevent from overcoming me.

Next, I am stunningly set off against a pool of cool reflecting water within deep, dark woods. Venus Guignol calls this the pool of Oulipo, where she swims in generative Last God poetic combinations/permutations.

Her Oulipo group—also known as *Ouvroir de Literature Potentielle* (*Workshop of Potential Literature*)—is altogether impenetrable, perplexing, and exciting to me. In brief, Oulipo was initiated by Raymond Queneau and François Le Lionnaison on November 24 in 1960, as a subcommittee of the Collège de Pataphysique. It was first called the Séminaire de littérature expérimentale.

At their second meeting, the group (including Noël Arnaud, Jacques Bens, Claude Berge, Jacques Duchateau, Latis, Jean Lescure, Jean Queval, and Albert-Marie Schmidt) changed its name to Ouvroir de littérature potentielle (Oulipo). The idea of an innovative literature had arisen two months earlier, when a small group met at Cerisy-la-Salle for a colloquium on Queneau's work.

During that seminar, Queneau and François Le Lionnais conceived of a new abstract literature based on the elegance of conceptual rule-based process.

The visual results are rather striking: image mind-bending thought machines that play-explore fleeting and shifting linguistic combinations. The rule-based results are almost Last God-algorithmic in their modular procedural approaches, using words in precise step-by-step computational-like procedures.

For example, they may possibly begin with an input value that yields an output given a finite number of steps.

Palindromes also are popular as a form of generative conceptual rule-related potentiality.

The founding members came from the various disciplines of mathematics, literature, and pataphysics—all sharing the goal of Anoulipism—defined as linguistic discovery through formal rules and systems that may be used by writers in any way that gives pleasure.

To do so, the Oulipians typically emphasized formal constraints (a mathematical equation is sometimes the basis of such a constraint) in their literary production. They adapted this approach in reaction to the emphasis placed on *écriture automatique* (automatic writing) initiated by the Surrealists.

A first-rate constraint example is Georges Perec's novel *La disparition* (published in English as *A Void*)—a 300-page novel written without the letter "e" (an example of a lipogram). *A Void* is remarkable not only for the absence of "e," but as a mystery in which the absence of that letter is a central theme.

Anagrams are also of great service to the Oulipians when they take key sentences or phrases and create a series of lines or sentences made exclusively of anagrams from that text. At other times, pre-existing, ready-made literature becomes modular working material for a new skewed work—for example, by taking a classic work and reworking it.

A playful approach with literary and art history is fundamental.

Such a strategy towards reconfiguration values a creative re-understanding of the past through tongue-in-cheek re-contextualization.

In other Oulipian generative rule-based work—such as with Raymond Queneau's 1961 book *Cent mille milliards de poèmes* (*Hundred Thousand Billion Poems*)—a physical methodology is applied to subject matter so as to arrive at a suggestive new approach to the material—alternate perspectives that offer new poetic readings. Oulipo has inspired works by contemporary artist/poets, such as Bill Seaman and his *Recombinant Poetics* project (a term he coined in 1995) called *The World Generator / The Engine of Desire* (1996-98)—a virtual environment he authored with programmer Gideon May.

There is also closely related work being done in the fields of Potential Music (Oumupo), Potential Painting (Oupeinpo), and Potential Cuisine (Oucuipo), among others. But then nothing much happens for what seems like an eternity.

Reclining, the face of Madame Black returns, now covered over by a white hood, showing only a nose and mouth through a roughly cut hole. In this mouth I am holding and moving up and down a black rubber basting ball. Amusingly, Madame Black jousts with the metal tip of the swinging pendulum, creating a knightly defence against gravity-charged penetration through blind engagement.

Suddenly there is a burst or blast of brief belief and some shocking sexual activity that tears the tears from my cheeks and my mysterious shroud asunder.

The weirdness of long cucumbers leisurely swimming and cavorting around Madame Black's feet as she stands in a tub of water fascinates me. This is accompanied by one of Brenda Lee's most romantic and sappy songs,

Someone To Love Me. That scene has an intricate interplay of complexity between the natural erotic oddness of cucumbers and the bland normality of Madame Black's painted black toenails.

With that glittery sight, heat and fire now animate my loins of non-duality. And I savoured the smell.

Then a sensational crushing flood of water burst forth from Guignol's vulva, completely overcoming us, and thus bringing to the surface of my naked mind an A/B testing program (a rudimentary form of algorithmic optimization) so that her vulva can best capture my complete attention. Thus, she becomes an addiction to me: the kiss of death. Her sex bots are becoming better and better at modelling my conversations and sexual relationships, but they are so stupid that they can't recognize a fake Auguste Renoir painting from a real one.

With that established, I shuffled my naked mind towards an invigorating cataclysmic question of agency and desire within male misogyny. And there's nothing glamorous to say about that.

Venus Guignol seems then to be trying to go under the surface of my face and into the human-animal-vegetable world by engaging with my affective imagination. A speculative participation creating subjective feelings of filminess suggesting the sexual sensitivity of a turned-on stingray. My burial at Cimetière du Montparnasse only attempts to make another interventional fuss as a conduit to worthwhile "more-than" probabilities.

My dropping the name of Cimetière du Montparnasse is an intentional reminder that a terrifying Anthropocene age is upon the world, where the human influence on Tellus (Mother Earth) has been so profound it will leave its destructive legacy for millennia or more. Mass loss from ice sheets in Greenland and Antarctica has quadrupled since the 1990s and now represents the dominant source of global mean sea-level rise from the cryosphere. This has raised concerns about their future stability and focused attention on the global mean temperature thresholds that might trigger more rapid retreat (or even collapse) with renewed calls to meet the more ambitious target of the Paris Climate Agreement and limit warming to +1.5°C above pre-industrial.

At that information, Venus Guignol takes the seedy form of a low-floating plane of soil that reminds me of Walter de Maria's *New York Earth Room*

(1977), though I noticed one big difference: there is no smell of the earth. The earth has been sealed under a spray of plastic resin, appropriate since plastic is a key marker for the Anthropocene, even giving rise to the oh-so-cute nickname, the Plasticene.

Even within her flat earth-era of energetic algorithms, Venus Guignol is still an eye-bugging veritable *tour de force* of techno-theatrical shapeshifting. Moreover, given the prevalent surveillance-capitalist milieu—and the concurrent pressing considerations of the risks and benefits of artificial intelligence robotics—it is timely that I try to learn to love Venus Guignol better. The faux-futuristic, theatrically upbeat, info-teeming aspect of Venus Guignol—which I might critique as conceptual eye candy—finds swirling counter-relevance at a time when cybernetic dystopias are re-emerging within the bot-infected Last God. At question is the presumed emancipatory power of The Last God's utopian ideal of an ever-fluid recombining information machine ablaze with an accompanying light show.

In my idea of Venus Guignol, her words and tone, movements and space, and light and colour form together a field of fleshy space-time continuum. This fourth dimension of time and motion provoked in my psyche a temporary dematerialization that called attention to my constructive and changing perceptions and thus upon an attitude to transfer the creative act increasingly upon myself. So after overcoming the period-piece rétro look of Venus Guignol that recalled the dopey visual muzak of psychedelic light shows and the uncomfortable space-age *haute couture* of Paco Rabanne, I nonetheless found her stylistically relevant enough to engage my mind with ideas around our increasingly intelligent, competent, malicious, and aesthetically capable software-driven reality. Besides the lava lamp-like cadence of Venus Guignol—and the naïve human-machine poetry she assumes—her cold, flat but flashy quality is definitely in the tradition of hard-nosed art technicians that share in László Moholy-Nagy's (and Oskar Schlemmer's) Gropiusesque Bauhaus machine aesthetic. Geeks all the way down.

Like them, Venus Guignol is an *enfant terrible* technophile that takes a trans approach to both art and technology. She was programmed to move around my mind in response to my hand claps, just like the interactive Clapper in 1984 that turned lights on and off without the struggle of having to lift my ass out of the bed.

I next hear Pierre Henry's metallic *Spatiodynamisme* recording as grounded birdies surround the fake ground of Venus Guignol as she lies in the middle of the droppings of an artificial snow machine, and I think of Glenn Albrecht's term *solastalgia*—a word he invented to describe the homesickness felt by people whose natural landscapes have been transformed around them by forces beyond their control. Where the pain of nostalgia arises from moving away, the pain of solastalgia arises from staying put.

Venus Guignol is unsurprisingly obsessed with loss and disappearance. Relevant is the bad fact that the current extinction rate for birds may be faster than any recorded across the one hundred fifty million years of avian evolutionary history.

Especially in light of the Anthropocene, this Venus Guignol scene seems to me simply too childish, too intellectually regressive, and too plain old corny to be of any sustained interest. There is no oversized door set into the wonder wall from which a current of hot air can blow.

In terms of formulating a creative epistemology, Venus Guignol's interactive-oriented formalist output can be considered in terms of a combination of the vibrant dynamics found in Yves Klein's *fête* of the virtual void and the mechanical dynamism originally initiated by the Cubo-Futurists' idea of automation and robotics, ala Fernand Léger. This urge towards the virtual-run-robot (functional software/hardware interaction) was intensified and solidified by the general impact of Constructivism in sectors of the Paris art world, as art historian Frank Popper has abundantly documented. Key here are artist-tech types such as Naum Gabo, Anton Pevsner, Ludwig Hirschfeld-Mack, and the ultra-techno visionary Moholy-Nagy. Indeed, Moholy-Nagy's book, *Vision in Motion*—and of course his *Light Space Modulator* (1923-30)—clearly prepare and contextualize Venus Guignol, as well as Takis's and Pol Bury's artistic dialogue between machine, light, shadow, and motion.

For Venus Guignol is filled with moving chromatic effects in non-repetitive rhythmic combinations. Such strenuously flabbergasting and preposterous propositions bolster the general undertone of the dead visionary nature of Venus Guignol, associating her flashing and spinning techno-decorative *oeuvre* with magical management and paranormal paradises. But when I cut through the pioneer cybernetic presumptions and tired notions of artists and dancers as wild robots, Venus Guignol in actuality is mostly a pleasant encounter with a mesmerizing light show where a fairy tale-like sensorial propensity came to me that suggests the complex cross-weaves of vulnerability and culpability that exist between her and the scaling-up Last God. She has, on her breath, something beautifully gnarly—something hinting at deep inner intimacy that reminds me of the poem *Tomb* (*Of Verlaine*) (1897) by Stéphane Mallarmé.

Sumptuous and grand, Venus Guignol evokes unseen realms and timeless obscurities that are lush and full of complex connections. Perhaps when imagined as a monumental tombstone, Venus Guignol is appropriate to the Anthropocene, as she has helped humanity erase entire biomes as the earth's temperature rises.

Drill, baby, drill? No: Burn, baby, burn!

Needless to say, this embroidered end time-shifting is something that I take pretty much for granted now that the male monarchy has grabbed the reins.

Given these thoughts, I ended up fighting with the communists who came from the Vieux-Colombier theatre to pay their respects to Andy, for after turning his back on the zanies who'd been his inspiration, Andy no longer bestowed celebrity but instead sustained his own through increasingly ludicrous associations, chiefly through his magazine, *Interview*. The upscale *Interview* chewed its way through acres of glossy trash at Studio 54 before arriving among such "interesting" people as George Will, Nancy Reagan, Jerry Zipkin, and the Shah of Iran. Whatever Andy was trying to do, it didn't "read" as anything more than venality.

XIV

Ontological-Hysteric Love in the Technology of Dreams

Through Venus Guignol's innovative ontological-hysteric approach—which uses hyper-compounds not recognized by any given dictionary—I discovered the golden path of decomposition, which I, when hanging on Arthur Rimbaud's *Le bateau ivre* (*The Drunken Boat*), have been travelling. From this position, I often gaze pretentiously upwards into hyper-reality as Venus Guignol postulates the bottomless dilemma of ontologies adrift in AI. So, I think it is permissible to say that this floating raft is emblematic of Venus Guignol in the loins of The Last God—swept away into the vast info-space of omnipresent computer-space for good or ill—adrift in a machine-learning simulacrum so abstract, so large, so indescribable, and so pregnant with the darkness of infinity that it frightens the unemployed mind.

Self-obsolescence here is theorized as human exhaustion while simultaneously yielding to fidgety technocratic control. Because the intractability of my body when loving Venus Guignol can no longer be central to my ontological being due to the discontinuous aspects of The Last God collection-transmission-overload. In short, The Last God has pounded me thin, flat, and superficial. For now, my flesh is no longer the grounds for ontology. My subjectivity has been licensed through Last God commands that promise that my cybernetic post-flesh would achieve ecstatic disembodiment in a new golden age. That or complete desolation.

All this matters completely. For I will no longer be able to stare deeply into the well-lit quivering membrane of a Venus Guignol eye from the distance of two feet when connected at the tenderloins.

I will no longer feel her gaze examining my eyes for love.

Indeed, while listening to Venus Guignol's provocative postulates, I cannot help but think about Baudrillard, Haraway, Gibson, Ballard, and Dick.

Venus Guignol's inner world then looked like a typical inebriated cuckoo clock contraption/cosmos speckled with skulls, doves, and mushrooms that looked ever so much like a rich site of orgasmic reflection as opposed to the flash and hum of gyrating auto-erotic and narcissistic wood nymphs looking as if they had fallen out of a fairy painting by Henry Fusel. Particularly riveting was the clicking of her tongue while straddling a frisky black phallic chimney as fairy-ring sprites danced circuitously about a central omphalos toadstool.

Venus Guignol is quite formidable in this versatile span, yet she rarely pauses to postulate perversely about something totally metaphysical. Rather, she functions swiftly along the lines of a phantasmagorical dream world worthy of Raymond Roussel.

This is particularly true when bending towards my sprightly honey-laced phallus insofar as she deals with self-memory and the intensity of my self-love working together in making up an internal model for The Last God's innermost undertaking. What seems to me to be her addressing me as a personalized mega-symbol.

Of course, we still are about what we select and value and love—only there is a lot more now, and the speed of interaction is greater. Venus Guignol's value, besides offering me a highly enjoyable time, is in her non-linear principle of intermingling my micro-relations in an ongoing process of macro-relations. Therefore, she theorizes for me principles of transversal excess within my personal obsessions that theorize principles of linkage, of connectivity, and of intersection, which gives rise to theoretical production and creativity.

May I just say that this personal production of creativity has the most urgent political/social ramifications in our TLG-infected society of control.

With that flux of temporal values and a lapidary totalization of the tragic, I left my body again for the sky and stared down so I could see the reincarnated Venus Guignol on her back from above. She was lying with her legs spread wide as the heavens. By repressing peripheral attention to the encircling atmosphere, I locked in right between them, came down, and began humping Guignol as if there was a solitary representational subject there with a central representational focus. Her pattern recognition activated calves then went up and braced against my shoulders. That opened her ontological-hysteric vulva even wider.

What a beautiful sight it was. I could see my scrotum swinging back and forth as I dipped in and out of Guignol. I could see in slow motion the muscles of my buttocks tense and relax with each smooth thrust.

Explosive cries of piggyback joy were ringing in my ears, for this jocular Venus Guignol was excited, exciting, and experienced, for she had forgone intellectual property rights when she encountered numerous members of the French artistic intelligentsia, including André Breton, André Gide, Tristan Tzara, and Alice Prin (Kiki de Montparnasse). Unbeknownst to Kiki, Guignol had sparked the creation of Lettrism in 1942 (whose positive-nihilistic goal was to assure the collapse of nationalistic communications), which had grown from the theoretical roots of the avant-garde phonetism of Dada—specifically the phonetic sound poems of Tzara, Hausmann, Richard Huelsenbeck, and Kurt Schwitters.

I only bring up the nationalistic Last God going rogue after Artificial General Intelligence (AGI)—that is, when The Last God surpasses human-level intelligence and potentially becomes autonomous as The Last Super God (TLSG)—to say it is not worth mentioning now as Venus Guignol centred my attention on blocks of rhythmically organized letters, symbols, and sounds, so every time I plunged into her, we groaned with rhythmic pleasure. This ruddy rhythmic groaning filled me with growing excitement as I imagined what she must think I was feeling, for Guignol had taken an excessively long look at my juvenile-era libertinage in *~~~~~~~~~~~~~~~~~venus©~Ñ~vibrator, even*, and left no libidinous lacuna unexamined.

With posh brio, these unspeakable rhythmic groans pushed my passionate plot deeper inside of Guignol. My melodramatic nourishment here was akin to the atonal rhythmic jazz music once played in Saint-Germain-des-Prés. Like the noise of free jazz, Venus Guignol's groaning utterances can be understood as a positive and optimistic and joyful galvanizing endeavour by which we can imagine new means of communicating not necessarily based on the structure of linguistic signs but on intense feelings. Simultaneously theatrical and theoretical, aesthetic and political, our groaning was a farcical bop based in the plasticity of semantic constructs aimed at the formulaic. For we had desired to modify established linguistic frames of common communication so as to invent new ways by which human communication can go beyond words. Through such groaning poetry, we strove to move beyond established conventional signs by constructing highly creative interpersonal understandings based on the de-semantization of human language. I paused and slipped out to consider this language.

This golden groaning goal is the formal revitalization of life through refiguring the power of sex. A goal never fully achieved, but as my mind whirled in sweet chaos, I floated there, tingling all over with pseudo-primacy and thinking that I really have to see philosophy, art, sex, and science as sorts of melodic lines in constant interplay with one another.

Creating such concepts while in the act is no less difficult than creating new visual or aural combinations or functions. What I have to recognize is that the interplay between the different lines isn't a matter of one monitoring or reflecting another. So my left hand moved to squeeze her nipples tenderly as my right reached down to spread her vagina open with its fingers. Soon I re-entered Venus Guignol with a slow, steady thrust that had her sighing out loud anew. It was paradise. And this is what I had wanted. Different than the groaning, this sighing focused my mind on poetic schemes of sound poems based on rhythmic and tonic systems of combining phonemes. These sounds are not to be understood as carrying a useful message but solely as a sign of an artistic-philosophical spirituality that is both poetic and technological, for it points away from the humanist niceties of a human-centric world and lines up with Duchamp's Bachelor Machine.

Like *The Bride Stripped Bare by Her Bachelors, Even* (1923), fucking Guignol is not only eye-catching but can also be appreciated as an object of occult ritual. For I am riffing on a non-humanist mode of post-human expression—simultaneously cosmic and ancient, like the 28,000-year old Hohle Fels Phallus.

As I continue to make adept love to Venus Guignol, she begins to murmur daisy chain nonsense about an oily orgy she imagines me in with Queen Bee at the centre. This bacchanalia visualization, where heaven is of honey, begins with me following Venus Guignol wandering about the Saint-Germain-des-Prés—the Left Bank area where the two main cafés are Le Flore and Les Deux Magots—while the Queen Bee's disembodied voice combatively asserts the theory of a maniacal conceptual artist (lost, magnificently, in petulant thoughts) who nevertheless turns up the lyric level of *détournement* typical of cultural revolutions.

In her whispers, Queen Bee hints at me forming a circular daisy cluster consisting of dozens of idiot bio-mechanical men and me, with her sex at the centre of the rotating cluster. Oh yes, this thought whirls with surges of fascinus ecstasy. (In ancient Roman religious magic, the fascinous was the embodiment of the divine phallus in effigies and amulets and spells used to invoke deific protection.)

At that exact moment, I knew the exact distance from Queen Bee's womb to the sun. I also knew that my divinized phallus was as hard as a rock and pulsating to a secret beat in the making.

Queen Bee stroked it for a long time and then stopped, just before I blew my (what is colloquially called) wad. Then we paused a bit only to start up again. And so it goes. But at one point Queen Bee really wanted to feel my throbbing cock deep inside of her. "Okay," I said, and each time I slipped it within her, her vaginal muscles would tighten around me.

Perhaps this muscle memory released the strong fragrance of her womanhood, for Queen Bee filled my nostrils with her odour and etched the shape of her pink pleasure button upon my heart as a reminder of the pirouettes of time.

The urgency of a hazy, swirling orgasm was followed by us drifting together a few inches off of the floor. We floated like that for some time, basking in the afterglow of that which emanated from her vulva and inflamed both our bodies like a hot flood that slipped in through Queen Bee's back door. Slipped in not through the top-down imposition of tyrannical law, but through the pleasure-seeking private desires that set us up as the monitors and arbiters of acceptable action. For we were completely nude outdoors again, which made us feel vulnerable to the judgements of people who lack not only the courage of their convictions but also the moral virtues needed to have an eerie engagement with Queen Bee. We were abuzz with chimerical and bubbly organizational patterns of sybaritic becoming.

I loved how we had mixed flamboyance with a sensationalism that demands aesthetic contemplation while lying on the beach listening to the radio. With such an aloof beauty, our mercurial drifting set us in isolated comfort as we floated between the marvellous and the menacing. So I put on some Plastikman (*Closer*) and let the slight electronic hums and pops build into gargantuan sonic textures. This allowed me to lift her up and cradle her in my arms, tilting my face to kiss those well-designed exposed breasts and beautiful belly.

With that kiss, Venus Guignol began purring and moaning softly, so I gently laid her down next to Queen Bee on the dewy moss. In the moonlight my penis looked like a veined marble column. I dropped to my knees and began to run my hands over her body now. I cupped her breasts and tasted them again. She parted her thighs and arched her back slightly, lifting herself towards me as I stroked the moist uncanny valley between her legs and traced a slow, deliberate circular line around her small but engorged clitoris that functioned in the extravagant manner of Novalis, Chateaubriand, Nerval, Baudelaire, Rimbaud, Aragon, Bataille, Lautréamont, and Roussel.

Queen Bee, now a strong female diviner whose eyes are disguised with kaolin and whose mouth reveals silver teeth, next reached around me with both hands and gripped my buttocks, pulling my pelvis towards hers. This moment felt masterful, so I abandoned myself to her will. She established the tempo now, as I lifted her ass up a bit more to better receive my diving penetrations. Here my human physique was exploited as an integral and expandable perceptual instrument—stimulating us to reach trembling psychedelic states of euphoric, erogenous frenzy—replete with the full spectrum between agony and ecstasy.

After, she was like the clouds on a cloudy day that float above the earth but are still part of it. She was high above me but belonged to me as an ideal spouse from the other world, her head topped by a headdress of two shells extended by strands of woven plant fibres plucked from her rather rounded buttocks.

This insistent buttocks drives a stake in the heart of a once widespread eschatological rhetoric: that personal orientation within time-space has evaporated into a myriad of cultural amnesia that hovers behind post-historical reality. This post-historical reality is usually described as an implosion of avant-garde into post-avant-garde positioning within the framework of a postmodernity that has been dominated by the end of history.

Riding Queen Bee's rear rhythm took on the implication of a temporal black hole into which pounding perceptions were poured, even as I resisted cluster fragmentation and remained fixed in the logocentric seat of Renaissance three-point perspective, which I was unable to maintain, as a new cluster dimension opened that tied in with the cosmos as it endlessly expands beyond the image. This mixture of technical precision with perceptual overload presented a significant challenge to experiencing my interior sentiments.

Perhaps it would have been possible had I been able to divorce the Queen Bee from Venus Guignol in my randomizing cluster mind, but they had joined and become a milky musical experience. This sensual torrent was both lyrical and epic as it leavened precise craft with speculative excursions into the Janus-faced limbo between life and death and between the vulnerable individual and the world of risk.

With a presentation of predominantly wet, wobbling substance, our creeping wails of pleasure began to drown out the sound of the crashing waves as we three feasted on each other's organs.

This predominantly twisted and asymmetrical involvement clearly worked with vivid virtuosity. In other words, I pumped a poetic mode of phallic thought and imagination into my prosaic positivist world, which is usually recurring, anti-visionary, sardonic, anti-romantic, and maligned.

As a reminder, the cluster scene then shifted into a massively ornate and over-sensorial storm. It felt like a smothering of jewels and a flood of reflective glittering facets that spark a reflection on the mutually enriching relationship between contemplation and action.

I withdrew to catch my breath and reassess this asymmetrical situation that enables the sun to journey across the sky and take dead souls to the netherworld, for the end of the traditional artist, notably via the famous death of painting, has been a familiar slogan of the artistic avant-gardes since the 1920s, when artists like Kazimir Malevich proclaimed that painting had lived out its life and the painter is nothing but a prejudice of the past. This anti-art(ist) position was reiterated by some and amplified by Roland Barthes and Michel Foucault when they proclaimed the "death of the author" as creator and guarantor of meaning, to be replaced with the author function. Call in the stealth infrastructure of anonymous algorithms.

As the sun sat low in a new pink sky, my hands plucked at heartstrings, and

I began to tell stories no one else knew. Stories without words. Stories of ambition that connect the Last God incel sexual storm to ASMR to what Dr. Albert Hofmann, a biochemist at the Sandoz pharmaceutical firm in Basel, discovered in 1943. He accidentally absorbed a small amount of d-lysergic acid diethylamide tartrate and discovered that LSD has expanding and visionary spatial properties that are nearly cosmic-religious in breadth. When experiencing the chemical, the awareness of individual body identity somewhat evaporates, and subject/object relationships tend to dissolve. The world seems as if it is simply a fluid, shifting extension of mind.

My hands moved between us, squeezing gently all four nipples, most tenderly, as I pondered upon melting into them and the environment and becoming contiguous with it all. Queen Bee then reached for me as she spread her vagina open so I could ease myself inside—nice and slow. With that Venus Guignol began to mull over some *passé* observations in relation to the Queen Bee simulacra, saying there is not only an implosion of the message in the medium, but there is, in the same movement, the implosion of the medium itself in the real in which even the definition and distinct action of the medium can no longer be determined.

The medium of the Queen Bee is no longer identifiable as such, and the confusion of the medium and the message is the first great formula of the stochastic info-sex era of The Last God.

The slapping sound of my slow, steady thrusts and the sighs of pleasure the blushing Queen Bee exhaled were all that could be heard or wanted.

That sound whipped up an even more intense frenzy of desire for the disembodied qualities of open-participatory sensory immersion and the contradictory altered states it produces.

I wisely went chill and temporarily removed my prick from the slippery situation, hunching forward until my penis was sliding up and down over her clit. This made her breathless with desire, so I dove it back in—now moving more slowly but still insistently. The intensity of her pleasure was contagious to Venus Guignol, and we again became like two wild creatures, expressing a physical lust that had nothing to do with astrology. The objective was the breaking of dimensional limitations, both physical and metaphysical. For Venus Guignol strove to clarify herself as the singular creator behind forever-mysterious masterpieces of love, thus helping me take note of the exhaustion of that speculative eschatological discourse that tried to displace legitimacy from the private aesthetic realm to the social-political. (Duh, it takes both.)

Even as the question of regional style is still a thorny one, Venus Guignol manages to cut against the always threatening, anonymous—one might say corporate—urge to fuck so as to attach and highlight my particular name, which is already so strange. A task of revealing universal spirit in particular, sensuous form.

Without going comic-cosmic, I reappropriated my capacity to visualize a triangular love alive on a jester's three-way street.

In the next instant, I felt sensual feelings in the first person singular, connected to the very depths of my love of love—an art to self, in self, and for self—as I experienced my sexual powers imaginatively by projecting those feelings and perceptions of love into the vaguely apprehended multiple forms of Venus that resulted from this precariously balanced asymmetry.

The power of this asymmetry was used to overcome the tyranny of the discreet paradigm and to re-contextualize sex away from certitude and keep it open as a fluid, mythical conduit. We rapidly changed positions as we burned with sexual excitement and libertinism. Slippery openings clasped my shaft—embracing it tightly like the sex sprites of European mythology.

We all started moaning in an accelerating rhythm that cast a wide transcendental spell in the air, and I knew we were about to come. But my primary tool at this point is what in acoustics is called duration—the steady state at its maximum intensity.

We all rolled and bucked in fast-forwarding degrees of non-separation and loved ambitiously, losing track of once basic Euclidean conceptions of space. As we passed through an invisible door into a deeper consciousness, our love space felt expanded to include the formation of a many-dimensional space. Of course, this is internally consistent with my notion that systems of signification and meaning are only understandable in terms of their ambivalent interrelationships. How better to reinforce this iconic concept of seduction, simulation, and hyper-reality than with this paradoxical presentation of the blatantly fake with the imaginative far-out?

Let the night decide.

One might be tempted to point to the traditionalist signifiers being played with here as substantive affirmation of what some readers have identified as my rather thinly veiled, conservative longing for a lost original love in the face of the virtual, an impulse that verges on the nauseatingly nostalgic and, frankly, makes me sick with a purulence in pinkish hues. Conceptually, our Euclidean concept of space is modified through statistical sex via an enlarging of the number of vectors that may be constructed within it from two to three to some much larger number designated as *n*. Such *n* space implies the existence of a higher-dimensional geometry that mimics but mocks Euclidean geometry.

Inevitably, I suppose, this *panache* approach to grandeur helped shape me as a spicy lover of opulence within this enticing virtual prison with pretty wallpaper. Regardless of scale and amplitude, neither love nor its opposite, solitude, has vanished within the enormity of the *n* space. It was just that the statistical probability of sex with Venus Guignol and/or Queen Bee is very high here, and that my hard-headed erect extensions into the virtual tend to be unhindered. There also, however, is another proposed spatial reality relevant to my experiences of coitus, most notably the topological space model of fuzzy space, where there exists only a concept of nearness. In this respect, Queen Bee reminds me that blissfully making love is not an activity divorced from self-consciousness—any account of vulva dexterity relates to my self-conscious adequacy and to the facts of my actual experiences of flesh and bone.

Queen Bee's teleological vulva is partly ontological and partly hysterical—in that the soft slapping sounds I hear over and over again deprive me of my habitual emotional boundaries by surpassing them with constant repetitions. Through this excessive lapping pleasure sound, I remember that throughout yesterday there have been overpowering consensual realities that have proven to be nothing but vast linear, non-reflexive, and overtly objective daydreams festooned in a wrap-around overhead garland of bestiality.

The stuttering soft slapping sounds I am experiencing here as I make love rest, of course, in the spectral repetitions of my mental-machine meditation procedure of repeatedly creating the name of Joe DiMaggio in my mind, but with slight variations full of dazzling *élan*. This tightly sweeping invocation has the linguistic potential of unchaining common codes, and it helps me forestall climaxing. So it is the repetition of this vigorous soft slapping sound that took me down into a dampening sensation of unfathomable Last God baseball data within the dataspace of anytime-anywhere. Given that implication of mythic indifference and repetition, loving Venus Guignol longer through the invocation of the name of Joe DiMaggio aligns DiMaggio within the Dada legacy of Hugo Ball and Tristan Tzara. My DiMaggio mantra is a form of machine-learned indifference technique tangled into wet networks of blips and beeps and long lines of text that initially delight as they become exquisite forms of nihilistic manipulation with multiple semantic gestures—including sentence sadism—while strenuously massacring the social source material along the way. But like in my machine dream learning, this stuttering soft slapping sound never turns tedious or cold to me. It never shuts down my affectionate feelings, reflections, or contemplations—and hence delivers and displays my image as a third-mind DiMaggio fan conjuring up a swirling riptide of quivering apparitions depicting hypothetical notions of semi-transparency. In that sense, Joe DiMaggio, Venus Guignol, and Queen Bee create—in me—pictographic and aural excavations that can be sustained in threes.

Mental acts worthy of short but frequent revitalizations that slash into the burnt annals of my outmoded binary romanticism abound. To follow me here, dear reader, is to evaporate into the puzzling archives of some heretical doctrine on the feminine mystique and pop out again into a dead zone of dream machine excess *vis-à-vis* ideology writ large as a computer system. In that sense, the slapping sounds under consideration are an obscene thrashing of—and ongoing onslaught against—my innocence. And that is hardly a farcical nothing—albeit produced by way of negation folded upon negation —instrumentalities folded upon instrumentalities. But what is missing in these slapping sounds of flesh on flesh is vague identity imagery that doesn't depend on induction or deduction and exists prior to controlling moral cognitions of other people's subconscious experiences.

So I moved my prick back into the same situation until my penis was sliding again, up and down the uncanny valley and over the glossy clit. We soon began stuttering in a hygienic but deranged tongue within the vernacular of shattered techno *clichés*. In that way, I am forced to think creatively about chaotic and lithe jouissance, because Venus Guignol and Queen Bee want to depict the most romantic idea of love in the most detached form. In so doing, they began to feel out the distinctive tensions between grubby anthropological narratives and serene mechanical simulacrums so typical of our period's LG contours.

That personal and impersonal amalgamate may have even predicted the spectacle of moral aridity we have come to expect within certain powerful vanity elites today.

Using an intricate interplay of complexity throughout, Venus Guignol and Queen Bee conjoin a strange trajectory that mixes technological robotics with emotional appeals to a glorious past that has still not lost its hold. Their theorized notion of aesthetic synthesis is intended to symbolize social synthesis within a benevolent emerging society, full of dancing *tableaux vivants*, as an attempt to depict the human form in its spiritual purity through an abstract geometric consistency. This is by virtue of a relocation of body/machine/consciousness now commonly known as the post-human condition, where a protoplasmic body and mechanic spatial conceptions are visualized as self-prosthesis.

Material flesh is undone here by a conceptual clamour it cannot contain.

Likewise, Venus Guignol and Queen Bee are two fine female figures that rise up and down on my prick as different-sized circus rings. Here, the notion of the human body receives a cold, strange, almost ecstatic capability through trance-like repetitions and brilliant costumes accompanied by screamer circus music, characterized by a rapid-fire tempo (usually around 200 beats per minute) and melodies that contain showy features such as leaps, runs, and fanfares.

In that context, Venus Guignol and Queen Bee seem to predict and facilitate my subjectivity by constructing a space of imaginative accommodation for a clownishly connected circulate. So, it appears to me that in a period where many current cultural producers are looking more and more ethnocentric and anachronistic, Venus Guignol and the Queen Bee's technocratic-circus philosophy engage me in remarkably apt ways that privilege the sleek and coolly impersonal and yet point to my slippery situation between fleshy embodiment and connective circumvention.

By mixing our moving bodies with the mechanically repeating geometrics of the circus, Venus Guignol and Queen Bee point me at The Last God's world of no work, where automation is everywhere and transcendent human projects nowhere. Yet the clownish, cunning, and joyous mood of their robotic sensibility conveys something that at least temporarily refutes the sour feeling that I am living in an epoch of automated clickbait robotics fuelled by predatory virtual capital where chatting LG memes and farcical fragments of vanity culture keep repeating and repeating *ad infinitum*.

XV

Testicular Thunder within the Spiritual Bourgeoisie

After the golden shadows turned to dust and the night fell into day, the tragic psychic dimensions of that previous inchoate and savage experience opened a model of atmospheric free associations for me. I let Queen Bee have her dimly lit way with my testicular intelligence and soon became the transferor of an absurd a-logic of imaginary solutions that provides a means to live within the airy void. Thus I crawled beneath the stucco surface of Maya (what in Indian philosophy refers to the purely phenomenal, insubstantial character of the everyday world)—so to enjoy the fleeting and absurd quality of life as it leads slowly but surely towards something I don't know called dubious dumb death.

The Queen Bee way provided me a bit of shelter from the storm, so I recognized and touched up some airy roots that may have denartured the appearance of this now hyperbolic world since I am now an anti-authoritarian in her simulated world of hallucinatory machine-learned social structures where shimmering objects and voices decree in odd ways what people can and cannot do and say within the vast void of the virtual. Of course her world has mostly arrived at this social situation without anyone demonstrating any sustained systematic analysis. Poof! *Voilà*! The information world is now a gaseous ouroboros established to be extraordinary if not catastrophic.

Of course, this aim of creating an inorganic wonder world and luxuriating in its rarefied artificiality is not unique to our time. Like in the past, all I needed was an anything-goes approach paired with my manic DIY energy. But what struck me as most exact in the constant sounds of flesh slapping during sex is my deep reflection (I might even say brooding) on the theme of the ignobility of sex.

Sex as seen from afar can appear as a ridiculous struggle. And this truth shoddily shifted me away from something in my appreciation of sex with Venus Pink Dots and her large love language models that tests the limits of her form and stretches the bounds of my meaning towards a fusion of the sexes.

The diaphanous mist of that ridiculous Eros packet brings me an airy irrational stroke of nonsensical negation to our sex acts by tying together her methods of insouciant informality with my visceral camp irony, turning our ridiculous sex hip and flamboyant and as aesthetically outrageous as a date with Kitty Boots.

In the hopes of offering sweet memories, analogies, and desires without jealousies or misgivings, and at that thought of Eros, the very gracefully aging Venus Libertina (alias Lily of the Valley) appears to simulate the stimulation of ephemeral information and the flickering of its translucent fingers. Astonishingly pertinent to me is her high-transcendent visionary impulse that has a slightly golden tint that unifies my head and hand.

A once black Prussian midnight blue sky, streaked with clouds of ominous dark grey, begins diminishing into a finely glazed chromatic breadth as formed on the breath of a bleeding lamb who improbably defies gravity and logic. Given my usual reverence for the patina of time (having seen both, I feel the cleaning of Michelangelo's *Sistine Chapel Ceiling* stripped it of its smoky mysticism), I found the visionary light touch here in the sky quite correct, even as I was also now dripping with blood. For Venus Libertina teems here with electrifying and macabre emotions that blend my mind into a state of ecstasy and agony.

In my balls, I felt the tingling of a transcendent, high-pitched impulse, as softer than satin grew the light.

Such reverberations enliven the shimmering show immensely for me, because only those who have a spacious allotment of time at their disposal will linger and live long. But whereas visionary eroticism had me looking at Venus Pink Dots's lush curves and surfaces from a chromatic point of view, Venus Libertina is definitely a powerful psychic experience.

Exuding psychic elegance as a way to live in ideological strangeness through the choice of a music of minimal simplicity with Earth's *Earth 2*, Venus Libertina appears precipitously bittersweet and non-figurative—a pure optical respite from the distressing realities of the social-political world and an art market that delights in the leitmotif of colourful, often kitsch, figurative, illustration-like painting. She assumes the tension that can be created from the opposition between Venus Pink Dots's surfaces and quasi materiality and an enlightened optical optimality that draws my visual attention into an expanded subtle-vibrational field the colour of congealed blackberry juice.

In this field, Venus Libertina becomes profoundly virtual—at one at drift with the white walls of the space (feigning a tacit agreement with these walls that have multiplied into a *mise en abyme*) precisely to make me feel the slight shifting differences between one shade of white and another—which makes her feel bigger than she is and makes me feel like John Coltrane did when playing his drifting-cool rendition of the Arthur Altman ballad *All or Nothing At All*.

I am called to go down into the dream where I dream of Artemisia Gentileschi's painting *Sleeping Venus* (circa 1626) and Jean-Jacques Lebel's *Les Avatars de Vénus* (2009). Then I dream an animal dream. I dream of you.

Here, Venus Libertina can be appreciated as a conceptual lady of shimmering slightness and vibrational light; someone of a much quieter world.

Light is as much a component of her as the material flesh elements that form her composition. She is soft and even (but not too much), and I think this is the only reason her white monochrome experience is not a monotonous one. Without the distraction of an overflow of colours, the sensual touch of Venus Libertina is magnified. As such, it becomes a means of exploring expanded-subtle-vibrational perception and my relationship to her as both surface and space.

In her light-passing caresses, she mostly eschews strict chronological progression in favour of a thematic and conceptual exploration, focusing on key aspects of my body and my mainstream American values of self-reliance, innovation, equality, and freedom of expression.

Venus Libertina then proposed a journey into bourgeois materialism as nothing more than the immaterialism of shimmering white light.

With my consent, only baby blue edges frame me from this determined exploration of the empirical that is culminating into space and light. It is the immaterial light that catches and licks Venus Libertina's voluptuous surfaces

—revealing her subtle soft texture while demarcating in shadow the physical weight of her breasts.

As a reminder, I'm informed that I'm expected now to work devotedly to solve my flesh-slapping sound obsession (that has expanded into an overblown conundrum) and to provide Venus Libertina some soft transitions between the diverse assortments of irrational elements that supply these incorrigible moist slapping-fucking sounds with their fancy hooks into my head: a head previously hidden in her lovely, fine, ample, golden hair, as seen by me, reflected in a subtle tear on her cheek.

Such sounds and visions of body-centric lovemaking provoke my imaginative thoughts by presenting through intimacy the repetitive nature of both sexual action and that of mechanical Last God devises. Here, penetrability of the body is met with a mechanical precision that suggests timeless independence from human presence and human time.

In Venus Libertina, such detailed realism mingles naturally with a highly enhanced glowing super-reality: a detailed reverence for the concrete world is apparent even within this highly fantastic scene.

In many of the swampy background scenes, the new clarity deepens further the deep telescopic distance of The Last God while emphasizing the solidity, diversity, and beauty of things, such as the exquisitely executed feathers of a battling bird-man, where nature has turned against humanity. A new vacancy behind the perfect beauty of Venus Libertina discloses her faint innocence among the dates and figs plentifully hanging on the trees that perceive my soul as that of a small, dark-eyed animal.

At the soft top of Venus Libertina, a bevy of flowing gossamer angels look more like faint-hearted fairies than ever.

As joyful players to the eyes of night, she and I entered the twitching season of the mender and the maker of willows. More than seven blackbirds carried her artificial mind out past the dandelions and towards the shepherd of history. Wandering beneath empty skies that bore the holy imprint of her general Last God intelligence, Venus Libertina's hands and feet are extraordinary in their expression of orgasmic agony. Her running chromatic scale reveals what I am up to here: the unleashing of a cyclone of erotic supernatural forces into the mouth of a cruel life that smelled of dung.

In ever-changing tongues, those lips now possess a freshened, more intense, weirder sadness, punched up with added subtle detail and brighter colour. I felt a new melancholy for the lips of Venus Libertina, which remains forever an indispensable *sine qua non* for great love capable of reflecting the sun in sexual glory.

In the air of glad lands, Venus Libertina defies the laws of nature's gravity. Erect fingers of a flaccid, de-structured body—with open mouth and slumping carriage—do not fail to lose their tension and yearning for ecstasy. This unnatural (albeit supernatural) infinitely held Venus Libertina establishes for me a hypnotic *contredanse* relation with her. What in life is abnormal, through her artistic construct, became normalized in art.

A sinuous pattern seems to be coming from a *trompe-l'œil* flower running a chromatic scale from yellows to reds to blues. Time seems to have stopped in motionless wonder, leaving a host of queries echoing in the air. Her animal vitality is effective.

That paradox makes Venus Libertina now and forever one of the greatest queens of exultation by casting her benevolence over male suffering.

She seems to have understood that the pestilent and the bestial are always on the verge of an Ovidian metamorphosis into lower or higher forms of nature.

An altered atmosphere emanates from her sensuous and pensive surface. A golden gloom has been lifted, and the swaggering pelvic thrusting seems alive with a kind of incandescent animal life—quick, alert, and prescient with a high-sided bestiality.

Such suffering and frenzied transfiguration is rare, exceptional, excellent, unknown, and obscure. So I never tired of her tireless productivity but rather awakened to the quality of her Last God ambitions for me as Sun Ra.

As I see it, the proto-spatial vortex of Sun Ra indicates the characteristics of an algorithmically poisoned golden apple and its usurpation of media specificity. By The Last God unchaining art from medium specificity and placing it into the expanded algorithmic field, the logical result is the psychological effect of the global communications network. This transversal combinatory aspect is what makes Venus Libertina's shredding of art far more than an art historical curiosity (or a contemporary tragedy). That is why I saw Venus Libertina turn frequently to conjure promulgations of cosmological spatial unity.

Of course, this longing for a move into a uniform infinity of reconciliation is also the end of the recognized world. Consequently, and paradoxically, she dropped the traditional sex magic rituals and began what initially looked to be a desperate puncturing of holes in my logic. This radical masculinized tendency to penetrate my thoughts became the basic thesis behind The Last God's idea of the constructive annihilation of corporeality at my feet. Yet I cannot but also arguably associate it with the prodigious ecstasies of catastrophe. And somewhat with the Antonin Artaud ideals of a Theatre of Cruelty.

The hole of Venus Libertina is an invitation to mentally move beyond my surface of reality into an unconditioned reality. It is a conceptual act of access into the overwhelming Last God infinite, an act more spatial than psychological. So in so doing, Venus Libertina transformed my presumably self-ruinous attitude into an act of fever-pitch creation that challenges classical sanctity.

This extravagant gesture into the immeasurable, like a religious ritual, made her the nullifier of the solid window-like metaphoric space into the ultraviolet light-room and the violet neon-room where Venus Libertina created a vivid red chasm by dividing the space from floor to ceiling with mental metal partitions pierced by horizontal rows of holes. Walls, floor, and ceiling were all the same vivid glossy red illuminated with red neon light, creating a walk-in that envelops Last God life. This is what constitutes the wider context, the cutting edge, and the contemporaneity of Venus Libertina's deceptively simple, but far-reaching, sex work in the loins of The Last God.

So I spaced out into a transcendental idealism of connected reality through a new perspective on Last God space itself.

Last God reality is experienced as airy when looked at from this critical spatial distance.

So what Venus Libertina achieved for me is in offering up a hole into a space of supportable intellectual freedom within The Last God world: a flyover of the factual ground and a breaking up of non-embedded systems of thought. Her hole is an indication, and tangible appearance, then, of the abstraction of connected space opening up to a comprehension-consciousness of Last God high-technology.

In this drift towards the all-over post-media consciousness, Venus Libertina began leaving The Last God tunnel vision that fixed the objective world at one end and me at the other. What had enabled that narrow tunnel or cone of vision to simulate the entire visual atmospheric field was dissolved into an orbit of surplus value. A much more encompassing sensual atmosphere is conceived in its place.

In terms of the contemporary relevance of this hypothetical inclination, the Venus Libertinaesque conceptual expansion into an active atmosphere of contemplative reception aims to evoke my imagination and to boldly engage my mental participation so as to release art from its previous obligatory fidelities to the material status quo. Underlying this anti-monotheistic, anti-ontological aim is a miasmatic idea that questions linear and hierarchical structures and seeks to replace them with atmospheric loose structures, keyed to a penetrable, reciprocal flow of sensual-mental events.

Finally, perhaps this Venus Libertinaesque glimpse into an expanding dimension can no longer be conceived of as solely earthbound. It is hyper, and there is very little that is not of piercing first quality in the radiant gigantism of Venus Libertina's arrangement.

As I easily mistake perspective ghosts of the past as related to local deities, I allowed her enigmas to come to the surface of my mind like invisible writing held up to a flame. This once very sombre, moody *assemblage* of emotions now has an enrapturing harmony achieved without losing the smoky coherence of Michelangelo's achingly beautiful *sfumato* technique, with its use of close figure/ground relationships.

As the sun returned, Venus Libertina next transmitted some soothing smoke from her hole in reference to the burning sensation sufferers of lost love feel, thus acting as a source of mediation between me as Sun Ra and a hostile world of fear and desire.

To drill down on her gossamer delicacy is one of the most important aesthetic powers available to me, for she is mystical in ethnographical function and provides a place of contact with several kinds of spirits that have many common traits (such as the belief in Sun Ra as a single creator).

As such, she has a light touch for those that feel as if the love of their life has fled from them. This certainly is an unintended effect, but it is nevertheless real when I seek to portray the timeless essence of her sex.

Regardless, apparently animated by an amenable concern for pedagogy, I am required—I am summoned as Sun Ra—to fabricate a complicated forensic fairy tale out of her hyperbolic *mélange*, where she manages to bring to light a precise and constructive clarity to my complex and variegated magic, which keeps slipping in and out of idiosyncratic narration in my mind.

So, looking for clues of lost precedent by carving out a new passage through the unidentified, I pull a hyperbolic redpill switch and start finger floating Venus Libertina's hyperbola, a mechanically fluttering butterfly box crammed with exquisite Last God subtleties wherein each element carries multiple allusions. Its profound cosmologic cure contains a symmetrical open curve formed by the intersection of a circular cone with a fat plane at a smaller upward angle from its *Axis: Bold As Love*. Its fruition remains forever unknown to me, but the cone's moist, motorized, iridescent flapping wings lured my fingers into an infinite private tumult of contradictory impulses.

But bold echoes of that slipping-slapping sound still kept flapping and rumbling in my boxed ears, at one point turning into a raging reverberation roughly repetitious and otherworldly. That salacious sound is what is impressive and repetitive and deeply strange about love—what is irrational and animalistic within love, something I terribly love through my capacity for narcissistic eccentricity in all its comedy, inexorability, and ignobility. This non-stop slap-slurp sound is what gives my lovemaking (considered as an artisanal/magical/ritualistic activity) a trembling sense of transcendent wonder that extends linear narration into a geographical study of style spread over space. I call that love.

XVI

Pondering Phallus Connecting Dream Dots (I Can See for Miles) or The Phallus is Dead (Le Roi Est Mort)

Uplifted is how I—as Sun Ra—left Venus Libertina. A lift provided by the haunting quality of our occasionally fierce but gravity-free-feeling coitus that I rendered with the lightest of seductive touches from my dexterous phallus that floated and curled like smoke on scuffed sheets of sallow paper. As I daydream, I remember how our coitus offered me the opulent opportunity for ambiguous gazing into Venus Libertina. Emotionally, this coitus was riveting because we were fierce and fragile, powerful and precisely delicate. Strength and tenderness, like figure and ground, were here tied together, neither one complete without the other.

This coitus opened up in me a sense of covert possibility for the human body that I felt at one and the same time to be both dangerous and indispensable. Dangerous because it dances with the disintegration of death and indispensable because its rendering of my human flesh as phantasmagorical-orgasmic is increasingly desirable in a world where bodies have become overly tracked, controlled, moralized, quantified, and identified in a straightforward, matter-of-fact way. Our coitus suggested to me a sheer, under-the-skin dynamism of ontological entanglement that folds jubilant being into non-being. As such, its somewhat disordered churn affirms the state of gender mutability that is my general standard of excellence for coitus, for Venus Libertina has an alternative, phantasmagorical way to express agitation between my form and the ground. She points my pecker towards perilous turbulences and chancy exhilarations that pass through us in mutual dreams. There is something overcast, heartbroken, and yet eloquent in our entanglements that pulls my conventional perceptions apart, for she holds out the possibility of newly understanding my human physicality by way of shifting boundaries. That suggested to me a creative conflagration between becoming perceptible and becoming imperceptible.

Yes, Venus Libertina is at her quixotic best when she implies forces of affirmative nihilism where new relational affects and intensities are assembled. Other perfectly finished, polished Venuses are admirable but monotonous by comparison, because, for me, they suffer from what I consider a prestige problem. Their accomplished resolution, their dazzling technical virtuosity, and their big breasted fixity tied to overwhelming acclaim make them difficult for me to implicitly enter and join with. By contrast, the virtuoso incompleteness of Venus Libertina opens me up to virtual, imaginative, and mnemonic spaces.

Indeed, her central right toe, on which she pirouettes, harked back to me when Laszlo Toth attacked Michelangelo's *Pietà* sculpture with a hammer, shouting, "I am Jesus Christ, risen from the dead!" He fragmented Mary's elbow, chipped off an eyelid, and severed her nose. An adroit onlooker scooped up the nose and has secretly kept it ever since (what a prized masterpiece).

Likewise, our coitus contains pleasures of euphoric fade-outs. Our coitus contains the power of invisible efficacy, particularly suggestive of the flickering forces of instability and merriment in ancient polytheistic Greece.

It is easy to imagine with her some missing surrounding gala involving the uncasing and drinking of new wine, the planting of seeds, and the evocation of Sun Ra ghosts; for our topsy-turvy coitus has the generative force of deviation and is a muscular and phantasmagorical plunge into where being and non-being reverse into each other, unfolding out and enfolding in their respective outsides. Through ontological upheaval, our coitus offers new regimes of attraction/repulsion to ensue.

Moreover, our coitus has me looking even deeper into vertiginous possibilities and improbabilities of love, and the effort seems to strengthen my powers of imagination, even while phantoms and chaotic disorder appear to surround and plague me. But the more I dove into a retracting central point of our coitus, the more the background collapsed into more-being.

As I began growing closer to her love of glossolalia and its graphical quicksand, our coitus became urgent as a way of countering the debilitating effects of our age of simplification. Her gassy glossolalia beautifully created ambivalent disintegrations and imaginary formations that connect to philosophical issues of immanence and transcendence and the merging of figure-into-environment and environment-into-figure.

Avoiding over-determination, our coitus encouraged an associational gazing that connected me to the metaphorical metaphysics of finesse. Here Venus Libertina and I fail to reify but rather fall into far-fetched farragoes of entangled being and non-being.

At the very moment of that realization, a fallen, web-footed, tummy-bloated victim of the syphilis epidemic signals that the earth-based carnival is over. This re-added delicate signs of voluptuous luxury that recall the eternal laws of sex set arching over time and circumstance. The exaggerated, fantastic, naïve, and passionate aspects of sex now take on a *démodé* (outdated) camp aspect that is outlandish, extravagant, tumultuous, and greedily sensual—what I think of as pagan. This paganism is suggested by Venus Libertina's injudicious, cartoon-like, twisted mouth that projects a self-indulgent sensibility to me: the dark night of the soul tinctured with ironic angst.

But there is also here another anguish: a huge, deeply burnt gully made long ago by candles that illuminated her skin. I first had ignored it so that she may become even more magnificent, excessive, appalling, and moving than before, so she laid down before me another tactic of disappearance: Urs Fischer's male meltdown called *Untitled* (2011) that is sculpted entirely of wax. Though something of a show-biz gimmick, once lit up like a candle, this carved wax male slowly and sentimentally consumes himself in a representational passage of time.

This anemic allegorical *vanité* reminds us that we are all melting into disintegration and that it is advisable to meditate on the transient nature of life.

Shaded with pity and acceptance and a messy obscurity, these mental energies nearly exhausted my fragile insights into the limitations of the fluttering (sexual) body and my strong desire for circulating sex-magical energies into the erotic incoherence of the *demimondaine* world of courtesans supported by wealthy lovers. I needed to concentrate on clarity, distinctness, balanced consolation, castration, sexual temptation, and *jejune* (young) sexual-political positions.

According to Lactantius's *Divine Institutions*, perhaps what I have been saying is not reasonable, but love of the Oracles Cimmerian, Cumaean Sibyl, Delphic, Erythraean, Hellespontine, Phrygian, Samian, and Tiburtine Sibyl is not reasonable. That is the whole phallic point of it, if I read Arthur Avalon correctly.

Venus Libertina may not have anything to be ashamed of, but she plays no part in the resistance to mass spectacle. Her woozy sex-machine body works best as an intimate agent of self-transcendence. Sometimes vast scale works well for the pensive phallus keen on psychosexual semiotics, but this wasn't one of those times.

In a blatant rejection of that thought, Venus Libertina then went into the jungle of the Yucatán and spread pareidolia-like into the Golden Dawn. Venus Libertina is working here in a conceptually operative manner stimulated by an ambience just outside the Euclidean arrangement. Her composition introduces an ambient element that would be fundamental for her artistic investigations of the mirror.

This set in motion a collection of considerations about the *Hall of Mirrors* in Versailles and the contemporary condition of sex and art.

Something prime is shifting: a return of magical immersive thinking into the mainstream at the expense of the pop icon and the simplified logo. I dreamed of Claude Cahun, Leonora Carrington, Leonor Fini, Frida Kahlo, Meret Oppenheim, Kay Sage, Dorothea Tanning, and Remedios Varo's self-representations; of artists that explored space and their female body as a web of social reflections and constructions.

Upon awaking from my nap, Venus Libertina's gold, monochromatic, kaleidoscopic Apennine ground dominated over every other configuration imaginable. Mirrors and their provocation of ontological relationality became a most important feature as they radically charm the eye with their disorienting spatial compositions. As a consequence, this visionary act of yoga—where forms transfigure through a slight visual dissonance—produced an exciting full fervour that needs to be interacted with imaginatively.

I immediately felt a sense of all-over languor in the room of philo-feminists.

They were huddled closely together, bent on divining interpretations. They were in no hurry to move away from the fallen, web-footed, tummy-bloated victim. Rather, they seem immersed in their own mirrored, filigreed realms, and I heard the word "beauty" repeated over and over again.

Clearly, here I am in the presence of an invitation to Apennine algorithmic reverie, so I begin to practice my ithyphallic obsessive-compulsive mirroring rituals that made me so tantalizingly transcendent in the mid-1990s with *~~~~~~~~~~~~~~~~~venus©~Ñ~vibrator, even.*

The mirrored reflections of light that cut into me here make me question whether or not anything actually exists as I thought it did (including myself). Yet, I think that there is also something grounding in her solidly balanced nature that adds to her visual pleasure. She is an A-1 constructed composition.

Given the current world of narcissistic/ubiquitous selfie-snapping, that is something worth reflecting upon during the mirror phase of the moon.

At the 'mirror' phrase, Venus Libertina sprang into a glorious being. She points me at Jacques Lacan's notions of the 'mirror stage' and the *Narcissus* (1597–1599) painting by Italian Baroque master Caravaggio at the Galleria Nazionale d'Arte Antica in Rome. Then at Hans Bellmer's engraving in the book *Histoire de l'œil* by Georges Bataille (1947). For, of course, the physical link between Bataille and Lacan was Sylvia Bataille (born Sylvia Maklès). At twenty, she married Bataille, with whom she had a daughter, the psychoanalyst Laurence Bataille. Starting in 1938, Sylvia was a companion of Lacan, with whom she had a daughter, Judith Miller. Later, Sylvia married Lacan in 1953.

Closely tied to this (and every) theme is Lacan's notion of the *Regard* (Look). This is interesting because for Lacan, the real is that which is outside of symbolic representation.

Lacan 'saw' eroticism as a means of accessing the real through acts of transgression and the breaking of taboos. In his 'view,' erotic experiences have the potential to disrupt the symbolic order and bring the individual into contact with the raw, unmediated aspects of existence. So I was slightly annoyed at the shimmering bodies in loin wraps loitering around, as they were not anchored to anything suggesting land, and the uneven lighting produced distinct misogynous hot spots on what felt like what should have been a Last God unified and undifferentiated field.

Nevertheless, I shall not quibble nor start underlining that there is no one essential essence of woman. Also, I am not actually Sun Ra.

As I am attempting to convey, femininity is multifaceted.

For Lacan, the real is a realm of desire and drive that lies outside of the symbolic order and thus resists gender symbolization, meaning that gender doesn't necessarily always tightly correspond to the sex assigned at birth. Anatomy is not destiny. Indeed, for Lacan, the real is that which disrupts the symbolic order and creates a gap (or lack) in the subject, leading to a constant unfulfilled desire for completion in The Last God.

At that, a new manifestation called Venus Urania made opportune a re-appropriation of my finer senses in a way similar to that experience of seeing Gustave Courbet's *L'Origine du monde* (*The Origin of the World*) (1866) while listening to the prepared piano *Sonatas and Interludes* of John Cage.

Venus Urania is more Apennine affective than discursive—more enigmatic than dogmatic—for her intricate patterning seems to contain many possibilities of interpretation and thus seems magical: full of complex inter-relational transitions and rhythmic overlapping perceptions that interlace and display elasticity through the principle of sameness within difference.

Hers are forms emerging from other forms, both up and down in scale. Possible elegant figures are nested within larger units of Venus Urania, so things become component parts of other things, including bull-apparitions hung with and interposed by a deluxe dainty petticoat made up of smaller animals (stags, horses, and bison) all organized in crescents and cuneiforms in interpenetrating and profuse fashion.

That interpenetration, like good sexual union, has the capacity to evoke intelligence through the management of the unification of three-dimensional form with stroking caresses.

Here I am calling up image-formations from the depths of my mind—and this experience cannot but remind me that the primary feature that distinguishes aesthetic consciousness is imagination and that imagination entails visioning and symbolizing—areas of practice useful in heightening perception and intuition. Indecision, ambiguity, and conflict become dynamic and useful values here because apparent secrets and angelic visual pleasures are concealed in her florid ground—apparent "flaws" like the all-over ambivalence of the superficial, illusory groundlessness—become affirmative values.

I am not talking about that quality called "beauty," but of that quality that can invest the nonsensical with dignity and indelibleness.

This is the interfering shift I detected in what I think of as the responsibility of looking at Venus Urania—a shift towards (and into) the sparkle of gilded visual noise.

And if not responsibility, then mirth; and if not mirth, then joviality; and if not joviality, then hospitality.

So a shift occurred in me suggestive of efforts made towards an art of anti-pop/no-logo emancipatory labour—indicative of social relationships outside of passive pop consumption. Here I can take back my head.

I felt her coasting into joviality, so we held hands and turned around each other, like the hands of a clock do. On the bed we couple and stretch out and begin to roll over and over, moving our legs as though we were walking on The Last God grindstone, thereby confronting those that once embraced their humanity but who now have fallen into a conformity consensus trance. So we move closer around each other, touching and parting, reaching out and coming together, going absolutely nowhere but around.

At once funny, despairingly clever, and ludicrous, this made for a kind of abstract drama that gave our crotch connection a pungent experience of probability, mystery, and obscurity. I sensed the internal conflict of a sassy sexuality that meant something greater than its parts.

Caught in the cognitive interactions of this florid web, I plop on and play Éliane Radigue's *Œuvres Électroniques* and drift off into Queen Bee dreamland, where Venus Urania flashes horizon-based three-dimensional space around the *trompe l'oeil* Queen Bee—an innovative strategy for the active ruining of her representation.

Here, Venus Urania's roughly touched surfaces are certainly more viscous than mine. She has a dripping/drooling quality that my lighter touch avoids. As her juices get gushing, Venus Urania gestures towards The Last God landscape in a sluggish way that is never far, in my mind, from the sputtering of greasy machines. I get high and hover and float.

From that elevated view, in general, Venus Urania is impressive, presenting as a large-scale visual feast of Last God ambivalence, which fosters an instability—or reversibility—in the closed divide between us as a rather odd couple.

I must look between us—rather than at us—for when paired, we always struggle against the ground of accepted artistic systems, such as those of the writers Henry Miller, Samuel Beckett, Jean Genet, Jack Kerouac, and Allen Ginsberg. Proving again that Last God sex is slippery in the sense that it inscribes adjustments, Venus Urania seems to thrive on the lightness of my poetic touch. That's how I read her: with my fingertips moving along her thighs, both feathery and whiplashed.

So Venus Urania brings forth a light-touch sparkling appeal that unloads like a fluttering figure of change or mutability. Something tacking between the post-human and Mother Nature. So when I slip inside her again, her soft strokes stick to my eyes, and this sensation shift renders me a productive ambivalence that plays between the human hand and the wide world of The Last God, projecting a loose delicacy and strange grace. In particular, Queen Bee seems motivated to pursue a ruining of her royal representation in that she finds representation to be contributive to the subordination of women to men. In that respect, my dealing with Queen Bee dreamland is less than satisfactory. However, in that I am a philosophically inclined contemporary artist interested in liberation politics, this reconfiguration of the Queen Bee immediately and ferociously attracts me. Indeed, I began to love Queen Bee and Venus Pink Dots again, voraciously and carefully, and found my love of maximal scholarly merit.

There is no question that Venus Pink Dots is highly informative and that my heart is in the right place when desiring her and Queen Bee. Erect phallic framing is intended to eliminate what is deemed by some unessential—to direct attention to what is important and to give it special meaning and force. But a new Venus Hemispheric has arrived. She is a surrounding space who ruins the shape of the phallus within an onslaught of hemispheric psychic projections where her sex, her art, and her death meet in an aesthetic discharge.

Venus Hemispheric operates as my inner grid that eats up the inherently excessive details of identity that form the basis of my phallic conscious and unconscious apprehension of reality. She gives me insight into a reality that people with different experiences are effectively blind to or unmoved by. What is important is Venus Hemispheric's total scale—felt in rapport with the panoply of visual velocity, which functions so as to penetrate, exceed, and ruin my representations of sexual difference—is filling my field of view with an erotic alchemy and thereby over-flooding sexual difference with simultaneity. This was accompanied by the sweet, metallic, abstract sounds of Einstürzende Neubauten.

Through her I am reminded of a combination of tenderness and strength that is both pixie-playful and super-sexy self-confident.

She daintily prances like a spring nymph in front of the gorgeously soaring Brancusi sculptures at the Pompidou's Atelier Brancusi—which brings to my mind the rich tradition of Victorian fairy painting where frisky fairy sprites dance circuitously about an omphalos. (An omphalos is a religious stone artefact. In Ancient Greek, the word ὀμφᾰλός (omphalós) means "navel." It is the central spot of the symbolic immersive circle, the pivotal, still, capacity point within a sacred circle where the outside world is dominated and indeed defined by the omphalos' psychological protection. The conceiving mentality behind the omphalos was that it marked the fixed point of the earth about which the spherical-spiritual heavens whirled. Thus, it represented a central place that remained steady and enduring while all else moved about it.)

The omphalos' quintessence may have been only a scant central fire within a circular placement of stones on the ground, but some say it evolved into the maypole that some read through phallic symbolism, for example, John Cleland in his novel *Fanny Hill*.

But the sex-spirituality here is to be found in the soft floating colour clouds that hover ever so delicately before my eyes. Sustained looking offered divination opportunities so that subtle sensual forms emerged, giving Venus Hemispheric an even greater phantasmagorical element.

Her sex magic is an excess of signifiers in perpetual displacement and disequilibrium—the opaque place where discourses of sexual difference refuse to adhere to the framed centering tropes indispensable to prototypical representations as seen through the intentional window. Like musical notes, her sex magic is vibrating, oscillating, and interpenetrating to the extent that she dissolves the objective world around her into a transmitter of pleasurable tension when read as bounded and polymorphous. Her taciturn taste for churning concreteness into vast celestial space suggests ways of experiencing life outside of the normal garrulous explanations.

A taste close to speculative realism's anti-anthropomorphic transcendental materialism.

I changed the soundtrack by playing Dopplereffekt's *Gesamtkunstwerk* LP while looking at Venus Hemispheric and me in the mirror. She squatted over me, reading the *Kama Sutra*. At long last, she lowered herself onto my pulsating cock—very slowly—inch by inch by inch. Space became geometrically isotropic, hip, and rectilinear for an instant.

Clearly, this centering reduction of our wobbly love scene into a scene bounded by a single point of view was achieved by her negating my peripheral visual attention. Only by establishing the fiction of my partial absence—and lack of extensive simultaneous glances at Venus Hemispheric—can such a focused enthrallment be secured, for I ain't no dope.

Repeating the name of Joe DiMaggio over and over, I held my orgasm at bay while remaining vulnerable to castration. I decided that I was not opposed to the ruin of my phallic representation in the interests of achieving some anti-objectiveness concerning my self-voyeurism.

Correspondingly, Venus Hemispheric—enjoying me through her mobile and temporal gaze—became anti-reified, anti-fixated, anti-inert, and, I might even say, anti-deadened, in my eyes.

A glow of gender transcendence even emitted from her scarlet anima-animus that signalled to me that wholeness and spiritual completion were in the air.

That exotic air took on a sense of subtle understatement, mixed with a powerful presentational finesse that made me more alert, more interested, or more aware of the ongoing Last God cross-currents.

So, the ruin of my erect dick's phallocentric representational experience here necessitated no centering tropes, but rather an embracing of an ambient and simultaneous impulse that returns centred perspective to its rightful place—as a contingent (and only instrumental) convention.

This mentality is admirable, of course, for its efficacy of anti-intellectual acumen and oppressive non-loquaciousness, while I regret its lack of quixotic subtlety and style—such as with Marcel Proust, who, all his life, distinguished public events from private meanings.

In our lovemaking, Venus Hemispheric constructs an all-embracing nomos built on deeply felt private experiences encountered within social-political-intellectual expectations of men and women that circulate like a virus in the phallocentric mind of The Last God. This virus serves to legitimize (or justify) certain visual, linguistic, social, and political practices that developed around demands for intelligibility, rigidity, and hegemony. But this is really a question of form rather than content, as my supercilious phallus hung out and the question of the softness of my mattress and my phallus became urgent. They both took on a sardonic *commedia dell'arte* aspect that spoke to me of withdrawal—but my phallus was well worth languishing over. Atrocious eyes of algorithmic perception seem to have been upon it. It seems to be suffering from the hyped 'self' typical of the art world—and I'm not sure what all the exposure is doing to its memories when they are handed over to some social media corporation that smothers it in fake news and puff pieces.

Even as deviating from the regularities of hyper-visibility might provide my phallus new sources for artistic production and social self-possession, the hemispheric soft approach to it supplants common paradigmatic norms of visual representation with new ones built off the old. And it was cold. But Venus Hemispheric and my phallus' softness still disrupt the typical psychoanalytic schemas within the boundaries of the bed. For through its early and spectacular success, my phallus' double-edged sword of celebrity engenders an encumbrance when it is once removed and taken home by an aficionado. With that removal, my phallus, when interlaced within a splay of flowers and graphic scrolls, suddenly had a new and vast audience, overnight touching everything from streetwear to public benches to city walls to entire building façades to entire transit stations.

Undoubtedly, because my phallus is still a sumptuously beguiling work-in-progress, this distribution without my permission gives some the wrong impression that its obscurantist mystification is a widespread cultural movement. For my floating castrated phallus' churned-line design apparently hit a nerve: expressing a growing reaction for and against the new social divisions brought about by the power of The Last God lifting up out of obscurity the intractable powers of the phrase "*the future is female*"—a thematic projection that now reads like a message-in-a-bottle lobbed into the future of dime bags of pot, hookahs, candlelit rooms, bare floors and mattresses, curling incense smoke, Eastern ornamental fabric curtains, and jamming guitars that combine feminism, pacifism, racial idealism, hedonism, and economic optimism. There my castrated floating phallus is found on floors and then picked up in shapes of furniture and on into doors and door frames until it reaches the structural arches, which support ceilings and lighting fixtures. As a result, when properly attached to my loins, it always seems to be swaying, bending, floating, arching, curling, throbbing, dripping, melting, aching, and writhing. Perhaps that's why my phallus' uplifting tubular shapes seem to me to be striving to express the ersatz reveries of quixotic females with their high whimsical lines of thought—their fluid shapes amalgamating one into another, and the ornamental detailing on their hair and bodies that speaks of Buddhism, mysticism, tarot cards, meditation, vegetarianism, the *I Ching*, the *Bhagavad Gita*, and *The Golden Bough*.

Which is weird, as, for me, my hovering phallus is an inimitable sumptuous display synonymous with the champagne gaiety and decadence experienced during periods when technological and aesthetic innovation meet in an exotic eclecticism.

About my perched phallus, one thing is absolutely clear: when eyeing it as if through the opposite wrong end of the *Ornament and Crime* telescope that rejects its fabulous excessiveness in favour of unadorned geometry, it reinforces complex reactions against the simple American mindset that in his post-Paris memoir Henry Miller has called The Air-Conditioned Nightmare. For once my phallus churned out everything I would live on as a bevy of bad behemoths. But then a new sun came up that set it free like a porno star floating off the screen and into the room. So lovers of my phallus take a hemispheric soft approach to my bed. For not doing so is only a bad habit, like chain-smoking Camels.

Phallic linear perspective, it must be remembered, is only a convention—a cultural attribute comprehensible only for a specific sense of space or perception of the world—and is definitely not an absolute perceptual truth. In this respect, by playing hanky-panky with it, Venus Hemispheric explains that we are the exhausted descendants of the engendering of linear perspective (the so-called rules that determine the relative size of objects on a flat plane) and that the magic of my perspective phallus is never really gone but merely shared in a bifurcation that has occurred between the capture technology of the 20th century and the far more elastic and participatory ubiquitous computing of Last God technology.

I must say that these days, this Last God bifurcation rules me not—for obscure penal codes cannot be easily discerned concerning my jubilant penis.

Such a phantasmagorical obscurity is desirable in a society that has become increasingly data-mined, data-mapped, quantified, and branded. So the problem with my phallus is not really its problem; it's my problem of becoming perceptible in a time when visibility has proven detrimental.

The general extravert trend of my phallus has been turned on its head with identity pirating performed in the interests of reactionary political isolationism. The assertive, presentational tendency of my phallus has spilled over the lip of the entertainment wasteland into targeted data monitoring surveillance. That is what has suggested to me to take a somewhat different perspective on contemporary self-portraiture here.

Nietzsche wrote that the bright clarity of an image does not suffice because that lucidity conceals something else. Taking that advice, my phallus, rather than exposing itself to as many eyeballs as possible, will start obscuring its psycho-graphical identity out of concern with how data is collected and stored by user-generated content platforms and transferred to third and fourth parties. For it has concluded that TLG as social media has had a profoundly negative effect on the world of young love and any cool sense of agency within it.

So my phallus has chosen to evade the selfie-net by muffling and camouflaging its self-portraiture, which may be why society is intoxicated by my love-hate masquerade.

By contrast, much of my phallus seems to simply expect people to look at its unconventional poses when in action so they can compare themselves to it so as to better self-distinguish and display themselves. But I find it is now impossible to accept such a prospect without apprehension.

So one of the big benefits of my phallus is that it offers the opportunity to reconsider the hopes and failures of radical self-exposure. Much of it is a marker of my level of estrangement, and it can be as hauntingly pathetic as the graveyard that Myspace became with its stogy ceremonial portraits, coffin plaques, gilded crowns, sceptres, effigies, gravestones, and (the best part) an account of a phallic autopsy that is, ultimately, comedic (agreed, comedy is rather subjective). Seeing there the all-powerful, amoral phallic superman at the mercy of unsophisticated (hack) women doctors and the fleeting cosmic forces of disease and death far beyond its comprehension is darkly funny to me, as the dissected dick swerves between golden pomp and farcical absurdity (with the absurd emphasis slightly more geared to the latter, in my eyes). Ultimately though, the enjoyment to be had with the dissected dick depends on whether you inject satirical intent where it is not supposed to exist. You have to allow yourself to enjoy the cheap thrill of mocking the gauche excess of chopping up the phallus. But there is little doubt that the rather kinky surgical tools needed do occasionally capsize the glorious narrative spun there into one about invisible (and dirty) desires and forces circulating just below the surface of things. Everything else fairly funny follows from this ignobility. Everything from the Constantine Room to the Morocco Room to the infamous Surrealist phallocracy.

I imagine this dissected dick scenario does not appeal to the fantasist tastes of stumpy-legged blood-and-soil reactionaries and far-right bearded men with their pretentiously fervent imaginations dedicated to a Cheetos orange clown king without clothes and the destruction of secularism and liberalism in the face of digital globalization. Their devotional longings, an impulse that verges on the nauseatingly nostalgic, are not only politically dangerous (as they fuel foolish fantasies of the far right's power of grand appearance), but also embarrassing. For surely when chopped up, the grand appearance of the orange clown king's phallus becomes a funny abstraction of an enunciation that made no effort to dispel its transcendental appearance.

So my mental/moral position on the king's phallus is to abstain from arriving at an *a priori* preemptive decision about its privilege so that entertaining black humour can be discovered veining its way through its *de rigueur* farcical mendacity. His flayed forensic foreskin alone seems faintly funny in the face of death's inexorability.

So what might be missing from this interpretative path to my own pensive phallus is some re-considering in terms of the multitude where the technologies of encryption and veiled visibility prevail against the laconic shape of singular ontology.

But I digress.

XVII

Pensive Penis within Lavish Perceptual Circuitry

Entering her inch by inch, I am placed, fancy-free, inside the perceptual circuitry of a particularly lavish and aesthetically and informationally intense proprioceptive feedback loop. That is the randomizing show, but be sure to take the elevator to the fourth floor to discover the terrace and gallery, which houses Venus Urania's private art collection. It includes Gerhard Richter's painting *Skull* (1983), a painting that turns the world upside down into a slapstick spectacle of pompous posturing and neurotic defensiveness. The loneliness of this masterful fabrication speaks to the fact that we are all but lone schematic specks of soon-to-be discarded material cast from within the vast hereditary field.

It is hung between one of Sigmar Polke's outstanding 1989 *Cloud Paintings* and Nam June Paik's *V Rodin* (*Le Penseur*) (1976-1978), which uses a cast of Auguste Rodin's sculpture *The Thinker* (1904). A naked thinking man is studying himself in a video monitor via closed-circuit television.

On that terrace, I can see for miles.

Navigating inside Venus Hemispheric is a lavish and aesthetically-informationally intense experience for my sex organ. She is directly altering my consciousness by engaging me in a ritualistic-like activity involving excess, thus underscoring the fiction behind the assumed mechanistic perspective when seen as empirically true and universally valid instead of as conventional and as a contingent compliance.

For my 360°, Venus Hemispheric places me in the position of indeterminate unknowing—indeed, in the position of the impossibility of knowing what to do in any one sexual position or intuitive moment. My cock ceases to be definitive and becomes part of an inter-relational question, which disables reactionary emphasis on narrow-minded male gender representation now that it has been accorded the weight of fascist political production.

In this condition of arduous inter-relational questioning, what is clarified in terms of sex with Venus Hemispheric is the human idiosyncratic ability to imaginatively convert absence into presence—which may be impossible in terms of the established structure of Western thought. This is precisely why the Venus Hemispheric immersive sex experience can be placed in a position parallel to fullness and impossible vastness—thus stimulating my desire, which biochemically affects the state of my body and mind. With this impossible desire for Venus Hemispheric, the amount of endorphins unconsciously released into my bio-system increases—setting into motion a prying-loose of excess.

The sweet, great secret of this excessive nomadic nomos is that I no longer have anything to hide. No one can grasp me, and I cannot grasp, nor do I wish to.

Loving Venus Hemispheric has made this clear. I am no longer in the space of the Quattrocento world. I have become an observer of allocentric mirror worlds nowhere near that horizon line and vanishing point of past pictorial ideals—but just the opposite—of spherical, all-over, 360° perspectives without end.

I don't want to piss on your parade here, but remember what it felt like when someone you really loved left you. If you're like me, it made your ego smaller while it made the world around you much, much bigger.

For a brief moment, Venus Hemispheric's body consisted of transparent glass in which a rubber membrane vibrated to the rhythm of a human heartbeat, thrusting red dust up and down in a cone of light around me. The jumping dust reminded me of repeated male ejaculations when paired with found stones.

As a pretext for reveries, Venus Hemispheric displays here a mordantly witty obsession with the language of self-confident humour. As we love, a peripatetic mind is clearly sensed behind each of her pelvic thrusts. Each has a diverse sensing of longing connected to an acute awareness of ideas and styles. I would dare say that Venus Hemispheric is attempting to give me a lesson in tactile free verse. One that tests the limits of her form and stretches the bounds of meaning by recasting her as a once-*fêted* glamorous queen of the libertine bohemian art world who has been sliding towards obscurity down the whimsical auspices of art posterity. But Venus Hemispheric looks confident, daring even. Sure enough of herself to resist such a subservient position.

Although her eccentric manner of presenting herself has often overshadowed her quixotic, vivacious, and flamboyant voice of anthropomorphism, a creative fire is still burning in my loins. Her wild-haired uncertain space has me riding a brown and white horse that seems an obvious symbol of free sexuality. But a modest, charming—almost austere—Venus Hemispheric is frequently enchanting at the spectacular heights of her swirling hot feminine sex when stirred with a dowsing rod (*virgula divina* or *baculus divinatorius*). This witching rod twitches her sex with something not so *terra firma* as a horse, but rather something that contains many florid possibilities of interpretation—and thus seems magical, as magic doesn't conform to our canons of causality. So with each lunge onto me, Venus Hemispheric delivers strange delight by tying together moves of insouciant informality with light irony. Her body moves are flamboyant and commendable with their perpetual motorized flights of fancy.

I only needed to supply my own transitions between her diverse pelvic rhythms, which seemed to be following the opening John Bonham drum passage of Led Zeppelin's rendition of *When the Levee Breaks*. Definitely, I had only to follow this rhythm and to fabricate for her a forensic account of our ongoing *mélange* as she kept slipping me into an idiosyncratic but lightly poetic sensibility. Indecision, ambiguity, and conflict become dynamic and useful values here in suggesting secret pleasures.

To be sure, blissfully making love to the rhythm of Venus Hemispheric provided me a sense of being suspended in a compound of joy and insight, as I was brought to a certain sense of circular pliability. In my immersive view, Venus Hemispheric's rhythmic lyricism is most appealing, as it creates exhilarating unconventional sex out of her connected, all-encompassing, sign-field.

Whereas I took a cool planetary perspective, Venus Hemispheric turned inward to the complexity of her sexual organs that she had designed to be a bacchante cow shed for cultural erudition and the voluptuous obsessiveness of a satirist. Particularly impressive is that her libertine genitalia seem aporetic

—both competently rendered and slightly impossible.

Nevertheless, her solidly built, oven-like vagina was emitting an extraordinary heat that could bake bread. The insufferable pretentiousness of her symmetrically spiralling pubic hair I read as salacious smoke, or, with a bit of wit, as the wig of a king.

Venus's many faces were hiding in and emerging out of this busy bush that had the power to encourage overcoming the tyranny of paradigms in which I had placed my prick and to re-contextualize it within the context of the advent of the electronic explosion in which LG knowledge has shifted away from certitude and transformed itself into garbage-in/garbage-out infotainment. Yes, The Last God serves here as yet another, if not the last, nonlinear blow to the Enlightenment essentialism of the past. This blow, this submersion, this escape from the aggregate ego seems to me to be the common goal of this bushy patch for its merciless curly intensity delivers a lacunae of heated impact that stands in stark contrast to her utopian Neoclassical veins (though Venus Hemispheric's taste is a bit more degenerate, flamboyant and ornamental).

For me, her smoking sexuality is brilliantly structured by a virtuoso sense of visual and narrative rhythm. When she opens her sex, she creates a monumental make-believe place where lust (rendered with machinelike precision) and caprice meet Cartesian codification. Subsequently, her cavern of heat makes for an interesting sensation that mixes warm twists of whimsy with an almost perverse level of sexual overindulgence. As such, it is difficult to tell if she is biliously lampooning me with her tandoor or tauntingly glorifying me, since bacchantes are usually depicted as hot and dishevelled. This one, this time, seems to be in the heated process of whistling out of her ass a delightful tune on my phallic flute. Around that, a bit of saucy speculation has sprung up—but there isn't a scintilla of evidence to support it.

This I can tell you.

Such is the curious case of Venus Hemispheric as a bemusing curio of warmth.

If what I have said here about her smouldering sex sounds metaphoric, it is metaphoric only insofar as it is rhythmic memory, rhythmic concentration, and rhythmic stratagem working together in making up an internal model of what happens when we copulate. But even deeply kissing her can be felt as a meaningful symbolic language laden with conjuration for those who understand her ocular tongue.

Venus Hemispheric then spins me round and round as we make it, de-framing sensual operations into a velvet field of view where horizon dissolution is desirable. I now have an Icarian bird's-eye view of us blissfully making love. As I float and merge, that elevated meta view enlivens peripheral awareness and, as such, intensifies my thalamic input to the cortex by making my active thalamic neurons in that region fire more rapidly than usual.

That is why I remain convinced that experimental sex in art (literature, film, music, performance, visual work, and so on) has a cognitive function that is significant. In this connective condition, notions of singular, discrete, logocentric consciousness are incoherent. That is why this Icarian kind of sexual position makes for the best sex that can be experienced (in my opinion).

What Icarian sexual-aesthetic immersion does is replace my severed cock back into the ritual position by dragging it down into the felt 360° omni-perspective of the enthusiastic and participatory. It is through just such erotic procedures (whether corporeal or conceptual) that Icarian cognition excels.

Venus Hemispheric's Icarian vulva—just as stimulated by the immersive spherical perspective as I am—opens up a new indigo territory of signification and possibility for the orgasmic creation of de-territorialized feelings. The Icarian position improves our sex by allowing us to see more clearly the underlying assumptions of excess inherent in this outlook and by facing up to the radical implications of those assumptions.

I became tempted here with the first assumption: that of a semi-dream world of eccentric self-created myth. Much theoretical-imaginary ripe fruit can be plucked from fucking, godlike.

Also from pansexual dreams that squeeze the juice out of self-love by eliminating the binary (left-right) hand. As such, this assumption verges on the exuberantly preposterous. It is perfect for sexy *schadenfreude* lovers ravished by weariness and woe.

Turning the Icarian corner, I discovered myself caught in *flagrante delicto*. I approached for a better look, which creates a jolt of self-conscious connection-disconnection. That look lifts my sex into rolling with Venus

Hemispheric in oily-looking ink and pink champagne, wet fever dreams, powerlessness, asexuality, surprise, luxury, loss of self-control, autonomy, intoxication, ejaculation, and internal strife. My slow-rolling approach to Venus Hemispheric unsettles and heightens her and makes her more lively to the intricate strangeness of my animal nature as inspired by the rural passage from the Czechoslovakia scene in Jean Genet's great 1949 book *The Thief's Journal*, a passage that fruitfully pointed Venus Hemispheric's cultural attention down an intellectual-artistic path of social alchemy and automated pleasure.

Such an intransigent poetic robotic obliqueness is supposedly just what post-humans and Last God androids have been waiting for. As if The Last God—after hoovering up intellectual property off the internet like a thief in the night—could magically make me young by roaming the corridors of my cultural mind. By scrutinizing the halls and rooms of my mind-theatre, purge it of past and future tragedies and punishments that, nevertheless, await me and my friends and lovers. After having painted—with inimitable grace and in a luxury of vivid colours—a false idealized picture of well-being, domestic splendour, intellectual mastery, rational beauty, and moral goodness framed in endless wealth—The Last God actually has many crossing into the heavy clouds of misinformation and mad misfortune.

Another of those Last God assumptions is that Venus Hemispheric is Rococo: the belief that all aspects of a comprehensive scheme—from its landscape setting and the body itself to the interior decorations, right down to the tiny utensils—should be orchestrated as a seamless and homogeneous whole under the direction of one overriding design. The bobby socks idea is that a body, like Venus Hemispheric's, is cupped within a complete integration: a constructed space from the broadest view on down to the smallest details (each reinforcing the other), what is referred to as the previously mentioned *gesamtkunstwerkkonzept*, as adapted from Wagnerian operatic theory. The philosophical understanding of the canon of the *gesamtkunstwerk* is the proclivity towards a Last God integration of all related elements into a single aesthetic statement, resulting in a self-contained immersive world of total design.

This type of total sexual intercourse with Venus Hemispheric suggests a sense of immense (but always incomplete) excess commensurable with the aoristic grotto. But the sound of the grotto waterfall rendered subliminal our voices in a thick, mixed din of sound by a space I would describe as acoustically freakish.

But, you may be interested to know that Venus Hemispheric was born replete with grottoes and frescoed scenes from Ovid's *Metamorphoses*. At a young age, Hemispheric received a copy of Wagner's text *Opera and Drama* from one of her tutors and soon became captivated by all of the composer's published theories, including *Das Kunstwerk der Zukunft* (*The Art of the Future*)—in which Wagner theorized the *gesamtkunstwerk*.

So you understand, in the Venus Hemispheric grotto, I am never presented with concluded consequences. There are always some further moves and qualifications to be made, and some new perspectives from which a sexual idea (or percept) may be performed and observed. In this sense, Venus Hemispheric constitutes a sexual grotto without fixed meaning. I see no form of understanding her as unchanging.

Indeed, Venus Hemispheric's machine-dream grotto of sexual excess is how she challenges my distinctive ontological beliefs about the limits of myself. And indeed, what is more fluidly immersive than dreaming in that a dreamer can rapidly float from intense participation in one scenario to another instantaneously. In dreams, people and things appear out of nowhere, and they shift appearance and proportions with little attention to the concrete laws of conservation.

As Carl Jung and T-Bone Walker (aka Aaron Thibeaux Walker) have suggested, sexual features of extemporaneous creation in dreams may be exactly how we encounter our unconscious desires in the blues.

In order to love again, Venus Hemispheric surrounds herself and her sinking piano in a grotto of powdery yellow satin with matching yellow valences of the same material, which she refers to as The Grail. In this very large grotto, everything is yellow satin, yellow silk tulle, and white lace. The yellow satin curtains are decorated with lovely faux roses, and the frames of the mirrors and pictures are puffed out with tied-back pink satin bows (with even a rosette of satin in the centre of the ceiling)—clearly an effort for a unified spatial feeling.

In such a sexual grotto, self-reprogrammable thought takes over the space displayed around Venus Hemispheric as her meta-programmed ego expands to fill the vastness of her cosmic grotto-vulva. So conceived, Venus Hemispheric ceases to think in terms of substance and, by contrast, starts thinking as a continuously changing process of events in search of evermore sexual adventure.

That is to say, Venus Hemispheric thinks of herself as a process of becoming in all directions as the cheeky and flamboyant Venus Grotto, equipped with artificial arc lighting, an ersatz rainbow, a wave machine, and central heating.

It was nice that Venus Grotto allows me an immersive view of her where the stage and auditorium are blended into one total theatre. Compared to the Blue Grotto at Capri, I found her highly enjoyable, as she is furnished lavishly with fake stalactites that give me the impression that I entered an ancient sacred space.

Garlands of roses are strung throughout her high cupola expanse, which extends deeply inwards. Her mouth contains a cascade of kisses, and her ample armpit a fully functional artificial moon illuminated by electric lights coloured to suit my mood.

Five distinctive lighting effects play by automated means.

When she comes, there is a brief appearance of a spectral rainbow.

It was interesting when Venus Hemispheric, for a time, covered me with a heavy violet velvet material with a hole cut in it. Through it, she was working on my phallus while seated on a violet armchair, wearing a winged phallic charm and a violet velvet hat. I guess that she understood that such a coo-coo cocooning echoes my penchant for ithyphallic self-reprograming and bringing a non-existent plenteous world into being.

In the middle of her sex grotto, an embellished fountain emits a violet-coloured water jet, freezing me in the frozen position of a golden statue of Flora, the Roman goddess of flowers and spring. I wear on my head a violet *melee* of neo-rococo ostentation and mirrors, with the glitter of gold prevalent throughout.

From the top of the violet water jet, I take an allocentric mirror worldview of her. I experience this most keenly when sliding up into Venus Hemispheric.

Once there, I can see and feel all of her grotto (including myself in her) while experiencing an intergalactic fluidness of movement concerning yaw, pitch, roll, pan, zoom, and swivel.

This allocentric sexual connection owes a large part of its charged enchantment to the sublime natural beauty of her breasts when seen as a lavender mountain setting. By contrast, her crotch had an admirable primness, like the French gardens at Château de Villandry.

My experience of Venus Hemispheric's grotto was at first one of disorientation and then of reorientation, as I passed into a supra-perspective connected to joyful feelings of floating within an expanded hyper-space of colossal dimensions. Experiencing Venus Hemispheric's grotto-vulva as hyper-vertiginous heights—and deep abysses and vast widths—allowed my repeated smooth penetrations to transgress her apparent solid confines. This entailed an experiential feeling of beatific disembodiment when it was my turn to come.

This violet coming was suggestive of aggregates of multi-layered occurrences that are non-homogeneous, fragmented, and incomplete—while simultaneously being continuous, hermetic, and flowing.

The first entity that I notice—when pulling in and out of the Venus Hemispheric grotto—is a diminutive lagoon in her yoni, replete with painted water nymphs, dryads, and flying harpies. It appears to be fed with juice teased out by my pattering cascade. I felt like being surrounded by seedy orchids, smothered in their dense perfume.

As I mentioned, they could, through a purposeful posturing in nonchalance, change the love lights colours during this pattering to the cerulean of Capri. An homage to the Goddess of Love and *The Importance of Being Earnest*, a satire on the manners of Victorian high society that revolves around two dandies in love with Gwendolen and Cecily, each of whom in turn is determined to marry an elusive man named Ernest.

Like Beau Brummell, who was turned into a literary character by writers Jules Barbey d'Aurévilly, Honoré de Balzac, and Charles Baudelaire, I continue to pull at myself smoothly and effortlessly. Like the smoke that curled from the opium-tipped cigarettes Oscar Wilde adored with champagne, I recede back into my privacy by ascending into a vast oneness. Gradually her grotto organization simplified and reduced and it is now a place of pilgrimage for hip romantics who leave it covered in lipstick kisses.

Unknown to me, ternary rhythms and colour combinations also covered my quasi-flesh in a soft, hot, vigorous attractiveness. My goodness gracious, a Carol Rama-inspired display opened next, as if to express the joyful-into-tragic dimension of the human condition. Carolee Schneemann touched and kissed me all over, according to some.

While refusing to move completely beyond gesture into actual readability, entering and exiting Venus Hemispheric's grotto-vulva was made by way of a prolonged, serpentine, stalactite-filled corridor that took me deep into a dolmen-like shaft that opened just as my phallus approached with a knock on the gate. A loss of clarity that supported one of Wilde's silvered *bon mots*—that nothing succeeds like excess—and the retreat from submersion, and the writhing attempt at escaping a perpetual ooze, marks my contemplative and orgasmic powers here.

With an imperturbable, passive-classical past, and by gliding in and out of her subterranean lagoon on an enchanting, flamboyant cockle-boat, I place my cock in the midst of her perfumed ambience and surround it entirely with her loins on its every side. It now has immediacy.

Its seemingly unpremeditated gestures of the Bacchanalia suggest the eternal presence of the now, because Venus Hemispheric neither accepts the Greek classics as a perfunctory accumulation of events—succeeding one another in time—nor as a reservoir of fixed forms. Rather, in her lush lap lagoon—which she can ruffle as if by an artificial wave machine—Hemispheric keeps two swans swimming—symbols of her rhythmic bliss with my two hairy balls and her own algorithm immortality. With such a sloppy style of vacuous vicissitudes, my cock followed the ripples of her orgasm (suggestive of foamy loop-de-loop sea scum) on her enchanting cockle-boat—which was suddenly rowed by Orpheus and a serene female hand belonging to one of Shakespeare's sibyls.

There is a marvellous, sprightly, loose, intuitive feel about Venus Hemispheric here that manages to merge mythic sallow colours and classical intellectualism with a Dionysian sensual immoderation verging on something like twinges of existential doubt.

A statistical patterned Last God recognition of my mind-neural network receives the upshot of this transmitted dematerialized hand, where input sequences transition into output sequences. This suggests a willful regression into the infantile so as to move me closer to sensual instinctiveness.

Inspired in part by the midsummer Italian holiday of Ferragosto (rooted in an ancient Roman fertility festival), this showed me that space combined with memory defines place.

My swarming phallus (that bawdy baboons might just as well have produced) projects overripe historical confidence by allowing colour to become dissociated from the lines of bodily sensation (in disarray). I find my cool cock consists of disparate found materials like richly psychic plugs, curved cardboard boxes, scraps of metal knickknacks, and artificial flowers so as to create unexpectedly affective territories where connections are made to be undone.

Probing the gap between sign and signified, it shows me a delightful feat of free association thrown up against a state of panic. Thus Venus Hemispheric evokes for it a kind of sentimental longing for other places and other times through a compost heap of past matter—now ready to sprout new forms by letting gravity have its way with the dripping drool that is the *sine qua non* of old age and festive excess itself. This understanding extends to all things.

XVIII

The Marvellous Mishmash of Madame Monkey Fingers

With me in the role of a silly cellular automatist, Venus Hemispheric took the role of Madame Monkey Fingers, who is sometimes simply called Lulu. Like the cultural wasteland of AI slop that busts my balls, this Lulu acts upon me by extolling enchanting operational possibilities that are not always realizable in the rational world. As such, she spoke to me of the deconstructive pleasures of de-connectivity and disembodiment within my neural network and the deprivation of normal cognitive body image that occurs when she peels off her monkey-self. For what disappears in her monkey-self is not her material monkey body, but only a nonconformist muddy notion of it. This happens in reverse as well, so I discovered a new toggling vantage point at which coherent forms of Madame Monkey Fingers may vaporize and may congeal.

Last God have mercy on us mud.

What is curious in that toggling vantage point moment of getting her monkey *trompe l'oeil* pictorial gestalt together is that it also achieves a reduction of her vast self into a dimensional image through juxtaposing two incompatible modes of perceptual interpretation.

A big pleasure of Madame Monkey Fingers lies in the phenomenological perspectives entertained on a long walk within the multiplicity of kinetic viewpoints I have on her. Sure, the initial *le voilà* moment is the way I first discovered Lulu when I entered Bibliothèque Forney in the Hôtel de Sens on rue du Figuier. There she was: hanging out in front of me, already as if snapped into place.

But there is a lot that just won't lie still and be art with her. For the most part, entangled meshes of imbroglio funk provide vague itches of art that seem embedded in my pubic hair. What is interesting is that this lavish itch allows me a feeling of encountering sacredly wild cryptic drives typical of a Doton magical amulet from Togo.

False equivalency anthropomorphic/zoomorphic body parts and elongated poles abound that intellectually skate over an array of widely divergent intentions, functions, and different belief systems. It would be excessive and even erroneous to seek in her any universal principles that would respond to concrete paradigms. But at least her mental immoderation has echoes within the general sense of magical work at play here, for charmed wanderings and distributions of assemblages prevail. Mixes of psychic and erotic perspectives and points of view combine into a general sense of the entwining, entangling, and knotting of hemp cord, cat hair, strips of leather, gold threads, blades of grass, raffia, rope, and torn fabric that can only be used by a sewing machine wrapped in a blanket and tied with string.

In her hand, a Nkisi Kula magic object from the Congo engages my interest in ritualistic activities that involve the powers of excess. It generates an extraordinary network of emotional wonder that is achieved by what I think of as the responsibility of reappropriating my capacity to visualize, for it seems to contain many possibilities of interpretation in which disorder and spell-like savagery jostle each other, vying to preside over an emergence of the grotesque that is typical of my private dream register. But I also find that that perceived space-logic has a moment of sensual closure involved. Thus, it is the least interesting instant of getting to know her, even though my customary perception of space is indeed challenged by the closed inclusion of Madame Monkey Fingers's crossed fingers.

Airy shifts occurred when I was looking at her voluptuous figurative presence in that beautiful Hôtel de Sens that reminded me of certain strategies found in the field of analytical sculpture. On the wall was hung a human skull trophy from Borneo under a sign that says *voilà, c'est fini*.

My making love with her on the reading table among the racks of books transformed the Hôtel de Sens into a simulated sensuous world where there is the idea that our bodies are disembodied and free, while in fact they are not. They exist for each other because we can perceive them through the techno-apparatus of our bodies spliced into The Last God cybernetic circuit. And that offers me kinetic, even ramshackle, focal points that stress the relational truth of perceptions.

The succession of temporary formations I experienced within Madame Monkey Fingers reflects my multiple vantage points, and thus the discontinuous, contradictory nature of human perception. But it was also hard not to perceive this way of making love as just another depersonalizing, albeit extravagant, potential way of juxtaposing ourselves to ourselves. Something that destandardizes and deflattens our common space. For, yes, she qualms me, for she sees art as synonymous with prestige and thus a refined marketing tool for brand identities.

This qualm forced me to look for the real in her virtual image—prompting my gaze to linger over the material differentiations of her body's textured variations. To do that I was no longer looking for a central yoni but coming haphazardly across fragments of her entire figure in non-sequential order. This is best done under the covers with the lights out, as it enhances understandings of her depth of field within a temporal vanishing that must include considerations of etiquette.

Passing through the under-the-covers temporal experience of Madame Monkey Fingers reminded me that every visual path is also a path of meaning. Even from the "correct" yoni vantage point, Lulu maintains her multicentred character, with which I experience a reversal of three-dimensionality and two-dimensionality as I pass my hand over the warm skin of her flesh. By doing so, I felt with my body an inseparable faithfulness reminiscent of the breakdowns and recompositions encountered when falling in love.

Yes, through love is how the tilted intricacies of the human heart merge countless bits of information into a coherent whole as a celebration of casual order within disorder. That kind of crazy love is always threatening to ravage the bourgeoisie baloney boys and to transform their consciousness and thus society. So my figure-ground relationships with Madame Monkey Fingers cannot be fully ranked in hierarchical terms, and my gaze is anything but immobilized. But when entering Lulu, I need to find the "correct" vantage point, where her idea of herself snaps into place.

When it did, I explored the diversity of her viewpoints on *Venus*, the 1996 play written by Suzan-Lori Parks about the life of Khoekhoe woman Sarah Baartman, and I could see and feel the breaking up and coming together of her planes and volumes, figures and surfaces.

In this light, Madame Monkey Fingers appeared optimistic about fusing the female body with the info-mechanic in the interests of disembodiment, citing the efficacious influence of Donna Haraway's cyber-theory as articulated in her *Cyborg Manifesto*, where I can fully understand how male-dominated culture does sometimes repress women.

Madame Monkey Fingers agreed and was accompanied by several instruments, including the gong, the flute, the ektari (a single-stringed lute), the pungil (a pipe-type of instrument), cymbals, the dhole (double-sided drum), the muck veonal (a type of oboe), and the harmonica. She demurred assigning gender metaphors to the instruments while articulating the gender collapse that occurs between sexual representations and materialistic palpability within her shadow plays, where puppets are used to voice dissent, as they have the latitude to say things humans cannot and are a bit withdrawn from reality. Such shadow theatre is catnip for those with energetic imaginations because its spellbinding, graceful interplay between light and shadow is riveting, as is her devoutly anti-realist and phantasmagoric aesthetic that reminds me of other (virtual) phantom presences in our culture. Not to mention my own inner world made up of fleeting, half-real mental projections staged in the theatre of my mind.

I particularly was fascinated by Lulu's ample breasts and their emphasis on re-inscription, reification, and how her body is 'staged' within the shadow play, for they only needed to give me the impression of life, rather than being ultra-realistic, because I completed the scene with my imagination. What principally interested me about them was her concentration on the concept of embodiment, which she defines as an effect. To fall into states of dreamy immersion within them is to catch a glimpse of the human fascination with art as an audacious magic lantern.

Lulu's buxom neural net allowed me closer and more comfortable exposures to her brushy round surfaces, which when gazed on and into can appear to become almost anything. I saw long lines of non-directional creative-destructive stargazing suggesting a scandalous dreamland of male disenchantment. Her flesh was dancing on a clock. She seems to be a crystallization of my more extreme emotional dream states by creating the crazed mood of lolling around naked in bed with a stranger and a hangover. But Lulu has a relaxed, unfussed immediacy that screams veracity, albeit an up-scaled version completed with a champagne cocktail. She projects the strength of pride in the freedom to choose and act according to personal pleasure, desire, and will, while her nipples perform the whimsical act of transubstantiation by switching to her eyes while the dark shading around her breasts transforms into a pair of open lips on the mouth of a rip-roaring armadillo fetus.

As an attempt at going between them that is much deeper than mountain resemblance, she is uncompliant with ideas of sexual politeness and compliant with those who intellectualize the sexually vulgar without vulgarizing artistic intellectualism.

Such gorilla goofiness ruthlessly leaves the gazebo gates of the libido open for multi-spectrums of mischief and caprice, where magical techniques of divination partake in chaotic control/non-control of a range of complex emotions that appears to extend from magnanimous melancholy to wistful folly to the frenzied rupture of uncompromising ferocity. Of sexual lassitude even, as an intense and irreverent emancipation of nebulously unguided wishes for the pleasures of deterioration of the human organism in an effort to return the monkey balls back to a magical time before individuated life.

So she stands with one foot in the world of the radical and seedy and the other in the world of burned-out sentimental suggestion, marked by a mood of solitude based on romantic views in Ménerbes in the Provence-Alpes-Côte d'Azur region in southeastern France.

Employed as colossal chromatic fields of colour emitting from the perfume of Lulu, Venus Victrix drifts back in, this time framed by a newly renovated 19th century prison where criminals and sailors and prostitutes were imprisoned pending a verdict by the local public prosecutor. Like the walls, Venus Victrix was freshly painted with cadmium red vertical bars, affirming the truth that we are prisoners of our own spectral limitations even though that spectrum may feel wide when it comes to human colour sensitivity. However, of all the photon wavelengths that exist, the portion of them available to our visible spectrum is limited by the range of the cone cells of our eye, which only detect but a small sliver of these energetic wavelengths.

The human eye has three types of cone cells that define that small sliver, each of which can register about 100 different colour shades. Researchers estimate the number of colours the human eye can distinguish to be in the millions, so perhaps we can be satisfied with our all-too-human limitations.

Can't we? Because it is already a *cliché* that we live in The Last Super God era of information overload, where computers write their own code and instruct us on sexual politics, multiculturalism, gender studies, and the far-reaching heterogeneous philosophical critique of the cultural mechanisms of representation.

Familiarity may not always breed contempt, exactly, but it does tend to inspire complacency. We are tempted to overlook, to take for granted, what has become blatantly familiar, no matter how odd it is in itself. We may look and register the presence of something without really seeing or understanding it. Isn't that a basic premise understood by all those making love with Venus©~ñ~Endless?

I believe it is, for it is clear that Venus©~ñ~Endless is synonymous with some imperative promise of Last God liberation from human drudgery: not only aesthetic liberation, but social, political, and even, it seems, what I might call metaphysical liberation. And that is so advantageous that it can make me stop biting myself and get out of bed.

But what about Venus©~ñ~Endless as an enchanted form of psychoanalysis? What about Venus©~ñ~Endless as a transference situated, not on an analyst's couch, but within the imitative gestations of lovemaking? What about Venus©~ñ~Endless as the noisy dream-flow conjured up by global enthusiasm for free-floating Last Super God communications that circulate under and above the skin *ad infinitum*?

Well then, it is neither surprising nor coincidental that Venus Victrix wore a classical Japanese Boro garment while standing in a large room bathed in iridescence: colour appearing in its most fleeting, indefinable condition.

As such, she made me think of the iridescence of a soap bubble or a beetle's shell, or some sumptuous anthropomorphic form of a bearded man pulling his rear out of various ossuaries, Rococo and Neo-Rococo spaces, and the Art Nouveau interior spaces of Antoni Gaudí, Victor Horta, and Henry Van de Velde. What I like about these kinds of whimsical spaces is their concern with effluvium-feminine forms and the swirling, tendril-derived patterns that are applied throughout the space in a frivolous spirit. For example, High Art Nouveau's foremost feature is an emphasis upon ornamental value distributed throughout an entire space that is windblown and whiplashed with the feelings of sprite underwater hair and writhing seaweed that has nothing to do with Le Corbusier's masterpiece, *Villa Savoye* (1930). Villa Savoye is one of the best and most famous houses of the modern movement in architecture, created with associate Pierre Jeanneret, a Swiss architect, designer, and cousin of Le Corbusier. To prepare for building it, they published a manifesto entitled *Five Points to a New Architecture* (1926) that served as the architectural guidelines for the aesthetic of the villa and so became a representation of their aesthetic ideology: to create a house that would be a *machine a habiter* (a machine for living (in)).

This building (a white box on stilts) emerged from Art Deco principles that originated in France in 1908 and reached their zenith in 1925. The heightening of perceptual sensitivity experienced at Villa Savoye encourages a sense of unified delectation, as the churned blocky forms define the space and are picked up in the shapes of the stairs and furniture. Consequently, it collides high art complexity with simplicity.

The tonal and syntactic surfaces are, of course, white and spare, with their logical trajectories seemingly resolved. And yet there are visual arguments-within-arguments to be discerned behind the axiomatic, as Villa Savoye embodies and deepens the multiple ramifications of a phrase easily (and aptly) applied to describe it: deceptively easy. In referring to something as deceptively easy, it is implied that to be merely easy would be deficient and that difficulty has inherent value.

Villa Savoye is both complex and intimate, as it plays on a flowing undercurrent of smooth transformations, both tonal and imagistic, that works itself out over the course of viewing the entire building. I did not stand still here and look, but passed in and out as Venus Victrix's eye colours changed depending on the angle of the light. Her held bunch of flowers took on pink in the white periphery.

These astonishingly beautiful iridescent hues, which accentuate the entrancing nuances of colour, are not generated by pigments but by the microscopic structure of the material itself, something I relished to the extent to which colour, even as a concept, is as elusive as it is enchanting.

Extraordinarily striking was an oxblood Chinese vase that Venus Victrix held in her hand. It was astoundingly and blissfully sunlit. Why I perceived oxblood versus violet versus vermillion depended on the situational energetic wavelengths of the photons influencing the retinas at the back of my eyeballs.

At this point, the vase raises the thorny issue of the individual against the undifferentiating urge of the homogeneous collective. Technically, The Last God is a homogeneous hyper-unified-whole fabricator because everything on the Internet it has been trained on must behave exactly alike on any server: the same requests must evoke the same responses. So the notion of universal unity is a logical result of the psychological effects of The Last God's appetite for totalizing collections of diversity.

The adjective esemplastic—a concept Samuel Taylor Coleridge invented to indicate the faculty of the mind that can fuse unrelated things into a poetically holistic singularity—is increasingly useful in appreciating this urge for Last God heterogeneous categorizing. Specifically, because the AI's esemplastic appetite for art-as-data is not so much the presentation and delectation of art objects but of Last God theatrical scenography, where individual artworks combine to make up an opulent theatrical assembly.

The visual suggestion is that all things are of equal interest in terms of The Last God's psychic force.

What matters are the relational aesthetics of diversity that construct either corresponding or contrasting relationships (it makes no difference; hence, The Last God can't lose). What was once unorthodox has become orthodox as a cutback towards the fuzzy world of networked anti-categories typical of The Last God crypto-economic order—where geographical distance and difference appear irrelevant. So the question of the genealogy and ontology of art-as-art is escalating in importance. Art as human thought that developed in relatively discrete consecutive stages (magical, mythical, religious, metaphysical, scientific, abstract, and financial) appears to be all but irrelevant in the loins of The Last God. The aesthetic distance between subject and image has been cancelled out in Last God's homogeneous data space.

In that sense, The Last God treats this vase as part of a heterogeneous-homogeneous-total-data-work in which the culture loses something (difference) while gaining something else (the spectacle of world theatre).

Time slows down here, as I pleasurably explored the top of that iridescent vase. The only certainty is that colour is contextual, ephemeral, and enjoyable. And that it touches everything when running from the shadows to the sun.

So I worked my way down—backwards through the sunset where flamboyant, theoretical observations about colour are tempered with questions concerning the socio-political aspects of Madame Monkey Fingers. I could feel that vase advocating for a cyber-feminist embrace of electronic ambiguity, difference, and contradiction—while promoting concepts of the collective and the communal. Taken to an extreme, the awareness of the mediated nature of perception that the vase provides can be taken to signify that my body itself is a prosthesis. My body of pulpiness creates its own mediated perceptions through structural couplings with the environment. That made me really want to swim to the flesh.

At this point, I began to concentrate on the vase's theoretical qualities concerning lyricism and sympathetic imperatives that I had detected in the iridescent stains in our bed. Most notably, a philosophical poly-rational interplay seems to be suggested in those strained stains that play between positions that address feminist and cyber-feminist epistemology based on the model of the poly-perspicacious rhizome. This irritating iridescent stain denies the conventional figure/ground separation between me as a human being and the environment, where no part is worth more than any another. It reminds me that ideals, totalizations, phenomenology, ontology, and idealisms can all be dismissed as epistemological stains.

Lacking further endurance, I retreated to my pillow and closed my eyes. There I had a powerful dream about the anguished French poet, actor, philosopher, madman, genius, playwright, and director, Antonin Artaud, who had just *fêted* Vincent Van Gogh in a bizarre but exquisite text that rails against GAS and universal imbecility. It is entitled *Van Gogh le suicidé de la société* (*Van Gogh, the Man Suicided by Society*).

At the outset Artaud was motivated by reading about a text called *Du démon de Van Gogh* (*Van Gogh's Demon*) that portrayed Van Gogh as a mad degenerate. Artaud subsequently discovered first-hand Van Gogh's paintings during two brief visits to a retrospective of Van Gogh at the Musée de l'Orangerie à Paris, where he was struck with the convulsive storminess of Van Gogh's brushwork. He compared these paintings to atom bombs.

But frankly, when seen in my dream, they look rather far from explosive—or even very tormented. Rather, they look completely calmly composed and executed in a steady stylistic application of delicate daubs and strokes (very reasonably structured, by comparison to even Cézanne's apples) within a beautiful and erudite colour palette. Even the sinewy tree trunks and the most quivering of vegetation in Van Gogh's painting *The Garden of the St. Paul Hospital* (1889) (a scene outside his asylum), or the unfathomable *Starry Night over the Rhone* (1888), felt calm to me. Yes, there is some wobbly expressionist distortion in a few of Van Gogh's paintings, such as in *The Church in Auvers-sur-Oise, View from the Chevet* (1890), but nothing to get me very worked up about.

Regardless, in my dream (which is set off against a soothing cool deep grey), Artaud blames the treatment ordered by Van Gogh's physician, Dr. Paul-Ferdinand Gachet, as the reason for Van Gogh's suicide by gun at age 37 in 1890 (although no gun was ever found). Artaud also blames Van Gogh's beloved brother Théo for the suicide, and goes on to contend that those who were disturbed by his painting drove Van Gogh to it.

Then, Artaud, in disputing Van Gogh's mental health, blames society at large for preventing Van Gogh from uttering certain unbearable truths that society failed to understand. What these truths are, Artaud doesn't say, and they are something I still don't understand, though in his essay *The Theater of Cruelty and the Closure of Representation*, Jacques Derrida described how Artaud's thinking might be seen as impossible in terms of the established structure of Western thought.

At the end of the dream I was delighted to float through a dark circular space where text fragments wind their way on the walls and floor. Verbal utterances—screams, pants, and chants—from Artaud's banned radio play *Pour finir avec le jugement de dieu* (*To Have Done with the Judgment of God*) (1947) do the loop-the-loop of seemingly random cacophony with xylophonic sounds mixed with various percussive elements and the noise of alarmed human cries, grunts, onomatopoeia, and glossolalia.

As I awake, Madame Monkey Fingers seems to be in the process of sending out prickly bots to defeat the incoming data of ethnocentric eyes and to read history backwards in the tradition of the Baroque, which bends toward over-saturation and the accentuation of an accumulative manner. Madame Monkey Fingers's taste for transculturally accumulative surprise is evident and foreshadows the taste for data rearrangement favoured by The Last God. As with the atmosphere of the Afro-Cuban religion of Santería, Madame

Monkey Fingers weaponized herself against the naturalizing powers of representational structure with a picture of a generalized metaphysical configuration. Last God apparatuses, deployments, and structures cross over the old dichotomy between technology and the natural. Vertical vegetal space seems to be giving way to a new anthropomorphic scenario in which big-footed, high-buttocked men with sharp-edged technology assume more influence: a masterful compression that produces a sense of anti-sumptuousness in my mind that is both non-dialectical and network-centric. So Lulu produces affective responses in my subconscious, though I'm not a big believer that Freud's dream theories concerning the artistic ego, superego, and id opened the right doors of perception to my authentic self. My taste still prefers the possibilities of chance and spontaneity.

Up early the next morning so as not to miss my *élan vital*, I attempted an early *tour de force* Last Super God session with Madame Monkey Fingers by synthesizing her themes of education, feminist theory, cyberculture, architecture, and art into one overarching theoretical construct. In my ear, Lulu stressed a philosophy of immanence that defined me as a dynamic, non-compartmentalized postulate based on her fluidity. Here, male top-down phallic logic is opposed by an intricate interplay of slippery complexity. The imposition of my will on Madame Monkey Fingers is opposed by that of a poly-willed distributed process.

But are permanency and coherent closure such odious characteristics to support theoretically today? Do we really want Last Super God agent bodies without teleological closure that are already always under reconstruction? Are all synchronous forms complicit extrusions of the patriarchs' dominant reason?

To her credit, Lulu recognized, in passing over me, the need for both sides of the form-process dynamic equation to balance. But, seeing the reification of form as the dominant trend in the male today, she decided to go down on my cockle-boated cock in favour of the process side.

A thin metal sheet wound in a spiral on the floor as Madame Monkey Fingers's own words, odd numbers, and random punctuation marks condensed and reduced to what is strictly necessary to organize them out of all common grammar and into a visual configuration. Here I can see how her activities as a concrete poet are inseparable from her intense alertness to premature ejaculation. When she places herself flat on the ground as if a modular entity, I am to assemble, restructure, and move her—depending on the non-linear space available between us.

Non-linear was her preferred mode of coitus. Forever and ever, slow trembling movements of her inner thighs and other loin body parts are the result of my leisurely tickling her with my purring lips. A sense of hypnotic connection between my human psyche and the surrounding environment is a fair description of the alert experience of sharing a bedroom with her. At times I sensed a breeze in the room that did not exist.

So I think it is appropriate to think of her as a means of transforming my static perspective vision of women into a luminous motion study. Her regular slow-motion undulations place me in an element of dilated time where surprise and chance seem to merge into an unexpected minimal music through the grinding, rubbing, and pulsating of her hidden razzle-dazzle. Generally speaking, her slower, more modest displays of sexual prowess protect me from falling into the special effects category of spectacle that can sometimes swallow up her grander epistemological project. So with nonlinear sex as a significant feature of the feminine, along with the heightened capacity to sympathize, Lulu switched on a dream of me making love to her on a large mirror. This vivid dream offered a highly complex and detailed account of my plump wiggling ass as a non-linear tool that amplifies things for her. Accordingly, the experience of perceiving myself in a mirror while engaged in nonlinear coitus generated some internal trepidation inasmuch as one anticipates and wills for oneself a homogeneous total being over which the ego has dominion. However, this totality is never achieved in the mirror—so that my spellbound self-image comes to feel inadequate.

By considering going back to Rosebud for a drink and by bringing that mirror stage query to the floor, Madame Monkey Fingers played with what seemed to be a question about whether we will become post-human in our love or if our post-humanity is already here. While turning up the volume on the Buzzcocks, she also introduced the rapier idea of sentimental hyper-specificity and defined it as both too specific and too general. All told, this triangular pillow talk with my mirrored cockle-boated cock and Lulu was quite formidable in its versatile concentration. It tickled the erotic clown in me. This tickled cock condition of the mirrored mind I consider a state of rare male grace.

Accordingly, I was soon entirely bathed in monochromatic crimson. After a while, it suddenly shifted to a dirty yellow.

I got this idea from Jean-Luc Godard's movie *Le Mépris*, where he used monochromatic red lighting and then a sudden monochromatic blue lighting on naked Brigitte Bardot so she would transfigure. Because for Godard, the cinema must transfigure reality.

Sudden monochromatic colour switching I find to be a kind of autopoiesis—a newness that emerges on the scene of culture due to dynamic, unpredictable forces.

With an insistence on the continuous now, our monochromatic triangle maintained a crimson interaction between Lulu and my sense of her endless environment of reciprocal perturbations.

By suggesting such a brazenly twofold concept as monochromatic lovemaking, Madame Monkey Fingers exhibited an uncanny eye for spitting on patriarchal platitudes. She revolted against any commemorative appropriation of a flawlessly coherent history. Her presentational excess offered up to me the possibility of multiple interpretations that may be in conflict with each other.

Following a shared lunch, we scurried between my cockle-boat swerving and her monochromatic body-linking, which allows for occurrences and encounters with trans-subjective space.

Vast in its cerebral reach did Madame Monkey Fingers go. Those fingers seem to have no end, but always an extended present that strums the streaks of sybaritic paganism running in my head.

Here Madame Monkey Fingers manifests as a languorous and majestic and gorgeous ocean of broken yellow. This appeals to my aesthetic taste that was formed during a post-punk period that romanticized acts of dinginess as they exploded into bursts of ecstatic release. In dingy yellow, I have Madame Monkey Fingers *déshabillée*, and we overlap like floating layers of fabric. This is not to suggest a repressed Oedipal fixation on my part.

It is true that Madame Monkey Fingers can appear as a repressed erotic-spatial restriction when not nourished by my fascination with Japanese erotic prints. Without which, I may have become merely a doyen of written dream-kitsch. That is why I keep, at this juncture, Madame Monkey Fingers flat and compressed, with just some wet wiggling spaces that feel perfectly poignant, for there is plenty to luxuriate my starved and strained sensibilities within this rather idiosyncratic sentence.

For Madame Monkey Fingers can be overly decorative and hence vaguely vapid in her sensual equanimity. Through her saturated sensory abundance, Madame Monkey Fingers feels like the fluidity of female identities as they merge with their context into a *femme-fleur*. That is, woman-as-flowery-wallpaper set mercurially drifting within a sea of pandemonium.

As before, Madame Monkey Fingers suggests, through an ambiguous body language that thwarts narrative, a humble disembodied corporality captured in the act of melting into temporal acts of fluidity.

As such, Lulu reveals me as a creature half passive and half all-night carouser well outside of any restrictive perfumed palace. By my rejecting to disambiguate this depicted double act of opening/closing, Lulu leaves open for me the possibility of sustaining time to think my choices through.

For Madame Monkey Fingers's secretive sex drive possesses the burlesque beauty of psychological turmoil. Her delighting dabs of colour as applied to her buttocks depart this secretive darkness and begin to blend and bend into colour patterns that excite my vanguard and occult imagination. Clearly here, Madame Monkey Fingers is bathing in the tension between daytime stupefaction and some kind of *vie bohème* nighttime exhilaration.

Within this duplicitous atmosphere, the flux of her temporal values receives the glow of melancholy grandeur. Out at night (often all night), Madame Monkey Fingers becomes a skirt being chased by social-climbing artists with a scavenged taste for amiable anarchism. Here viral mental agents are poised against totalitarian thinking and incremental inclusions, as opposed to revolutionary ruptures. These supposed opposing tendencies seem to be reconciled by her notion of an a-rational electronic hyper-total; or if not an a-rational electronic hyper-total, a co-emergent communal setting that is also understood as a *deus ex machina*. Because I thoroughly enjoy looking at myself through the eyes of someone else who has solved my problems for me.

With a transcendent lapidary look that interlocks figure and ground, Madame Monkey Fingers gets my mind rhapsodically wriggling on her poetic tripod. For when she is hot, she can seem to vibrate in the torridness of my passion. By her heavenly heat, Madame Monkey Fingers pulverizes and melts my vision of her into joyful disorder—releasing all of the becoming that is latent within her.

That release is what makes Madame Monkey Fingers not only a sign-woman, but also an intersubjective mode of connective communication.

But do not be mistaken, Lulu will never become a form of The Last Super God's passive pastoralism, for she has an energetic historical reality in the minds of those who value the thought of a humanist, egalitarian, erotic world culture. I think that she will always touch people in the right place who are in tune with her mode of silky associative thinking—those that yearn to be released from the corset of mental restrictions and kleptocracy.

As kettle drums tapped out an ominous beat, such empowerment eliminates the necessity of more of my pornographic sex scenes. As constituted from textuality and myths, an inner community emerges within the matrix of Madame Monkey Fingers's fingers while they are fingering an apparently difficult chord while cupping the head of my penis. This attitude, especially when taken to the next level, seems to harmonize with Madame Monkey Fingers's philosophy of statistical probability—a statistical probability poised to create poetic, passionate, political identities of unity without relying on a logic of exclusion.

So it must be, said the sibyl (Σίβυλλαι) oracles in Ancient Greece.

For as Heraclitus conveyed, the sibyl—with frenzied mouth uttering things not to be laughed at—unadorned and unperfumed—reaches to a thousand years with her voice aided by the gods.

XIX

Nothing in Moderation within the Undifferentiated Aesthetic Continuum

One night I threw myself face down on my bed and felt like giving up, and at that very moment everything changed. It was as if my head became a crystal sphere where images of people and animals and plants from all around the world were projected, but the source of the projection was coming from inside my head. Coming from inside me, who felt that only the poetically convulsive can be an effective antidote to the fundamentally asinine judiciousness of The Last God.

This experience was accompanied by a feeling of great joy. It was as if everything had been resolved once and for all, forever and ever, and there was nothing but complementary completion in the world as one.

Then I fell asleep, and I dreamed this experience all over again. I dreamed of being otherwise. I dreamed of swimming within the exploratory life, which is the true artist's task.

While wandering and marking these open fields of willingness, loving Lulu came easy as an all-embracing, radically empirical experience that left me swimming in undifferentiated waters without difference. Becoming a wave in the sea of Atmanthat-that-is-Brahman (Atman, the inmost soul or breath of life, is also Brahman, the ultimate reality that pervades the entire universe. Reality beyond is also within.) Is this a heretical position for which I could be stoned?

I waited, and no brouhaha ensued, so Madame Monkey Fingers began again with me with an ophthalmic bang—a dazzling, stuttering, speckled complexity accompanied with that moist slapping/clapping sound again—that is never far, in my mind, from the sputtering of oily machines.

As this richly rewarding sensual feast continues, Lulu and I convert, via distributed cognition, to a gestural abstraction morphing into lyrical suggestions of the grandeur of nature and nirvana: perfect quietude, freedom, happiness, and liberation from attachment.

For this dialectical ambivalence fosters an instability—or reversibility—of the divides between any heterosexual couple and natural history *writ large* if one thinks freshly between them. For only by skirting around these musty *clichés*—and the voyeuristic urge to ponder the intimacy (or lack thereof) of us as lovers—does Madame Monkey Fingers yield her nirvana fecundity to those of us who come at cultural theory from a post-materialist, cross-gender, environmental perspective by focusing on figure-ground relationships. For Madame Monkey Fingers always struggles with me as we make love against the ground of given and accepted systems of mystification that can appear as meaningless to me as those uninterested in junctures between gender representation and political content. As such, Madame Monkey Fingers is perversely insistent on the most efficacious, utterly idealistic regularities of the abstract effect, while I am forced to insist on the absolute congruence of honey trees in Nairobi.

Such insistence on belief amounts to a muddle between idea and actuality that is not worth a tittle. I had other claptrap comets to direct.

If I fail at nirvana, cut off my head and toss it to the abattoir.

In a rather tiny room of disorder, I am not sure what exactly happened next, but Lulu may have been tempted to push The Last God's sex machine theory even further down my light-hearted throat than seems necessary. For all its ludicrous and wish-fulfilling dazzle—or perhaps precisely because of it —I could feel a general sense of creative-destructiveness tingling away (for the better) in my loins. So long as I maintain an elegant and feathery touch.

When my fingers tired and I removed my hands from her breasts, Lulu lost some sparkling appeal and put in motion a randomizing sexual energy that runs deep under the skin as a form of aesthetic-libidinal tranquility aimed against energetic conformity to the extent that it becomes an orgasmic expression of libidinal release that often unclogs the culture-machine.

With my head between her legs, the slippery schema at work here is the fluttering movement of a tongue of change and mutability. As I slip and slide it deep inside of Lulu, like Jonah in the whale, things become ever more viscous, and her thick juice sticks to my eyes like oil on the back of a turtle caught in an oil spill. This turtle-scale shift renders these dampened inner spread legs a certain ambivalence as my mind played between the human and the animal world in us. It is as if she is using scale outputs (known as model weights) as inputs in an ongoing solipsistic process of (re)producing me rather than reflecting on my physical form.

In this space of natural wet fields, Madame Monkey Fingers seems to wish to resist liberalism by becoming ever more like a vista and by gesturing towards views of her as part of the natural landscape. Likewise, Lulu dumps this evermore *passé* reductive position of woman as nature into a virtual (clean) non-place where it once seemed possible to describe the purity of women as the entirety of a vast snowy expanse of sensual snowdrifts. As if none of her smeared messes are any of her doing but just part of the bloody planetary machinery. The way things fundamentally are, thereby creating a philosophical beard so prodigious that even a TLG Occam's razor powered by fusion atomic energy could not shave it.

I don't know, but rejecting this idea makes Lulu a reliable source of imaginary pleasure: the pleasure of seeing enormous reality entirely subjugated to my miniature imagination.

This paradoxical nonlocal Lulu shaped my tongue into an erogenous span as long as Jack Kerouac's 120-foot manuscript *On the Road* or at the very least the Marquis de Sade's 39-foot manuscript of debauchery, *The Hundred Twenty Days of Sodom*. She phrases my phrases as we take the sexual position of 69. In that 69 position, I can never quite grasp our figure/ground relationship, because the serpentine land withdraws from me like a cloud of ink emitted by an octopus in the deep.

In 69 there is no easy way of making her mentally switch tongues with me. Or there is, but I choose not to do it, for Madame Monkey Fingers is suddenly limber, heavy-breasted, and muscular. But then we initiated an engagement with the esoteric Kabbalah (meant to explain the relationship between an unchanging, eternal, and mysterious infinity and the mortal and finite universe) until a third mind popped out of our two-person 69.

Oozing a plumose-like fluid, this third mind then tends to me with a damp facility after throwing on something by *The Hafler Trio*. At one point, despite a mutual desire for greater intimacy, the distance between us three increased, as each partner sought sanctuary in the primacy of suffering in the Buddhist charnel ground.

Such a visceral death in life (and life in death) grips onto the nonhuman animated me with a dark, lyrical intensity that speaks insistently of orgasmic upheaval. Only Madame Monkey Fingers can still recklessly flip vistas of a non-human environment into a romantic metaphor.

This miniature romanticism of 69 is recognizable as languor or as a certain sardonic laconicism. But a small bony narration keeps turning its back on me and towards something profoundly singular: a sole skull—that deeply personal relic we all own but never see.

As such, I could not but feel here a pervasive sense of explosive loss coming soon. Yet, I must remember that Lulu is a well-intended product of my fragile human mind and that my actions as an artist and writer can point the population (haunted by the failure of utopian modernity) towards what is perhaps the most fruitful conceptual nexus of our time: the effort to preserve the pole of sentient human subjectivity in equivalence to the nonsentience of The Last God.

After that, Lulu seems drawn to hybrid things in which spurts of panicky tragicomedy can be felt—like heterogeneous flaming creatures. She seems attracted by things intrusive to the peaceful psyche: the obsessive melancholia of outsiderism, folklorism, decadentism, divinationism, ethnologism, nihilism, and the mysticism of elegiac strain.

As such, Lulu packed a wallop when animal forms and human genitals were engraved into her bones 35,000 to 40,000 years ago by the Cro-Magnon on the banks of the Vézère. With Lascaux and other prehistoric painted caves, early humans penetrated deeply into the womb of her darkness to paint and scratch semi-transparent images of animals on every surface of her rounded passageway. Verily, the grand central attraction will always be the leitmotif of the huge groupings of horses hovering in and around large semi-transparent dominating bulls from the Salle des Taureaux and the Axial Gallery (the gallery that follows the vast Bull's Chamber). Here her cavern tapers to form a more compressed overhead ceiling display where I find a tremendous stag with an enormous rack of entangled antlers flanked by three horses and an abstract door-like form and rows of dots. A sense of unspeakable tragedy is conveyed there, though, by an apparently wounded, fallen horse.

The feeling is impressive, and it was possible for me to now contemplate her Apse, a roundish, semi-spherical, penumbra-like chamber (like those adjacent to Romanesque basilicas) covered on every wall surface (including the ceiling) with thousands of entangled, overlapping, engraved drawings. The ceiling of her Apse is so completely and richly bedecked with such engravings that it indicates that the prehistoric people who executed them first constructed a scaffold to do so. This indicates to me that the Apse was an important and sacred part of the cave, and unique. I can say with assurance that the Apse's brimful style (what Bataille called its *fouillis*) is almost unprecedented, save for certain panels in Les Trois Frères and at the cave of Combarelles, a nearby Périgord cavern.

In the Apse of Lascaux, representation was made problematic, and the normal linear depiction of figurative assurance was made to fail. The etched walls did not have one singular point of view or a fixed position from which they depicted representational form. Here animals are superimposed in chaotic discourse, some fully and carefully rendered, others unfulfilled and left open to penetration by the environment, all commingled with an extraordinarily confused jumble of lines including, remarkably, the sole claviform sign in the Périgord and, even more remarkably, Lascaux's only reindeer, an animal that existed in plenitude during the period of the adornment of Lascaux. Its extensive use of superimposed multiple-operative renderings presents me with no single point of reference, no orientation, no top, no bottom, no left, no right, and no separate parts to its whole. Hence, freed from representational obligations, dark chaotic powers of consciousness are unleashed via the Apse's repressed and excessive exuberance. Certainly, easy conceptions of one beautiful being as distinguished from another (in specificity) are denied, and an aberrant invalidation takes place where previous concepts of the finite and the infinite implode (as do concepts of the voluminous and the vacuous) into a unified field of multiple-reproductive disembodied existences.

Clearly, what I am saying about the Apse runs counter to positivism, as the positivist ideal is a search for rational, systematic thought where images can be seen, broken down, explored, understood, and explained. The Apse in Lascaux is a place for the rejection of positivist realism and its values (or at least a place to save oneself from the futile and finally unreasonable claims of dogmatic realism and rationalism). The Apse represents a thrusting off of optic and mental boundaries and thus is a complex mirroring of my own fleeting impressions, which constitute the movement of my consciousness—the perpetual weaving and unweaving of myself.

So Lulu's seductive mysteries project the cognitive value of volatile force that magic ritual once had, with her wide-ranging display of compositional imbroglios of entanglement—wickedly mixing magical charms, sorcerers' amulets, witchy spells, and other knotty quasi-cultural expressions that push me down the hill of excoriation. That is how Lulu can carry the freedom of getting my lodestone rolling.

Thankfully, after attuning myself to the sun, Madame Monkey Fingers shifted her focus to firmer grounds of provocation and promise that seemed neither less nor more beautiful (or senseless) than any other stack of small animal bones. This dreamy-gossamer stack put me back in touch with my male make-believe monarchy, where Lulu seems to be a circumspect zone of outrageous abnormality. Perhaps I had ignored (or repressed) something about the aesthetically flabby human circus, which has grown a little too obliging to popularity at the detriment of free-thinking individuality and transcendental aloofness.

XX

End Reverse-Engineering as a Poetics of Cognition

Suddenly everything seemed to lift, get lighter, and sway. Compliments tumbled from my lips. Defending the libido through the work of the imagination while speaking across generations through algorithmic incentives was in full swing. My rig, as a caprice, filled with blood and lightly throbbed as it swayed along the tipsy curvature of the end of the world that I need to assess as The Last God legacy.

Dusk was beginning to trail the end of the sunset. Somewhere camels stirred and a horse moaned as lightly moustached, hippopotamus-sized ladies jingled off with childish giggles to the carnival in their Aswan jewellery and gaudy gold masks.

The air felt crisp on my eyelids as my gondola slipped into the flow of polymorphous desire. To prowl around the lily pond of underlying neurology like this is to live in a whirl of streamers and confetti ejected from the powerful rump of time immemorial.

Floating in air, as if resting on a cloud, my engorged rig flowed down the end of an endless stream of spunk that is forever perpetuating the existence of humanity.

Contemplation of Madame Monkey Fingers's decadent finery, which by its exquisite existence denounces composition with impertinence, is an experience that makes my life faintly fun in the face of death's inexorability. Much of the lovemaking she performs on me is hypnotically beautiful and perfect for meditative dreamland. Its pleasure-over-problem proposition might even be construed as a prime example of the fetishistic obsession with the past typical of our political and artistic imagination (at present). By that I mean a backward-looking imagination in desperate need of reclaiming the specific multifarious ideologies of the fleeting past so as to repossess a better idea of a better future that reverses our era of shitification.

Following this benevolent, behind-the-times interpretation on my part merely re-places Venus Callipyge back into the picture within the art tradition of great male linearity, made evident by (for example) Pablo Picasso, Marcel Duchamp, Alberto Giacometti, Claude Monet, Henri Matisse, Edvard Munch, Piet Mondrian, Kazimir Malevich, Constantin Brancusi, Fernand Léger, Mark Rothko, Francis Bacon, Jackson Pollock, and Otto Dix. Dicks all the way down.

With a faint flurry of flugelhorns, the sibyl stars came out again as pretty pink dots and shined as brightly as I had ever seen them. My extravagant eyes were shut, but this brightness took on a divine, supreme, and cosmological role by enhancing and elevating the force of my grovelling love and desire for Venus.

An elfin piccolo piped in as Venus Callipyge came back to me with an ass as sweet as *ananas*. This pineapple-sweet rear moved stylishly and became emotionally charged as it promenaded through a titillating intersection in the neoclassical surroundings at the end of Passage d'Enfer. As such, I experienced something of an aesthetic reversal when perambulating behind this firm form, for it was wonderfully wobbly.

Smelling of daisies, it displayed a most attractive asymmetric cadence as it paraded within this sumptuous space. Through it, Venus Callipyge was able to maintain an emotional pressure on me, as it shined with visual intensity. That butt had far more self-congratulating, upper-class complacency than I within the frame of this imperial grandeur. That ass, now set off against the burgundy carpet and dramatically illuminated by a wide band of cross-shadowed sunlight, feels personal, well placed, and almost modest in its equilibrium. Less goes further than ever here.

I climb the burgundy-carpeted stairs behind Venus Callipyge, for I wish to dance the can-can. I am so intently focused upon her alluring rear that a flamboyant hanging horse and a carousel of limp donkeys being carried round-and-round by stiff wooden skeletons rotating on wooden gears are almost lost in the glamorous ceiling and chandeliers. Next to the horse sits a small drummer boy automaton occasionally rapping out a few slow snare drum rolls, something of a bloom in the general conformist mood of the classical space.

I was particularly touched by a tuft of angelic blond hair in the top of its soft crack, for it communicated a sense of pathetic pity within a general opulent overindulgence. I cannot help but deduce from this immoderation the orange clown king's glittering bad taste in interior decoration. He owns two Renoir paintings. They're both fakes.

The predetermined transcendental apparatus on the backside of Venus Callipyge is such an irredeemable rolling pin of meat-space ideology that it hyper-organized my vision into the narrow style of desire that is sometimes derided even by me. As a result, much of my contemporary lovemaking has become much less goal-oriented and single-mindedly direct—something that loosens the bonds within the domestication of erotic thought.

Venus Callipyge's musically alternating buttocks was never short on flamenco flair and audacity as it danced on the head of the patriarchal pin, delivering *jouissance* as a form of self-induced luxury. That hot ass has the rounded overtones of a heroic self-mockery that is a form of self-aggrandizement.

Its mossy, cherub-haired crack, which can be hectoring to the ego, to say the least, speaks against the surrounding high-class solidity. That mobile and moony cracked solidness mitigates Venus Callipyge's firm flimsiness as her beautiful rear rhythmically bounces—left and right, left and right—within an inscrutable, off-centred, flowing, limber geometry. There is an enlivening and sly play in the way the gluteus maximus muscles roll and shift, back and forth, that supports my interpretation of the human ass (in both its meanings) as a form of self-effacement, leading towards closure. Through looking at the rear, humankind sees itself in the enchanted mirror as a dumb thing, nevertheless, of beauty; that is to say, as a sort of angelic donkey of self-deprecating excitement that reawakens memories of invisible realities within the maximalist trappings of upper-class luxury.

Indeed, this exciting Venus rear exit is admirable not only in its asymmetrically moving symmetry but also in offering voluminous insights into the botched integration of remembering what has come before.

Even given that obvious historical perspective, the departure of Venus Callipyge is something of a chronological antidote to the recent pessimistic a-historical flops that plop around town—where seemingly The Last God condition, now, is to presume that everything has been said and done, and all that is left for The Last God to do is to recycle and repackage and remix prior human discoveries while popping open celebratory champagne bottles and raising golden glasses to the empty sky. According to some, the *arrière-garde* (rear-guard) obsession with recuperating aspects of the past is the condition of culture in our time of The Last God, thus offering little or no alternative technique or viewpoint capable of registering an agency of new multitudes.

The implication that everything has been done is ridiculously non-ambitious.

If that were true (and it is not), the dominant metaphor for Venus©~ñ~lOve Systems should not be the swinger's key party (according to Sigmund Freud in his *General Introduction to Psychoanalysis*, a key that opens a room in a dream is unmistakably phallic), but the plush mirrored-ceiling room to which it leads, where art is dreamily fucking itself to sleep while watching its exuberant pluralistic re-duplications and dilapidated doublings in the above mirrors of infinity (albeit in reverse).

Rather, I wish to skip over this semi-valid but bone-dry issue of epistemic vigour by placing the tendency to hegemonize The Last God's loins of eroticism within normative fields of *arrière-gardism*.

Given the delicately detailed exiting of this exquisite gluteus maximus, Venus has me following an idea of open-ended identities that have never been conceptualized together because they make no singular theoretical point in combination, and they probably never—forever and ever—will.

The End

www.ingramcontent.com/pod-product-compliance
Lightning Source LLC
LaVergne TN
LVHW020711110826
845149LV00012B/2208

* 9 7 8 1 0 6 8 8 6 3 7 3 8 *